Range
of
Motion

A Novel

Mary A. Agria

She is not gone. She is everywhere.
In loving memory of my mother Lydia
and to John and our daughters,
the loves of my life, with gratitude
for all the memories and support. Without you, this novel
could never have been written.
And with special thanks to Ellen for her infallible
advice and support.

**visit Mary Agria online at www.maryagria.com
for excerpts from her work or agriainc@msn.com to arrange
for live author chats or signings**

Other Novels from Mary Agria

Time in a Garden
Garden of Eve
From the Tender Stem
In Transit
Community of Scholars
Vox Humana: The Human Voice

. . . and for lovers of gardens and gardeners:

Through the Gardeners' Year:
52 Weekly Thoughts on Gardens,
Gardeners and the Gardening Life

Second Leaves: Growing Young Gardeners

Available online from Amazon, Barnes &
Noble or on order from your local bookstore.
For sample chapters and more, visit:
www.maryagria.com

-

ALCEA ROSEA, HOLLYHOCK, is a member of the Malvaceae family. Known as *holyoke,* it somehow migrated to Europe from China pre-1400.

Plants don't move. They root themselves. The very expression 'to plant' means to set firmly in one place. Except life doesn't end there. Plants bend and recoil, sometimes to the point of breaking when a random footstep or the purposeful blade of a scythe makes contact. Come hail or heavy rain, plants fold in on themselves, waiting out the storm. They grow toward one another, sharing space, building the community we call a garden. Plants stretch upward toward the sun. They dance on the wind. We can learn a lot from plants.

Maggie

She began to spin on tiptoe as children do. For the sheer joy of it. Her bare feet made no sound on the damp earth. Alone at sunset in her grandmother's garden, the girl spun and spun. The gauzy skirt of her nightdress billowed out like hollyhock petals in bloom along the white picket fence behind the family cottage.

It was the height of summer in Northern Michigan. The waters of Little Traverse Bay thirty miles south of the Mackinac Bridge were calm and glassy, tinged with bands of purple and teal. The girl's name was Maggie. Maggie Aron. She was eight.

"*Hollyhock* . . . our sandy soil is perfect for growing them." That very morning her grandmother had laid a fallen blossom in Maggie's outstretched palms. "Years back, we used the flowers for dolls. Look—here's the head, the doll's wide circle skirt."

Brow knit, Maggie tried to make the circlet of petals dip and twirl. "A funny name," she said.

Hol-*ly-hock.* **Hol**-*ly-hock.* Waltz time. A word just right for twirling. Like the sound of new patent leather Mary Janes clattering on the wood floor of the cottage.

It was getting dark before young Maggie had a chance to experiment on her own. Hair still damp from bath time, Maggie crept out into the quiet of the garden, chanting the magical word over and over under her breath.

5

Hol-ly-hock. Spin, spin, whirl. She began slowly at first, then faster. Her long chestnut brown hair flared outward. The dying rays of the sun set each silken strand ablaze with red and gold.

Heedless of seasons or calendars, little Maggie Aron spun on and on, turning in rhythm with the revolving earth and the moon rising over Little Traverse Bay. Arms stretched out and head thrown back, she surrendered to a steady circling that left her at once breathless and dizzy, giddy with youth and its endless promise. The high gable of the cottage seemed to be whirling with her, its intricately cut wooden gingerbread melting like icicles from a wintery roof.

After a while, Maggie fancied herself floating lightly above the yellow border of evening primrose. Their petals curled inward, anticipating sleep. The pungent scent of lavender stung her nostrils.

A childhood paradise. All hers, hers alone.

Except she wasn't, hadn't been for some time. That fact didn't register until finally, her balance faltering, Maggie took a couple of wobbly steps, another, then collapsed with a squeal of pent-up energy and laughter on the damp ground of the garden.

And there he was. Watching her. Flustered, Maggie half-sat up. Her world appeared to be spinning wildly out of control in the gathering darkness.

A gangly, suntanned boy in cut-offs, tee-shirt and sneakers was standing behind her grandmother's white picket fence. His hands were braced on the gate installed mid-fence to access both garden and cottage from the alley. A baseball glove was slung over one of the pickets.

"Hey, there!" He sounded out of breath. The ballfields were a good half-mile up the hill above the lakeshore. "You hurt yourself?"

Suddenly embarrassed, Maggie picked herself up as best she could. She busied herself with brushing the stalks and stems, the fine dusting of pollen that clung to her nightgown.

"You okay?" the boy repeated. "Whatcha doin'?"

He had to go and spoil it, Maggie scowled. "None of your beeswax."

Silence stretched between them. Then she saw him shrug.

"Well, g'night, then," he called out to her retreating back.

An ordinary night, the culmination of a childhood day. It ended with an exchange over the back fence between a boy and a girl, a scene no

6

more or less remarkable than the dozens and hundreds, nay thousands of children frolicking in the endless twilight of a Northern Michigan summer.

Care-less. Children at play, blissfully oblivious. And yet the memory of that solitary summer's dance in the garden would stay with Maggie Aron into adulthood, for six decades and beyond. It would resurface even as she drew her last halting breaths.

Young Maggie found herself looking for the boy after that, scanning the knots of kids in the morning day camp, at crafts, at the waterfront. More often than not, she took the long way back to the cottage so she could pass the ballfield. She felt foolish doing it.

The two never spoke again. Years later, as a teenager, she often spotted him on the lifeguard stand at the beach. Surrounded always, Maggie thought with disgust, by giggling blond girls with their braces and just revealing enough bikinis. He was even taller then, tanned and with the lean muscles of an athlete. His smile, although not aimed at her, was troubling, made her look away.

"Jake" the girls called out, flashing tubes of suntan lotion in his direction. "Jake Faland, do my back."

Jake would just shrug. Supremely above it all.

Everything in its season. Childhood innocence ended in resort country with the impersonal sound of a time clock recording the minutes and hours spent behind the scenes in the kitchen of a local inn or restaurant. Washing dishes. Busing tables. Quickly it became time to go to college. Get a *real* job. Settle down. Buy a house. Raise a family. Maggie did all of these.

Time and age creep up soon enough on both the wary and unsuspecting, child and adult, plant and gardener alike. And with each memory come the aches and pains accumulated from a life well and truly lived.

"Art-right-us," Maggie's grandmother called it.

The eight-year-old Maggie Aron didn't understand the joke. Whatever *art-right-us* was, it didn't sound fun. Who would want to stay stuck in one spot when everything around her was gloriously growing and changing, spinning off wildly into the unknown?

§§§§

Decades pass.

Her hair more salt than pepper now and tucked into a tightly braided bun, Maggie Aron stood stock still in the middle of that selfsame Northern Michigan garden in the July twilight. A storm was forecast. As she stood there in bare feet and tie-dye silk caftan, Maggie only had eyes for the slumbering garden, the newly-painted white picket fence.

She had left much of her grandmother's garden intact over the years. But eventually those stalwart perennials were joined by hybrids, exotic Asiatic lilies and David Austin roses, a creative genetic mix of old fashioned garden roses and more prolific modern varieties. Whimsical pocket gardens linked by a network of random limestone slabs now wound their way around the cottage. And after a slow start, densely tufted dwarf oregano had begun to encroach upon those stony islands like a pale, unbroken sea.

The gardener in Maggie embraced continuity and change, made the garden truly her own. And yet, when it came to the landscape of her own life, she found it far harder to put the milestones, the many contradictions in any kind of perspective. Married, widowed in her sixties, she retired from a successful career in public agency work, having raised a grown son and daughter she saw far less than she would have liked. Hers had been a full life, by any standards.

Yet in times like this in the still of her garden, Maggie Aron quietly found herself wondering, "Is this what it means to bloom where I'm planted?"

On impulse she bent to snag an errant strand of bindweed. It took a split-second to right herself again, though at least the pesky interloper was gone.

Roots and all . . . and without a digger, Maggie hummed tunelessly to herself. When it came to weeding, a gardener declared victory where and whenever possible.

Through a sliver of daylight between the neighboring cottages, she caught a glimpse of the beginnings of whitecaps on the bay. The great lake *Mishigamaa* was stirring. "Big Water" the local native tribe called it, shallow for its size, but formidable when riled. Over time, the Ojibwa name had stuck, for the state as well as that vast inland sea that helped give Michigan its unique topography.

America's so-called Third Coast, the state is rimmed by more shoreline than the entire Eastern seaboard from Maine to Florida, the only state among the fifty to qualify as a peninsula. Technically two peninsulas, cartographers say, separated by lakes Huron and Michigan at the narrow and treacherous Straits of Mackinac then bounded to the far north by Lake Superior.

A thousand legends had sprung from the deeps of these ancient waters, formed by the slow advance and retreat of the great ice sheets that had covered half a continent. Hemingway walked these beaches, fished these waters. Tiny Beaver Island once housed the nation's only indigenous king. And the gales of November still struck fear in the heart of captains and crews on the ore ships dodging the shoals and shallows.

From childhood on, Maggie knew the stories. By comparison, cottage life in the tiny enclave of summer homes along the lakeshore was prosaic and unassuming. Maggie filled her days with plants and quilting, painting out of doors with a group of local art and garden lovers, long walks along the network of bike trails. She rocked on the porch. She settled down with a book after dinner, then bed.

This summer night was no exception. But the predicted storm, straight-line winds and dangerous lightning, never materialized. Maggie watched at the bedroom window as the ominous line of squalls skirted the bay entirely, venting its fury instead over the midnight expanse of the Great Lake itself. Silent strobe-like flashes from within the cloud bank betrayed its path, north and eastward toward the Straits.

Maggie shivered, arms bare in her pale flowered nightgown. The floorboards sighed and flexed as she felt her way back in the darkness to the brass and iron bed that once had been her grandmother's pride and joy. Eventually deemed too old-fashioned, it was relegated to the cottage, left for another generation to discover and love.

The message light was blinking on her smartphone lying on the night stand. Maggie broke down and checked it. The text message from her daughter had a terse finality about it:

Fourth of July homecoming not in the cards. Am shooting
for August. Hugs, Holly

On a sigh, Maggie found the Power Off button. *The usual workaholism*, she wondered. *A love affair gone south*? There was no knowing with Holly. She would find out eventually.

For now, Maggie had plenty of Fourth of July get-togethers to keep her busy, starting with a block party and parade. And when her friend and fellow-cottager Sonia bailed on watching the fireworks on the Fourth, Maggie headed off on her own. As long as she could remember, she had made the selfsame pilgrimage to a quiet stretch of beach along Little Traverse Bay to take in the annual fireworks competition between Petoskey and Harbor Springs. She wasn't about to miss it now.

The two resort towns lay directly opposite each other along the bay. In the right spot, beachgoers could see both displays at once, vivid bursts of fire blossoming over the dark waters. Legend had it, a card game among the civic leaders settled which community shot off the first volley. And every year the prime viewing spots grew more crowded with beach blankets and kids with their sparklers darting like fireflies along the shoreline.

Twilight came late on this far edge of the Eastern Time Zone. By the time the crowd on shore heard the final staccato volley of mortars and approving chorus of boat horns echoing across the bay, it was way past eleven o'clock. In the pitch darkness, parents struggled with crying kids as they navigated the sand and scraggly dune grass. To cross the traffic-clogged narrow road lining the waterfront was to take your life in your hands.

Caught up in that sea of humanity, Maggie didn't even see the pothole until she stumbled into it. When she started to career forward into the unknown, there nothing to stop her descent.

"Dear God," she gasped. Visions of broken hips, months in traction—or worse—flashed before her eyes.

And in that moment, an arm shot out of nowhere. Stunned, Maggie felt herself awkwardly half spun around, drawn tight against the buttons of a shirtfront, more or less upright.

"You okay?" a voice rumbled, male and unfamiliar. "Treacherous going out here."

Maggie stood on her own, but too unsteady for niceties. "Way, way too close for comfort. I could have done us both in."

"No problem."

The glare from oncoming halogen headlights did little to help her put a face to her rescuer. *Seventies*, she guessed. As old as she, mortifying when she thought about it. No question, the guy's reaction times were a heck of a lot quicker. If she had encountered those weathered features and tight cropped hair before, she certainly couldn't recall it.

"Stupid. My own fault. I forgot a flashlight."

He flicked on his smartphone, flashed a wry grin her direction. "Will this do? If you're on foot, I'd be glad to—"

"It's a short walk. I think I can—"

"Get home in one piece? Probably," he tweaked her. "But who knows what else is lurking out there."

Maggie laughed, couldn't help herself. "Just the thing a serial killer would come up with."

"Guilty. You got me."

They were laughing together now. The surreal-ness of the moment struck Maggie like a dull jab to the ribs from a passerby caught up in the melee around them. A car honked somewhere behind them. Increasingly impatient, pedestrians and SUVs were jockeying for the right of way.

"I suggest we get out of here. It's getting ugly."

Maggie suddenly felt too tired to argue. "The cottage is just a block from here, through that alley."

"A shortcut, you're telling me?" Peering off into the darkness, he didn't sound optimistic. "I'll take your word for it."

He raised a hand to signal their intent to cross the road. The other hand at her elbow, he steered them both to safety on the lawn of one of the sprawling cottages along the lakefront.

"I'm serious, you really don't have to feel obligated to walk me home."

"Walk each other," he said. "It's not out of my way. I left my car back there somewhere."

The screen of his smartphone cast off a surprising amount of light. What looked like a single massive lake-front cottage turned out to be two. A narrow walkway ran between them, half hidden in a thicket of Annabelle hydrangea.

"You up for the summer then," she wondered.

Her ankle had begun to twinge, badly. She was not about to let it get the best of her. Gritting her teeth, she tried not to limp.

"A month. Maybe more," the guy said. "Getting ready to put my Dad's cottage on the market. He broke a hip a couple of months ago, wound up in assisted living. I'm staying at the Perry downtown while the workmen are tearing up the place."

"Hard to go through that, for him—and you," Maggie said. "But he's recovering?"

"Tough as nails. They threw away the mold when they made that generation."

True enough. Maggie's grandmother had passed at ninety-two—still gardening until the end. At ninety-nine, Maggie's mother was still living independently in a senior living center downstate near the family homestead. When the cottage stairs no longer proved navigable for her in recent summers, Maggie continued to bring her north during the season to a retirement complex just outside of Petoskey.

She owed her mother a visit. "Good genes," Maggie said. "They run in my family, too. Kinda scary when you think about it."

Her rescuer chuckled. "What's the old saying?" he wondered. "If I knew I was gonna live so damn long, I'd have taken better care of myself."

The alley quickly dictated single-file. Maggie was glad her escort took the lead. She was limping now, couldn't avoid it. The throbbing of her ankle didn't make picking her way over the uneven ground any easier. Whenever it came time to dodge tree roots or random rocks on the path, the light from the cell phone swung her direction momentarily. It was enough to keep going until the next obstacle loomed up ahead.

Finally the two of them emerged on an open patch of lawn and the unpaved alley beyond it. The cell phone threw off just enough light that Maggie could spot the white of grandmother's picket fence

"Up ahead there, beyond that garden . . . home sweet home."

At that the stranger stopped dead, abruptly turned and flashed the light from the cell phone her direction. Half blinded, Maggie just barely managed to avoid plowing into him.

"Maggie," he said slowly. "Maggie Aron?"

When she didn't acknowledge it one way or the other, he chuckled softly, shook his head. "Of course, should have guessed. You do these face-plants often, do you? As I recall the first time we met, you were attempting a vertical takeoff in the middle of that garden up ahead."

Maggie blurted out the first thing that came into her head. "Do I know you?" Ridiculous, because she did.

"Jake. Jake Faland," he said. "You had to be—what, back then? Nine. Maybe ten."

Eight. She would have corrected him, but the shrill ascent of homegrown fireworks, unnervingly close, took them both off guard. A shower of gold and silver sparks, followed by a loud flash-bang illuminated the entire back yard. It seems that local fireworks laws or not, the neighborhood kids weren't ready to pack it in for the night.

"Not too swift," Jake swore softly. "With all the dried out cedar around here, the siding, even support posts in these old cottages, we're talking major fire hazard."

"You probably haven't been up here in a while," Maggie said. "Resorts around here go all-out for the Fourth. But then we're supposed to stick to patio lighting and no open flames."

"You hung out some lanterns, too, I see."

"Hard to miss," Maggie laughed. The dozen round white parchment lanterns suspended from the rafters had been a fixture on the porch for a decade. The faux Edison-bulb patio lights in between them were new this season. "Forgot to unplug the light show on the way to the fireworks. Can't imagine what the neighbors are thinking."

"Nice. Homey."

"Nice for you to get me home in one piece, that's for sure." *Nice,* Maggie winced. Her daughter's favorite expression for any and all situations—good, bad or indifferent.

The latch on the garden gate never stuck before. It did now. "Can't imagine what got into the darn thing." On a sigh, Maggie stepped out of the way enough to let Jake take a crack at it.

"No problem," he said. "Good seeing you again . . ."

"Good luck with your renovations."

Despite her ankle, Maggie took the narrow walkway through the garden double-time. The last thing she saw before she closed the cottage door behind her was a dim outline of Jake Faland standing at the fence where she had left him. She flicked the porch light twice, hoping that would send him on his way.

Enough of that. Her ankle had morphed from twinges to a steady,

13

ominous ache. Teeth clenched and hanging on to rockers and end tables when and where she could, Maggie limped to the refrigerator.

"Empty, of course." She set the offending ice trays on the counter without refilling them, then grabbed a bag of frozen snow peas as a makeshift ice pack.

Ten years ago, no one would have locked their doors, but a rash of break-ins last summer changed all that. Maggie checked the locks, then scoured the medicine cabinet for the most potent pain killer she could lay hands on.

"Where's the medical marijuana when I need it," she gritted her teeth, tried to favor the foot as best she could.

The mirror and unforgiving lighting in the bathroom didn't help. In that moment Maggie Aron felt every one of her seventy-two years. A network of lines and furrows traced the contours of her still high cheekbones. The pinched and tired face staring back at her from the glass bore no resemblance to the Maggie Aron who had twirled and spun and frolicked in her grandmother's garden all those years ago.

For everything there is a season, a time for every purpose. The quiet rhythm of the Pete Seeger tune played itself out in her head as she left herself drift off to a troubled sleep. *A time to be born and a time to die. A time to dance and a time to mourn.*

Turn, turn, turn, the ancient text whispered to her gardener's heart. *I swear it's not too late.*

ALLIUM SCHUBERTII. - Native to Israel, Palestine, Syria, Lebanon, Turkey and Libya. Called the 'fireworks plant' or Persian Onion. Despite its lowly pedigree, this member of the onion and garlic family makes a spectacular statement in any garden.

Nostalgia

Memories can play tricks on a guy, Jake Faland found his hadn't done justice—not by a long shot—to the traditional Petoskey and Harbor Springs fireworks extravaganza.

For one thing it was more crowded. Blankets and lawn chairs sprouted like tufts of beach grass along the Little Traverse shoreline waiting for nightfall. When the fireworks finally erupted, locals and tourists alike ooh-ed and ah-ed, applauded and cheered the glittering blossoms unfolding over the dark waters, only to watch them vanish like smoke into the night sky.

And afterward? No one had warned Jake about the traffic. After he saw his erstwhile neighbor back to her cottage, it took him five frustrating minutes just to find his Dad's wreck of a car, a rusted-out twenty-year-old Toyota. *Cottage wheels.* Fly in to Pellston, retrieve the car from a storage barn, replace the battery and the clunkers were good to go. Tan must have been the model of choice back in his dad's day which certainly didn't make locating his family's particular junker any easier.

Through the gridlock and annoying blaze of headlights, a nagging thought kept roiling in his head. *Maggie Aron.* Jake was still shaking his head over that one. Now *that* was a blast from the past.

It wasn't surprising they hadn't recognized each other after all those decades. As kids they ran in very different circles. But then nobody chooses what resurfaces as one of life's *deja vu* moments.

Magical, the poet in him realized these many decades later. It was as if Maggie Aron's solitary dance captured and preserved for him the spontaneity of childhood, blissfully unrehearsed and before life intervenes.

The girl in the garden always seemed to be popping up in his field of vision after that. Once he caught her lugging a loom home from the craft building. Heavy white cord and long strips of blue jean material from the partly finished project trailed out behind her like bread crumbs in some bizarre fairy tale. During swim lessons down at the waterfront, she always seemed to stand shivering on the periphery, wide-eyed and solemn, refreshingly oblivious to the groupies clustered around his lifeguard stand.

Years later on one of his rare forays home from college, he thought he recognized her again. Now a leggy teen, Maggie had joined the wait staff at one of his parents' favorite inns, a Victorian treasure with cabbage rose wallpapers, exotic turrets and porch trim. She was juggling trays of planked whitefish and chicken with morels, cherry soup and berry-laden salads.

Rather silly, awkward looking, he concluded at the time. But then anyone would be in that get-up. A long-skirted green dress, frilly white apron and weird puffy cap. When she smiled, he caught a flash of silver. *Braces*.

A lot of miles had piled up on the odometer in the intervening years. At seventy-five, if Jake Faland had any regrets at all about his childhood spent along Little Traverse Bay, it was only how short those days seemed after the fact.

He couldn't complain. The years had treated him well. No heart issues or cancer. At worst a cranky thyroid and the usual wear and tear. He still taught online after a distinguished career as professor specializing in endless courses in Western Civilization at a small but respectable Midwestern liberal arts college. A handful of relationships had ended badly, left him vindicated in the end that he had not been hell-bent on marriage. His kids were the students who populated his classrooms. To steer them past snippets of Chaucer and Milton on their road to adulthood was challenge enough.

"Well one thing's for darn sure," Jake told himself. "Strolls down memory lane are way too exhausting."

The traffic gods must have heard him. In that moment, the post-fireworks gridlock eased for a split-second. *Carpe diem*. With a sharp twist on the wheel, the Toyota shot into the Gaslight District near the hotel.

Parking spots were in short supply. When Jake finally found one, it was in the hotel lot, the very last place he was predisposed to look. Beyond worn out, it wasn't until he tried getting out of the car that he realized he hadn't escaped the night unscathed himself. Hands braced on the car's door frame, he gingerly stretched, waited for the twinges in his back to subside before he headed for the rear entrance to the hotel.

"So much for heroics," he muttered.

In the far distance, a last staccato burst of firecrackers trailed off into silence. The night air felt damp, heavy with a lingering acrid smell of gunpowder. Of the dozen-plus resort hotels that once dotted the Petoskey landscape, the Perry was one of the lone survivors. Its elegant lobby was all but deserted. Jake's room overlooking the glass-ceilinged rose garden seemed a tranquil paradise after that bumper-to-bumper road rage out there.

But sleep only came fitfully, punctuated by chaotic dreams and long bouts of staring at the ceiling. Odd flashback fashion, Jake found himself a kid again, jogging break-neck fashion toward Little Traverse Bay under a spreading canopy of trees. Out of breath. No sense of where he was headed or why.

Eventually a subtle gray began to tinge the windows. To let himself doze off again at this point seemed an exercise in futility.

"Hells bells," Jake groaned. *Five-thirty*.

Bleary-eyed, he fumbled for the Off button on the wind-up travel alarm staring out at him from the bedside table. He had salvaged the clock from the cottage. It was the old fashioned analog type with the minutes and hours circling its face, spelled out in oversize numbers.

"For the record, I'm not a digital kind of guy," he always told his classes as he plunked his watch down on the lectern to get his bearings at the start of every new semester. "We need clocks with faces and hands if we're going to make sense of time passing, put the measure of our lives in some kind of human context."

Right now, that act of humanizing meant getting the cottage updated and on the market, pure and simple. A hot shower took care of his still aching back. The day-old stubble along his jaw line would have to stand. Shaving wasn't on the agenda. Jake doggedly pulled on jeans, work boots, faded tee-shirt and over it a vintage pastel madras shirt he had found in his dad's closet.

Swashbuckling, he grimaced as he caught his reflection in the ornate mirror just inside the hotel room door. *It would have to do.* Worn for only several months a year, a cottager's wardrobe lasted for decades, eventually finding itself back in fashion in a quirky sort of way.

Jake was in no mood for sit-down menus. Claiming his car from the hotel lot, he made a beeline for the nearest fast-food chain. An egg-white sandwich to go and a scalding oversize coffee in hand, he drove back to the hotel, parked the Toyota and set off for the Petoskey waterfront.

A lone jogger nodded a greeting as Jake ambled along the breakwall toward the harbor light perched at the walkway's end. Ballast rock lined the path, flat enough in spots for a makeshift seat and table.

His sandwich was soggy and cold, the coffee scalding. An anticipated sunrise failed to materialize. Shore and bay lay shrouded in a dense fog. Out on the glass-smooth water of the bay, a lone trolling motor sputtered and caught, lost in the gray of the landscape.

No beach weather today. A couple more early risers were venturing out to the harbor light. A kid with a fishing pole held what had to be his grandfather's hand as he shuffled along in Jake's direction.

"You usually catch something?" Jake said.

The kid just grinned, a study in optimism. In the process, he revealed a conspicuous gap where his two front teeth should have been.

A guy after my own heart, Jake thought. Knows what he wants and goes after it. Well, what he wanted was to make sure those carpenters would be on the job at his dad's cottage by eight. Time to get going.

The construction crew was trickling in, visibly worse the wear after a long holiday weekend. *They had their work cut out for them*, Jake admitted.

Most of the cottages including his dad's had begun as single downstairs parlor with the open second floor space above it subdivided into bedrooms. Kitchen and bathroom add-ons appeared with the demise of communal kitchens and outhouses. Over time each and every one of those additions had begun to shift and settle at its own pace.

An issue, granted. But to Jake's mind, progress on the dry wall going up over the bare studs seemed painfully slow. "Problems, I gather," he said to the contractor.

"Not a single straight wall in the place," the man grunted. He was trying to put a level on a row of studs, with little apparent success. "These centers are all over the map—eighteen inches, twenty-four. So much for craftsmanship back in the day. To build straight, ya gotta build crooked."

Jake laughed. "If it works," he said, "do it. Some Old Timers still think putting in insulation like this is a sacrilege, as bad as TV sets and central heating. You saw that old floor furnace. If a kid wasn't careful, the hot grill would brand these painful waffle-weave designs into the soles of your feet."

The contractor just rolled his eyes. "Camping indoors ain't my thing. I'll take a tent any day."

A new energy-efficient furnace was already in place underneath the cottage floor. Jake could empathize when the workmen complained about crawling in the sand among the cedar posts holding up the building to finesse the job. He had been under there often enough himself as a kid, chasing down the family cat or stashing the bikes for the winter.

For a hundred-plus years those raw bare boards between the studs had served both as exterior and interior walls Few of the cottages in the area were winterized, even today. No point when the entire enclave virtually shut down every fall, boarded up and unoccupied. On one of Jake's only mid-winter visits, most of the streets were unplowed, piled thick with snow, passable only to snow mobiles or cross country skiers. He spent the weekend in a local motel.

"*Brigadoon*," Jake told the contractor. "As kids we thought the whole world rolled up the sidewalks every fall. And that somehow back home in summer everyone did the same."

Signs of the twenty-first century were obscuring those glory days of childhood. Gone were the tube and knob wiring throughout, the burn hole in what had been his bedroom ceiling, mute testimony to a long-vanished stove pipe that had gotten too hot. Wood beadboard now covered all that and the cobwebs left behind by a stubborn colony of spiders. In most cottage kitchens, ready-made oak cupboards took the place of the original open shelves or dented metal Westinghouse cabinets rusting around the edges. But in the Faland cottage, the cabinetry was custom-made hardwood, worth restoring.

"Sure got a lot of old stuff around here," the workman said. "We haven't done anything with one of the bedrooms upstairs—just too darn much furniture."

Jake looked sheepish. The crew wasn't exaggerating. He had stacked the room full, floor to ceiling, with contents of the rest of the rest of the cottage rather than move it into storage. No easy feat.

"I figured your crews would prefer that," he said, "over working around the stuff spread over the whole house."

"You're right on that one," the workman said.

Jake found himself fingering a crudely painted wooden boat sitting amid the clutter on the fireplace mantel. The sails were missing. When Jake turned it over, on the keel he saw the faded initials, JDF, 1991. His nephew James Donohoe Faland must have made it in the craft club back in the day. Jake would have bet good money that kids still slaved over the same project, twenty years later. Some of the old bottles decorating the corner shelf on the far side of the kitchen probably went back to the original owner in the 1890s.

"A tradition from way back," Jake explained to the workman, unaware of the wistful edge as he said it. "Contents and cottage went on the market together. Complete with puzzles and games and pots in the kitchen, linens in the cupboards, sometimes even food in the fridge—vintage now, that's for sure." Except for a few treasures he planned to keep, Jake would let the practice stand.

The carpenter eyed the wreck of a sloop cradled in Jake's hand. "A time capsule, I guess you'd say—"

"Something like that."

Jake set the boat back in its wonted spot, clearly visible thanks to the absence of dust where it had stood. *All this chit-chat wasn't doing a thing to help speed up the renovation job*, he decided.

"Guess I'll get going," Jake said, on a frown. "I'm not much use here at the moment."

"You could pick out the fixtures for the half-bath," the contractor offered. "Burt might get to it this week. If you're going on the cheap, there's a Habitat resale on the way to Harbor Springs."

A plan, Jake told himself.

By any ordinary standards, this was not going well. But then construction in Northern Michigan was a seasonal business given the long, harsh winters. All of the workmen were over-committed. And all of them wound up hopelessly behind. More often than not, the job slated for completion in November usually materialized by the next June. If a guy was lucky.

Jake made a mental note, the sidewalk in front of the cottage was heaving. And while he was at it, he would investigate clear vinyl roll-ups for the three exposed sides of the two-story front porches, up and down. It would keep snow off the porch floors in winter and add two what amounted to all-weather rooms for the place. A plus with buyers judging by the number of cottages using them.

A thin veil of mist still hung in the air, coating porch furniture in a chill, slippery glaze. He felt it on his skin, the hint of stubble along his jaw. Without thinking about it, he set off on a stroll through the yard, then intrigued by the strange foggy light, ventured beyond into the neighborhood.

Spent fireworks lying in the grass was proof positive the weekend of the Fourth had come and gone. With it went a fair share of the tourists. Cottagers who remained behind were laying low, sleeping in, waiting out the thick blanket of gray. The Chamber of Commerce had the formula for tourism down to a science, and for the most part, the weather cooperated. Raining? No problem. By four o'clock the sun would reemerge, just in time for one of the region's Million Dollar sunsets—the estimated tourist intake on any given day in the region.

This particular fog was proving so dense, Jake had his doubts.

As he worked his way on foot through a maze of cottages stacked three-deep between the shore and the first thoroughfare of any size, he found himself unintentionally back in familiar yet unsettling territory. More often than not, vehicle alleyways serviced the backyards and rear kitchen entrances while only pedestrian walkways passed between the cottage fronts. The Aron cottage was no exception.

Maggie was in the garden. She was wearing something long and tie-dyed, the colors of a tequila sunrise on a gloomy morning. Her long silver-gray hair was out of the way in a tight braid that hung well below her shoulders.

One of a kind—an original, Jake smiled to himself. With her back turned, she didn't see him coming. He had caught her deadheading.

"You're up with the birds," he said.

22

Maggie turned, startled. "Ditto."

She was barefoot. When she took a tentative step in his direction, she winced. Jake noticed an elastic bandage on one ankle. It appeared she hadn't come off unscathed last night after all.

Maggie gave him a quizzical look. "It's . . . what? Around eight o'clock."

"Going on nine. I was just checking out the crew over at Dad's cottage. They're all moving a bit slow this morning."

"They aren't the only ones."

"Your ankle? I noticed. Sorry about that."

"Among other things. I must have wrenched something in my back when you tried out your fireman's carry. Not that I'm complaining, not one bit. If you hadn't reacted so quickly, this could have been a heck of a lot worse."

He chuckled, laid a hand on the garden gate. "Still, you've made it out here, I see."

"OCD," she said. "Runs in the family. See a weed and pull it. I had some pretty tough role models."

"Impressive," he said. "Whatever the motivation. That garden of yours is a show-stopper."

"Credit for that goes back way before my time. But thanks."

"Well, good you. Some traditions are definitely keepers."

They were running out of small talk when Maggie intervened. "I've got a pot of coffee on the back burner. Some rhubarb-strawberry bread in the fridge. Homemade. And I owe you one. You probably skipped breakfast—"

"Junk food actually. But if you think you're up to it—"

"It's the least I can do."

Jake followed her down the path past a clump of pretty impressive looking rhubarb bushes mixed in with a jungle of perennials straight out of a seed catalog. At the top of the porch steps Maggie paused, clutching at the slender hewn porch post momentarily for support.

Hurting more than she let on, he thought.

From the look of it, she had kept the Aron cottage as was. Living and dining areas flowed at right angles to each other, separated from the kitchen only by a wide arch trimmed out with a wood ball-and-rod transom. The exposed upright studs made the rooms seem larger than they were. Anybody much over six foot would have trouble with that doorway. The place seemed a jewel box compared to the grand scale of the Faland cottage.

"Open concept," he marveled. "And a good century before anybody in the HGTV trade ever thought of it."

Maggie laughed. "Not so behind the times after all, those ancestors of ours."

Studs and board walls were painted an arctic white. And in between the studs hung pictures and objects of all descriptions, from souvenirs of travels past to kids' artwork from the craft house, positioned one over the other, floor to ceiling. The hodge-podge gallery looked all the world like wallpaper. No high-end minimalism here. The history of a family came alive on those walls everywhere you looked.

"Unique," he said in passing.

"As in weird. The ultimate throwback."

"Nothing weird about it," Jake said quickly. "In a world of over-designed and lifeless interiors, your life is on these cottage walls. Honest, out there for all to see. Nobody could argue with that."

One particular snapshot caught his eye. It was of Maggie as a young mother with her arm around a girl in a tutu and leotard. On the other side of Maggie slouched a boy about nine, looking very irritated at the whole business.

"Your kids?" he speculated. "Your daughter looks just like you."

Maggie's smile seemed vaguely uncomfortable. "That's Holly. Grandmother Aron loved hollyhocks. I thought the name made sense. And that very disgusted guy with the crew cut is her older brother Tony ... Anthos really. You can blame that on my obsession with gardens too, by the way. 'Anthos' is the Greek word for *flower*. My son wasn't impressed—routinely complained, *Mom, what were you thinking?*"

Jake laughed. "Hollyhocks. Those tall things, back by the gate."

"You noticed. Another gardener?"

He chuckled, but couldn't get past the fact that whenever he started to press her about family, Maggie changed the subject. "Me garden? Not hardly. A Ficus in the living room back home—"

"Which is . . . ?"

24

"Right next door. Wisconsin—Fox River Valley. Cheese head country."

"Lot of paper mills around there."

"At one time. Now it's mainly insurance, specialized tech industries. And higher education—my stock-in-trade, by the way."

"Business?"

He frowned at the thought this was her assessment of him. "Western and World Civ," he said. "A mad mix of art-in-the-dark, comp lit and history. It's about as esoteric as you can get."

"I wouldn't have pegged you as—"

"A nerd?"

Maggie laughed. "That wasn't the word I would have chosen. But then I can't pretend my own career path sounds all that practical. I changed majors a couple of times, then wound up loving comparative literature myself for my Master's degree. Not many job descriptions demand that for a background. Before I settled into a job as office manager with a not-for-profit, I clerked in a book store for a while. Lots of *Curious George* and Jackie Collins."

So, careers celebrating the glories of printer's ink then. For the both of us."

Finally, he thought, their shared laughter sounded relaxed. Maggie had begun to busy herself with a vintage coffee maker. Rummaging in a fridge from about the same era, she also retrieved a foil wrapped loaf of what looked like amazing bread.

"Strawberry rhubarb. I hope you're not allergic to nuts."

"Earthy-crunchy sounds perfect right now."

The two of them sat at the kitchen table. Outside a percussive burst of firecrackers told them the locals finally must be getting up for the day as well. Michigan's green light for homegrown fireworks displays expired twenty-four hours after the Fourth. Time, apparently, to shoot off whatever remained from last night's stash.

"And you," Jake wondered. "Where do you hang your hat when you aren't baking rhubarb bread and weeding away out there?"

"Downstate." She raised her hand, mitten fashion, and pointed to a spot roughly east of Lansing, naming a familiar suburban community in the process. "I inherited the homestead down there—lodged smack in the middle of the suburbs now, unfortunately."

"Ah, a native Michigander I see . . . "

"You mean using the hand for a map? Force of habit. My folks lived in Illinois until I was six months old. So technically I guess that makes me a *perma-fudgie—*"

Jake laughed out loud. "I've heard *Fudgie*—the way locals razzed us tourists back in the day. But *perma-fudgie,* that's a new one."

In young adulthood, Jake bristled at the local habit of labeling even the life-long summer cottagers for the sticky-sweet concoction that got its start on Mackinac Island and spread quickly through the region as the souvenir of choice. An implied dismissal of seasonal residents seemed harsh, on some level. Like many summer cottagers, this felt like *home* to him. But then he also had seen ample evidence in recent weeks of the impatience and imperious mindset of some summer cottagers—hard for anyone to take without some sort of backlash.

"You *haven't* been here much lately," Maggie shook her head. "We multi-generation cottagers seem to have worked our way up the food chain. They now call us *perma*– or permanent Fudgies. Though I'm not sure where I fit on that scale anymore. Since retirement, I spend a month in Arizona with my daughter in winter. I was expecting her up here over the Fourth. But now it might be closer to Labor Day . . . "

Again, something in the way she talked about her daughter, wistful, made him wonder. Perhaps mother and daughter weren't as close as Maggie would like.

"Fascinating how labels matter up here," she said finally. "All in good fun, mostly. You know, of course, that folks living on the Upper Peninsula answer to *Yooper—*"

"Makes sense. Try saying *U-P-er.* I do remember seeing a lot of Yooper bumper stickers over the years."

"Well," she flashed a mischievous grin, "you should also know that all of us down here qualify officially as *trolls* now."

"Trolls."

"As in living down south—'under da bridge'."

"Ya gotta love it," Jake laughed, shook his head.

In Northern Michigan, Mackinaw was the measure of all things. Mackinac the bridge, Straits and island, Mackinaw the City. For all the vagaries of spelling, pronounced exactly the same. *Mack-I-gnaw.*

26

"So, are a lot of the old gang still around up here?" he wondered.

Maggie hesitated. "Some. Most of my buddies hang out on the community garden crew. Not that I need more weeding with that jungle outside. You probably know Sonia, I imagine. Sonia Gunderson—Adelskold now. But a lot of cottagers are newcomers these days. I'm not really in with the beach crowd or the bridge groups. Never was. Not my thing. The garden keeps me busy."

"Better than I've been doing. You're right—I haven't been up here more than a weekend in years. And then mainly to help Dad open and close the cottage. He hoped, I think, that I would take over the place when I retired. *If*, I should say. Moot now with the place going on the market."

"You're still teaching then?" She sounded surprised.

"Online and occasionally in the classroom. I seem to have cornered the market on freshmen who think The Beatles represent the greatest achievement in British culture. Which means I can travel now and again. There are worse ways to spend one's retirement."

Maggie laughed. "Honestly, I didn't picture you as the type to die in harness. Not when you could be out there climbing a mountain somewhere, playing seniors tennis—I don't know what. But not grading endless essays on ancient civilizations."

"Ouch," Jake winced.

"Then again," she added quickly, "I wasn't always the best judge of character. So, your family's good with it—your choosing not to retire, selling the cottage? A lot of people would be reserving prime spots permanently on the beach at this point."

"On my own on that one," he told her. "No spouse in the picture to weigh in on the subject. Though I came close a time or two, just never got around to saying the I-do's. My brother lives in Thailand—runs an eco-tourism business. He's out of the picture. My sister is currently babysitting our dad. Since Mom's gone, Dad's been losing ground for a number of years now—bottom line, the cottage hasn't been a family thing in a long time."

Maggie averted her gaze, visibly embarrassed. "I wasn't intending to pry."

"No problem. I volunteered," Jake said, savoring another bite of strawberry rhubarb bread. Multiple cups of coffee on top of the megadose of caffeine earlier were starting to take their toll. It was probably time to get going.

"Still, it must be hard to let the place go. You spent your childhood here."

Jake hesitated. A muscle worked along the edge of his jaw. "True, I did think about taking over the place ten or fifteen years back. For five minutes, anyway."

He hadn't intended to sound that negative. Maggie picked up on it immediately.

"Why do I think there's a story lurking behind that one?"

He forced a smile, tight and utterly without humor. "You're right, of course. I was dating a woman from India at the time, a faculty colleague in economics. Eventually we spent a weekend together at Dad's cottage, checked out some of my old haunts. Except out of the blue a 'well-meaning' neighbor pointed out to her that there aren't 'many of her kind' around here. So much for the relationship—and nostalgia. After that, I never looked back."

Maggie looked shocked. "Beyond awful."

"Yeah, well . . . let's just say, I've decided it's way too monochromatic around here for my taste. I just don't feel comfortable any more with what that represents."

"I honestly hadn't thought of it that way," Maggie told him, her distress evident. "To me, the area always seemed oddly eclectic . . . quirky. It's hard to pin down exactly *what* the political climate is when we've got the Michigan Militia, left-leaning folk who live off the grid and retired CEOs from all over the Midwest staking out turf around here. I suppose some might see that as a potential quagmire for issues we thought we left behind us decades ago . . . "

Jake decided not to trot out some of the harsher labels that had bubbled to the surface in recent public discourse. Racism. Bigotry. Anti-Semitism. Nothing that hadn't been said about the larger national arena, except far more personal and devastating in rural areas, where the scale was so small.

"Tragedy is" Maggie persisted, "these tiny communities always prided themselves on being so safe, so welcoming. Where kids still could run off on their own from morning to night without—"

"I get all that." Jake drew a long breath, let it out slowly. "But at what cost—for starters, to racial and ethnic diversity, inclusiveness? Problem is, I'm not a kid anymore."

He could tell from her face, he had struck a nerve. Her eyes said it all, an expressive amber-flecked green that held a guy's attention. There was a great deal of intelligence behind them. *Underestimate it*, Jake thought, *at your peril.*

Maggie abruptly began clearing the table. Back turned, she was making a project of stacking the dishes in the oversized enamel sink. When she turned to look at him again, her face was sad.

"A pessimist," she said.

Jake shrugged. "Realist maybe. We all pick our battlegrounds. This one isn't mine. Life's way too short. There's one heck of a big world out there."

Tension crackled between them. The silence was uncomfortable. Scorching hot weather was forecast for the next few days, sweltering humidity. *Close*, Jake's mother always called it, like the air itself was closing in, stifling everything it reached and touched.

Jake stood up. His chair made a scraping noise on the bare plank floor of the kitchen. "Unfortunately, we aren't going to solve the problems of the universe, even our little corner of it, in a morning . . . or even a summer for that matter," he said. "But I appreciate the chance to talk, catch up on—"

"Glad you enjoyed it. If I can help over there . . . anything that might help with renovating the cottage, be sure to keep in touch."

"I may take you up on that," he said. "The yard is a mess, nonexistent really. Mainly moss and horrifying overgrown bushes straight out of an Addams' family cartoon. But with your gardening skills—"

Maggie laughed. "Even skill can't do a lot with yews, tree roots and deep shade all over the place. That said, I guess there's always hope."

"An optimist."

"A gardener," Maggie said, suddenly dead serious. "Though maybe they amount to the same thing."

She walked him to the door, stood outside on the porch as he started threading his way through the garden to the gate. He closed the latch behind him then turned to wave, half expecting to see her back at her weeding. But she wasn't. She stood there leaning on the porch post, a splash of tie-dye sunshine against all that impeccable white siding.

In the flattering filtered light of that foggy morning, he could have pegged her for a good ten years younger. Good bones. Those deep-set amber-green eyes and faint dusting of freckles on the bridge of her nose. Maggie definitely had a timeless air about her that had outlasted the pert and perky of adolescence.

Enough, he decided, to make a guy regret the turn their conversation had taken. But then politics had a way of doing that.

"A flower child back in the day," Jake chuckled to himself. "And one who genuinely loves flowers. Go figure."

IRIS, common yet uncommonly lovely, this genus of showy plants numbers around 260–300. The name comes from Greek for 'rainbow'. The plants' rhizomes and gnarled roots give no clue to the elegance of the plant itself or the showy blossoms that result. Subject to leaf spot, a fungus that thrives when plants become too crowded and air cannot circulate among the rhizomes.

Neighbors

"Well, that was different," Maggie concluded.

As she stood watching Jake Faland pick his way through the garden toward the alley, she tried to picture the modest Aron cottage and its setting through his eyes. Technically what he had experienced was the back not the front facade. Visitors rarely saw the supposed main entrance door at all. That was accessed only from a narrow central sidewalk which cut through between two rows of cottages, all stick-built and with no two alike. It was always Grandma Aron's garden that had given the so-called 'back porch' of the Aron cottage its unique identity and charm.

No excuses. By force of habit from that vantage point on the back porch, the gardener in Maggie quickly took over. From where she stood, her grandmother's showy iris—vintage two-tone gold and purple varieties that had been the staple of homestead gardens all over the region—had gotten hopelessly out of control. Maggie had struggled spring and fall for years to weed out the quack grass popping up amid the cluster of gnarled horizontal rhizomes. But from the look of it, avoidance and stop-gap measures no longer sufficed.

"Time had come to break out an axe or machete." Maggie was not looking forward to it.

The distant ringing of her cell phone made the issue moot. Limping prodigiously, Maggie managed to locate it on the kitchen counter just in time before the caller gave up.

Sonia, the caller ID read. The voice on the phone sounded way too cheerful for the morning after a very late night.

"Maggie . . . hey, gal, you're up! What a bummer to miss the fireworks last night—but then I'm up to my ears in house guests, wouldn't have subjected you to that craziness," the caller rattled on by way of greeting. "How are things?"

Sonia Gunderson, Adelskold since her marriage, was what her peers' parents privately described as a 'healthy girl', tall and sturdily built. A Golden Girl incarnate, she had worn her thick, fair hair styled in the same long bob ever since she was ten, just a tad too blond these days considering the fine network of lines etched into Sonia's otherwise still high cheekbones. She and Maggie Aron had been summer friends, inseparable, for as long as either one of them could remember.

"Up to no good," Maggie laughed. "You wouldn't believe it if I told you, Sonia. I'm just about to clean up the kitchen after an hour-and-change entertaining a gentleman caller."

"Gentleman *who*—you're kidding right? I'll be right over."

The phone went quiet. Maggie chuckled softly to herself, knew full well the response her 'teaser' was likely to get. If she hustled, she could finish hand-washing the breakfast dishes before Sonia showed up on the doorstep.

It took only seconds to run a sink full of hot soapy water, plenty of time for regrets—starting with how the morning's visit with Jake Faland had ended. Maggie wondered wryly what her friend Sonia would have made of that confrontation. At worst the guy must have thought her a bigot. At best, woefully naive. All now water over the proverbial dam.

When in doubt, Maggie told herself, *dispose of the evidence.* Whatever the crisis, dispatching a stack of dishes had qualified as makeshift therapy ever since she was a girl. "Ma'am," the plumber who opened the cottage every spring hinted, "if you're wondering, that water system of yours *would* handle a dishwasher."

Maggie would just aim a skeptical look in his direction. "Can't believe it. The community pipes are so shallow they have to be drained every winter—down to every single cottage hot water heater, sink and even commode. Don't want to risk messing with that."

"Suit yourself," the guy would tell her. "But no need to be a martyr here." His reassurances or not, the thought of a dishwasher just didn't seem to fit the lifestyle. Maggie slipped the last plate into the wooden drying rack on the counter. Four minutes, tops, was all it took.

Maggie had her estimates of the job down to a science.

"Knock, knock!!" a voice warned her through the screen door. Sonia didn't wait for an invitation. A woman on a mission, she crossed the checkered linoleum and drew her childhood friend and neighbor into a rib-cracking hug.

Maggie grimaced. That Sonia finally noticed, along with the ace bandage on Maggie's ankle. "What on earth have you been doing?"

"Fell in a pothole last night—well, almost anyway. Coming home from the fireworks. This guy fished me out or I could have taken quite a header."

"Okay, give!" Sonia said. "Name, rank, serial number."

"You'd never guess." Maggie hesitated. "A neighbor of ours. Apparently Jake Faland was at the fireworks last—"

"*The* Jake Faland? Lifeguard, jock of all trades, driving all the girls crazy back in the day."

"The same."

"So . . . that was last night," Sonia cocked an eyebrow in her friend's direction. "And he wound up here this morning at the cottage exactly *how*?"

Maggie told her a highly edited version of her near wipe-out in a pothole on Bay Lane, the surprise rescue followed by the great reveal at the garden gate. "My guess, this morning? Jake just happened to be out and about—that, or the workmen over at his cottage kicked him out. I decided offering him coffee was the least I could do."

Sonia looked genuinely stunned. "No accident, kiddo—the guy's showing up here. Couldn't be. Come clean, what really happened . . . the truth now !"

"Nothing."

"Say again."

Maggie wasn't about to describe her tense go-around with Jake on the subject of cottage life. Sonia had no such qualms. And it occurred to Maggie for all her own defensiveness about tradition, she couldn't guarantee her brother or children were any more intent on preserving the family cottage than the Faland clan.

"Zip," Maggie told her. "End of story. The guy finished off half a loaf of rhubarb-strawberry bread and several cups of coffee. I thanked him again. He left."

"Wow!"

Maggie didn't react one way or the other. What started out as casual banter was beginning to feel more than a little uncomfortable.

"Still as gorgeous as ever?" Sonia prodded.

"Define gorgeous. Jake was older than us—has gotta be at least seventy-five."

"Out of shape probably. As many creases as a leather shoe."

"Actually no. On both counts. He still has most of his hair, though it's cut too close to tell for sure. And decent reflexes or I would be over in the ER right now, waiting for multiple scans and a month of rehab."

"Is he single?"

"No clue. Oh wait . . . yeah. Says he came close but no cigar. Which says a lot right there."

Sonia sighed, shook her head. "Maggie, Maggie—"

"And what possible relevance could all that have at this point? The whole bunch of us left our so-called primes behind us a good decade ago. Jake may be footloose and fancy free, but you and I are grandparents."

"You make it sound like we've contracted some terminal disease. If a chance at some quality time with a Jake Faland would just happen to land on *my* doorstep—"

"You'd laugh him out of the room. Sonia, I know you."

"Not as well as you think."

Maggie shrugged. "Well, if you're looking for action, he's spending the next month at his dad's cottage, getting it ready for sale."

"No way," she said. "Not when you've had a thing for this guy as long as I can remember."

"Ridiculous!" Maggie snapped, tired of the whole conversation. "He and I talked more in the last two days than we did in the past sixty years. He's dead set on selling the cottage. And I have one goal right now and one goal only . . . to age with some semblance of grace. And to be able to straighten up again the next time I bend down to weed the daisies. Anything else? Way too much work.'

Sonia didn't look convinced, but didn't protest either when

Maggie offered her a slice of leftover rhubarb bread as a peace offering. "Well anyway," Sonia said as the two of them settled down at the table, "for the record, Jake Faland might not be the only one selling out one of these days."

Maggie's brow tightened with concern. "You've heard from your tax accountant about the cottage?"

"No, I haven't. And in this case, I'm thinking no news is *not* good news. With the state uncapping of the cottage assessment after my parents' death and the tax bite that goes with it, I'm beginning to think selling is inevitable. Although lots of luck with that. There are a slug of cottages all over the area on the market. Not much selling either, I've been told."

Maggie frowned, shook her head. "Why do I get the feeling that I'm going to wind up all alone here, surrounded by strangers or rentals. I can't even imagine what I'll do, Sonia, if you aren't—"

"No worries. Have you got a spare bedroom . . . wait, you do," Sonia laughed. "Up those incredibly steep and narrow stairs. But then we could always install a chair lift."

Not funny, Maggie wanted to tell her. Instead she bit her lower lip, dropped her gaze—distracted by the convoluted meanderings in the wood grain of her grandmother's old kitchen table top. At some point in its history, the oak drop-leaf with its delicately turned legs had been demoted to a so-called 'canning table' common on the porches of farm houses in the area. Weathered and etched by countless blades that missed the cutting board, the vintage wood was tinged a deep amber, with intriguing looking berry stains that left random darker patches behind.

Battle scars, Maggie found herself thinking, *can make for one beautiful patina.* Time, it seemed, had a way of creating both.

Cottage life was no exception. To his credit, Jake Faland had seen immediately what that world meant to her, the minute he walked in the door. Long conversations on the porch. Curling up with a glass of merlot and a good book on a cloudy afternoon. Memories of family and beach time with the blistering sun of early August overhead. Long walks through leaf-strewn streets glistening from a gentle autumn rain. Her girlhood played itself out and still lived on within these cottage walls, a powerful constant in her world.

But at what cost? Once Jake Faland shone a light on what she knew in her heart to be true, Maggie knew she would never be able to think of the life she had built for herself here in quite the same way, ever again. Sonia worried about dollars and cents. All the while Maggie was wondering, *does this lifestyle make any sense at all*, especially if preserving the past depends upon shutting out others.

Maggie shivered. "Sonia, I'm sorry you're struggling. Totally understand, believe me."

"I assume Jake is more or less in the same boat."

Not exactly, Maggie thought but didn't say out loud. There didn't seem to be any point in rehashing the real issues behind Jake's decision to sell. Sonia was feeling bad enough as it was.

Suddenly glum, the two friends finished their tea, hugged, went about their respective days. "Anyway, keep me posted," Sonia said on the way out the door.

"Posted?" Maggie said quizzically.

"You know. About Jake."

Maggie just laughed.

Not smart given the state of her ankle, but Maggie spent the rest of the morning and into the afternoon in the garden. Clad in jeans, lightweight long-sleeved top and with the rigid support of an ancient pair of work boots, she took on that iris with every tool in the shed. Success came hard and in increments, a hunk of fleshy rhizomes liberated here and another clump there.

Living proof of what happens when putting down roots turns into something far more destructive. Maggie found herself beating back the recurring thought Jake Faland's visit had planted in her brain. Her own life had become no less firmly entrenched over the decades.

At what cost? A question worth asking.

Finally sweaty and exhausted, she soaked in the tub. It occurred to her that with that ankle of hers, after a half hour in scalding water she might not be able to stand up again.

It took a lot of false starts, but she managed. Tossing her gardening clothes in the wicker hamper, Maggie pulled on fresh jeans and an ancient navy sweater. The vintage wicker glider on the porch had thick flowered chintz cushions—heaven. Maggie poured herself a stiff drink and settled down with the novel that had been obsessing her for the last couple of days. It was only then she noticed what she had been using for a bookmark. Someone had slipped the three-fold flyer under her door. Assuming it was just another Fourth of July calendar of events, Maggie hadn't even bothered to read it.

She did now. Reread it twice, still unable to believe its contents. In a word, it was a hate letter dressed in pious phrases about God and country. With the November elections coming up, it said, those of us who love this part of the state can't afford to be complacent. It was time to take a drastic stand against all the talk of religious diversity, blended families, same sex unions. Life as we knew it would be replaced by crime in the streets and terrorists lurking behind every tree and bush. The organization behind the flyer was unfamiliar, its intent patently obvious.

Maggie sat up bolt upright on her grandmother's wicker glider. Never one for profanity, she used it now, out loud.

Some of her distress if not the actual vocabulary must have transmitted itself to the stranger strolling down the alley. At any rate, the guy turned, eyebrow raised as if a firecracker had just gone off underfoot. Flushed and heart pounding, Maggie watched until he was out of sight.

Fighting words, she thought. "Back to Ozzie and Harriet—? They have got to be kidding! If this kind of hate mongering succeeds, decades of social change are out of the window for women, gays, people of color—all of us."

Her first instinct was to call Sonia. Instead, she found herself hobbling, letter in hand, in the direction of Jake Faland's bay-front cottage. It never once occurred to her that he might not even be there. But he was, spade in hand, trying to dig under the roots of an overgrown yew that was all but obscuring one wing of his family's cottage.

He looked up, saw her coming and stopped. "Maggie—?"

"Did you get one of these, too?" she said.

The puzzled expression on his face spoke volumes. "Did I get—?"

"This."

Jake had laid down the spade. She thrust the by-now crumpled flyer into his dirt-smudged hands. He just stood there, holding it, as if somehow all he needed to know was written on her face.

"I can't believe it," she said.

Jake started to read what she given him. The slick paper was now mud-streaked as well.

"Okay . . . ," he said slowly. The undercurrent of anti-Semitism, racism and xenophobia were enough to take anybody's breath away.

"You were right about the climate," Maggie said, "Did I tell you that? Well, unfortunately you were."

Jake's mouth was compressed in a tight line. "The thing's blatant, I'll say that. Worse than I would have thought."

"Well, I said a lot worse when I first read it, trust me. Scared some poor soul walking down the alley a minute ago."

"When did you get this?" Jake said.

"Dunno. Last week, last couple of days. Somebody must have slipped it under the screen door on the porch. I never even bothered to read it—thought it was some kind of sales pitch. It is, I guess. But Holy Smokes!"

Jake shook his head. "Gotta say, whoever wrote this knows how to play the Parade-of-Imaginary-Horribles card. May I keep this? A friend of mine from grad school works in Lansing. He would want to see this."

When she nodded in the affirmative, Jake folded the flyer and slipped it into his jeans pocket. "I'm sorry," Maggie said. "You said you didn't want to get involved in this sort of stuff."

Jake frowned, reached down for his spade. "The principle of the thing," he said. A muscle worked along the edge of his jaw as he thought about it.

Maggie asked him to keep her posted. "All right, then."

But things weren't all right. That was the problem.

For all the tree-canopied streets, the waters of Little Traverse in their gun-metal splendor on a gray July afternoon and the memories that drifted like last season's wood smoke, Maggie realized with awful clarity that things hadn't been all right in her world. Hadn't been for one very, very long time.

§§§§§

Maggie could recall with an odd clarity the rite of passage, the day her childhood ended and girlhood began. She was ten years old. Her mother, Lillian, stood in the cottage living room holding a thin, rectangular box. When young Margaret opened it, cradled by a layer of

39

tissue paper lay two hunks white cotton fabric sewn into the shape of her hands.

"Your very own gloves, Margaret," her mother told her. "Try them on."

Awkwardly, young Margaret tugged at them as she had seen her mother do as long as she could remember. Progress was slow. The gloves fit tightly. For trim, each glove had puckered lines of stitches that fanned out where the tendons on her bare hands would have been. The trim extended from the base of her fingers almost to her wrists.

"Funny looking," Margaret said.

"Young ladies wear them. And white shoes—but only from Memorial Day to Labor Day. Then you wear black or maybe brown."

Exactly why, young Margaret had no idea. From that moment she was expected to don both shoes and gloves on the way to services on Sunday mornings. Despite assurances from the neon green outline around the dark shape of her feet in the department store x-ray machine, the shoes pinched. By noon the pair were relegated once again to the dark recesses underneath young Margaret's brass-plated iron bed. The gloves went into their tissue lined box in the lone dresser that fit in her tiny cottage bedroom. The drawers smelled of moth balls and lavender.

"For the mice," her mother said.

Margaret wrinkled up her nose. "The mice won't like it."

Her mother laughed. "That's the whole point. Otherwise in winter they'll nest in the cupboards and closets."

Even in the summer, clothes in those drawers smelled of naphthalene. And no amount of washing seemed to help.

The rules of childhood to this point in time had been so simple. Daylight seemed to linger forever. A teeth-jarring plunge into the great lake Mishigamaa in June became the very definition of 'glacial'. There was no swimming or crossing of the main thoroughfare through their summer enclave without an adult present. No yelling if you played kick-the-can in the gravely alley in the evening or on lazy Sunday afternoons. Disputes over TV time weren't an issue. The cottage simply didn't have a set at all until Margaret, now Maggie, was grown and in her fifties.

If you were bored, you read. If you were sleepy, you napped on the wicker day bed on the porch. The battered upright piano always had music displayed at the ready on the rack. Wainscot cupboards were full of games, puzzles. If you were hungry, wild raspberry bushes along the old railroad right-of-way were ripe for the picking.

Up until now, many of the Thou-Shalt-Nots were of young Margaret's own making, holdovers from the toddler days when No likely as not meant Yes. *I'm not tired*, said with a yawn. *I'm not hungry*, on the one day she decided not to forage for wild strawberries in the scraggly patch of grass that passed for a front yard.

But with the arrival of the gloves, all that began to change. On the cusp of adolescence, the rules began multiplying exponentially.

"You're growing up now. And young ladies don't play in the mud," her mother said. Or run sock-footed in the garden. Or hang upside down from the cast iron pipe suspended between two large old maples in the cottage side-yard where a swing used to be.

It became taboo to hang out evenings with the neighbor boys visiting from Detroit. The two were overheard using the F-word and had taken to smoking down on the waterfront. And it wasn't appropriate to seek refuge with Esther, the neighbor's housekeeper. A large woman of color in a white starched seersucker uniform, Esther, for years had provided lemonade and a porch swing whenever young Margaret felt the urge to run away from home—to escape even momentarily a world in which the rules became ever more demanding, baffling, capricious.

Friendships became fraught with mystery. The older twins summering three cottages down the alley were considered too 'fast', though Margaret beat them regularly in the rec program's races. And only once did she remember playing with Esther the housekeeper's granddaughter.

Esther helped out at the neighbor's. Her granddaughter was older than Maggie, at least eleven. "Up from Chicago for the week," the girl said with some pride, "on the train."

She was dressed in a frilly dotted pink pinafore. Her hair was braided in a style Margaret had never seen before. Each braid ended with a pink ribbon that matched the color of the dress.

"Cornrows," the girl drawled when Margaret quizzed her on the subject.

Nothing, Margaret thought with a thrill of curiosity, like the small stands of field corn growing in most gardens downstate. If the adult Maggie had ever known the granddaughter's name, she had forgotten it.

41

Their acquaintance was short-lived. It ended abruptly as the girl taught Maggie to turn a simple blade of grass into a piercing whistle that eventually drew adult attention.

"Margaret," her mother called out from the porch. "Time to rest up for dinner."

Young Margaret Aron felt anything but tired. Scuffing the toes of her blue canvas boat shoes in the dirt, she reluctantly complied. At the garden gate she looked back toward the alley, but the girl was gone.

Maggie never saw her again. The housekeeper herself disappeared a summer later and in the decade that followed, Maggie could count the people of color in her cottage world on the fingers of a single gloved hand. In the sixties, the adopted biracial son of another cottager spent several years in the crafts program, never to return. A random African-American speaker came and went at community programs and events. A rainbow diversity flag flew over a cottage or two in recent years.

African-American. Black. Queer. Gay. Only the language seemed to change, never the demographics.

Outside her cottage world, an older and more worldly Maggie Aron never saw herself as prejudiced. She feasted on Thai food, developed a love affair with Cajun bands and Bob Marley records. She bumped elbows, built friendships with colleagues of every conceivable background.

All of which made the disconnect with cottage life all the stranger. In this childhood paradise, lawnmowers still didn't break the Sabbath calm. But Jake Faland's question about the rectitude of that tranquil world kept haunting her. *We don't see what isn't there*, Maggie told herself. But Jake had made her aware of that invisible bias, loud and clear. Any answers or excuses that came to mind made absolutely no sense. No sense at all.

Regardless, most likely she would never see much of Jake going forward, Maggie told herself. She couldn't blame him if he avoided contact—not given his opinions about the cottage life to which she had clung so tenaciously over the years.

Would everything prove as easy as getting the iris under control. Maggie quickly finished reading her novel and had moved on to a nonfiction book about the young Hemingway in Northern Michigan. Together she and Sonia went to the foreign film night, a depressing saga

42

of family turmoil in wartime Bosnia.

"Enough to make a guy lose his appetite," Sonia shook her head. And yet they wound up afterward at a popular local fifties style custard stand just before closing.

When in doubt, weed. It was one of those rare humid days when the surface of Little Traverse Bay lay heavy and still.

"Ya gotta get outta that sun, kiddo !" Sonia called out, obviously on her way to the State Park beach. She had a couple of visitors in tow from out of town, judging by their utter lack of tans. They were armed with faded seventies era towels and bulky wood-framed, striped canvas lawn chairs several decades older than that.

"You're welcome to join us," Sonia said.

Maggie felt awkward refusing. But then Sonia knew she had never been much of a beach goer. "Way too much work."

Sonia laughed. "Weed on, McDuff !"

A few minutes later, Maggie heard Sonia's old soccer-mom van rattling down the alley. Weeding already had lost some of its appeal. By the time she worked her way around to the shade garden on the southwest corner of the cottage, Maggie was tired, cranky.

"Crazy hosta," she groaned.

A good dozen of the sprawling plants were elbowing one another to carve out space for their enormous ribbed leaves. It really wasn't the time of year to divide them. But then hosta would take just about anything.

Maggie liberated several of the smaller ones with a few deft spade- thrusts. She had seen Jake Faland's yard. Whatever plans he might have for landscaping, hosta were about the only things that would thrive in such dense shade. Rummaging in the utility shed, Maggie came up with enough black nursery pots to house the plants. While she was at it, she threw in a couple of ferns, then loaded the whole mess into a rusty Radio Flyer wagon that was pressed into service as a garden cart.

Better safe than sorry. As an afterthought she cut back the sprawling fern fronds and all but a few of the shorter hosta stems before potting them. Jake said he wasn't a gardener. He would be tempted to leave the lush foliage intact. Not smart when the plants needed every bit of energy they had to survive the transplant. The pruning accomplished, she started off down the alley, awkwardly towing the wagon behind her.

The forecast heat wave had arrived. When she found Jake in the front yard he was dressed in a sweat-soaked tee and mud-covered jeans and work boots. From the look of it, he was still wrestling with the same recalcitrant tree root. By now the size of the hole around the rootball could have accommodated a small swimming pool

Maggie chuckled quietly to herself. Stenciled on Jake's faded navy tee were silk-screened portraits of the Rolling Stones. She had to hand it to the guy. When it came to wardrobe, he wasn't a stickler for resort chic.

"Hi, neighbor!" Maggie said. "Beware Greeks bearing gifts."

He looked up, startled. Awkwardly he grabbed a denim shirt slung over one of the yew branches, used the sleeve to mop at his sweat-drenched forehead.

"Dead plants," his brow creased in a puzzled frown as he gestured toward the contents of her Radio Flyer. "Are you trying to tell me something?"

"Ferns and hosta," Maggie laughed. "They may look it, but trust me—they're not dead, just resting."

"Aha!" He shot a bemused look her way. "Another Monty Python fan?"

"Their Dead Parrot sketch. You know it? I just couldn't resist." Maggie dropped the handle of the wagon and headed his direction, hand outstretched in greeting.

Jake hesitated before reaching out to take it. "I'm covered in dirt."

She laughed and shook his hand. "A true gardener, after all. Whatever you're planning for that giant hole you're digging, I thought a hosta and fern garden might be a good start. I had to cut them back, so maybe the plants won't look like much this season. But by next year they should be in great shape. Meanwhile you could always get some instant color with a few annuals if and when the realtor starts showing the place."

"Whatever you did for that agency where you worked, you must have been one heck of an administrator," he chuckled. "See a problem—solve it."

Maggie flushed. "Right now I see a backhoe in your future. You've been at this rootball a week."

"Not quite. But yeah. Time flies, fun or not." Jake winced as his hands flexed on the shovel handle. "Blisters galore "

44

"Hypocritical since I never use them myself, but gloves do help. Sometimes anyway. I certainly wasn't intending to make even more work for you with this cartload of greenery."

He laughed. "I'm not complaining. I've got to fill this hole with something."

"No need to be a masochist about it. You've got time. The plants will survive several days in these pots if you keep the roots wet."

Jake started to say something, reached instead in his jeans pocket. He retrieved what looked like several now crumpled, equally mud-streaked tickets.

"Actually, I've been meaning to come over myself," he said. "Was downtown earlier. On a whim, I picked up two passes to next weekend's Bliss Fest. For Sunday. Thought you might like to go."

Maggie just looked at him. "You're . . . I'm—"

Her jaw clamped tight. The last time a guy offered to go anywhere with her, it was a neighbor downstate who volunteered to chauffeur her to her cataract surgery. And Bliss Fest wasn't like a pass to the local cinema. The folk and rock festival outside of Cross Village had become popular enough in recent years that anyone who didn't have tickets beforehand was risking a shut-out. Spendy, too, from what Maggie had heard. Jake's expression gave absolutely no clue to what he was thinking.

Meanwhile, the time for polite excuses about checking calendars had long since passed. "Can I take it, that's a Yes?" Jake said.

The only response that came to mind sounded lame even as Maggie threw it out there. "I haven't gone in years."

"Neither have I," Jake shrugged. "Couldn't resist. Posters are plastered all over town—*Find your Bliss*, right? It's not as much fun going solo and somehow I guessed you might enjoy it. Sure beats digging all weekend in this stony ground."

"Tickets are on the high end of things. I would reimburse you, of course."

"No way. My idea. This one's on me."

Maggie caught the finality in his tone. She drew a long breath. "All right then. Yes. It sounds like fun."

"Sunday. I'll pick you up at nine."

"See you then."

At least she had the presence of mind not to say, "It's a date." The whole transaction was beginning to feel like a pending root canal.

"Good," Jake nodded "Meanwhile, I've got a heck of a lot of digging to do."

"You can hang on to the wagon for now, if that would help. Keep the plants damp and stash them up against the cottage. Actually, that wouldn't be a bad place to plant them either. Take advantage of the deep shade—"

Rambling on and on, it occurred to her. Jake stooped to grab the handle of the wagon. With some difficulty, he steered it and its precarious load toward the spot she was suggesting. "I can't guarantee I won't kill 'em," he said. "But at least it's not on purpose."

Maggie laughed. "You won't know for sure whether you did until next season."

"New owner's problem. Not mine."

They had traversed this particular ground before. With an awkward wave, Maggie turned and hurried her way through the alleys between the cottages. Halfway up the garden path, a familiar twinge stopped her in her tracks.

Lower back. Maggie stifled an oath. "Sciatica—lovely."

After all that digging, she had it coming. *Piriformis syndrome.* Inflamation of the sciatic nerve. Whatever the formal diagnosis, she knew the drill. Stretch, then stretch again.

She couldn't manage it where she stood. Breathing hard Maggie gingerly picked her way up the cottage stairs. Once on the solid ground of the porch, she braced a hand against the porch pillar to steady herself and leaned into a brutal stretch that she felt all the way from hamstring to calf. Seconds passed. Twenty-eight, twenty-nine, thirty.

Repeat the process. When Maggie finally straightened, the pain was all but gone. She took a cautious step, then another. It felt as though she had grown an inch.

The doctor's prognosis in March was blunt. "You're going to have to live with it. Bottom line, you're fighting to maintain range of motion, the degree of flexibility it takes to change positions, get in and out of cars and chairs, among other things. Painful, I'll give you that."

Maggie scowled. "You're saying I've been overdoing it—the parts are wearing out? That I need to cut back on—?"

"On sitting maybe," the doctor said. "The culprit isn't overuse. It's our sedentary lifestyles. That, and age. Can't do much about that last one. Parts wear out over time."

Maggie had the sudden urge to smack the guy. Late fifties, she guessed, and not an ounce of sub-cutaneous fat anywhere in sight. So much for her strategies for killing time during those long Michigan winters. She had given up cross-country skiing when she did in her knee five years ago. Plan B was to keep busy reading, painting and doing needlepoint. Except for gardening in the summer and periodic walks along the Bear River or Wheelway trails, everything revolved around hunkering in one spot for hours on end.

"You say I'm going to wind up stiff as a post?"

The doctor shrugged. "That's up to you."

Rigid in more ways than one, Maggie thought looking back on it. Only some of the symptoms were not going to show up on WebMD.

Where had it all gone off the rails? She had never been one to avoid issues. As a student and young professional, she had picketed in support of migrant workers, had marched against a variety of wars. She had sanded woodwork on teams that built houses for the displaced and homeless. Even after retirement, in the narrower confines of her cottage world, Maggie had prided herself on her book group and garden club memberships, the caffeine-fueled discussions of 'causes' ripped straight from the headlines. And yet all around her, the global world she had come to cherish was under siege, right under her very nose.

Down the alley, her plants were undergoing a dramatic transplant in someone else's front yard. She expected them to survive. Was she as capable of rolling with the punches? Maggie could only hope so.

Sonia had left a message on the answering machine of her land line. Cell phone era or not, some habits die hard. "We're cooking out tonight," Sonia said. "Would love to have you join us."

The phone felt cold and hard in Maggie's hand as she punched in her friend's familiar number. "Thanks for the invite," she said. "But I'm really tired." It wasn't a lie.

"Gotcha," Sonia sounded disappointed. "So tomorrow then. Lunch—we could go into downtown Petoskey?

Maggie hesitated. "Eleven-thirty," she said finally. "We'll beat the crowds."

Coneflower or ECHINACEA is a colorful medicinal herb common in butterfly gardens. Plants such as Coneflower rely on diversity for their survival. So-called *alternation of generations* in their reproductive life cycle is just one such strategy. A garden limited to a single species is vulnerable to the catastrophic spread of plant diseases or marauding insects.

Generations

Rolling Hills, the retirement complex on the outskirts of Petoskey showed no signs of stirring when Maggie pulled her ten-year-old boxy green Scion into the parking spot marked Visitors Only: Violators Will Be Towed. She shut off the ignition and retrieved her keys. If she was going to be back in time for lunch with Sonia, she was going to have to cut her mid-week visit with her mom short.

Inside the imposing red brick main building, the corridors were equally deserted. Maggie's footfalls echoed on the gleaming tile floor. She took the elevator to the second floor. Tucked half-way down the hall, her mother's tiny apartment was even further out of the mainstream. It was one of the few furnished units available for rental every summer.

The door to the nearby nursing office looked just like any other apartment, a subtle way of minimizing an institutional feel to the place. Maggie knocked, didn't wait for a reply.

"Ms. Aron," the aide looked up from the paperwork on the desk in front of her, gave her visitor a hearty "Good to see you".

"Don't get up," Maggie said. "Just wanted to check on how mom's doing."

"Fine. She joined a Christmas in July party in the lounge yesterday and the bus took her along with a bunch of residents to the fireworks the other night. She seems in good spirits."

Maggie felt a twinge. The aide wasn't hinting, but the woman's blow-by-blow reminded her just how long it had been since the last visit. "Crazy-busy everywhere. You have a great Fourth yourself?"

The young woman looked pained. "Pulling double shifts," she sighed. "We've had some staff out on vacation. I'm saving mine for the kids' fall break. So you can guess who winds up covering—"

"Hang in there. This too shall pass. I'll let you get back to business. But thanks for the heads-up."

Her mother's door was unlocked. Maggie stuck her head in the door and called out a warning, "Halloooo!"

"In here," a voice called from the bedroom.

Maggie found her mother sitting on a floral-upholstered love seat on the far side of the bed. Her red-white-and-blue outfit had to be the staff's doing. Despite ongoing reminders, last count her mother still was convinced it had to be Easter. Lillian's striking silver-white hair also was impeccably styled, Maggie noticed. The every-other-week pattern she had arranged with the on-site salon seemed to be working.

Always a fastidious dresser with a keen sense of style, Lillian Aron had risen from two years of business school and the secretarial pool to executive assistant in a multi-office law firm in the county. In an era when most women gave up professional life after marriage, Lillian's determination to 'stay busy' had been a powerful influence on her daughter over the years. Maggie vowed long ago to do what it took to keep the tiny dynamo of a woman's dignity intact. It was the least she could do.

"Reading I see," Maggie said.

Her mother looked up, flashed a wicked grin. "Excitement, huh."

Maggie caught the title, a *Times* best-seller, albeit a couple of seasons back. "Staff said you saw the fireworks."

"Past the curfew around here," Lillian sniffed. "But I persisted."

"Good for you."

"About all you can expect when your memory's shot, eyesight's going and you come down with a case of selective hearing."

"At least you haven't lost your sense of humor. I'll take that," Maggie told her. "Sorry I haven't been around for a couple of days."

By force of habit, she noticed one of her mom's nylon knee-highs had picked up a snag. Commandeering a notepad and pencil from the night stand, Maggie started a list: more nylons. She would check the fridge for juice and warm-up breakfasts, the bathroom for tissues. The snack dishes salted around the condo also appeared empty.

"Working on a novel?" her mom wondered.

Maggie laughed. "Not hardly. Just a grocery list. You aren't the only one who needs a gentle prodding now and again."

Rousting herself, Maggie launched into a heavily edited account of her own Fourth of July festivities. When it came to Jake Faland, she assigned the whole sequence of events footnote status. Even so, she saw her mother's eyebrows arch.

"I knew Jake's dad," her mother said finally. "Quite a character.'"

"As in—?"

"Nobody's fool. He wanted what he wanted. A real chain rattler."

A knowing look greeted that pronouncement. "It seems the apple doesn't fall far from the tree," Maggie said.

"Jake? Cute kid, if I remember. The spitting image of the face on the Campbell soup commercials. Shook hands like an adult. You liked him."

Maggie shrugged. "I guess."

"Nothing wrong with that."

"Mom, *really*. I'm seventy-plus."

"Don't remind me. I'm way too young to have a daughter that old."

"Time does it to a guy."

Maggie's mother shot her a pointed look. "They had an old duffer come in last week and fuss at us about staying young. *Nurturing your inner adolescent*, he called it."

The speaker must have made quite an impression for her mother to remember. "Sounds exhausting."

"Maggie honey, I may not know what month or day it is—but one thing I know. Aging doesn't get any easier with time. As I see it, you can either spend the so-called Golden Years picking out a headstone or keep on a'moving. I'd rather be pegged as working on my second childhood than sitting in a wheelchair staring at the linoleum."

Maggie looked uncomfortable. It was nothing she hadn't been telling herself of late. Ever since the doctor hit her with the pep-talk about the consequences of sitting too long in one spot.

51

"So, you wanna do lunch?" Maggie said. "I'm meeting Sonia downtown Petoskey in an hour or so."

"Thanks, but no. You go ahead. If I skip lunch, the crew at my table starts to assume I'm dead."

Maggie laughed. "Don't want to get the gossip mill going."

The route downtown was less than two miles. It took a record twenty minutes. Traffic was bumper-to-bumper in spots, parking non-existent. Maggie needed two full stoplight cycles to traverse one particular intersection. By the time she hobbled the block-and-a-half to Northern Lites, a trendy new restaurant on Mitchell Street, her bum ankle was aching again. A headache had emerged full-bore behind her eyes.

Sonia already stood in line out in front of the narrow storefront. Her straw hat, imported leather huarache sandals and sorbet-toned green and ochre sun dress stood out in the knot of shorts-clad tourists around her. She was fanning herself with a menu, visibly out of sorts.

"Sorry," Maggie tugged at the waistband of her gauzy geometric-pattern peasant skirt trying to look more put-together than she felt. "I took a detour to see Mom. Big mistake. Even the back roads look like parking lots."

Sonia groaned. "Remind me never to suggest lunch downtown anywhere near the Fourth again. Right now, I'd go for a round of margaritas on the porch, veggies and humus—in the shade anyway. How's your Mom doing?"

Brow knit, Maggie tried to put her visit in context. Sonia probably was just being polite. But of late it was hard to take the question that way.

"Same old mom," she said finally. "More forgetful with every passing day. But she hasn't lost an ounce of spunk in the process."

"You're lucky, you know. Most of our friends lost their parents a decade or more ago. Me included."

"I know. Mom was and is my best-friend—nothing personal, Sonia."

"I envy you."

"Don't," Maggie said quickly. "Am I selfish, I wonder, willing Mom to hang on beyond the point she seems happy with her life. With her short-term memory all but gone, she's forced to live almost entirely in the moment. Tougher than we think—this business of living in the *Now*. Don't dwell on the past. Don't worry about the future—"

"Sounds like a feel-good Facebook post."

"True enough. But watching Mom struggle, I never appreciated before how much our memories matter when it comes to who and what we are. It's enough to disorient anybody. As for the future, the things we anticipate can also define us. And without *either*, yesterday or tomorrow, life can become a flat, unending routine. *Boring.* Lately on bad days, Mom uses that word a lot. Though the staff says she's going non-stop, she doesn't remember a bit of it."

"Heavy stuff."

Maggie winced. "Aging isn't for sissies, Mom keeps saying. Right now my ankle's killing me and I have a heck of a headache."

"At least the line's moving," Sonia chuckled sympathetically. "Turns out, this place doesn't take reservations."

The crowd around the heavy oak hostess station was getting impatient to the point of surly. A visibly harried young hostess in black dress slacks and tee shirt worked her way down the line in their direction.

"Sonia?" the woman wondered.

"That's us."

"If you don't mind sitting on the patio out back, we've got a table for two."

"A view of the alley wasn't exactly what we had in mind," Sonia frowned.

"It's in the shade," the hostess said.

"Sold," Maggie chimed in.

The three of them threaded their way through the noisy interior of the restaurant with its original tin ceiling and bare brick walls. Once outside again, the air felt downright cool. The decibel level proved equally refreshing. Across an adjacent public parking lot, they were treated to a view of a mural of the historic downtown. Sketchily drawn sailboats danced on the waters of the bay visible between the buildings.

"Not as bad as I feared," Sonia said.

W*orse*, Maggie quickly concluded as they settled down at the table. A half dozen wrought iron tables stretched along the back of the

53

restaurant, separated from the public walkway by a matching iron fence. And at one of them sat Jake Faland. With him was a gorgeous blond who had to be at least half his age.

Now why wasn't that surprising? Maggie hadn't seen the guy in decades and suddenly she was imagining a script straight out of a stalker-movie. Though which one of them was the stalker seemed less clear-cut.

About that point Jake caught Maggie's eye. He smiled over at her, nodded a greeting. The young woman and he seemed about finished with lunch. After retrieving his credit card, Jake headed their way. His companion, ash blond and sporting chic business casual, trailed a few feet behind.

"See you two got stuck out here in outer darkness as well," Jake said. "Though the food was worth it."

"Everyone in town seems to have the same idea," Maggie's mouth felt stiff. Sonia was looking at her expectantly. "By the way, I think you know our neighbor, Sonia. Sonia Adelskold. You knew her as Gunderson, of course."

"Jake Faland." Sonia shot a thinly veiled gotcha-look in Maggie's direction. *Way too pleased with herself.* "I heard you were in town."

"Treating my niece to lunch," Jake said. "Though we sure weren't expecting this kind of madhouse. Anne is an administrator at the hospital—one of those kids who summered here and never left."

So much for hasty conclusions. Maggie felt a flush spread along her cheekbones. She made a show of bending down to rescue her napkin. Her silence was conspicuous.

"Anyway, good to see you." Jake flashed a grin in Maggie's direction. "Be sure to polish up those dancing shoes by Sunday."

She just stared. Jake took his niece's arm, steered the two of them across the alley toward the parking lot.

Sonia's eyebrow arched. "*Sunday?*"

By now a fiery red, Maggie mumbled under her breath. "Bliss. The Bliss Fest is running this weekend."

"And you're going—the two of you."

Maggie didn't bother to answer that one.

"And just when were you going to share that little tidbit of information?" Sonia prodded.

The arrival of the waitress cut short the third-degree. Sonia ordered a vegetarian Reuben—a ridiculous culinary concept as Maggie saw it. Maggie herself chose a kale salad with an exotic-sounding mix of unfamiliar nuts and seeds and cheeses.

"Maggie, Maggie—"

"I thinned out my hosta yesterday, gave Jake a few. His yard's a mud-hole. Turns out, he had a spare Sunday pass for Bliss, that's all."

"And I just won the Powerball lottery."

Maggie frowned. "Hardly in the same category."

"Whatever. You go, girl."

"You're starting to sound like my doctor."

Sonia just laughed.

The rest of the week crept past, ample time for Maggie to reconsider her plans for the weekend. Finding her Bliss with Jake Faland seemed less and less appealing every day. After nonstop exposure since the Fourth of July, it was as if the guy had disappeared abruptly from the planet. A half dozen times, phone in hand, she contemplated calling him and begging off on his invitation. But then that would have involved even more grilling and teasing from Sonia.

Better just let things stand, Maggie decided. *And then stay as clear of the Faland cottage as possible.* The joke would grow old with Sonia. Life would resume and no one would be the worse for any of it.

Want-ads in hand, Maggie spent Thursday morning hitting the garage sale circuit. She found a half dozen children's books for her brother's grandkids. That meant a trip to the post office, but first a hunt for a box in which to ship them. Friday was a standing date with a friend from the garden club, the weekly perch-fry at a popular Greek restaurant north and east of town. The Mediterranean decor and tiny deck out back were welcome respites from thoughts of pending tie-dye and drum circles.

Saturday morning meant volunteer time on the community garden crew. By noon when the team of gardeners packed it in, the public beds were duly dead-headed and there wasn't a weed in sight. Maggie joined a few of the other sweaty crew members for lunch at a popular sandwich spot in downtown Petoskey. An afternoon at the State

Park beach was cut short by a cold front barreling through. The cooldown was welcome after a hotter than usual Fourth.

Jake was picking her up at nine next morning. Early to bed made a lot of sense. Instead, Maggie treated herself to a decent merlot while she prowled through a shelf of family albums. Looking for what, she had no idea.

Summers dominated the photos—three generations' worth. For much of Maggie's childhood, she had spent a month or more with Grandma Aron at the cottage while her Dad Benjamin and Mom Lillian held down the fort downstate.

Grandma Brigitta Aron, known to her friends as Bidey, was a formidable presence. *Stately*, her friends described her. Broad, high cheekbones and olive complexion gave her face an exotic cast that never quite fit with the 'hundred percent German' claims on the family tree Maggie put together as an assignment in biology her freshman year in high school.

Maggie owed Grandma Aron her greenish eyes with the subtle amber highlights. She also inherited the woman's sharp vision and long arms.

"Perfect for weeding," Grandma said

Her granddaughter wasn't impressed. To Maggie's dismay when the rest of her fit into a size nine, those broad Aron shoulders required an eleven. And it wasn't fashionable in the fifties to have inherited chiseled features that could be described as Teutonic or Wagnerian.

The war was long over. With it went the undecipherable Low German conversations among the adults at family gatherings whenever the children weren't supposed to hear. And by junior high school, a tall-for-her-age Maggie quickly discovered that 'stately' also was 'out'. All the cheerleaders suddenly were petite and perky-featured, fair-haired and with surnames like Wilkins and Cavendish.

So when Maggie enrolled in German in high school, it wasn't so much from an urge to reclaim her roots. The French and Spanish teacher was originally from Georgia and she spoke with a southern accent that bore no resemblance to English much less a Romance language. By the time Maggie achieved a level of fluency in the Mother Tongue, Grandma Aron was the only one left in their extended family who could still converse with her in High German, the language of Goethe and Schiller and the Brothers Grimm.

Grandma Aron's stories were in another realm entirely—rambling, fascinating tales of living in an isolated German-speaking enclave as a girl. Highpoint was being chased by gypsies on the wagon ride home from the nearest general store and losing her buggy whip in the process. But most amazing of all was the lexicon of expletives that accompanied those adventures—arcane and bawdy songs and phrases that would never have passed her lips in English.

How much simpler though if "Aron" had been "Smith" or "Jones", Maggie privately lamented. She made the mistake of expressing that just once in earshot of Grandma. Never again.

A woman in a neighboring cottage had made a point of repeating the surname quizzically after their first public introduction. Maggie squirmed as the woman looked her up and down in the process. "Aron," the woman said. "Isn't that a Jewish name."

It wasn't a question. Grandmother's amber eyes crackled with an intense flame when Maggie told her about the encounter.

"Never be ashamed of who you are, Maggie Aron," she said. "Or where you come from." Fierce words for a girl of nine, words it had taken Maggie half a lifetime to comprehend.

For all that, Maggie's most powerful memories of her grandmother were in the garden, above all her fierce love for the earth and green things growing. When it came to the attire chosen for the job, things for Maggie became more fraught.

Keeping off the sun was the sole objective. Even on the hottest days of mid-summer, Grandma Aron always wore a broad-brimmed straw hat and mid-calf length cotton house dresses with long sleeves. And in an era when no one wore full-body gartered corsets with metal stays anymore, she shed hers only when working among the perennials. In its place she donned these strange undergarments she called 'draws' and darned but wearable Sunday stockings rolled down and fastened with an elastic band just under her knees.

To Maggie's chagrin, kids in the cottages next door found the getup vastly amusing. Whenever her grandmother bent to snag an errant cluster of grass or wild mustard popping up among the onion sets, the whole neighborhood was treated to a glimpse of those baggy knit bloomers that reached nearly to mid-thigh. Mortified by the audience, Maggie would finish her own daily chore of patrolling the weeds as quickly as possible.

Mission accomplished, she and Sonia would head for the beach, a world populated with fair-skinned blonds intent on baking themselves to a crisp. The black and white photos of Maggie and Sonia in the family album had yellowed. But Maggie still recalled the powder blue of her detested one-piece suit as if it were yesterday. The thing looked all the world like her grandmother's corset, ill-fitting and shapeless. Maggie's naturally pale coloring and the pallor produced by Lake Michigan's teeth-numbing cold did little to improve the overall effect.

The hardest photos for Maggie were the shots of her husband Joe. His death just weeks before retirement came both as a shock and an abrupt end to so many assumptions about Maggie's future in this place. Joe had aged along with her, shared the quiet, loving adjustments that come with time in a relationship. Literally overnight Maggie's identity had changed to widow, a woman of a certain age no longer loved or remembered for who she had been or become in her husband's presence—perhaps the cruelest loss of all. Ten years later, time had blunted the pain but not the reality of her situation.

Maggie could lay claim the titles of 'mother' and 'grandmother'. She had childhood friends, mainly women, who were still a major part of her life. But when it came down to it, she felt alone.

Self-contained, she liked to think of it when she felt depressed. *Independent.* But then rationalizing has its limits.

The years sped past with each turn of the pages. On one particular snapshot, Maggie thought she spotted Jake Faland at a distance on his lifeguard stand behind her and Sonia, though the photo was too grainy to tell for sure. The lifeguard's awkward grin seemed out of synch with his official stenciled tank top that reached nearly to the hem of his baggy swim trunks.

"Uncomfortable in his own skin," Maggie muttered after she studied and restudied the photograph longer than she would have wanted to admit. "Who would have thought it?"

Through all the ambiguity, summers past lived on most reliably in the craft projects strewn about the place and in the inches and dates pencilled on the kitchen doorframe. MAGGIE ARON, AGE TWELVE, FIVE FEET FOUR INCHES. AGE THIRTEEN, FIVE FOOT FIVE AND A HALF.

In 1955 the now-faded jottings with Maggie's name on them stopped. So did the growing—outwardly anyway. By the time she went off to college, she was average to short among her classmates. Even so, the stereotype remained embedded in her deepest perceptions of self, the Amazon of her youth, never quite fitting in.

"Willowy," Maggie's husband always described her in their newlywed days. She never entirely believed him.

Over a decade passed before the notations on the doorframe resumed, an odd family tree that survived numerous paint jobs and retouchings over the decades. Another generation had begun to leave its mark indelibly on this place. Nineteen seventy three was penned in blue ink next to the name, Holly. Maggie's daughter was four. Landmarks for her brother already had begun to pop up two years earlier.

Maggie found the practice quaint, even arcane, but then how *does* a person quantify the act of growing? Candles on a cake. Notches on a doorframe. Albums chock full of memories.

The dusty photos reminded Maggie of an old-fashioned zoetrope she had built years ago for a science fair, the forerunner of the modern animated film. Like summers in the garden, the images viewed through the zoetrope's cardstock drum blurred together at whatever speed the viewer chose to turn the crank—a moving, unending time warp.

Rainfall varied with the seasons. A late spring led to an explosion of flowering condensed dramatically into weeks not months. Summers were cool or too hot, the growing season short. Mid-summer nights on the far end of the Eastern Time Zone went on forever. Inevitably fall came, then winter.

Cottage shutters went up late September. School and downstate life resumed. Graduations, birthdays, first jobs, children and grandchildren arrived in turn on the scene—a thousand and one grounds for celebration or grieving.

Grandma Aron passed when Maggie was in graduate school. It was midwinter and the ground was hard. The backhoe had struggled, the funeral director said. Grandmother would not have approved of the piles of bare dirt lining the cemetery plot.

"Too much red clay," she would have sniffed. And so it was.

As the crowd around the open grave shivered in the chill December air, Maggie felt her thoughts drawn to the sandy soil of the cottage garden, made rich over time by generations of perennials and leaves, egg shells and coffee grounds folded lovingly into the earth. Epic battles with tree roots were fought and won. Traps were set out for the slugs that left glistening trails on the cement slab at the base of the porch.

"Living on garden time," Grandma called the journey.

With the generation's passing, it began to make sense. Ninety-two seemed light years removed to Maggie in her twenties. But at seventy that kind of gap had become far smaller.

Garden time flowed into the unknown like the quicksilver of the Bear River salmon run plunging into the enigmatic waters of Little Traverse Bay. Never still, never resting, its range of motion was infinite.

Native to Asia, Europe and Western North America, PEONIES are so-called perennials, plants that live two years or more. The average perennial lifespan is three to five years. Surprisingly, flamboyant, quirky, ant-friendly peonies are among the hardiest. Many of them can thrive for the span of a human lifetime.

Bliss

Sunday arrived and with it Jake Faland. Maggie woke up groggy and disoriented at the sound of the wind-up alarm on the bedside table, as if she had somehow overslept. There was no time for coffee and scant opportunity for her morning ablutions. Luckily, she had laid out her wardrobe the night before. She got dressed, twisted her hair into a tight up-do. And with precious little time to think about what might lie ahead, Maggie found herself fumbling with the passenger side seat belt in Jake's ancient Toyota and headed north and east out of town.

The route Jake chose out of Harbor Springs bypassed the Tunnel of Trees, a historic narrow highway along the bluff to Cross Village that drew tourists by the busload every fall. It was far too slow—an outing in itself. Instead, he took an inland route north through the sparsely populated interior of the mitten.

Maggie found herself looking with new eyes at the tiny farmsteads, rolling hills, pastures and forest land that flowed across the landscape. The open waters of the Great Lake were nowhere in sight.

Traffic seemed unusually heavy for an otherwise remote country byway. Eventually they turned right onto a narrower secondary road. Nothing prepared Maggie for the sea of humanity camped out in lawnchairs, tents and recreational vehicles across an open hillside. The comings and goings into the hardwood forest at the crest of the long sloping meadow hinted at an even larger venue beyond.

"Bliss," Maggie felt a knot of excitement in the pit of her stomach. The line of cars waiting to turn into the festival grounds stretched a good half-mile along the narrow road. Plenty of time to think about what lay ahead.

"Pretty much as you remember it?" Jake grinned as he shot a glance her direction.

"Bigger," she said. "That's for sure."

"Apparently there are more concert stages now, a kid zone, crafts and a drum circle in the woods. Most of the campers seem to hunker down out here in tents or RVs for the whole weekend."

"Wow, I think." Maggie found herself hoping the spontaneity and Woodstock atmosphere she remembered hadn't suffered any in the process.

They parked. Jake opened the trunk and hauled out several vintage webbed aluminum-frame lawn chairs, a cooler and a bentwood picnic basket. "I figure at this stage in life, it pays to forego the blanket-on-the-ground routine," he said. "This isn't exactly grass out here."

Maggie insisted on carrying the basket as they headed off in the direction of the Main Stage. "What have you got in here—rocks?" she said.

Jake laughed. "Sunblock. Bug repellent, just in case. I've thrown in a decent bottle of red, some cheese from this new shop downtown, gluten-free everything—"

"I don't remember picnics being so complicated back in the day. What is the world coming to?"

"Older. For starters."

It hadn't occurred to Maggie, but as they picked out a spot off to one side of the crowd, they were surrounded by a fair share of gray hair. A few guys around their age were sporting impressive pony tails.

Maggie laughed. "Guess we aren't the only throwbacks reclaiming their roots. I don't feel so much like a latter day hippie."

Jake arched an eyebrow. "I'm disappointed. I really was expecting that tie-dye of yours . . . "

Maggie flushed. Anticipating the lack of shade and stubble of the festival's new-mown hayfield, she had slipped on a pair of jeans and a gauzy white peasant-style tunic. In the back of her closet she found a pair of thin leather lace-up ankle boots—dusty, but salvageable. Last minute, she grabbed a straw gardening hat that hadn't seen the light of day since the last time she had come to Bliss. A satin ribbon silk-screened with cabbage roses stretched around it as a band.

"I was going for funky," she said.

Jake shot an appreciative look her direction. "In a classy sort of way," he said.

"Well, I've been coveting your shirt. Vintage Bliss."

He had shown up in jeans and a well-worn Green Bay Packer ball cap. His earth-tone tee was silk-screened with a cartoon of a seedling dancing wildly in front of a stylized seed packet. The date read 2005, the twenty-fifth anniversary Bliss Fest season. From the look of it, the shirt hadn't gotten a lot of wear.

"Yeah, well—as you gather, it's been around a while."

"Some things never change."

True enough. Maggie caught herself swaying in time to a high-energy reggae beat. The band on the main stage was just ending its set. From the look of their drums, Latin rhythms were the group's specialty. Up next was an acoustic guitar and folk duo with credentials that went back to the nineties.

Maggie eased into one of the beach chairs and began to scan the rest of the Sunday program. "Zydecco," she read out loud.

"As in, Cajun," he wondered.

"The same. I love it. Ever since I heard the soundtrack for *The Big Easy*."

Jake chuckled. "I should have guessed—another film buff."

"Dennis Quaid and Ellen Barkin. Protagonists older than teeny boppers. And the music in his voice when he called her 'Cher'—what's not to like?"

In the far distance, they could hear the sound of mike tests and what sounded like a double-time tune, weaving its way from major to minor keys and back again. Waves of heat shimmered over the open field. The aroma of patchouli, stale beer and fried sausage was overpowering.

"Deja vu all over again," Jake said. "I could swear I just caught a whiff of pot coming from somewhere behind us. A flashback that's for sure . . . the drug of choice at some of my wilder grad school bashes in Madison back in the day."

Maggie chuckled knowingly. "Too chicken myself . . . beyond a few epic experiments in college. Though I'll admit to my share of smoky bars in Ann Abor with pitchers of dark German beer and some guy totally stoned over in the corner."

"Could have been yours truly," Jake chucked softly. "Though the University of Wisconsin was another world entirely. We never knew when clouds of tear gas would chase us off the streets."

Maggie shook her head. "Surreal."

Jake's jaw tightened as he thought about it. "At the time . . . but even now. The question has never gone away. What was it for—the war, all of it? I suspect you must have seen it . . . in recent years *The Times* has run several series on Southeast Asia. Hard to believe, but tourism to the Mekong Delta and Cambodia is skyrocketing. Apparently what Agent Orange and napalm couldn't accomplish, trade agreements have."

"And after all the censure when he was younger, Bob Dylan, our generation's poster child for protests, has been named a Nobel laureate. Who would have guessed?" Maggie hesitated before broaching the obvious. "I never heard whether you—did you get caught in the draft back then?"

Jake was looking out toward the horizon, his face inscrutable. "In a word, *no,*" he said. "Ostensibly I cruised through to the doctorate on a string of academic deferments. But then I sometimes suspected that Dad also had friends on the draft board."

She couldn't read his tone. Guilt? Regret? "You lost friends over there."

"My best buddy from high school actually enlisted, talked about free college down the road. Instead he wound up MIA and his girlfriend married some jerk from Milwaukee. The guy showed up with her once at a class reunion, driving a rag top with an air horn blaring *My Way.* The whole night he tried to hustle life insurance to anyone in earshot."

Maggie took a deep breath. "Some of my classmates got called up, too. Eventually one of them wound up living on the streets in Arizona or New Mexico. We never knew for sure either, but a good friend of my brother—the story was he went to Canada. After a while he just dropped off the grid. His parents . . . we all were devastated when we heard ten years later that he had been killed by a hit and run driver."

"Vietnam," Jake said finally. "Tough way to define a generation.

Pretty much a lose-lose, all the way around."

They sat for a while in silence. In the distance, random notes had resolved themselves into a driving Cajun rhythm. Jake slowly got out of the lawn chair and extended a hand in Maggie's direction.

"We seem to have some New Orleans vibes going on over there," he said. "What say we check out the band?"

The route to the dance tent was tricky. It meant picking their way across the stubbly field while dodging lawn chairs and coolers. Uneven furrows in the newly shorn hayfield made the footing dicey in spots. Now and again Jake's hand shot out to cradle Maggie's elbow.

"Who's holding up who?" she said finally.

Chuckling, he tucked her arm through his. "Does it matter?"

No, Maggie found herself thinking. *It didn't*. She took Jake's gesture for Old School chivalry. Somehow that felt okay.

"On the subject of changing times," Jake wondered out loud, "I gotta ask. How did a free spirit kind of gal like you wind up spending her working life as a bureaucrat pushing paper and punching a clock?"

Maggie was on the verge of a caustic retort, thought the better of it. The two extremes—aging Hippie and dull as dishwater public servant—were about the last character references she would have chosen for herself.

"You make it sound so Kafka-esque."

Jake laughed. "No offense intended."

"Actually, there was no master plan at work," Maggie said after a while. "I always drifted with the flow more or less. In small town life, it's pretty much a necessity. Forget degrees and job titles. If there's decent work, you take it and worry about credentials later. There certainly wasn't much call for literary buffs, that's for sure."

Jake aimed a pointed glance in her direction. "Why do I think you're underestimating yourself."

"Honest, that's all. When my kids were little, they got very bored with people asking them what they wanted to be when they grew up. And given my own career path, I could certainly empathize. I finally told them to think like a plant. Tell 'em, you just haven't gotten your second leaves yet."

"You lost me," Jake said.

"Gardening 101. Never try to weed when the first green pops up in the garden. As plants first sprout, they all look more or less alike. Most likely you're going to pull out more flowers than weeds. You have to wait for a plant's second or true leaves to know what you're dealing with."

Jake grinned. "The Fountain of Youth if I ever heard it. Personally, I've always felt so-called growing up is vastly over-rated, if not impossible."

Maggie shot him a knowing look. "Now and again, we all need to be reminded of that."

Space in the dance tent was at a premium. The air was heavy with the smell of straw and canvas. Strobe-fashion through the crowd, Maggie saw a handful of dancers lost in the moment. Style and substance were irrelevant. Energy prevailed.

"So what say, we just go for it," he said. Jake's hand was extended in her direction.

"As in—?"

"There's a waltz rhythm in that beat somewhere. How much trouble can we get into?"

"I haven't danced in at least a decade."

Jake flashed a sympathetic smile. "Never too late to start. I'm told it's like riding a bicycle—"

Maggie hesitated, then laid her hand in his. "No guarantees."

Jake laughed. "Never are."

Uncomfortable at first and strangely light-headed, Maggie followed him onto the wood plank dance floor. As Jake swung them into the crowd of dancers, she began to lose herself in the strident wail of the accordion and fiddlers. She didn't need a translation to understand the lyrics—the pain of love lost or unrequited, the sad realities of living. Yet for all that, the powerful rhythms and melodies soared relentlessly onward into the unknown.

Jake's hand against her back steadied her as they dipped and twirled. Protestations aside, he was a good dancer. *Sure of himself*, she thought. *No longer young, but still confident in his athleticism.* That hadn't changed.

Safe in the anonymity of the moment, Maggie let the dance carry her seamlessly from tune to tune. The world spun past in a rush of bodies, the bare wood of the dance pavilion, the musicians' glistening faces in the still air—whirling, turning to the changing rhythms. When the set ended, Maggie felt both out of breath and a rush of disappointment.

She started to disentangle herself. Jake's intense steel-blue eyes, unsettling close, stopped her in her tracks.

"Had enough?" he said.

Maggie laughed. "Unless you're sure there's a first aid tent, I'd say, Yes."

Her hair clung to her damp forehead. A few strands had escaped the bun piled high on the crown of her head. Her face felt hot.

"I've got beer in the cooler," Jake said. " Or hard cider if you prefer. We've earned it."

Maggie leaned a hand against one of the wooden pillars supporting the roof of the dance tent. The thought of leaving the music behind was oddly painful. "Give me a minute," she said.

"I get it, trust me. You realize, we're both going to feel this tomorrow."

I hope so, Maggie thought.

Retracing their route back to the lawn chairs would have challenged a GPS. The crowd had begun shifting like a wheatfield, ripe and blowing in the wind. Blankets once empty of occupants ceased to be landmarks and new clusters of lawnchairs had popped up like morels after a spring rain.

"Worse than looking for your car in a Walmart parking lot," Jake said as he finally located the spot they had staked out for themselves.

"I was thinking the same thing," Maggie laughed. "In fact, I've gotten in the habit of pressing the emergency alarm on my car keys in desperation on a regular—"

"Gotta love it. So, you're the one whose car has been levitating, door flying open and closed, headlights flashing and horn blaring."

Maggie chuckled more uncomfortable than amused. "Guilty. Though fortunately, my son taught me to snap a photo with the smartphone to get my bearings. It's a lot less drama. Except there's way too much coming and going here to make that work."

"Well, it seems some things never change," Jake said, half

wistful and half amused from the sound of it.

Maggie followed his gaze. Twenty feet or so beyond them, closer to the main stage, a young couple were settling down into a double-wide sleeping bag, way too hot given the sun blazing down on the open field. Only the crowns of their heads were visible, the intent all too obvious.

Love knows no season. Love knows no time. Maggie struggled with recreating the rest of the lyrics, gave up. Composer and name of the tune were proving equally elusive.

Jake had rummaged in the cooler, popped opened a cider, slipped the can with its striking image of a twisted tree into one of those foam sleeves and extended it in her direction. "I think you told me you're an Angry Orchard fan. But if you prefer beer or Perrier, I have both."

Maggie just looked at him. It was the cider that did it. At the oddest moments, images of past summers kept bubbling to the surface. The strange melange of then and now wound up discombobulating to say the least. On a bare budget tour of Scotland with her husband months after their marriage, they had lived for two solid weeks on cider, fish and chips. "I'm starting to grow gills and fins," Joe had grumbled. Over forty years later, Maggie couldn't even pass a seafood restaurant without remembering.

Meanwhile cider in hand, Jake was looking at her strangely, waiting for an answer. "Cider's fine," she told him quickly.

He opened an amber IPA for himself. Local, Maggie noticed from the label before the can disappeared into another foam sleeve touting the efficacy of an area savings and loan. *Long defunct.*

"What goes around seems to come around," Maggie told him. "There was always that brewery on M-119 and then for a while it was anything but. Now they're back in the beer business again and the cars out front, you wouldn't believe."

Hard to keep up with it all," Jake said. "Thai food and Cajun on Mitchell Street—quite a change of pace from the burgers and pizza back in our day. At least most menus around here still offer planked whitefish, I'm happy to say."

They settled into a comfortable rhythm as the afternoon unfolded, with the minimum of awkward seven-minute pauses. At times it seemed like two dancers circling each other, this business of getting to know one another. *Reconnect*ing, if Maggie wanted to get technical about it.

But for all the shared childhood experiences and for the most part compatible adult perceptions, she couldn't pretend to know this man who had been the boy next door. Nor he *her*, for that matter. Too much living had intervened, had drawn its subtle veil over those early formative years.

Time does that, she thought. *Sometimes mercifully so.*

The day melted into the record books as effortlessly as butter melting on a warm griddle. Bands came and went, storytellers and periodic drawings for door prizes. Maggie and Jake wandered the vendor tents. She bought herself a new tie-dyed caftan, serviceable cotton and marked down as the day went along. They feasted on stuffed grape leaves and humus, salads heavy with sprouts and seeds and dried fruits from one of the food trucks.

It was nearly midnight when they decided to pack it in. Sunburned and sleepy-eyed, Maggie settled back in the passenger seat for the long drive home through the isolated farmlands and occasional forested stretches. Except for a random yard light, any houses or buildings were lost in the murky blackness beyond the reach of the headlights.

"Better keep an eye out for deer," Jake said.

Leaning forward toward the dash, Maggie tried her best. The headlights from the Toyota weren't revealing much. Newer cars would have used halogens.

"You're right. That tall grass along the ditches could be hiding just about anything," she told him.

Jake stifled a yawn. "Slow going, then. Rather safe than sorry."

In the end, all that threatened their progress was a family of racoons about five miles north of Harbor Springs. Strung out along the thin strip of gravel next to the roadway, four pairs of eyes caught the headlights. At the sound of braking, the little convoy stopped, turned and melted back into the undergrowth.

Maggie chuckled. "Decided not to make a run for it."

Jake's hands flexed on the wheels. "I'm glad you didn't either when I asked you to come," he said. "You were certainly thinking long and hard about it."

Maggie flushed, grateful that the car's dark interior didn't betray her. "I had fun," she said. "This was special. Thank you for that."

"Well named," Jake told her. "*Bliss.* Who knew that retreating to our generation's hippie roots even if just for a day could recharge the old batteries! It's enough to make you think Thomas Wolfe was not necessarily on the mark when he said you can't go home again."

Surprised, Maggie shot a veiled glance his direction, half-convinced he was putting her on. Jake's face in profile was impossible to read. She always considered him an onward and upward kind of guy and was on the verge of tweaking him on the subject. Changed her mind.

"I've always volunteered a No," she said finally, "if someone asked me whether I would ever want to go back and have do-overs on childhood or college. As if somehow those were the best years of our lives. But yeah, when you think about it, writing off our pasts can be pretty cynical . . . if not impossible."

"Not much of a prognosis for the future either. So-called second childhoods late in life always sounded like a put-down to me—less about fun than a prelude to senility. But then maybe I'm starting to rethink."

An odd conversation for two people pushing eighty, Maggie thought. And certainly on what some might consider a first date. She wasn't in any way, shape or fashion willing to go down that road. Still, whatever Jake's motives for inviting her, she had to admit to herself, she found them flattering.

Conversation dwindled after that, stopped entirely as they started passing the familiar landmarks. Maggie ticked them off in her head starting with the airport, the log cabin night spot that used to be known as Flying Dutchman (popular years ago for its live dance bands on weekends), the State Park, the old brewery now in business again, the State Police Post.

When Jake eased the car into the alleyway behind the Aron cottage, the business of leave-taking abruptly took on an awkward edge. The entire neighborhood was dark and still except for the porch light Maggie had left on earlier in the day. *No time for prolonged farewells.* Jake must have been reading her mind. He cut the headlights, but left the engine on idle.

When Maggie noticed his hand on the driver side doorhandle, she anticipated him. She quickly threw open the passenger door and

71

started getting out on her own. "Don't bother with Emily Post," she said. "I can see the path through the garden well enough."

Jake hesitated. "If you're sure then."

"Safe home," she said. "And thanks again."

Her last memory as she shut the door behind her was of Jake staring straight ahead out the windshield, his hands flexing on the steering wheel of the Toyota. The leather of the wheel covering had a fragile air about it, had begun to wear thin and shred in places.

Funny what we notice, she thought to herself.

For all her bravado and disclaimers about making it safely to the back porch on her own, Jake waited. Even with the help of the porch light, it took Maggie a while to pick her way through the greenery to the back steps. She didn't hear the Toyota lurch into gear until she clicked on the kitchen light.

LEDs flooded the gleaming painted hardwood floors of the kitchen, apocalyptically bright after their time in the midnight of the countryside. Everything in the cottage was thrown into sharp relief, as she had left it, as generations before her had left it, down to the handful of dishes in the sink waiting to be washed.

Like Rip Van Winkle must have felt, she winced, *waking from a long sleep.*

Last summer Maggie had traded out all the remaining incandescents at the hardware downtown for the brighter, more energy efficient, longer-lived LEDs. Standing in the check-out line and scanning the manufacturer's claims on the packaging, she had felt a bizarre, stomach-in-knots rush of awareness.

If the hype was to be believed, these bulbs would last for a good twenty years, maybe more. In all likelihood this would be the last time in her own lifespan that she would replace one.

Proof positive of her own mortality. A sobering thought.

At day's end, Maggie found herself seizing on another epitaph entirely. When it comes to age, the baseball legend Satchel Paige once said, surviving is a question of mind over matter. *If you don't mind, it don't matter.*

Not exactly a blissful prognosis for the future either. But it seemed to fit.

Columbine or AQUILEGIA is native to Northern Hemispheres and high altitudes. Because some varieties are short-lived, in the 'flower lexicon' Columbine can be used to symbolize 'sorrow'. Its name comes from the Latin word for 'dove'.

Mortality

The call came at three in the morning. Much later, checking the Recent call log on her smartphone, Maggie was able to piece things together. In fact, the assisted living center had called three times within seven minutes of each other. Sound asleep after all that sun and exercise at Bliss with Jake Faland, she hadn't heard the first two ring-tones at all.

"It's your mother," a woman's voice said from the other end of the line. "She's fallen—"

Whatever followed was drowned out by the roaring in Maggie's head. "Is it a hip?"

"We don't think so. But she's in enough distress that we're recommending x-rays."

"I'll be right over."

The caregiver didn't need to spell out the short-term prognosis. No way would her mother Lillian agree to ambulances or hospitals. Thoughts racing, Maggie threw on jeans, tee and sweatshirt, whatever came to hand. Nights had been in the low sixties in Northern Michigan the past week. There was no sense in shivering through whatever was likely to follow.

Maggie found her mother lying on the bed in her apartment. A visibly frazzled caregiver was trying unsuccessfully to make her comfortable. The woman was young, wide-eyed—overwhelmed. Maggie couldn't imagine the conversation that had been going on between the two of them.

"Mom," she said.

74

Lillian strained to see in the dim light from the cut glass lamp on the night stand. "What are you doing here?"

Maggie silently counted to ten. "You fell, Mom. They think you need x-rays."

Her mother's chin hardened. "No hospitals."

"Mom, I promise you, you won't have to stay. But the caregivers need to know how to help you."

"You say that *now*—"

Lillian's eyes riveted her daughter's. Message sent, message received. What her mother was demanding, Maggie knew, went way beyond pinkie swears or fingers crossed behind her back. There was a Do Not Resuscitate order in place, filed in the assisted living office, but she had never put those clinical demands into context before.

"I promise." Maggie's voice was low.

The silence that followed was deafening. A full thirty seconds passed before Maggie was able to bring herself to move beyond that unspoken connection between them.

"Go ahead and dial 9-1-1," Maggie told the caregiver.

The woman keyed something into her phone. 'We need a pick-up," she said. "X-rays after a fall."

Mid-call, the woman wandered out into the hall. She seemed to be giving directions to the first responders to help them locate Lillian's apartment.

"I'll be fine," Lillian said after a while. "You look worn out—ought to pack up and go back to bed."

Maggie sighed, took her mother's hand. "You were up without your walker again. And I can't seem to find your life-alert."

"Don't know why you pay for the darn thing. It's heavy. Hurts my neck."

This wasn't going to end well, Maggie realized with shocking clarity. Maybe not this time, but next week, next month were likely to be a different story.

The caregiver came back into the room. "They're on their way."

Lillian glared. "Don't need an ambulance."

"We've been through this, Mom. If you say that, the staff says they won't take you for x-rays."

75

The caregiver nodded her assent. "That's right, Lillian. They won't."

Again, silence prevailed. When Lillian tried to roust herself, shift positions, Maggie saw her grimace. *Hurting more than she let on.* Scared, too, though trying to put a brave face on things.

There were three EMTs in the squad counting the driver, a lot of bodies in Lillian's tiny bedroom. Two of the crew clearly worked out big time. When the gurney wouldn't fit through the door, they used a backboard to get Lillian out into the short hall that led to the living room and beyond it the front door of the apartment. The emergency squad made short work of the process.

Lillian said nothing. But then again, Maggie admitted, her mother's expression said it all. *She was doing this, but under protest.*

"You promised," Lillian shot her daughter a long pointed look when the EMTs seemed ready to wheel her out into the hallway.

Maggie nodded. *Yes.*

A quick exchange with the driver confirmed the logistics once the ambulance arrived at the hospital. "I'll follow you there," Maggie said.

The lobby of the emergency room was packed. *Odd,* Maggie thought, *at four o'clock in the morning.*

On the fringes of the waiting room, several families clustered around wheelchair patients in varying stages of dress and undress. Maggie and the caregiver had helped Lillian into a bathrobe before the EMTs arrived. It seemed a small price to pay for her mother's consent to the whole business.

Seated across from Lillian and her gurney, a young mother and a toddler were sandwiched in between a tattooed biker holding a bloody towel around a gash in the sleeve of his leather jacket and a visibly disoriented older woman with stringy gray hair that reached well below her shoulders. The toddler's nose was running and in between sobs and yawns, was coughing prolifically.

One by one the rogues gallery emptied until only Maggie and her mother were still waiting. The green-garbed staff that came to get them looked exhausted. Maggie could empathize.

"It'll only be a few minutes now," one of them sighed.

Maggie was skeptical. Ushered into a curtained cubicle, she and

Lillian were confronted by an aide with a clipboard who asked the same questions Maggie had answered already twice before, for the benefit of the ambulance crew and then the original triage staff at the hospital. The x-ray room was too small so Lillian was wheeled off on her own while Maggie stayed behind in the curtained cubicle.

Another hour passed before everyone returned. A doctor was with them. This time Lillian was in a wheelchair.

"Hairline crack of the pelvis," the doctor on call said. "Normal procedure is rest, no undue stretching or straining. There's no way to splint it. I'll write a scrip for painkillers if you give me the name of your pharmacy. "

"So I can go home," Lillian demanded.

The doctor had zoned out, looked capable of falling asleep on his feet. "Which is?"

Maggie quickly supplied the name of both the assisted living facility and pharmacy. "Mom can count on 24-hour care," she says.

"I suggest staff check on her hourly to start. She shouldn't be running around at night alone to go to the bathroom. Does she have a life alert system?"

Lillian's chin tightened.

"Lots of luck getting her to use it," Maggie said.

Her mother just glared.

With some difficulty, Maggie and the hospital aide in charge of the wheelchair managed to ease Lillian into the car without major incident. The drive across town and back up the hill to Lillian's apartment was a lot less dramatic than the trip to the hospital had been.

"So, did the ambulance use the siren?" Maggie wondered as she guided the car out of the emergency room parking lot.

Her mother was staring out the passenger side window. "I told you going to the hospital was a waste of time," she said.

Maggie managed an even tone. "At least the staff will know how to deal with things, make you comfortable," she said. "I promised you I wouldn't make you stay, no matter what."

Lillian didn't react one way or the other. The rest of the trip passed in tense silence. At the care center, the usually full parking lot was still empty except for the facility van that took residents to events around town. Maggie pulled up right in front of the darkened building, shut off the ignition and doused the lights.

"You stay here," she said.

"And where would I go?"

Beyond arguments, Maggie let that one pass. While her mother waited in the car, she set off to track down help and a wheelchair to cover the distance back to the apartment. From what she could see, the only signs of life on her mother's floor were open doors at the nursing station and a resident's room down the hall beyond Lillian's apartment.

Maggie's footsteps echoed in the deserted hallway. She was still contemplating where staff might have gone when a burly male night attendant with a close-cropped reddish beard emerged into the hall from a resident's room. He was pushing a medications cart.

"We're back," Maggie said.

The guy just looked at her.

"Oh, you don't know. Lillian fell earlier. We spent the night in the emergency room." Maggie rattled off the diagnosis verbatim. "I'm going to need help with a wheelchair and getting Mom out of the car."

"Gotcha." The attendant dropped off the cart at the nursing station. Then together the two of them retraced Maggie's route downstairs to the car. Along the way, the attendant snagged a wheelchair. In the interim Lillian had dozed off, still buckled into her seat belt.

"Mom," Maggie said as she leaned into the front seat from the passenger side. She was having trouble releasing the seat belt. "You're going to have to help us here."

Too groggy to respond, Lillian let herself be half-carried and deposited as gently as possible in the wheelchair. Once she was safely ensconced in bed, Maggie waited around to make sure the prescription for painkillers was on its way.

"They are just ordering enough of a dosage to take the edge off," the attendant said after he checked the scrip's status. "Not enough to encourage mountain climbing or a 10K, Lillian."

Lillian wasn't amused. "Would I ever?"

Maggie and the attendant just looked at each other. Some things are not worth contradicting.

By the time Maggie got back to her car, the velvety night sky had already faded to flannel gray, tinged with streaks of pink and coral. She had left the car doors unlocked, but fishing for her keys at the bottom of her purse proved a major operation. Mentally and emotionally she felt like she was sailing in uncharted water.

Without consciously plotting a route back to the cottage, Maggie wound up headed down 131, the long way round. It was all downhill from there, literally. Cresting that last steep hill into Petoskey, she could see the sleeping village spread out like a canvas with Little Traverse Bay behind it. The gunmetal expanse of water was shrouded in mist, all but indistinguishable from the far shoreline and rolling hills beyond.

There was no escaping it. Maggie's route once again took her past the sprawling hospital complex. "Freud would be having a field day with this one," she muttered under her breath. It was as if somehow instinctively she needed to confirm what she already knew to be true. Lillian had fallen—likely one of more such episodes to come.

When she passed the exit marked ER, the wail of a siren startled her. Coming or going, she couldn't tell. Maggie watched the rear view mirror, but the ambulance and its flashing lights never materialized.

Other emotional landmines loomed on the horizon. On the right, the yellow and white facade of the old turn-of-the-century resort hotel, the Perry, caught the first rays of the rising sun. Jake had mentioned he was staying there. In the merciless light of morning, their day at the Bliss Fest had receded with the cold efficiency of hitting the fast-forward arrow on a television remote. It seems that some things are just not meant to last or even savor.

A lone jogger was stirring as she passed the Bay View Inn. He was using the picket fence screening the parking lot to stretch. About to run or done for the day? There was no way of telling.

The cottage turned out to be unlocked, also out of the ordinary. But then in crisis moments, it is said we revert to what we know. There was a day when no one locked their doors, kids roamed the streets from morning to night unmonitored. In this corner of the world, the habits persisted longer than most, but here too they were under siege. The stream into which we step is never quite the same for all the attempts to contain its course.

Life happens. It ends. What lay beyond, Maggie was in no mood to speculate. The Great Eternals lay outside the realm of human control. Maggie had never run head-on into her mother's vulnerability in quite that way before, much the less her own.

Too tired even to undress, she eased herself back into bed and burrowed down into the covers. The next thing she knew it was one o'clock in the afternoon. She had thrown off the bedclothes and her mismatched wardrobe from the night before felt sticky and stiff. A long shower did nothing to deal with the dark circles under her eyes.

Pointless, Maggie muttered, as she tried to get her hair into the usual bun. She gave up and used a twistee to secure it in a makeshift pony tale at the nape of her neck. The first thing that came to hand in her closet was a vintage teal and green sun dress that had seventies written all over it.

Yin and yang, Maggie recognized the swirling pattern in the fabric. Even the most opposing forces in existence are interrelated—life and death, joy and sadness, everything in between. *There had to be an irony in the timing.*

Breakfast was no longer an option. Lunch sounded unappealing. A cup of warmed-over coffee and half an English muffin would have to do. Right now fresh air seemed like the only tonic with any potential.

The screen door yielded to her touch. Eyes narrowed at the flash of sunlight, she didn't spot the obstacle in her path until she stumbled over it. Water sloshed against her ankles.

"What the heck—"

Sitting in the middle of the porch where she couldn't possibly miss it was a two-quart blue canning jar. *Square Shoulders*, the raised lettering on the glass read. The jar was chock full of daisies, Queen's Anne lace, chicory with its notched, baby blue petals and tall wildflowers that looked like they might bear a distant relationship to CAMPANULA OR Canterbury Bells.

No card. Obviously hand-picked. Maggie's throat felt tight.

Jake. Not a lot of other options came readily to mind. She hadn't heard anyone knock, but then maybe he intended it that way.

"Hiyah, kiddo! You busy later?"

Maggie's head snapped up. Sonia stood in the alley outside the gate to the Aron cottage, obviously headed for the beach. Righting herself and the mason jar, Maggie quickly set the flowers on the white wicker table on the porch. She knew better than to call attention to them. Mopping up the porch floor would keep.

"Mom wound up in the ER last night," Maggie said. "I'm pretty much a wreck."

"Sorry to hear that. Is she okay"

"Hairline crack in the pelvis. Painful, but it could have been a lot worse. She's back at her apartment— "

"Still," Sonia said, "you'll have your hands full for awhile."

Maggie had thought of nothing else for much of the wild night behind her. "I'll keep you posted," she said.

"Let me know if I can help." By now the freckled, red-haired boy in swim trunks and carrying a sand bucket and shovel alongside Sonia was tugging at the sleeve of her gauzy red beach cover-up.

"You've sure got your hands full yourself," Maggie laughed.

Sonia grimaced. "Grandson Number Four is up for the week and rarin' to go. I could use a nap, that's for sure. Unfortunately not in the day planner." The two of them started off down the alley.

The puddle around Maggie's bare feet from the wildflowers was spreading across the porch floor. A mop proved close at hand in the utility closet just inside the kitchen door. She made quick work of the mess then turned her attention to the mason jar and its contents. That water from Jake's makeshift vase would need replacing and soon.

Once common on the sand hills along the bay, field flowers had become scarcer over the years. The encroachment of civilization had taken its toll. For years Maggie and her daughter too had kept the kitchen table of the Aron cottage well-stocked. But as the wildflowers became scarcer, she started feeling guilty for denuding the landscape. When she gave up the practice. Holly didn't seem to mind.

"There are lots of flowers in the garden, Mom," Holly said. "Without having to cruise around the countryside."

"Not the same," Maggie said. Though in the end her environmental ethos had prevailed.

And then much to her surprise on the drive up to Bliss with Jake she had noticed the wildflowers were back—with a vengeance. So, it seems, had Jake.

Maggie's hand closed around the cell phone in the pocket of her sun dress. But then it occurred to her, she didn't know his number. *Just as well*, she decided. 'Thank You' took two seconds. Beyond that, she had no idea what she would say to him.

Last night's drive alone through the empty streets to the Emergency Room and all that came after had given Maggie plenty of time to think. Nothing in the future that loomed so large for Maggie in the months ahead included Jake Faland.

Short term, the plan was to keep Lillian from overdoing things. Mid-afternoon en route to checking on her mother, Maggie stopped off at the grocery and picked up a few new word search puzzle books—Lillian's favorites—just in case. Parking lots at the senior complex were crowded to overflowing, a popular family time since the call to dinner became a natural cut-off point for visits. Maggie had discovered some time ago that as Lillian's memory failed, taking such issues of structure into account became increasingly important.

"Mom's not the only one who's losing it," she muttered to herself as she fumbled around on the floor of the car for the goodies she had brought with her. In the course of the chaotic day, she had taken time to pick a bouquet of zinnias for her mother from the garden. To keep them fresh, she had stored them in water in an old biscotti container on the kitchen counter in the cottage. Which is where, Maggie realized to her chagrin, they were still sitting.

Harried, disgusted with herself, Maggie caught a glimpse of her reflection in the rear view mirror. She hadn't bothered with makeup and her hair hadn't improved since her attempts to tame it several hours ago. She felt as if she had aged at least five years overnight. Fact or merely perception, the thought took her aback.

She had brought her mother to Northern Michigan with the best of intentions—ostensibly to keep Lillian involved, engaged as long as possible. For the first time it occurred to Maggie to wonder if that trip was really for her mother's benefit, or for *herself*. Had she been in denial over how frail Lillian had become, what toll that summer trip north really might be taking?

Guilt closed its powerful vise-grip around her heart. Suddenly apprehensive at what she might find at her mother's apartment, Maggie grabbed the plastic shopping bag with books and headed toward the facility elevator.

"Consider the lilies of the field." The Biblical admonition about these plants is just one of many literary references to these stunning flowers. The word LILIUM comes from the Latin via Greek and the Coptic Egyptian word for 'flower". Lilies are known for their dramatic 'painterly' markings and showy blossoms. White lilies have come to symbolize immortality in the Christian tradition.

Matriarch

Maggie opened Lillian's apartment door, but saw no sign of her. Normally by now her mother would be ensconced in the overstuffed brown rocker in the corner, intent on a puzzle or novel. Instinctively, Maggie closed the apartment door quietly behind her, skipped her usual warning Hello.

Down the short apartment hallway, the bedroom door stood wide open. Lillian was lying on the bed, eyes closed. Fully dressed in black slacks and a familiar pale blue sweater with beaded trim, her hands were folded across her chest.

As if she were in her coffin. The image popped in Maggie's head unbidden. Once there, it was one she would not forget. The slow rise and fall of her mother's breathing did little to reassure her.

As Maggie moved into adulthood, she had never thought about the reality of a daughter's need to separate herself from her mother. Content with being her mother's daughter, there was never a moment, day or year, when she could say, "Aha, now I'm independent. Now I'm totally my own woman."

And there was no mountaintop experience when they passed the watershed from parent and child to friends. That, too, simply happened, quietly like the garden at dusk when the bird sounds fade and the last whispers of the breeze fall still.

Even a seemingly requisite adolescent rebellion had never been a source of friction between them. Which is why the changing dynamic in recent years was all the more shocking. Helping her mother move out of the homestead into assisted living two years ago had been a shot across the bow, a nightmare for them both.

Subtly but surely over the decades Lillian had become a packrat. Squirreled away in the basement of the sprawling homestead were taxes going back to 1939 when Lillian and Maggie's father Ben first married, multiple artificial Christmas trees and decades worth of National Geographic magazines. Treasures and furnishings inherited from past generations and books galore crammed the shelves and closets. Somehow Lillian imagined all of this would fit in a one-bedroom apartment in the senior living community nearby.

"Once I'm out, you can sell your bungalow, move into the homestead," Lillian told her daughter. "Keep this place in the family."

"It's never going to happen—taking all this stuff with you," Maggie said as she finished a quick and dirty survey of the house chock full of her mother's things. "Not without a *heck* of a lot of downsizing."

And so the simplification of Lillian's life began. The piles of items to be donated grew mountainous. Rooms became impassable. The fate of every lamp, every end table, the antique pickle crocks and appliances dusty from lack of use became grounds for vocal protests. While Maggie won skirmishes, the war was another matter entirely.

Lillian's eyes darkened. She thrust out her chin. Her choice "to save" or "not to save" grew non-negotiable.

"You're getting rid of everything," she said, an underlay of bitterness in her voice. At issue on the kitchen counter sat a pasta machine unused for at least two decades.

Exasperated and back aching, Maggie stood mid kitchen with hands on her hips. "And you're going to wind up on the other end with furniture all over the lawn of the senior living center," she said. "Trust me."

It was clear that deep down Lillian *didn't* trust her, not on this one. The struggle grew ever more contentious. They had only weeks not months to get the job done or lose the spot at the senior center.

Some things were harder to handle then others. In one nondescript carton in the back of the attic Lillian had carefully stashed a trove of items from her husband Ben's childhood—report cards going back to kindergarten, his Scouting medals and badges and a model sailing ship he had built in high school. The varnished tissue paper sails had become brittle with time, had begun to crack and crumble.

The randomness of such emotionally charged finds hit Maggie like a gut punch. She quickly chose not to share their existence with her mother. Instead, she simply labeled them Family Treasures in thick black marker pen, taped them shut again and set them aside as 'keepers'.

Everything considered irredeemable wound up in bags in the garage. Finally, on one bitterly chill March night, Maggie and one of her mother's neighbors loaded the trunk of his Mercedes with the bulging trash bags. Together they started around the circle drive, trunk open, through the neighborhood. At each huge curbside garbage container, the neighbor would stop long enough for Maggie to shove as much as she could until each plastic bin was full to overflowing.

Eventually Maggie would knock on the driver side window. "We're good. Time for another load," she said, teeth chattering.

"Righty-o," the neighbor said, way too cheerful given the circumstances. The two of them headed back to her mother's open garage for another load.

Emptying the garage of trash took two hours. The neighbor had the foresight to wear a quilted ski jacket, wool ear muffs and insulated gloves. Gloves or not, by then Maggie's hands were numb.

"You're going to get frostbite," the neighbor told her. "At least I've got the car heater going for me."

Maggie tried to laugh. "Heaters aren't much good with the window open on a regular basis."

When they finished the final run, they found Lillian standing alone in the driveway in her bathrobe in front of the empty garage. She was minus coat, hat or snow boots.

"Mom, you're going to catch your death."

"I should be so lucky," Lillian muttered. Her face was like a storm cloud. "This is ridiculous—all of it. Why don't you just shoot me."

Maggie couldn't agree more about the craziness of the situation. "I was actually thinking of doing us both in!" she said. "You realize, in another month, I'm going to have to go through all the stuff in Joe and my bungalow if I'm going to move in to the homestead. While we were at it, you and I should both have settled for a condo."

But she had promised her mother to keep the old Aron farmhouse in the family as long as possible. And that Maggie was determined to do.

The only thing that saved mother and daughter through those awful days was the winter Olympics. Exhausted and sullen, often by eight o'clock or later, Maggie and Lillian would raid the pantry, freezer and well-stocked liquor cabinet in the homestead basement.

"Eat it, drink it, or pitch it!" Maggie said.

They poured the undrinkable down the drain as they went along. Jar after jar of fifteen-year-old homemade strawberry preserves met the same fate in the garbage disposal.

Fortified with whatever they could salvage, Maggie and her mother collapsed in front of the television. For the next two hours, the two of them watched skaters dance and soar, ski jumpers hurtle airborne and athletes in sports neither one of them had ever seen before competing within an inch or their lives.

Who won or lost was irrelevant. Mindless spectacle was just what the doctor ordered.

By the closing ceremony, the job of downsizing was as done as it was going to get. The rooms of the homestead were empty except for the things the movers were going to pick up on the following day and those items Maggie agreed to keep herself. As the strains of the Olympic hymn poured out from the television's speakers, Maggie filled two large tumblers with a serviceable German red, one of the few wines left.

"Here's to us" she said. "We did it. Awful, but we did it."

Mother and daughter made eye contact as the rims of their glasses clinked. For a long time Lillian sat silent, glass untouched in her hand, staring blankly at the TV screen. Unshed tears threatened to fall any second.

"After all that . . . ," Lillian's voice was shaky, low. "After all that, are we still friends?"

Maggie's throat tightened. The words didn't want to come. But tired as she was, the deeper truth in her mother's question struck at her very core.

"Of course," she said quietly. "You're my best friend. Always will be. You knew me when there was no *Me*, before I took my first breath."

"And you . . . ?" Lillian's tone was matter-of-fact, devoid of any trace of self-pity. "You'll be there at my last."

Maggie had to look away. A silent pact had been ratified between them. *Down the road*, she told herself. *I'll deal with all that later.*

And that was that. Until last night and Lillian's fall.

In an instant, Lillian suddenly qualified as frail. Her fierce energy and determination to preserve her independence had become the Enemy, no longer the driving force behind her life. And there was precious little Maggie could do to change what was bound to follow.

Though her mother's losses had become harder to ignore, Maggie had been able to compensate behind the scenes without the feeling she was intruding upon her mother's dignity. The fall suddenly escalated the challenge.

As Maggie saw it, she had several choices, none of them good. She could try to bubble wrap her mother, cajole Lillian to use her walker, urge staff to check on her more frequently, make sure she was drinking enough, eating enough, the list went on and on. Or she had to let go, admit that being a parent's keeper however loving had its limits.

The *later* Maggie once had applied to her mother's situation had abruptly become a *now*. In her heart, she was not prepared for that seismic shift.

Lillian had always loomed larger than life as long as Maggie could remember. Her mother ruled the kitchen, gardened, painted, sewed her own clothes and young Maggie's much of the time. Together with husband Ben, she had traveled, exposing Maggie and her brother to the world with a relentless curiosity. And in an era when other women left the labor force to raise families, Lillian persisted. Remarkable as that biography was on so many levels, it seemed as natural as breathing.

From the first time young Maggie walked into the law firm of Stroch and Beadle and saw her mother in her professional element, she realized how extraordinary all this was. A surge of incredulous pride dominated every other memory of her mother going forward.

Lillian's office was housed on the fourth floor, a novelty in itself in a town where ten stories was considered a skyscraper. Plush blue-gray carpet underfoot in the executive suite dulled every footstep. Diplomas and great wood and brass plaques on the walls created a kind of shrine to competence and power. And in that inner sanctum behind her great mahogany desk, sat Lillian. No longer just Maggie's mother, here she reigned as gatekeeper supreme.

Those periodic girlhood lunches with Mom Lillian, often around the year-end or Easter holidays, stayed with Maggie as some of her oldest memories. The downtown Five and Dime had the best hot dogs in town, piled high with kraut and relish and brown German mustard. Maggie and her mother ate at the counter, standing up. Afterward they trudged several blocks to the emporium where an overhead pneumatic trolley system carried payments upstairs and out of sight to the accounting office. Windows of the jewelry store down the street came alive with animated displays that changed with the seasons. Miners in miniature rode a tiny ore car through a tunnel studded with faux diamonds. Elves in a workshop fashioned treasures under a foot-tall Christmas tree. Magical.

Not until years later, on her first visit to Fifth Avenue over the Christmas holidays had Maggie put those adventures with her mother into larger perspective. It also would take decades for two-income families to become the norm. Meanwhile, Lillian Aron's status as role model loomed large as the most precious gift she ever gave her only daughter. That, and the will to live life flat out, pedal to the metal.

All of that shared history came flooding back as Maggie stood in the doorway of her mother's bedroom. Even a shell of herself and in pain from a cracked pelvis, Lillian's force of personality radiated like a homing beacon.

"Mom," Maggie said quietly.

Lillian's eyes snapped open. For that split-second, Maggie sensed her mother didn't know where she was.

"I was resting," Lillian told her.

Maggie nodded. "Yes, I saw that. I didn't want to wake you, but wondered how you were feeling."

"Old. I'm feeling old."

Maggie laughed in spite of herself. "At almost a hundred you're entitled."

Lillian stirred and with some difficulty started to sit up. When Maggie rushed to help her, she brushed her daughter's hand away.

"Ninety-nine. And I can manage myself."

It took every bit of willpower not to intervene as her mother eased herself off the bed. But Lillian's walker wasn't within easy reach. At that Maggie drew a line.

"Here, Mom." Maggie retrieved the walker along with her

mother's life alert pendant which was lying predictably on the dresser top alongside the bed. "Neither one of these things will do you any good if you don't use them."

Lillian glared. "You're not my mother."

No, Maggie thought, *I'm not.* But exactly what was she called upon to be? That was not so easy to answer. The tacit cease fires she and her mother had negotiated during Lillian's ten days of Olympic-scale down-sizing had emerged from a finite job and a tangible quit date. With Lillian's fall, the situation abruptly had become open-ended, changing rapidly.

For starters, when Lillian tried to move from a seated to standing position, Maggie noticed her mother's lack of balance was alarming. Wincing and holding on to the walker for dear life, Lillian made it from the bedroom to the corner chair in the living room, but barely. Maggie followed close behind, though not so close as to draw her mother's ire.

Lillian must have sensed some of her daughter's distress. They talked with relative ease about everything and nothing. Eventually a loud male voice over the public address system warned that dinner was being served in the dining room. This time when Maggie offered her mother a hand up, Lillian didn't protest.

"Thanks for coming," she told her daughter. Clearly meant it.

"I'll be back tomorrow."

Maggie told her she loved her. Lillian reciprocated. Together they navigated the hall to the dining room. Maggie stood outside the massive glass doors for the longest time watching her mother pick her way through the clusters of residents to her assigned table. *Cautious, hesitant, trying not to show it.*

As Maggie got out of the elevator en route to the exit, an older woman in street clothes staffing the reception desk pulled her aside. She sounded oddly rehearsed, choosing her words deliberately. "The medical staff put a note in Lillian's file. After your mother's fall, staff really felt it is becoming . . . *appropriate* to think about registering with hospice."

"Hospice." Maggie just stared at her, uncomprehending. "That means . . . you're telling me Mom—"

"Needs more help and hospice can provide that. They can monitor Lillian's medical condition, arrange visits by a social worker for further assessment. Volunteers help with memory care."

When she got no reaction, the woman quickly added, "Of course if Lillian's condition improves over time, she would 'graduate' from the program. But for now, the extra support could be very beneficial."

Maggie swallowed hard. Her mouth felt stiff. "I assume you want some kind of . . . there's bound to be paper work."

By way of answer the woman handed her a packet out of which she retrieved an intake form. "A signature here can get things started," she said.

Maggie scanned the document, not once but twice. A Mackinac Island mug on the desk held a stash of pens affixed with a gaudy assortment of neon silk daisies. Finally on a sigh, Maggie plucked a pen from that unlikely bouquet. On autopilot, she scrawled her signature above the yellow highlighted line at the bottom of the form.

"The hospice team will want to meet with you and Lillian together," the woman nodded. "The point is not that staff believe Lillian would be . . . passing anytime soon—just that the added support will be useful in her ongoing care."

Hospice. The woman at the desk had kept stressing quality of life. In Maggie's mind, the word conjured up 'death sentence'.

Once out in the parking lot, she sat in the car a long time before she even tried to maneuver the key into the ignition. Maggie's throat was tight. She felt short of breath.

Anxiety attack. She knew the symptoms. After her husband Joe died of a heart attack, she found herself struggling with them on a more or less regular basis. Time eventually proved the only cure, the deceptively simple act of putting one foot in front of the other.

Her son and daughter had completed college and were off on their own, leaving Maggie alone in the family home with her grief. Lillian came for a week and stayed for a month. When Maggie wouldn't get out of bed until noon or later, Lillian started running the vacuum in the bedroom until she did—whether the floor needed it or not. She dragged Maggie down to the community pool to swim laps. She was merciless.

Maggie knew she needed her mother's intervention, just as now she knew with brutal clarity that her turn to reciprocate had come. She turned the key in the ignition. The car's engine roared to life.

Across town an empty cottage was waiting. Grandmother's

garden was ablaze with color, lifted straight out of a picture postcard. *In the face of life's uglier realities*, Lillian once said, *we take beauty where we find it.*

Maggie started up the porch steps, stopped. Those field flowers in their mason jar vase still stood on the wicker porch table where she had left them. She didn't give herself time to reconsider.

With a determined stride, she navigated the flagstone path to the alley, turned left. A backhoe was parked in the front yard of the Faland cottage. Jake Faland and the machine's operator were standing vigil over a gigantic yew now lying on its side with its roots upended. Gnarled and tough, those ties to the earth had not let loose easily from the look of it.

Beyond the hole where the overgrown bush had stood, Maggie saw her Radio Flyer wagon. Jake must have been watering the roots of the ferns and hosta she had given him. Most of the deadheaded clumps showed signs of rallying.

Jake looked up. His face lit up when he saw her. "Maggie."

"You broke down and got help."

He laughed. "I took your advice, first thing Monday morning."

Yesterday, Maggie realized with a shock. Their Sunday at Bliss seemed a lifetime ago.

The backhoe operator was starting to look antsy, impatient to get going. "With the hoe protecting the site, Mr. Faland, I think the yard is safe enough until tomorrow," he threw out there. "Finishing the job—clearing out the brush in the backyard, getting in fill dirt, leveling the lawn is another couple of day's work. A week at most. Eventually you can bring in the sod, bushes, whatever."

Jake nodded. "See you then."

The guy made a beeline for his pickup with the now-empty trailer behind it. Jake took one last look at the work in progress, then joined Maggie at the edge of the public sidewalk.

"You look tired," Jake said. "Gotta say, I'm not too perky myself. So much for finding our Bliss."

"I wouldn't have missed a minute of it . . . *considering.*"

And then she told him about Lillian. In the calm retelling, Maggie felt her angst slowly begin to retreat again to the cave where all life's darkest fears reside.

Jake listened, compassion and concern in his eyes. "Rough," he said finally when she had finished. "I'm sorry. Back then—when we were kids—your mom always took notice, had something to say when I passed your place. Not all the neighbors did."

"She remembers you too. Something about an abundance of manners. That rated high in her book."

Jake seemed amused by that. "Making small talk was an art form at the Faland cottage. Sitting at the kid's table or not, we were expected to hold our own. My brother and I learned right quick to hold a door open for our elders or a woman. Different times."

"Which is why I came," Maggie told him. "To say thank you. I found your house gift on the back porch. Tripped over it actually. Water everywhere but nothing broken. The flowers are beautiful."

"Creating havoc—not exactly my intent."

Maggie needed to know. "Which was . . . ?"

"If anything more personal bothers you, call it a plant rescue," he shrugged. "The backhoe was going to mow down a perfectly decent patch of wildflowers along with several more trees out back. Seemed like a shame to waste 'em. And there were all these blue jars in the shed."

"Your timing was perfect, after a night with Mom in the ER."

Jake hesitated. "I'm sure you're worn out, but it occurred to me . . . have you got any plans for dinner?"

Maggie just looked at him. "Dinner . . . "

"You, me, food. Downtown somewhere. Two neighbors, neither of them in the mood to cook."

Maggie laughed. The guy could read her like a book. "When you put it that way, how could I possibly refuse?"

"Okay, sounds lame, I'll admit," Jake told her. "Point is, no strings or agenda here. I wanted to be clear about that."

Clear as mud, she thought. "I'll admit the thought of rummaging in the refrigerator sounds positively dreadful."

"I ought to shower first, change. The backhoe guy and I have been at this all day."

"Have you taken a good look at me," Maggie said. "I got home from mom's at dawn, slept in until noon or thereafter. By the time I pulled myself together to go see how mom was doing this afternoon, I couldn't have cared less what I wore."

"The dress code most places around here is nonexistent."

"Fine by me."

And so they went. Maggie didn't bother with a purse or locking the cottage. The two of them piled into his dad's beat-up Toyota and headed west along the shore of the bay.

A booth in back at one of the pubs in the Gaslight District offered plenty of anonymity. The place was dark enough that Maggie found herself hanging on to the furnishings as they followed the host through the sprawling cavern of a room.

"I've had enough of falls and falling to last a lifetime," Maggie said with a sigh of relief as she settled down on the bench seat. "I don't know about you, but I can't see a darn thing."

"I was thinking the same thing."

Jake fished in his pocket and pulled out a disposable lighter. The wick of the candle on the table in front of them flickered, caught.

"A smoker?" Maggie wondered.

"An ex-Boy Scout." Jake chuckled softly "Some habits die hard. I guess that beats you thinking *obsessive compulsive*."

In the steady glow from the amber glass of the candle holder, Maggie saw the deep furrows around his mouth, the crinkles at the corners of his eyes soften, relax. *Patently unfair*, she couldn't help thinking, the double-standard at work here. While a man of a certain age might be described as "rugged" or "distinguished", no one would say the same of a woman.

Suddenly self-conscious, she brushed at a strand of hair that had escaped from her makeshift pony tail. "I could use a mirror," she said.

"You look amazing."

Maggie just stared at him. "You're kidding, right?"

"Wouldn't dream of it."

An awkward silence settled in between them. "For the record," Maggie said finally, "you confuse the heck out of me."

"As in—*good*, I hope."

"Bad, indifferent, I'm not sure what applies. Add up the years and the two of us belong somewhere in the realm of dinosaurs walking the earth."

Jake chuckled softly. "Doesn't bother me, if it doesn't bother you."

"Except for that epic mastodon in the room. We've seen more of each other this summer than we did in the past sixty years."

"And that's a bad thing?"

"No. I don't know. Time seems to be a problem for me lately."

"The fact of it."

"The lack of it," she said. "Mom always reminded me she's older than dirt. I had started to assume longevity is a given, the permanent state of things."

"And now you don't."

"Pretty much."

"So, Maggie Aron, *carpe diem*," Jake toasted with his water glass.

Seize the day. They both chewed on that one for a while. The waiter brought them a huge bowl of popcorn and took their orders, a cider for Maggie and a Horny Monk for Jake.

"Freudian slip," he laughed when he saw her eyebrow arch at the name. "We may be pushing senility. But then neither one of us is dead either—"

"*Yet.*"

"Promise me you won't consider the possibility between now and dessert."

"Done."

"Which leaves us exactly where?" Jake shot her a pointed look.

"Confused."

"Back there again. And racing for the exits?"

Was she that transparent? "Too much furniture out there in the dark, remember?" she teased. "A minefield."

Flirting wasn't on the menu. But whatever was going on, their laughter felt good, easy. Both of them settled on fish and chips. They ate, talked, had a second round of beer and cider. They split a tiramasu.

Eventually Maggie stifled a yawn. Jake checked his watch.

"Ten o'clock," he said. "No wonder we're becoming comatose."

"Dear God. I had no clue."

Signaling the waiter, Jake paid the tab. Maggie let him, without a word of protest. When he helped pull back her chair, she stood and linked her arm through his, also without comment.

"If we go down," he told her, "we go down together."

The Toyota was parked just across the street, the drive home uneventful. This time when Jake eased the car into the alley, he both doused the lights and cut the engine.

"I'm walking you to the door," he said. "Just so you know."

Maggie processed that declaration in silence.

"And if there's a neighborly hug in our future—or anything else in that department, I'm counting on you not to deck me."

"Deal." Laughter bubbled up in her voice as she said it.

With that Jake opened the driver side door. Maggie waited until he had a chance to do the same with hers.

The garden path wouldn't permit anything but single file, but the light from Jake's cell phone was enough to help them both. At the top of the porch steps he turned and waited for her to follow.

What came next was as natural as breathing. Maggie slipped into his arms, head resting on his shirt front. The night air was cool against her flaming cheeks. As they stood there in silence, she felt her breathing gradually steady.

"Now, that wasn't so bad," Jake's voice was low.

Maggie levered enough distance between them that she could see his face. But this time there was no porch light to help. Whatever he was feeling was lost in darkness.

"Tonight was . . . *thank you*, for all of it."

"I'll stop by tomorrow," he said. "See how you're doing."

"I'd like that."

With that he let her go. The door was unlocked. Maggie slipped inside and flipped on the kitchen lights.

"G'night," he said through the screen.

Illuminated by the porch light, Jake's features were no longer in shadow. What Maggie read there was too complicated for easy dissection, except to say *unmistakably positive.*

"Back atcha," she said. Quietly she shut the door behind her.

A popular cut flower, gladiolus is a member of the iris family and is native to the Mediterranean region, tropical and southern Africa. Its name comes from Latin GLADIUS or *sword*. For all the longevity of the flowers themselves, the plant is vulnerable (some might say, high maintenance) in Northern Michigan gardens. The plant grows from corms which must be dug up or 'lifted' and stored in colder climates in order to survive.

Daughters

It was as if both she and Jake needed a break, Maggie concluded. The next morning and a chunk of the afternoon rolled around and she hadn't seen hide nor hair of him. But then she hadn't felt compelled to initiate the contact either.

Around four o'clock she planned on making a trip across town to visit her mother. Meanwhile she was out in the garden, trying to keep up with the weeding. The skid of tires on the sandy strip of grass that passed for a parking area behind the cottage put everything on hold.

Maggie wasn't expecting company, had never seen the black Lexus before. Its tinted windows revealed nothing.

After an awkward pause, the driver emerged. The slender woman, early forties, was juggling a trendy woven rag handbag and a bouquet of orange gladiolas in one hand, a small overnight case in the other. Her tailored jeans and coral summer-knit sweater had resort chic written all over them.

Maggie's throat felt tight. "Holly," she called out.

In a few strides she closed the distance and drew her daughter into a tight embrace. The cellophane around the flower soaked through Maggie's sweater, felt damp against her skin. A few of the petals had crunched around the edges in the process.

"They're beautiful," Maggie said as she accepted the gift, obviously fresh from the market down the road. "Based on your text, I wasn't expecting you until—"

"Fall. I know . . . changed my mind," Maggie's daughter said.

"They said these flowers are gladiolas—"

"Glads, for short. I always loved that name, though I never grew them. It was just too much trouble lifting the bulbs every fall."

Her daughter's gaze darted from the day lilies massed against the house to the 1890 historic marker in one of the windows, the moss accumulating on one of the north-facing roofs. Most of the cottages, including Maggie's, still rested on the original sawed off cedar trees that held up the entire structure. The lilies had probably been in situ nearly that long in front of the lattice that concealed the crawlspace.

"I see the hollyhocks are still taking over along the fence," her daughter noticed.

"*Of course.*"

Seeing her daughter standing there like her namesakes, tall and strong, looking out over the garden, Maggie felt a surge of quiet pride. *Turns out, the name absolutely fits*, she thought.

At five foot eight, Holly had inherited a fascinating blend of her Greatgrandma Aron's broad shouldered Germanic genes and her dad Joe's lanky New Englander's frame. The freckles and fair complexion, her reddish blond hair cut pixie style gave her pronounced Aron cheekbones an almost elfin impression.

For all that, she was clearly her mother's daughter. It was the eyes that did it. Deep set, more green than amber, the quirky laser-like wit and intelligence behind them was all Maggie.

"I see, though, you finally got rid of the trellis over the gate." Holly sounded wistful, remembering.

From childhood Holly knew the stories—how her dad had scratch-built the lattice structure behind the family cottage in time for his own wedding day. And how Maggie had rescued creeping myrtle from the nearby woods to wind in and out of the white lattice slats.

Maggie and Joe. Theirs was anything but a childhood love story. They met at the Field Museum in Chicago on summer break when she was twenty-one. Joe was two years older. The two of them were standing in line for tickets to a popular exhibit. Instead the two wound up talking their way through the dinosaur exhibit and the dioramas on the emergence of civilization, the gems and minerals. Joe even put up with the half hour Maggie spent in front of Colleen Moore's dollhouse, a magical fairy castle of an exhibit that most guys would have found mind-numbing.

Joe got her phone number, though trips for him to Ann Arbor where Maggie was starting graduate school were few and far between. An engineering student, he had enlisted before he could be drafted, wound up a radar specialist stationed at the Great Lakes naval station in Chicago. But they wrote, prolifically. And within the year they were married with Grandmother garden as a backdrop. Their honeymoon consisted of a day trip to Mackinac Island before Joe went back to his post and Maggie finished grad school. She kept her maiden name, rare for that era—*Margaret Aron*, but then so had her mother Lillian. Months became years, almost a decade. Maggie and Joe had all but given up on having a family when their son was born. Holly followed two years later.

"Stuff happens. The trellis just gave out, honey," Maggie told her daughter. "We patched it up for ages but finally the winters just got to it. I found one almost like it in a catalog, just never got around to—"

"I miss it."

"We had to do in the myrtle, too—much too invasive. It's ruining the native plants in the woods around here."

Mother and daughter stood for a while in silence. A lone black swallowtale, nominee for official state butterfly, swooped from the astilbe to a low-growing stand of blanket flower. Somewhere a cricket was drumming out a plaintive rhythm to the sky.

"I keep forgetting how *green* it is up here," Holly said finally. "Looking at Greatgrama's garden, I get the feeling I'm carrying coals to Newcastle every time I show up with something floral. I suppose rather than gladiolas, a bottle of wine would have made more sense."

Maggie laughed. "All good," she said. "There are two box-wines in the fridge, a chardonnay and a merlot. If it's quality you're after, you've come to the wrong place. I have some hors d'oeuvres. We could sit out on the porch if you like. Bet you're hungry by now."

"My bags are still in the trunk," Holly hesitated.

"We'll get them later. Did you fly in to—"

"Grand Rapids. All I could get for a rental was that boat of a car. Traffic was a nightmare. Fortunately, most of it was going south."

"Fourth of July stragglers headed home," Maggie said. "We'll have another flood of tourists in early August. Then once families start gearing up for the new school year, it settles down considerably."

Together mother and daughter raided the kitchen and carried the wine carafe, glasses and a plate of appetizers to the porch overlooking the garden. Maggie had been experimenting with thin fresh sheets of dough to create simple but elegant lavosh mini-pizzas. Holly bit into one of the crusty, mushroom, onion and olive-covered slices.

"Mmm," Holly closed her eyes, savored another bite. "Fabulous. How do you it?"

"Four minutes on the grill. About as low-maintenance as it gets."

"Could have fooled me. I could eat these things seven days a week."

Maggie laughed, gestured toward the small veggie garden sandwiched in among the perennials. "Trust me, I do. We've got a whole bunch of options growing out there. Chard. Beets. Spinach. Basil. All considered ornamental now as well as practical, by the way. Add some cheese, oil and balsamic vinegar and we're all set."

"Simple or not, a winner." Holly sighed. "But I don't expect gourmet fare, you know. Lately I've become the queen of TV dinners."

"You sound tired."

"Tired. Disgusted—"

There was more. Maggie sensed it. Her brow tightened. "Do I sense an agenda here?"

"Yes . . . no. Maybe."

Holly hesitated, then fished around in her purse and came up with an article obviously pulled off an online blog. The post exposed in blunt terms the undercurrent of discrimination, racial and religious animus bubbling away under the surface in Michigan politics.

"I hadn't intending on coming right out with it like this," Holly said.

With a shock, Maggie recognized the headline and text. Root and branch, it reflected the same message in the flyer she had found on her doorstep earlier in the month.

"Where did you get this?" Maggie said.

"Online. Hateful stuff." Her daughter drew a harsh breath. "It's nothing I haven't heard lately in our neck of the woods in the Southwest, Mom. But the timing of the article right before my visit kind of brought things to a head. I've been thinking for years now that maybe it's time to cut our losses."

Maggie's heart sank. "As in—?"

"Sell the cottage. I know you've wondered why I don't show up here very often. Truth be told, this is it. The vibes—frankly—have gotten borderline creepy. It's gorgeous here. I have nothing but the happiest memories. But times have changed and all of us with it. Whoever wrote that hate mail obviously sees white-bread, Ozzie and Harriet America as under siege. As I look around me up here, I keep wondering, where is the cultural, ethnic and religious diversity—where is the melting pot?"

"Harsh," her mother said.

"Maybe. Maybe not," Holly sounded pensive. "I know how you feel. Our family has summered in this area for a long time."

"Four generations, counting you."

"We've had a good run. My brother Tony and I've been talking about it for a couple of years now. Grandchildren don't exactly abound on the family tree. I never got around to starting a family and at my age, with my Ex out of the picture permanently, that ship seems to have sailed. Tony and his kids live in Hawaii. There isn't a 'next' generation to—"

Maggie started to protest. The few times Tony's kids had made the trek to the cottage, they truly seemed to love the experience. Holly cut her off.

"Mom, it's a big world out there. Your fault . . . you taught us to love it."

An awkward silence followed.

"I hope you won't take this personally," Holly said finally.

"You're being honest about where you stand. It's hard to argue with that," Maggie said finally. "Your reluctance to come here—not knowing why? That I *was* taking personally.

"This isn't about you, Mom. Never was."

"I realize that—now. And I guess I shouldn't be surprised. When it comes down to it, one of my neighbors pretty much told me the same thing, barely a week ago. Meanwhile poor Sonia down the alley has been struggling to hang on to her family cottage, one step ahead of the IRS. There's got to be an irony in that somewhere."

Holly sighed, shifted in her chair. "Mom, I'm sorry, truly I am. Maybe I'm naive. This 'back to the fifties' groundswell is going on all over. I guess the upcoming election will tell."

"Most important, you're here. For that, I'm grateful."

Holly taught at a high school in Tempe, language arts and ESL classes at night. Summers, realistically, were the only time she could get away to visit. In recent years, those visits to Northern Michigan had become fewer and farther between.

Had I been so mesmerized by the image of cottage life over the years, Maggie wondered, *that I hadn't seen how uncomfortable it was making her daughter?*

"There's someone I would like you to meet by the way," Maggie said after a while. "The neighbor I was talking about—this guy I knew as a kid. Jake Faland. Politically you and he are pretty much on the same page. He's actually in the process of selling his Dad's cottage . . . "

Holly's eyes narrowed. "Do I detect the faintest hint of something *interesting* going on?"

"As in personal? I'm not sure I know . . . or want to know."

Holly turned the disclaimer over in her head. "Mom, you've been alone since Daddy died, for nearly a decade. For the record, I don't think there's a thing disloyal about—"

"Thanks for that. Truly," Maggie sighed. "But believe me, at my age, I have no intention of entangling myself in anything."

"I'm a fine one to talk, I guess."

"You *have* been divorced a while now. And I remember something about a relationship with Tom . . . wasn't that his name? Working in health care, chiropractic, something like that."

"*Dick*." Holly winced. "An orthodontist. And at the risk of sounding glib or crude, the name pretty much says it all."

"Where do these guys come from? You're tall, gorgeous, smart—"

"And likely too picky for my own good."

"Better safe than sorry," Maggie told her. "In any case, you don't hear me clamoring for grandchildren. Two are fine—I'm not in some kind of contest. Though I wish I saw them more. You'll get around to all that in due time. Or not. Either way, I'm proud of you."

"I know that. My theory is, if and when it happens, it happens. Panic at the prospect of never finding Mr. Right doesn't accomplish much—just adds to the worry lines. And goodness knows, there's enough of those already."

"You're still young."

Holly laughed. "All relative."

The sky was graying as they talked. A light rain had begun to fall. Silent, it coated the leaves and blossoms in the garden with a shimmering glaze.

"I've been meaning to tell you," Maggie said. "Your grandmother fell a couple of days ago."

Holly's face tightened in a frown. "Is she okay? She's here, isn't she?"

"Yes. At Rolling Hills. Though after this summer, I'm not sure she's up to making the trek from downstate any more. She'll hit a hundred soon. But I guess the best way to put it, she's failing. I just signed the forms to get hospice involved."

"You're telling me she could—"

"I don't know. No one does. That's the point. Somehow I expected the bad stuff, when it comes, to happen all in one blow. A heart attack, stroke and it would be all downhill from there. But it doesn't always work that way. One day your grandmother is pretty much fine and then the next she falls or she seems confused or she's tired, depressed, sick of it all . . . "

"Sounds like an average week in my day planner. It's life you're talking here, Mom."

Maggie chuckled softly. "I guess it is."

"So, we had better go see her."

"I'll clean up, you take the time to get yourself settled."

Holly didn't protest. While Maggie cleared the remnants of their impromptu feast off the porch table, her daughter hauled a large suitcase from the trunk of her rental car. It took a bit of noisy maneuvering to get it up the steep and narrow stairs to one of the upstairs guest rooms.

"Need help there?" Maggie called out.

Holly groaned. "I deserve this, trust me. When I decided to come, I more or less threw everything and anything I might need into this clunker of a roll-on. It's no weekender, that's for sure."

Red-faced and sweating Holly joined her mother in the living room. "We never talked about—you haven't said how long you can get off," Maggie said.

"A week. Then I'm on to a conference in Vermont."

"I'll take it. I can't remember the last time you spent more than a long weekend here." Maggie hadn't meant to sound judgmental, though she sensed the minute she said it, it could have been taken that way.

Her daughter looked sheepish. "The visit hasn't gone exactly as planned either. I was intending to spend the first few days softening you up, before arguing about what to do with the cottage. I realize this might have come across as hostile or—"

"Better this way, just get it out in the open. Though I'm not in any hurry to think about selling. Let's just leave things like that."

Maggie quietly had drawn a line in the sand and neither one of them seemed predisposed to cross it. When her daughter suggested using the rental car to chauffeur them out to the senior center, Maggie didn't object. Before she had her seatbelt fastened, Holly had punched Rolling Hills into the car's elaborate GPS and pushed start. The screen built into the car's control console flickered to life.

"Ten minutes," Holly noted.

"More like fifteen. Twenty if there's traffic. I see that gizmo takes you via the highway. I always take the back roads, which for once turns out to be a bit of a shortcut."

"In a quarter mile, turn right," a woman's voice insisted from the GPS speaker system. Holly complied.

Simpler that way, Maggie thought. Navigating had always been a sore spot with Holly's dad. The first time she and Joe tried using a GPS on a trip to Pennsylvania, they wound up in the driveway of a plumbing and heating shop instead of at the Jim Thorpe memorial in the town of the same name.

When she shared the story with her daughter, Holly laughed. "So totally you, Mom . . . ," she broke off with a puzzled frown. "And wasn't Jim Thorpe that Native American Olympic runner who—"

"Lost his medals . . .yes. Technically they said he was a professional," Maggie nodded. "After the scandal, his home state of

Oklahoma wouldn't erect a statue in his honor. So folks in that Pennsylvania town offered to change the name of the place to 'Jim Thorpe', bury him there complete with monument. Made sense, in a way. Jim Thorpe began his running career in nearby Carlisle . . . so despite some nasty lawsuits, they dug him up, moved the grave back East and covered it with soil from his native Oklahoma."

"Wow."

Pretty much, Maggie found herself thinking. Who's to say in the end what constitutes *home* or where our roots really lie?

Holly was maneuvering the car into the senior center parking lot. "Home sweet home," she said looking around her. "A gorgeous facility,"

"Grandma Lillian's been happy here," Maggie told her. "Up until she fell, she was participating in a lot of activities. The Fourth, trips down to the bay. Though I'll admit, it was tough motivating her to move up here this year."

"She was always big on routine—I remember that from summers up here. But then we all have our fair share of OCD in this family."

"Multiply that tendency by a dozen for every year one of us accumulates on the old chronometer."

Holly shot a puzzled look in her mother's direction. "Chronometer?"

"The Cadillac of watches. As if anything can measure what goes into a life with any kind of accuracy."

Holly laughed. *A trifle anxious*, Maggie thought. Most likely Holly too wondered exactly what they would find when they got to Lillian's apartment. She needn't have worried. Lillian was back in her familiar spot in the living room, newspaper in her lap.

"What are *you* doing here?" Lillian's face lit up when she saw her granddaughter.

Holly laughed. "I came to see you, Grandma."

"Pretty far for a weekend, isn't it. Alabama."

"Arizona—a bit farther west. But yeah, Grams, I was planning to stay a week."

"Don't think they'll let you stay here."

"It's okay, Grams. I'm down at the cottage with Mom."

Lillian frowned. "But they would let you have dinner with me.

106

Any time."

"I'll make a point of doing that . . . soon," Holly said.

Maggie could sense her daughter was taking in the place, picturing her grandmother making it her own. "I see you have some of your paintings on the wall, Grams," Holly said.

Lillian looked around at the walls, as if seeing them for the first time. "Your mom's idea, I guess. Don't know why she schlepped them along."

In a word, *continuity*. Maggie and Holly made eye contact. What Maggie read in her daughter's expression made her throat feel tight. Quietly, without fanfare, Maggie had tried to keep life as stable as possible for Lillian through all the moves and ups and downs of the past several years. Her daughter instantly recognized the forethought all that had taken. Approved.

Time was passing. A booming voice from the intercom announced the call to dinner.

"You can stay," Lillian said.

Maggie shot a quick glance in her daughter's direction. "I think Holly's pretty tired, Mom," she told her. "How about tomorrow?"

"I would like that." Lillian had moved on, was struggling to corral her walker. "But I've got to go. It takes a while."

Gingerly she stood. *Still in pain*, Maggie realized, though not about to show it.

Maggie and Holly accompanied Lillian down the hall to the glassed double doors of the dining room. Inside, white linen tablecloths and bouquets of silk daisies gave the room a festive air.

"I love you, Grandma," Holly gave her a makeshift hug.

With that her grandmother was off and headed toward her assigned table. Mother and daughter rode the elevator to the ground floor in silence.

"Same old Grams," Holly said when they were back in the car.

"In flashes," Maggie told her. "Yes. She never was one to feel sorry for herself—or admit she needs help. But you sensed that."

"I'll come over alone for dinner with Grams some night while I'm here. Just the two of us," Holly said.

Maggie nodded in approval. "She really would like that. And it would give her a chance to air any or all of her frustrations with having me as a daughter—bullying her at every opportunity."

Holly laughed. "I can imagine."

They made short work of dinner themselves, leftover pasta salad and cold cuts. The dishes done and kitchen back in order, mother and daughter retreated to the back porch, watching the garden shut down for the night. The showers had blown over. Morning primrose curled in upon itself, its short lifespan ending. Heightened by the rain, the smell of lavender was overpowering. All was calm, quiet.

Which is why a cheery Hallooo! from down the alley startled them both. *Jake*, Maggie recognized the voice. Privately she had been hoping that Holly and Jake would meet later than sooner. There was no avoiding it now.

"Hi yourself! You out for an evening constitutional?" Maggie called out. She got up from the loveseat, set her wine glass on the porch rail.

"Or something. Though I see you have company."

"Come meet my daughter Holly."

Jake's hand was already on the gate latch. "Look forward to it."

Maggie shot a quick glance back at her daughter. The raised eyebrows spoke volumes.

"He's gorgeous," Holly muttered under her breath.

Maggie flushed. There was no point in protesting. In those chinos, penny loafers and button-down collar blue dress shirt open at the neck, Jake could have been on his way to a sunset sail over in Harbor Springs. It hadn't occurred to Maggie, but she had slipped into her new caftan after dinner. Fan of tie-dye or not, Jake could be under the impression that her wardrobe needed serious up-grading.

"May as well get comfy," she had suggested to Holly.

Her daughter took her up on it, after a fashion. As she joined her mother at the porch rail, her off-white brushed cotton lounging pants and long-sleeved boat-neck shirt had casual elegance written all over them.

Jake's attention was on the path in front of him. "You've had a few casualties out here," he said.

"Sorry about the delphinium—didn't mean to create a tripper," Maggie told him. "The wind earlier this afternoon knocked 'em over.

I intended to stake them up, but didn't get around to it."

"Those gusts slowed down work at dad's cottage, too. Nobody was about to go up on that steep roof this afternoon."

With that Jake rounded the top porch step. Before Maggie had time to think about how it might or might not look, she and Jake had exchanged hugs.

"My daughter," Maggie said. "Jake Faland."

Jake took Holly's outstretched hand in his, made eye contact. "Your mother's daughter," he said.

Holly laughed. "So I'm told."

"You up for the weekend?"

"Not really feasible for an Arizonan. I'm on my way to Vermont on business. It was easy enough to take a detour."

Jake chuckled. "You know the drill, then. Anybody headed for Northern Michigan better like commuter airlines."

Taking the measure of each other, Maggie realized with a shock, for all their good-natured chitchat. She would have expected that from her daughter. Where Jake was coming from was harder to read.

"We've got wine," Maggie said. "Red or white. Boxed but drinkable. On a par with two-buck-chuck anyway."

"I'm in," Jake said. "Thanks."

Too much could go wrong in her absence. Still, Maggie found herself heading into the kitchen for an extra glass. As the screen door shut behind her, she drew in a deep breath. *That could have gone worse*, she decided. At least Holly wasn't giving the guy the third degree from the get-go.

While Maggie was at it, she rattled around in the refrigerator and put together a tray of hummus and multi-grain chips, several varieties of olives, fresh mozzarella. Occasional waves of laughter could be heard from the porch. By the time she got back out there, her daughter and Jake were absorbed in a dissecting the upcoming national elections.

"Dangerous business, politics," Maggie said.

"Not around you two," her daughter contradicted her. "For the life of me, I would have assumed growing up when and where both of you did, you would be buying into all the back-to-the-fifties nostalgia."

"Ouch," Jake winced. "But you forgot the magic leaven in the lump—Vietnam. Not everyone in the Upper Midwest and collecting social security is destined to weigh in somewhere to the right of Attila the Hun."

"Not exactly what I meant . . . "

"But close enough."

Maggie caught the laughter in his voice. "Trust me, Holly," she said, "the fifties weren't all that much fun the first time around. Can't say I personally would want to relive any of it. The sixties was our generation's way of saying, 'You have *got* to be kidding.'"

"We want the world and we want it now." Jake turned the phrase over in his head. "It all started out well enough. Unfortunately, these days, I find myself gritting my teeth whenever someone our age starts grousing about having to pay taxes because they don't have kids in the schools or get stuck with insurance premiums when they aren't going to get pregnant. *I've got mine—to heck with you.* Makes you wonder what the tipping point becomes from youthful idealism to end-stage selfishness, narcissism."

Sciatica of the soul, Maggie thought, a painful rigidity of spirit. Was that going to be their generation's epitaph? Sad, coming on the heels of the Greatest Generation who had lived through the tail end of the Depression, fought the second Great War and lived to tell about it.

Silence descended like the coming night. The sunset glowed a fiery red between the neighboring cottages across the alley. Gradually the sliver of Little Traverse Bay was lost in darkness.

"The witching hour," Jake stood, stretched out the kinks in the process. "I better be heading out."

"Good to meet you," Holly told him.

Maggie walked him to the garden gate. "Thanks for stopping by," she said.

Jake stared down at her, quizzically. "Becoming a habit—my hanging out over here," he said evenly.

"Is that such a bad thing?"

"You tell me."

Maggie hesitated a split-second before responding. "No. Absolutely not."

Hens and chicks are a hardy, low-growing succulent in the family CRASSULACEAE. Native to southern Europe and northern Africa, they grow like rosettes with the leaves forming around each other. They spread by means of offsets: daughter plants clone themselves from the mother without pollination. They begin as buds and establish themselves close to the mother plant.

Local Color

Maggie stood peering off into the gathering night as Jake picked his way down the alley. The glow from his cell phone grew ever fainter, finally disappeared. She knew what was coming next even before she climbed back up the porch steps, sat down next to Holly on the loveseat.

Holly didn't disappoint."Mom, that guy really likes you," she said.

"Possible."

"And I suspect you like him."

"We hardly know each other."

"You grew up together."

"Past tense. That was sixty years ago. And we weren't really close even then."

"No time like the present."

"*For*—?"

Holly turned in her seat and made eye contact, not about to be put off so easily. "Your call, Mom. Trust me, it isn't every day of the week that a guy comes along truly worth the effort."

Maggie drew a deep breath, sipped thoughtfully at her wine. "The world is full of people who—"

"Challenge us. Surprise us by just being there. Mom, I can smell the platitudes you're likely to throw out a mile away. And commendable as all of them are, they aren't *attraction*. Which is partly what we're talking about."

Maggie laughed. "You've read too many novels."

"And apparently you haven't read enough. Not lately anyway."

"What was your favorite expression . . . ?" Maggie told her. "That ship has sailed?"

"You could have fooled me."

Maggie's hand shook as she set the wine glass down on the wicker coffee table. Once her daughter got going, there was no stopping her. "I'll make you a deal," Maggie said. "I won't try to play matchmaker, if you promise not to do the same."

"*Mom . . . !*"

"I appreciate the gesture. Truly I do, but—"

"*Butt out.*" Holly sounded genuinely hurt.

"It's you I want in my life. Your brother. Those gorgeous grandkids in Hawaii, Naomi and Dan. Nothing can compete with that—ever."

Holly didn't reply. From down the alley toward the Gunderson cottage, the sound of children's voices and car doors slamming broke the silence.

"Sonia must have more company," Maggie said finally.

"Your friend. I remember her."

"You and her daughter Lena used to play together."

"We almost set their upstairs bedroom on fire, as I recall. Trying to learn to light book matches."

Maggie's eyebrows arched. "You never told me that."

"Too embarrassed, I guess."

Which probably explained why Sonia herself had never said anything either. "So, what happened?"

"We burned a hole in one of their quilts. Finally Lena grabbed a pitcher of field flowers on the dresser and dumped the contents—water, flowers, the whole works—onto the bed."

"Was Sonia home?"

"Downstairs. The smoke got her attention. But by the time she got upstairs, we had put the fire out."

"To which she said?"

"Not much, considering. When Lena handed her the soggy

packet of matches, Sonia just stared at it for a few seconds. You know better than that, she told us. Though I wasn't likely to forget the way she looked at us as she pocketed that matchbook. Printed on it was, *Tip-Top Tavern*. All these years later, who remembers something like that?"

You'd be surprised, Maggie thought. It was only through a magazine article of recent vintage she learned that in the forties and fifties, the Tip-Top Tavern on Mitchell Street in Petoskey had been a Blacks-only bar. The 'Black and Tan' she heard her dad call it. She always wondered as a child about the two names, was fascinated by the steep exterior stairway to access the place. But something, a subtle sense of the taboo prevented her from asking.

Over time those memories of her youth receded along with the sight of the uniform-clad black men waiting alongside sleek touring cars in the summer outside the dime store downtown. "Drivers" her parents had called them. By the time Maggie was exposed to college courses talking about Jim Crow and 'sundowner' laws, the disconnect to the world of her childhood had become all but complete. And with the passage of the Civil Rights Act of 1964, Black Americans, even the blue-clad 'maids' in the park in Harbor Springs on their Thursdays off vanished as inexplicably as the disappearance of Maggie's playmate with the corn-rows in the grassy alley behind the cottage that long-ago summer. Never to return.

Only the myth of a childhood summer paradise lingered, ephemeral as the wisps of smoke from a dying campfire. Maggie's daughter couldn't have known what that soggy matchbook represented. Nor would Holly have guessed how close to her own mother's heart or current state of mind the story had struck.

When Holly went to bed, visibly worn out from a day on the road and all that came after, Maggie found herself glued to the internet until long into the night. The google entries were few and far between, but there for the finding. Maggie unearthed a brief account of the Payne family who ran the Tip-Top. She found bits and pieces about John West's Rainbow Inn on the edge of town—the first hotel in the area open to anyone including people of color from 1950 to 1965 when it succumbed to an out-of-control kitchen fire.

Maggie scoured *The Negro Motorist Green Book* available online from the New York Public Library, stunned to find that in 1939 only thirteen communities in the entire state of Michigan advertised bars, restaurants, hotels, gas stations and boarding houses open to 'people of color'. Petoskey, Harbor Springs, Charlevoix and Traverse City—iconic resorts along Grand Traverse and Little Traverse bays—were not among them.

By the fifties, villages listed as safe havens for Black Americans had increased. Still, that crack in the unspoken racial wall came at a time when Maggie and Joe and their own children were traveling freely from coast to coast with a different set of roadside service directories entirely. They never needed to give basic accessibility to motels or campgrounds a second thought.

It had not always been so. A small community of just under a thousand Blacks, Maggie learned, lived in the county surrounding Petoskey in 1860, most likely a stopover on the Underground Railroad of pre– and Civil War days. But ten years later that enclave and its Black population too were gone. The most recent census revealed that less than one percent of the county's permanent residents were Black, Caucasians ninety-seven percent. And in this part of the state where deer still outnumbered people, three 'hate' groups singled out by the Southern Poverty watch list had sprung up quietly in their midst.

Her ignorance, Maggie realized, *was boundless.*

In her youth, the marches in Selma and scenes of bloody violence on the covers of national news magazines had seemed as remote as the Kasbah in Algiers or the Taj Mahal. All the while in a world Maggie thought she knew, dark currents had flowed under the surface, troubling the calm teal and violet waters of her beloved Little Traverse Bay from deep within.

The sky outside Maggie's bedroom window was beginning to lose its dark velvet texture when she finally switched off the Power button on her laptop. Even then, for a long time she stared wide-eyed at the ceiling.

When sleep finally came, the dreams accompanying it roiled and surged like mountains of spray over-topping the breakwall during a late summer storm. Sunlight filtered in through the windows. The smell of bacon frying and muffled footsteps in the kitchen finally got Maggie's attention. Her daughter must be up and making breakfast.

"Ten o'clock, sleepyhead," Holly called out as her mother wandered into the kitchen.

Still barefoot and in her favorite summer nightgown with the spaghetti straps and tiny flowers embroidered on the bodice, Maggie yawned. "Tell me about it. My watch read 3 a.m. and I was still wide awake. I ought to be making you breakfast."

"It's fun," Holly told her. "I don't get to do it for anyone else very often now that the Dick is no longer in the picture. Earlier I took a jog west along the bike path as far as the waterfall and marina. By the time I got back it was getting pretty sticky."

"We could try a run out to the State Park later. Not on foot, mind you. I have one of those license plate stickers so we don't have to pay for a day-pass."

"I brought my suit. Just in case."

"We've got beach chairs and a sun umbrella in the shed. After a run-in with carcinoma, tanning is definitely not in my future."

Holly's brow tightened with concern. Her tone was serious. "You have a clean bill, though?"

"Three years now. But I'm done with taking chances."

"In Arizona, everybody tests out low in Vitamin D. It takes the snowbirds a while to figure out you cover up even for a stroll to the mailbox."

Change, Maggie found herself thinking, is not always by definition 'good'—the conspicuous shift in the climate among them. While she had tinkered and weeded in her grandmother's garden, the very air she breathed, the sunsets and sunrises had not remained untouched. Some areas of Northern Michigan were now rated two zones warmer than maps developed in 1990. Even the venerable Northern Michigan maples were visibly showing the stress. The Ag Extension people had been warning gardeners in the region for years that the escalating swings in temperatures were only the tip of the rapidly-melting icebergs.

Overwhelming, Maggie sighed. To live in the *Now* of subtle racism and Climate Change Deniers had become problematic, especially knowing what she now knew. On every front imaginable, the landscape of daily life had altered beyond recognition. The past wasn't what the once eight-year-old Maggie remembered. The future seemed murky on so many fronts.

"Zombie apocalypse," Holly teased as she set two plates of

116

scrambled eggs, bacon and hash browns on the kitchen table. "Earth to Mom."

Maggie chuckled politely. "Zoning out, was I? I promise, I'll get my act together. That coffee I smell brewing should work wonders."

She shook off the bleaker images that keep surfacing. Her landmarks might be changing by the minute, but Holly was right. Life goes on and somehow she needed to move with it.

Mother and daughter shared a leisurely breakfast, then strolled together through the garden. It was a beloved morning ritual, passed from mother to daughter through four generations, as long as Maggie could remember. The sky was cloudless. A great day to pack a hamper full of goodies and head for the sandy beach and dunes of the State Park.

Jake Faland was way ahead of them. "Up and at 'em, I see," he called out from down the alley.

"Up . . .I'm not so sure about the rest." Maggie felt herself flush, most definitely under-dressed for the occasion. *Thank God,* a voice in her head told her, *at least she had the sense to slip a bulky cardigan over that filmy nightgown on the way out the kitchen door.*

If Jake noticed the potentially revealing get-up, he was too polite to comment. "A beach day if I ever saw it," he said.

"My thought exactly," Holly chimed in. "Sounds like a plan."

"So why don't we join forces. I've got swim trunks back at Dad's cottage somewhere . . . "

"We'll come up with lunch," Holly threw in for good measure.

And just that casually they had committed to spending the day together. Shell-shocked at how the whole thing came about, Maggie forced herself to concentrate on the issue of a swimsuit. Four at least hung on the wrought iron hooks behind the bathroom door, in some cases for decades. One was too small, another too skimpy for public consumption. A third looked positively psychedelic.

That left a basic black one-piece with an overskirt. Safe enough, Maggie decided. She pulled on an oversize gauzy blouse for a beach coat and called it good. It wasn't the only crepe-iness on display. Between that and the hint of love-handles, there was no point in looking in the mirror. It was what it was. Last minute she snagged a straw sun hat from the bedpost. The ring of silk flowers on the band looked a heck of a lot more jaunty than she felt.

Blooming where a guy was planted could be exhausting. But then in retrospect, Maggie realized the summer cottage season had always been that way. A lifetime of experience crammed itself into roughly fourteen weeks. This summer was proving no exception.

Like the lifespan of a fruit fly, Maggie grimaced. *Frenetic and harried while it lasted. And bound to end.* Of that Maggie wasn't allowing herself any illusions.

Jake was waiting on the back porch of the cottage. He had pulled on a pair of cargo shorts and a Key West beach shirt, topped it off with a Detroit Lions ball hat and tired-looking flip-flops. "Want me to drive?"

Maggie fought a smile. Her daughter was right, the guy could have made a gunny sack look good.

"I have a park permit on my license plate," Maggie said.

That settled the logistics. Before she could weigh in on the subject, her daughter had taken up residence in the back seat which left the passenger seat up front for Jake.

"I'd be happy to sit in back," he offered, "if you want to sit with your Mom."

Holly laughed. "I'm good right where I am."

Maggie stayed out of it. Traffic was awful and demanded a lot of concentration. By cutting through the mini-mall east of town, she was able to use a light to get onto the highway. Cars waiting for the turn lane to M-119 heading north along the bay stretched a good quarter mile.

"Looks like everybody has the same idea," Holly said.

They hit another queue at the turn for the State Park. Once under City of Petoskey's administration, the state park was *the* spot for locals as well as tourists to take advantage of both sandy beach and the chill waters of the bay. Finding a parking spot was going to be a nightmare.

Except it wasn't. "Wow," Maggie breathed as a spot opened right in front of them. "The parking gods are with us. Who'd have thunk it?"

Jake shot a glance her way. "Great reflexes," he said. "I probably would have shot past it."

Maggie laughed. "Sometimes being old and farty has its perks."

"*Mom . . . !*"

"Grandma Lillian pretty much summed it up—if you don't laugh, you die. Most of the time we take ourselves way too seriously."

Jake's eyebrow arched but he didn't protest.

Unpacking the trunk took ten minutes. "Hamper, towels, beach blanket, sunblock, beach chairs, umbrella." Maggie ticked off the inventory. "We look like a Salt Road caravan."

As they maneuvered their way past the concession stand to the shore, an ongoing scan of the beach confirmed they had rejoiced too soon about the logistics. It was tough to carve out a spot among the forest of beach chairs. Finally they trudged south and west through the sand along the shoreline. Away from the park pavilion, the crowds thinned out a bit. They gave up on the umbrella. The wind made spreading out the beach blanket an adventure in itself.

"Okay, worn out now—time to head home." Out of breath, Maggie settled down into one of the vintage aluminum tube beach chairs. "If I get down on that blanket, I'll never make it up."

Holly laughed. "The water actually seems clearer down here."

"Makes sense," Jake said. "The current pushes the algae and debris toward the head of the bay. Over here we're out of the line of fire."

A campground nestled above them in the dunes. Maggie remember staying there in her youth. A weathered wooden stairwell towered over the sand to protect the fragile dune grass and other vegetation from the beach-going foot traffic.

Out over water toward Harbor Springs on the right and Petoskey on the left, the view was breathtaking. The passing front yesterday had left its mark on the bay. Off toward the horizon, the Great Lake itself had responded with a vengeance. Lines of white-capped breakers, some cresting at six feet were coming ashore, creating near-surfer conditions.

Only a handful of swimmers were struggling with the swells. Over the crashing of the waves, the brave souls laughed and called out to one another as a random wave caught them unawares.

Jake stood and took several steps toward the water's edge. "You game?" he said.

Maggie frowned. "The water's probably still sixty degrees out there."

"Actually sixty-seven. I checked online before we left. We lifeguards used to tell the little kids in weather like this that we had turned the heaters on in the lake earlier, just for them!"

119

On a sigh, Maggie stood and shed her makeshift beach jacket. "And nobody, of course, really believed it. Then or now for that matter. You coming, too, Holly?"

Her daughter had stretched out on the blanket, made a show of settling in for the duration. "Pass. You two go on ahead. I'm gonna catch a few rays."

Just a trifle too casual, Maggie thought. Almost as if her daughter had planned it. About ten feet out in the water by now, Jake had turned, was waiting for her.

"Have fun, you two," Holly said.

Maggie started to reply. Her mouth clamped shut again. Whatever her daughter thought she was doing, this was neither the time nor the place to confront it.

"Holy Toledo!" Maggie said. When it came to Lake Michigan, putting the equivalent of a toe in the water took on a whole new meaning. "Good grief, it's cold in here."

Up ahead, Jake's pace through the breakers had slowed considerably. "An understatement. You can see sandbars ahead where the water changes color. Maybe it'll warm up."

"I wouldn't count on it." Maggie was hanging on to her balance as a larger-than-usual wave sent a tide of freezing water to her waist. "Usually you can get out a lot farther than this before you're getting much of anything wet."

"Lake level is up eighteen inches."

"A regular encyclopedia Britannica," she grumbled. "I'm not sure how knowing all this makes getting in any easier."

"Doesn't. Sometimes you just have to go for it."

With that, Jake dove in to the trough of a massive wave coming at them—surfaced almost immediately, only to catch the incoming crest behind it which swept him off his feet. He went under in a surge of swirling water, took his time coming up just as another wave knocked him off his feet.

Maggie laughed, couldn't help it. Jake's erstwhile career as a lifeguard made the wipe-out all the wilder.

"Spectacular. I hope that wasn't for my benefit," she wondered out loud between choking bursts of laughter.

"It's damn cold," he muttered as he took a swipe at the sand he had picked up along the way. "If you don't believe me . . . "

He was headed her direction. From the look on his face, Maggie suspected she was at minimum in for some purposefully splashing to get her wet. She decided to take her fate into her own hands and went under herself, more of a dunk than a dive. The water temperature drove her instantly back on her feet. Mercifully, she had found the lull between crests and was able to stay upright.

"Hells bells," she sputtered.

"Told'ja." Jake was close enough now to pitch her back into the surf if he chose. Something in her face stopped him.

"Two old fogies," she said. "And we are out here, *why?*"

Jake grinned. "Because we can."

Maggie mulled that one over for a second or two. "Profound, come to think of it."

What had her daughter told her? It was *life* she was sensing in the chaos of the last few days. Like a full-on plunge into the icy cold bay, enough to rob you of your breath and set your teeth on edge at any given moment. But life nonetheless.

"You're one of a kind, Maggie Aron," he told her. "Most women I know would be coming out with these high pitched whining sounds and heading for shore—that is, if they even had ventured out here in the first place trying to spare their perms from disaster. And there you stand soaking wet and freezing, the weight of the universe on your shoulders, wondering if or how it all makes sense."

Maggie's teeth were chattering. "Gee thanks . . . I think."

"Compliment intended."

"All right then. We're in here. We may as well—"

It would have been an exaggeration to say what happened next was intimate or romantic. Maggie's back had been to the surf. There just might have been a rogue wave at work. But the *what* of it was indisputable.

Jake abruptly caught her bare shoulders in his two hands and drew her toward him in the roiling surf, steadying them both. In that same instant the wave lifted Maggie off her feet as the crest broke over them. Jake's skin felt slick and cold to the touch. His breath was warm against her hair.

"Maggie, Maggie," he said.

Her mouth seemed stiff. Words didn't want to come.

Meanwhile the force of the undertow was relentless, drawing them with it toward the bay. Jake held them both more or less upright as their bodies clung awkwardly to one another. Eventually Maggie's breathing adjusted to the powerful ebb and flow of the water. On tiptoe she found she could stand on her own again on the sandy bottom.

"What *are* we doing?" she gasped.

She had broken the spell. After a few seconds, with visible reluctance, Jake let her go.

I have no idea," he said. "But I'm not complaining."

Maggie had been trying so hard to keep her balance in that turbulent water, she hadn't thought how any of this roughhousing was bound to look to her daughter lying there on the beach blanket. "Seriously, we aren't kids any more."

"No, we are aren't. Which makes this—whatever *it* is—all the more—"

"Ridiculous?"

"I was thinking, *surprising*," he said.

Standing less than arms length from one another, she could see the fine droplets glistening on the down covering his bare chest. Gray no longer blond of course, Maggie smiled to herself. *No, they weren't kids any longer.*

The admission should have put a damper on the moment. Somehow, it didn't.

"My daughter is going to get the wrong idea if we keep this up," she said.

One of his eyebrows shot skyward. "*Is* she? Or more to the point, does that possibility bother you?"

Maggie hesitated. "I don't know, to tell you the truth."

"Fair enough. But I suggest if you don't want to give her more fodder for speculation, we could try to swim in this stuff before we freeze solid out here. More like body-surf, but it could be fun."

She laughed. "Okay, then."

With that Maggie took off. Striking off parallel to shore, she got in about a half dozen awkward strokes before another wave caught her.

She rode the crest several seconds, struggled back up on her feet again.

"Don't laugh," Maggie said.

Jake stood watching her, an amused expression on his face. "Better you than me—though I suppose as an ex-lifeguard, I really ought to make a stab at it."

He covered the expanse of water between them in a few powerful strokes, kept going for another handful of yards. "Tricky," he said as he found his footing again, stood waiting for her to catch up.

"The breakwall downtown would be better when it's rough like this," she told him.

"Too much like work."

He reached out a hand as she struggled toward him. Maggie took it. "Had enough?" he wondered.

"I think I'm going into shock," she told him.

Laughing, hand in hand for much of the way, they worked their way back to shore. Every time Maggie glanced up to clock their progress, she caught a glimpse of Holly sitting bolt upright on the beach blanket. She was watching them intently, her amusement apparent.

"Do I catch a not-so-subtle hint of PDA going on here?" she said when Jake and Maggie came within earshot.

"Public Display of Affection?" Jake laughed. "I'd say more like Lifesaving for Dummies. If you're going to drown, make sure you have company."

"You two couldn't pay me enough to get in there," Holly said.

"One thing for sure, a guy can sure work up an appetite just trying to stay upright."

When in doubt, eat. Face burning, Maggie had begun rummaging in the picnic hamper. "I've got tapas-size plates and napkins. But we're likely to get sand in everything," she said.

"So, let's forget the niceties and pick away at stuff right in the containers," Holly suggested. "Mom, you used to do that with us when we were little, just home from vacation when everybody was too tired to break out dishes and utensils Camping out in the living room, you called it."

Turns out, the plan involved a goodly amount of contact and jostling, despite Maggie's decision to put the impromptu feast between herself and Jake. Fishing out a stuffed grape leaf still in its original carton, she glanced up to see him smiling over at her.

"Seeing your mom in action, I'll bet she could have weathered a hurricane without batting an eye," he said.

Holly laughed. "Bingo. Though I've seen her lose it a time or two. You don't forget those moments in a hurry."

"Do I sense a tell-all in the works?"

"I was six," Holly volunteered. "We were headed out of state to visit my Dad's parents for Thanksgiving. It was quite a drive but my parents had left enough time—or so we thought. Except when we got to the airport, there wasn't a parking spot to be had, Nada. Not in the long term or short term lots. Time was passing. Finally Dad pretty much tossed us out at the curb and told us to make a run for it. It wasn't a loading zone which got the security guy mighty ticked off."

"Oh, Lord," Maggie said. "Do we really have to hang out all the old family laundry—on a public beach, forty-plus years later?"

Holly ignored her. "And we ran, trust me, hauling our luggage. Everybody for themselves. Mom was scolding my brother and lugging this carry-on. A wheel broke off, but so help me she just kept going."

"You made the flight."

"Nope. They shut the gate early, wouldn't budge. Every flight thereafter was full. Mom went to the counter at the gate and I thought she was going to have a cow. In between chewing out the agent and trying keep my brother and me from wandering off, she had created quite a stir. A crowd was gathering. Red in the face, the agent finally checked the computer and came up with a later flight. We're going to lose a whole night with our elderly parents, Mom kept saying—pretty much recited a litany of every reason you don't do that to an older couple who sees their kids and grandkids once a year."

Jake laughed, shook his head. "I can imagine."

Holly wasn't finished. "Anyway, I think mainly to shut Mom up, they gave us all passes to the VIP Lounge and three hours later we were on our way. To this day my brother still calls it Mom in Ride of the Valkyrie Mode."

"Hojotoho!" Still laughing, Jake quoted the Wagnerian chorus as he raised his plastic wine glass in salute. "What I would have given to witness that one!"

Mortified, Maggie passed the grape leaf container in her daughter's direction. "Happy now?"

Holly seemed way too pleased with herself. "You could say that. Figure Jake has a right to know who he's dealing with."

"*With whom*," Jake volunteered as he snagged the last grape leaf, then set the container down on the blanket.

"Oh, God," Holly said, "don't tell me, you're an *editor*. Mom never let my brother and me forget that particular skill set on her resume."

"Worse," he told her. "I taught, still do once in a while. Every Freshman's least favorite course, Western Civ. Though I'm currently down to one course a semester, usually online. At least the poor students don't have to put up with my obsession with Indo-European sound shifts in the flesh, so to speak."

"I sure could have used you in German 101," Holly said. "Mom's idea—when I could have taken Spanish instead, much more useful down in Tempe these days. At least I survived the darn course somehow."

Maggie quietly counted to ten before risking a sigh of relief that the conversation had veered off in a slightly less embarrassing direction. Although every now and then, something Holly said was tinged with the same unmistakable undercurrent. In his own laid-back fashion, Jake Faland had scored major brownie points with her daughter. And apparently in Holly's mind, some kind of relationship with her mother was totally A-Okay.

By early afternoon the breakers were calm enough to venture out into the bay again. This time Holly joined them. With the three of them struggling around out there, Maggie had an excuse to keep her distance. Eventually the sunlight took its toll.

"Siesta time," Holly said with a yawn. "At a hundred fifteen degrees, nobody spends this kind of time outdoors in Arizona in the summers. I don't know about anybody else, but I'm ready for some skinny margaritas on the veranda."

It was only two o'clock but it felt more like early evening. The sun blazed incandescent in its path toward the horizon. Packing up proceeded in slow motion and involved a lot of sand shaken out of beach towels and shoes and redistributed everywhere else.

Even the trek back to the car seemed longer. Maggie carried the hamper and her catch-all beach bag with the car keys. Her water shoes kept coming off as they sank deep into the unstable beach underfoot. Holly dragged along as if sleepwalking.

Jake alone seemed unphased by it all. When Maggie felt the car keys slip from her fingers on to the asphalt, he was on it like a flash.

"I can drive if you want."

Maggie shot him a pointed look.

"Just an offer," he laughed. "Night of the living dead, the bunch of us."

She got them back to the cottage in one piece, no thanks to a monster truck tailgating her and the guy ahead driving ten miles an hour under the speed limit. Passing wasn't an option. Traffic was as bad this direction as in the morning out of Petoskey. It took two lights to make the turn on to the highway at the State Police post.

"Sixty thousand cars a day," Maggie muttered. "And most of 'em picked *now* to get out there and make sure MDOT counts 'em."

Jake laughed. "I would be snoring at the wheel right now," he stifled a yawn. "Amazing what a hefty dose of sun, surf and sand can do. I used to sit on that lifeguard stand in a coma most of the time with my super-cool aviator sunglasses, just praying nobody decided to drown on my watch."

Maggie's quick glance in the rear view mirror caught her daughter with eyes closed, cat-napping. "Holly and I stayed up late last night. To boot, I had trouble falling asleep."

"Insomnia?"

"Something like that." Maggie hadn't meant to sound so grumpy. "Well, it should cool off later, better sleeping weather. They're predicting a fifty-fifty chance of scattered showers."

So we're back to chatting about Doppler radar, she thought. But after the three of them retrieved the beach gear from the trunk and were saying their goodbyes, Jake made it plain if it were up to him, he wasn't going anywhere.

"We up for dinner later? Nobody seems in the mood for cooking."

Maggie looked at her daughter. Holly's expression gave no clue to what she was thinking.

126

Jake persisted. "There's a folk singer downtown tonight. I noticed a flyer in the hotel lobby when I drove over this morning."

"Sounds good," Holly piped up before Maggie had a chance to protest.

Which left Maggie about four hours to get her head on square, starting with a shower and a nap that left her groggy and even more out of sorts. "One beer and I'm going to be face down, snoozing on the table," she told her daughter. "Folk music or not."

"Naps. Early to bed," Holly frowned. "Since when?"

"Since I turned seventy-two and stay up half the night on a fairly regular basis," Maggie sighed. "You realize, of course, we aren't likely to get over to see Lillian today either."

Holly registered surprise. "You go every day then?"

"No." Maggie admitted. "But since she fell, I've—"

"Mom, you're entitled to a life. For that matter so is Grams."

"Easy to say."

"No," her daughter said, "it isn't. I realize that. Though I also remember what Grams used to say when you got on our cases as kids."

"That mother doesn't start with an *S*. Except the habit of smothering someone with attention, as Lillian sees it, has skipped her generation entirely and landed on yours truly."

"Don't let Grams fool you," Holly laughed. "In that department you simply learned from the best. I spent summers here at the cottage with her and I know, trust me."

Maggie drew in a long breath. "I assume you've also heard of the 'sandwich generation'. Now with that I *can* empathize!"

Her daughter looked pained.

"Okay, so I know you're only trying to be helpful," Maggie said quickly.

"And not succeeding, obviously."

"We aren't going to the mattresses over this. I get it. You've decided you like Jake . . . think I'm missing something in my life—"

"Slight correction. You're entitled to have fun. You've earned it. And yes, I do like the guy. If 'fun' includes some companionship of the male persuasion, why not go for it?"

"I don't like feeling pushed into—"

"Nobody does. But a gentle nudge never hurts. I've been grateful for one or two in my life, as you know."

Maggie had been on the dispensing end of several of them. "Apparently what goes around, comes back to bite a guy."

"Hungry are we?" Holly chuckled as she looked at her watch. "By my watch, Jake's going to pick us up in fifteen minutes."

The bathroom mirror took Maggie off guard. She was expecting the worst and instead saw that despite the sunblock and oversize straw hat, she had gotten a bit of color at the beach. Tired as she felt, even the dark circles under her eyes had faded. With a few practiced twists, she wound her hair into a sleek knot at the nape of her neck. She added a hint of pigmented lip gloss and a pair of silver clip-on earrings she had left on the shelf above the sink.

"Good as it's gonna get," she told herself. The turquoise teardrop in the earrings fit with the teal overblouse she had thrown on over a black sleeveless top and black dress slacks. It simply was what Maggie found easily at hand, but the combination worked.

Holly meanwhile had slipped into a black tunic and broomstick skirt in a wild black, neon green, gold and rust print. Her pair of black strappy sandals had beach-goer written all over them. One thing Maggie hadn't appreciated before—fluff-and-go haircuts like her daughter's certainly made things easier.

The two of them had barely ventured out on the back porch when Jake's ancient Toyota came rattling down the alley. Holly scrambled in the back. That left the passenger seat.

A couple, Maggie thought. By default that was what was happening. Holly's nudges were maneuvering her over a line that she hadn't planned on crossing.

She had opportunities to date after Joe's death, had gently but firmly turned them down. One was a former co-worker, the other a long-time family friend. Their ties to her past made her uncomfortable. She had been privileged with a long, happy marriage. To have aspired to another relationship seemed somehow greedy, pushing her luck.

Jake's connections to that part of her life were tenuous at best, even though technically Sonia and Lillian were right. As a girl, Maggie had a crush on him for years. But then the Jake Faland of the past few weeks was nothing at all like the Jake of memory and imagination, the seemingly self-absorbed jock she had worshiped from afar.

In fact, the man was thoughtful, self-deprecating. Most of all—*spontaneous*. Maggie found herself putting that portrait together with what the doctor had told her about going for the gusto in her life. Settling for the status quo may be safe and comfortable. It can also subtly diminish a life in the process.

Jake shot a searching glance in her direction. "You okay?"

"Me . . . ? Fine. Tired but a good tired."

His gaze was on the traffic ahead, but the crinkles around his eyes had morphed into a smile. "You look stunning, by the way."

Maggie's laugh sounded awkward. She managed a mumbled, "What you see is what you get."

Jake laughed. "For a couple of old duffers, you're thinking."

Scary, Maggie winced. The guy was a mind reader. For once even the commentary from the back seat was not forthcoming.

Traffic was erratic—grounds enough for silence. Downstairs in the pub, the decibel level more than made up for it. A crowd was beginning to gather. Just off the bar, a small stage was furnished with an alarming assortment of mikes, cords and industrial strength speakers.

Maggie already felt the beginnings of headache. The booth Jake reserved mercifully turned out to be in a relatively quiet corner, close enough to hear the musician but not in the thick of things.

"They serve bar food," Jake said as Maggie and her daughter started thumbing through the menu, "but well done."

Maggie ordered a hard cider. Holly and Jake weighed in for local IPA beers on tap. Jake threw in a starter of breaded cauliflower. "To take the edge off," he said.

Turns out, the folk singer used an acoustic guitar and didn't amplify either voice or instrument to the nines. "Thank goodness," Maggie said. "I was wondering if they were going to supply ear plugs."

"Not stuck with hearing aids yet, either one of us I see," Jake said. "But you gotta feel for folks when the bands really crank it up. It sounds like a flock of smoke alarms going off all at once."

Maggie laughed. "My nemesis is the light in these places. There's never enough of it. Cataract surgery helped. But still—"

Jake flicked on his smartphone and concentrated the light on her menu. "I'm with you there," he said. "Doc is threatening me with the surgery coming up in fall. Have any pointers?"

"Start scrambling for a ride now. Otherwise, No."

The singer turned out to be young, in his late twenties. Intent on looking 'folk' as advertised, he had shown up with close-cropped beard, pony tail and a leather vest that smacked of the sixties.

"Have you noticed," Maggie wondered out loud, "how so many professionals nowadays tends to look like pre-teens? Especially artists and medical staff. Disturbing actually."

"I'm still mystified that vinyl records are back," Jake chuckled. "I never got around to pitching mine and suddenly I'm sitting on a goldmine."

"And when entertainers are appropriating our wardrobe from back in the day, it makes me feel even older. I'm not ready to be pegged as quaint or Lord help me, *retro*."

Jake chuckled, shook his head. "I gave up on that one a long time ago . . . the day the first low-slung jeans, thong and a tramp stamp showed up on a coed in my classroom. Moment of truth. I realized how out of touch my button-down collars had become. Maybe it's why language changes so fast. *A gas* instead of *trendy*, or our generation's *camp* instead of *old school*—however we finesse our way around aging, it tends to sound a heck of a lot more glamorous than it really is."

When the folk guitarist announced a Bob Seger tune, Maggie found herself intrigued, wondering for a split-second if that was any relation to Pete. Turns out it wasn't. The guy made a joke about it.

"*Against the Wind*, a classic out of the eighties," he said as he played a riff.

Classic. By the eighties Maggie was married and a mom, twice over. She didn't know the piece but it quickly drew her in. The lyrics told of young lovers running into the wind, not realizing how their differences, time and fate were working against them.

"Wish I didn't know now, what I didn't know then," the line kept recurring. The text fit Maggie's mood—introspective, rethinking her life choices. Adolescent fantasies seemed like ancient history.

She had nothing to regret, except perhaps too little time with the man she had loved, who had loved her. Maybe selective amnesia is a blessing in disguise, she concluded, as the refrain repeated itself. *Against the wind. Against the wind.*

"Earth to mother," she heard her daughter say.

"I've been in la-la land," Maggie said.

"Pretty much."

"I was thinking about that surf earlier." Sunlight had turned the crests to blinding waterfalls of spray and foam.

Jake was looking at them both. "Cut from the same cloth, you two," he said.

"There was a point I would have punched you out for that remark," Holly laughed.

"Part of the deal," he said. "My dad and I had an interesting relationship to say the least."

Holly looked at him quizzically.

"Dad's a banker—was I should say. He's in a nursing home now," Jake explained. "For a son in our family, a lawyer would have passed muster, maybe an accountant. But me a teacher specializing in Great Books, that definitely was not on the top ten list for career choices."

"And now?"

"Late twenties when I was slugging it out for tenure and trying to make ends meet on an Assistant Professor's pay, Dad seemed like the epitome of capitalism at its ugliest. I will say, two years ago when I started handling his finances, those choices began to make a lot more sense. And vice versa. Maybe grudgingly, but Dad had to admit I wasn't as impractical or clueless either as he assumed all those years."

Maggie laughed. "That's Mom and me. In a nutshell."

"Family," Jake said, raising his mug of IPA in a toast.

"To family." The three of them echoed in chorus.

Contrary to her direst predictions, Maggie did not fall asleep on the table. Jake's invitation seemed less like stalking and more like prolonging the moment.

"Seems like yesterday, but it was long ago." The words of the not-Pete-Seeger tune kept cropping up in Maggie's head. "What to leave and what to leave in, runnin' against the wind."

Jake drove them home around ten. It had been a long day. The streets were largely empty. Cottage life had its own informal curfew.

131

Holly hopped out the minute the Toyota ground to a halt in the alley behind the cottage. "Stay put, Mom. We forgot the porch light again. I'll get it."

So there they were, she and Jake in the front seat, alone and pushing within hailing distance of eighty. Maggie had never appreciated the logistical challenge of intimacy in a car with bucket seats, wasn't expecting it when Jake leaned over and drew her toward him. Gear shifts proved more hostile to intimacy than adult children could ever be.

For all that, Maggie felt his hand warm against her face, tilting her mouth to meet his. His breath was warm, the touch fleeting as kisses went, discreet. But as the porch light clicked on, Maggie saw Jake's face. And what she read there took her breath away.

"G'night, Maggie Aron," he said.

For a split-second she felt the familiar twinge inside, the heady exhilaration of the girl in the garden so many years ago. Her world was spinning like the core of the universe, suns and planets revolving to a rhythm as old as time.

On impulse with a free hand, she tentatively reached out and connected with the strong plane of Jake's face. She felt the stubble along his jawline, the warm sense of his presence. And then just as abruptly she was gone, fingers grasping the latch of the car door, and so out into the night.

The air was cool. Mist was rising in the garden, a damp cloud at her feet. The fallen delphinium and bloomed-out creeping phlox brushed against her bare ankles. Thick lavender perfume drifted from the border on either side of the path.

Holly was standing in the kitchen doorway. Her smile was knowing. But whatever she was thinking, she kept it to herself.

"Tired?" Maggie said.

Holly leaned past her and flicked the light switch, twice. *Her mother's daughter indeed*, Maggie took renewed comfort in the thought. In the alley, Jake slid the Toyota into gear.

Side by side inside the screen door, mother and daughter watched the taillights disappear into the darkness. Holly's arm wound around her mother's shoulder.

"I'm glad I came," Holly said. Maggie didn't have to wonder if she meant it.

What's in a name? COREOPSIS or tickseeds have nothing to do with ticks at all—are especially attractive to bees and butterflies. The elegant botanical name comes from the Greek words for "bedbug" (koris) and "view" (opsis). After flowering, the flat, dry 'fruits' of the plant resemble bugs. Showy petals of the plant are sawtoothed, usually a deep yellow or yellow with red highlights.

Empty Nests

Maggie didn't need the calendar on the refrigerator door to remind her summer was fleeting. August was just around the corner. The season was ending in a few short weeks. Fall wouldn't be far behind. Maggie would be headed downstate and her cottage friends would scatter to all the corners of the earth. Jake Faland's family cottage was about to go on the market.

But that was then. This was now and goodbyes came hard. The fourth week in July, Maggie's daughter left for her conference in Vermont. Their time together was the best Maggie could remember as mother and daughter in ages.

"I'll treasure this," Maggie told Holly, her voice breaking at the admission. "I'm going to miss you."

A wistful smile teased at the corner of Holly's mouth. "It's good to know you won't be alone."

No, she wouldn't. Maggie flushed at the undertone in her daughter's voice.

They hugged each other once more before letting go. Fighting back tears, Maggie watched Holly maneuver her rental car down the alley. The walk back through the garden to the cottage was tinged with a rush of memories, raw and bittersweet. Once inside, solitude filled the empty spaces of the kitchen, the wicker-furnished living room. It took up residence in Maggie's heart.

Leave-takings were nothing new. Holly and her brother had been off on their own for decades. The thousand-and-one goodbyes—from the first day of kindergarten to the first day of college, the first live-in relationship, the first child to marry—were long in the past. Still, in moments like this, the reality of life's empty nests hit home with a vengeance.

In the first terrifying rush of parenthood, privacy seems forever a thing of the past, even the prospect of a solid night's sleep. The turbulence of adolescence becomes nature's way of helping parents muster the strength to urge and in desperation even gently push a child out of the nest into a life of their own. If and when offspring return, it is on very different footings.

Son Tony in Hawaii had put not just half a continent but half the globe between them. For a die-hard surfer, even the most ferocious of Michigan's storms and swells just couldn't cut it. Daughter Holly at long last admitted she felt this visit as if she truly had 'come home' again. That had not happened in a good long while. But in the end if Holly had reversed her opinion about selling the cottage, that change of heart remained unspoken.

Losses, all. But from some of life's leave-taking, there *is* no return. With her mother Lillian's fall still recent history, Maggie found herself revisiting the loss of her husband Joe, felt the distancing from adult children even more acutely.

Somehow inexplicably, Jake Faland had become a part of that equation. "For what it's worth, I think Jake really cares about you, Mom," Holly had repeated on the way out the door.

Maggie didn't need her daughter to tell her that. Hearing it was both reassuring and unsettling. The Faland cottage was on the market. Another era was passing. Inevitable.

Maggie's kitchen wall clock read 9 a.m. The coffee was gone. Grasping for something to do to keep her mind off the empty cottage, she brewed a fresh pot. The rich aroma of South American beans clung in the morning air.

Like memories, Maggie told herself as she sat at the kitchen table with the mug of potent brew clutched in her two hands. Our senses trigger reminders of time well spent, how finite life is.

Her day with Holly and Jake at the State Park turned out to be their last sustained beach time for the week. The rest of Holly's visit it rained. Temperatures dropped into the sixties. Under gray skies one day the three of them drove along the Tunnel of Trees from Harbor Springs to Cross Village, had lunch at historic Legg's Inn. The legendary Polish restaurant's Bigos or Polish hunter's stew was the perfect comfort food with the wind howling out of the west. Even in the rain, the gardens were beautiful against the backdrop of the open waters of Lake Michigan. On the horizon, a lone ore boat was riding low in the water, too distant to figure out which way it was headed.

Like every long-time summer resident, Maggie knew the pilgrimage spots by heart. A trip to the lavender farms west of Petoskey in between showers was a treat for the senses. On their stroll along the pier at Harbor Springs to see the yachts moored at their slips, the deep green waters were momentarily still enough to catch a glimpse of the towering columns of seaweed reaching upward toward the surface. Biking on Mackinac Island under troubled skies left them tired and wind-burned. Holly's week was almost over.

The rains eventually became serious enough that they settled down in front of the massive stone fireplace in the cottage instead of venturing forth at all. Holly broke out old games from childhood—Skigammon, King Oil and Trouble. They started but didn't finish a thousand-piece puzzle of wine corks of the world.

"Cottage life at its best," Jake admitted as he poured them all another round of merlot.

Holly was looking pensive. "Childhood revisited," she told him. "That doesn't happen much any more anywhere else—for all the game nights penned in on my friends' day planners. Most of the time it means sitting miles apart on a couch playing video games or online solitaire."

"Partly it's the place, I'll grant you," Jake said. "But it's also an acquired mindset that either becomes internalized or it doesn't. I've always felt the trick is to live in all three time zones wherever we find ourselves. The past, the present, the tomorrows. But mostly we have to start where we are—in the *now.* "

Maggie started to chime in, decided against it. That didn't keep her from trouncing both of them at a round of Trivial Pursuit.

"No fair," Holly said. "You always kicked our butts at this, even back in the day."

Maggie rummaged around in the cupboards and came up with a more recent creation. Point of the game was to reconstruct song lyrics, everything from Elvis tunes to Bob Dylan and then sing them. The three of them quickly gave up on competing and rewrote the rules so they could collaborate on recreating the random lines and phrases.

"If I could save time in a bottle " Jake sang in a creditable baritone when it was his turn to guess words and tune.

"Jim Croce," Holly broke in.

Maggie laughed and helped the two of them finish, in an approximation of two-part harmony. "I've looked around long enough to know you're the one I want to go through time with."

Jake was right. Time warps and wraps itself around us, Maggie thought in retrospect. And keeping our balance in its vortex begins and ends in the moment.

Holly had left. And in the new normal, life goes on.

Stashing her empty coffee mug in the sink, Maggie strode quickly back to the bedroom and threw open the closet door. Her life story of summers past was on that rack. Retrieving a mid-calf length blue jean dress with French metal military style buttons down the front, she got dressed.

Her garden clogs were waiting by the back door. Weeds were intruding even worse again along the path to the gate after all the rain, but she didn't let herself be deterred. She got in the car and drove along the lakeshore toward downtown Petoskey. With a deft twist of the wheel, she maneuvered her way into a tiny strip mall.

The barber shop advertised Unisex Haircuts, fifteen dollars. Three padded chairs stood empty. A single stylist was fiddling with his smartphone at the counter. When Maggie entered, he looked up.

"Can I help ya?"

Maggie grimaced. It had to be some kind of conspiracy. *Twelve, the guy couldn't be a day over twelve.*

A couple of style magazines were protruding from a rack near the cash register. Grabbing one with a conspicuous amount of gray hair on the cover, Maggie thumbed through it quickly to a photo.

"That one," she said. "Can you do it?"

The kid just looked at her graying pony tail that even in a twistee fell well below her shoulders. "Are you sure?" he said.

"Positive."

The kid gestured toward the middle of the two barber chairs. "This is going to take a while."

"I've got time." When Maggie slid off the twistee, her hair cascaded around her shoulders.

"It's thick," he said. "Got a lotta body."

"That's good?"

The kid nodded. His eyes were the size of pie plates. He picked up a shears and comb and stood holding them.

"You can start any time," Maggie said.

He did, tentative at first. Hair began to accumulate in great patches and clumps on the black and white linoleum tile of the floor.

Maggie took one last look at her image in the wall-length mirror in front of the chair. Then she closed her eyes. From outside the salon, the occasional screeching of brakes and car horns told her the traffic was piling up again on the highway. Time was passing.

"Okay," the kid said after a while. "Whatcha think?"

Maggie opened her eyes. What she saw left her speechless.

"It's *short*," she said. Spiky, like the jagged-edged petals of the coreopsis in her garden.

"Ya gotta use product with a cut like this."

The salon keeper rubbed a white foam into his two hands. With his fingertips he teased at the longer strands on top and at the back so that they arched into a feathery wave. In front, he spiked the shorter hair to give it height and fullness.

"Sure looks different," the stylist said.

"I like it," Maggie said firmly, though her voice quavered at the end. "Just what I wanted."

The floor around her chair was ankle deep in hair. While she studied her image with the hand mirror the salon keeper had given her, he used a broom to clear a path for her.

"That'll be fifteen dollars," he said.

Maggie gave him twenty-five. "I'll be back," she said.

Shell-shocked he stood there holding his broom. "See ya."

As Maggie opened the door, the breeze ruffled the strands of hair that had escaped the attempts to tame and shape it. The sensation felt like being caught in an updraft, flying.

Armed with a sense of accomplishment, she headed east again. The bevy of construction trucks in front of the Faland cottage left hardly any room for parking. Maggie pulled off the roadway as best she could and got out of the car.

She had plenty of sidewalk in front of her for Jake to see her coming. Maggie spotted him first. He was wrapped up in an intense conversation with a landscaper holding a hard-tined garden rake.

It didn't take much skill in lip-reading to decipher his reaction when he saw her. "*Wow . . . !*"

Maggie flashed a smile, waved. Her pace quickened.

"Thought I'd stop by and see how you're doing," she said.

"You got your hair cut."

She laughed. "You like it?"

"Amazing. You look—"

"Ten years younger, I hope."

"Like *you*," he said.

"Well, I'm in the mood to celebrate. I'm taking you to lunch."

Jake just looked at her. "When?"

"Now."

The landscaper had been watching the exchange with a quizzical look on his face. "We can finish this later," he told Jake.

"Just what I was going to suggest."

"All right then," Maggie said.

Jake walked alongside her to the car in silence. "I'm filthy," he said finally. "You sure you want to be seen in public with me?"

Maggie laughed. "You'll do. I thought we'd go downtown. I've been told there's this place—they supposedly make great lamb tacos. And we can have a gelato afterward."

"It shouldn't be too crowded."

When Maggie tried to ease the key into the ignition, her hands were shaking. "We can hope."

Conversation was awkward, starting and stopping like the traffic around them. Buoyed at first by an adrenalin surge after her adventure at the salon, Maggie felt a lot less confident with every passing block. It took her ten minutes to parallel park. To his credit, Jake sat without comment until she cut the ignition.

"I've got change for the meter," he told her.

It took him a while to piece together enough coins for two hours. By then Maggie was standing on the sidewalk, watching his progress. "Should do it," she said.

The walk to the café was barely a block. They finessed it while keeping a safe distance between them. The restaurant gods were favorable. Wait staff seated them right away outside at a corner table overlooking the long and narrow park that had once been a railroad right-of-way. A white bandstand and cannon surrounded by hosta broke the sprawling expanse of green lawn.

Maggie looked up from her menu. Jake was watching her with an expression on his face that could have been appreciation or stunned confusion. It was hard to tell.

"It made sense," Maggie explained, "what you said the other day. Life starts with the *now*. After Holly left this morning, I was feeling colossally sorry for myself. So I had a cup of coffee—and it hit me. This was a new day and I was going to live it."

"You succeeded," his voice caught. "Big time. You look . . . your hair is—"

"Crazy, huh."

"Not the word I had in mind. When your hair was long it reminded me of when we were kids. But this is a side of you . . . it was always in there, I suspect. But now, it's visible."

"Reckless."

"I was thinking *irrepressible*. The girl in the garden, all grown up—out there in the garden at nine o'clock in the morning with her adult daughter in a nightdress that would have stopped traffic anywhere . . ."

So, he had noticed after all. Cheeks burning, Maggie looked down at the menu. "For the record, I had a bit of a crush on you back in the day—truth be told."

"You hid it well." Jake chuckled softly.

"And you aren't exactly that dude with aviator sunglasses on the lifeguard stand anymore, I have to say."

"Bottom line, we both seem to have cleaned up nice."

"Something like that."

"So where now, Maggie Aron?"

The arrival of the wait staff to take their orders gave her time to think about it. "Game for splitting those lamb tacos you talked about?" Jake said.

"Sounds good. Portions are always so big. I either wind up with doggie bags that might or might not get eaten, or I finish them off and regret it later."

The young woman taking their order looked disappointed. In a system where tips are based on the bottom line, a shared entree was a substantial come-down. Meanwhile, Jake's question was still out there, unanswered.

"When do you leave for Wisconsin?" Maggie said.

Jake shifted in his seat. "Mid-September. Maybe later. The exterior of the cottage is starting to come together. The crew starts painting next week. But the interior still needs a lot of work."

Maggie didn't ask him about putting the cottage on the market. "Time marches on," she said.

Avoiding his gaze, with one hand she began to deploy her napkin. With the other, she nudged her silver ware into a ragged line, more or less the requisite half-inch from the table edge. Etiquette class in junior high school had left a permanent mark.

"A carpe diem moment, you're telling me." With that, Jake casually reached across the bistro table and closed her hand in his.

Flustered, Maggie made eye contact. Her throat felt tight.

Jake turned her hand over and studied her palm. "Promising," he said. "A long life line."

"Anything else?"

"You didn't stop to weed before we left."

Maggie looked puzzled. "Mind reader . . . ?"

"Not exactly. No sign of chlorophyll."

As he released her hand, their laughter felt good, clearing the air. They talked effortlessly after that with no evidence of awkward seven-minute pauses. Maggie discovered Jake loved photography. She revealed her passion for hunting morels in the spring.

"I breaded, fried and froze a bunch of them this season. A couple of pounds all total. Come over to dinner Wednesday night and I'll unthaw a few. We can go to movies at the library afterward."

"Two days from now." Jake started to say something—stopped.

"You have a problem with that?" Maggie said.

"I was hoping you might be free later," he said evenly. "Short notice, but I could pick up Chinese to-go. And we can still take in the movies—sample the morels—later in the week."

'I guess . . .yeah, sure," Maggie stammered. "We never finished that puzzle, the one we started with Holly with all the wine corks. The morels just need to be thawed. I'll make a thin crust lavosh with stuff from the garden to go with 'em."

"And I'll supply the vino. White or red?"

"Riskier I know, but I'm fonder of white."

"Good to know," Jake nodded. "I'll pick up a couple of bottles of a decent chardonnay, maybe a moselle."

While he was pondering the possibilities, Maggie had snagged the bill and paid it. "Is 6:30 too late?"

"You've got a date."

Flustered, she found herself calculating the tip twice. In desperation she tacked on twenty percent and called it good. This time on the way to the car, Jake took her hand in his. It felt comfortable, *like two old shoes.*

It wasn't until Jake laughed that Maggie realized she had said that last out part out loud. "Sandals or velcro sneakers?" he said.

"The sturdier the better," she said. "I took one of the scariest tumbles of my life trying to hop around on one foot slipping into a pair of wedges without bending over."

Driving gave her an excuse to ruminate. Jake fiddled with the radio, came up with a station of Golden Oldie's.

Maggie recognized a favorite, "Fields of Gold", even without a modern car radio's digital ID system. Sting's lush voice made the lyrics sound as if they were aimed straight at her.

"You'll remember me when the west wind blows upon the fields of barley . . ."

The stubble feel of the new mown hay at Bliss and the harsh sun overhead scrolled through Maggie's imagination as the song unfolded. "I never made promises and there are some that I've broken . . . ."

But then there comes a point in life when vows and contracts mean little to nothing. *It was enough to be,* she thought. And as Holly said, to know she was not alone.

Back at the Faland cottage, the crews were on lunch break. As she and Jake said their goodbyes, they had an audience. Maggie cut the engine, looked over at Jake only to catch him studying her face intently.

"See you tonight then?" she said.

He smiled. "Wouldn't miss it for the world."

§§§§§

The garden was waiting for her. Maggie changed into a pair of worn denim capris, a red boat neck shirt and plastic garden shoes. For a solid hour she weeded as if her life depended on it, taking a break only long enough to stake up the miscreant delphinium that had taken a pounding during last week's storms.

Mid-afternoon she settled down on the wicker chaise in the living room with a book of stories about Great Lakes ore boats. Before she knew it, she was sound asleep. In her dreams she was making her way through a field of tall grass. Her hair was floating on the breeze, the ends bathed in a gold light. The grass gave way like the waters of the bay, then closed again behind her.

When she awoke the book had slipped to the floor. Her watch said four o'clock. She had veggies to chop and a table to set. First things first. A quick shower dealt with her morning at the salon and workout in the garden. Toward the back of the closet she found a red knit floor length sun dress with fish stenciled at the back of the open neck, the hem of the skirt and on a random pocket.

The flushed face in the mirror with its close-cropped hair bore no resemblance to the Maggie Aron who had started out the day grieving her daughter's departure. In truth, she had not seen this woman in decades, if ever.

Bohemian, if she had to give voice to the change. Comfortable in her own skin.

143

It was also a very different looking Jake Faland who popped up on the back porch of the cottage at 6:30 on the dot. His navy slacks and button down collar dress shirt, open at the neck, were straight out of a Brooks Brothers catalog.

Their hug was awkward. Jake was juggling two bottles of white wine and a vinyl bag stamped with undecipherable Oriental characters. Maggie took the container he extended in her direction.

Sushi," Jake said. "They were making these fresh at the market. Couldn't resist."

Maggie peeked into the depths of the shopping bag as she took it from him. "I love sushi," she said. "How did you know—"

"You had a takeout menu posted on your fridge."

"Oh."

Jake shrugged. "Anyway, I was thinking all of this should go with a dry white. The moselle this time. Though the combo of morels you promised and California rolls aren't your usual appetizers, I grant you."

"Yum." Maggie plated the assortment of sushi with the modest stash of breaded wild mushrooms. Jake fiddled with the wine cork. At up to fifty dollars a pound, even several morels as a garnish counted as a luxury and worthy of mention on a menu.

"The lavosh is ready to go," Maggie said, "but I haven't baked it. Just minutes in the oven and it's done"

"If we want to mess around with the puzzle, you can put it on hold for a while," Jake suggested.

"Sounds fine to me."

Maggie had moved a brass goose-neck lamp next to the card table where the partially-completed puzzle stared up at them. The outer frame was done and a random patch of shadowy corks distinctive because of an unmistakably violet cast. Most of the remaining pieces—corks bathed in bright sunlight—were yet to find a home.

A contact sport, Maggie quickly discovered. Even concentrating on different sections of the partially finished scene, the close quarters led to a conspicuous touching and jostling. She was finding it oddly hard to catch her breath.

"Who knew there were so many different kinds of corks!" she muttered as she hooked together two pieces. When assembled the printing on the cork read, *Illuminare.*

"I was wondering if somebody actually sat down and drank all this stuff," Jake said. "One heck of a hangover."

Maggie's laughter felt tight. She took a break to clear her head while she sipped at a glass of the white Jake had brought. "You're right about this moselle," she told him. "It's not bad."

"Inflation has hit the world of two-buck Chuck. But it's amazing what's still out there in the two-for-ten range. For once I actually notched the options up a bit."

"I haven't been one for drinking very much," Maggie said. "At least not after that first wild flush of hedonism in college. My husband Joe used to tease me about being a 'cheap drunk'."

Jake made eye contact, chuckled politely. "I'll keep that in mind," he said. "You and he . . . you were married a long time?"

"Forty years. He died of industrial lung cancer ten years ago, just six months after retirement. Not that uncommon for engineers, I'm told."

"I'm sorry about—"

"A long time ago," Maggie said. "At the time you think your life is over. And then one morning you wake up and realize the rest of the world is going on, business as usual. Somehow you do, too."

"You had a good life together?"

"He was gone a lot for his work. Honestly, I hated that. But when he was home, he stayed close. We traveled together a lot as a family, even when the kids were little. I think I miss that the most . . . seeing the world through someone else's eyes."

"Travel's addictive, I agree. Since I stopped classroom teaching, I've been on the road a lot—Europe top to bottom, the Middle East, Central and South America."

"That was the plan," Maggie sighed. "After Joe died, I thought about taking a small ship tour in Europe, but then kept procrastinating."

"It's never too late."

Maggie fitted another cork together in the puzzle. *Mis en bouteille.* She had in truth been bottled up too long, first with her grief and then with her dogged quest for independence. Her daughter had told her as much.

"Do you travel alone—or with some kind of group tours?" she

said.

"Both," he told her. "And yes, I'm always up for company, in case you're wondering."

Maggie sat in stunned silence. If he was kidding, she saw no evidence of it. Jake just kept working on a section of the puzzle where all the corks were labeled with German wineries or varieties of grapes.

"There are some great small ship routes along the Mosel and Rhine or the wine regions of France," he persisted. "But if you don't mind changing hotels fairly often on a land trip, there's always Tuscany to consider . . . "

Way too much and way too fast. The thought came to Maggie like that wave breaking over them in the bay, out of the blue, making it treacherous to keep her footing.

She could count on the fingers of one hand the anxiety attacks she had weathered in her lifetime—her first night alone in the dorm freshman year in college, the night before her wedding then again coming home to an empty house after her husband's funeral. Most recently, fear of the unknown had reared its head after a night with Lillian in the emergency room. None of those had prepared her for the full-bore wave of panic suddenly bearing down on her.

What in the heck do you think you're doing? World travel together? Truth was, for all that had passed between them in the last several weeks, she and Jake Faland barely knew each other. Any response she could muster seemed lame at best, insulting at worst.

"I guess most people accumulate a bucket list," Maggie admitted reluctantly.

"And tops on yours?" he persisted.

"Monet's gardens at Giverny . . . "

"There you have it. The Loire. I'm game, if you are."

The sushi and morels were gone. Their glasses were empty.

When in doubt, ignore or deflect. "Nice thought. But right now I would settle for a walk to the bay," Maggie said weakly "That sunset isn't going to wait. I suggest we take up residence on the porch for dinner— ?"

At something in her tone, or maybe it was the abrupt change of subject, Jake shifted in his chair. They made eye contact.

"You would be one awful poker player," Maggie's husband had told her more than once in their years together. What Jake read in her face must have spoken volumes. His wry hint of a smile flickered and was gone. He had gotten the message.

Flustered, Maggie dropped her gaze. Her face felt hot. Hand trembling, she laid the lone puzzle piece in her hand on the table between them.

"And I don't know about you, but I'm starving," she lied as she clambered to her feet. "You can go ahead and set up camp outside. I'll bring the munchies."

She didn't wait for him to respond, turned instead and hustled toward the kitchen. Taking her time, she started to preheat the oven for the lavosh, then arranged a small platter with an assortment of olives and sweet peppers.

Jake, meanwhile, had beat a strategic retreat. He was encamped at the table on the porch, nursing his glass of wine and looking out over the garden. At the sound of the screen door opening, he ventured a guarded look her direction.

"I could help if—"

"No need. That's it really, we're good. Except for the lavosh."

Jake drew a long breath. "Well exotic places aside, we're certainly going global tonight. Local morels, the Far East, German wine—not sure where lavosh originated, probably Manhattan. A far cry from the meat and potatoes culture we knew as kids."

The edge of sarcasm in his voice was impossible to miss. Maggie retrieved the lavosh and in damage control mode, settled down on the opposite side of the table.

"By the way," she wondered out loud, "you never mentioned home . . . what it was like growing up. Not counting the family cottage, of course—and your Dad's job. Banking wasn't it?"

"A blip on the map in northern Indiana," Jake shrugged, "typical white bread suburb. Dad wound up president of the town's only bank—but then you knew that. Classic big fish in what amounted to a birdbath. I got as far from the place as scholarships would take me. College and doctorate in Madison, as it turns out. A year studying in Berlin."

"Western and World Civ, you said. An unusual career path," she told him. "Impressive."

"Thanks, I think," he told her. "Unfortunately Dad pretty much said the same thing—vaguely effete as he saw it. Elitist and not in a good way."

Maggie flushed. "No offense intended. I can understand the stereotype. My classes in the lit department back in the day were certainly two-thirds women."

"And the *professors*?"

"Men, of course. All but one anyway and that particular woman had been there forever, a giant in the field of classical English lit."

"You didn't ever think about going on in the field yourself?"

Maggie hesitated. "For a doctorate? It occurred to me. I loved medieval studies, took tons of early English and the old Germanic languages."

"*But*—?"

"I went to the English department chair with a 4.0 average and asked about scholarships. *We don't scholarship women*, he said. Flat out, just like that. *You'll just get married and never use it.* My day job at the university library eventually helped to finance my master's in comp lit, but by then I had met Joe. And we got married. So I guess that department chair's assumptions were not that far off."

Jake's jaw tightened. "Or by shutting the door, that Neanderthal in the English department made the outcome inevitable."

"I never thought of it that way."

Another lie. It was one of her few regrets, despite a career that would have produced envy in most of her former classmates.

"A life lesson in how discrimination works," Jake's voice was hard. "I sat on the tenure committee and trust me, that kind of stuff still goes on. A lot subtler maybe. Few fight it, though they should."

Whether or not Jake meant it that way, Maggie perceived in his words a hint of unspoken disapproval. She dropped her gaze. The subtle gulf between them was becoming a chasm.

"Different times," she said softly.

Jake let it drop, softened his tone. "Anyway, I really wasn't out to get Dad's goat—or prove anything. Not consciously at least," he said. "Basically I couldn't decide on a major. Global studies wound up the

148

only thing that tied together all those random courses in art, music, lit, history."

"A lot to master."

Jake shrugged. "A jack of all trades and master of none is closer to the truth. I thought about History at one point, but it seemed way too specialized. So, what to do with all those random credits? The Big Picture always seemed more interesting than a slavish rehashing of dates and wars of succession."

Silence lengthened between them like the shadows creeping across the garden. *This was not going well.* Finally Maggie got to her feet, an empty stoneware platter in her hands. "Speaking of time passing, from the look of it we're going to miss the sunset."

"So we are," Jake said, "Unless—"

He stood, took the platter out of her hands and gently set it back down on the wicker table top. "What say we go for broke and catch as much of it as we can."

It wasn't a question. He extended a hand in invitation in her direction. *A peace offering?* Maggie hesitated but took it. "All right, then."

Together they made their way through the garden and down the alley toward Little Traverse Bay. As they rounded the corner of the last cottage before the lakeshore, Maggie could see the nightly ritual of sunset watching had been spectacular by any standards.

"Wow," she breathed, took off on her own toward the shoreline. Flaming orange, the sun already had plunged half-way below the dark water on the horizon. Even so, intense shafts of reds and purple still illuminated the cloud bank spread out above it.

Maintaining a calculated distance between them, Jake stared out over the horizon. "Breathtaking."

"Although from the look of those clouds, we could have rain tomorrow." It wasn't her intention to come across as a perpetual wet blanket, but she seemed helpless to prevent it. "Seems to work that way. Sunsets over Little Traverse often go over the top like this when there's a storm brewing over the big lake."

Jake didn't react one way or the other. The sun sank to a sliver. Then it was gone entirely.

Maggie shivered. The light was fading fast and with it any

excuse to prolong the moment. As if by mutual agreement and mostly in silence, the two of them started back toward the alley and the Aron cottage. What had sprung up so easily and naturally between them over the past weeks all at once had become strained, self-conscious.

"Getting cooler," Maggie ventured. When he didn't respond, she found herself rattling on, anything to fill the silence. "I can't believe it's the end of August. Fall's coming. . . sooner rather than later. This morning I noticed that huge maple along the highway has started to turn."

"I remember. As kids it was always the first."

They had reached the garden gate. Jake hesitated, stood with a hand on the latch.

"I should be going," he threw out, just a trifle too casually. "The guys are coming at seven in the morning—trying to make up for lost time after all that rain last week."

Jake was only doing what she wanted. He was backing off. Maggie was having trouble meeting his steady gaze. "Don't work yourself to death over there."

"Not hardly," Jake shrugged. "Tonight was a great break. Thank you for that."

The gate creaked as it swung open. "You're welcome any time," Maggie said.

Their hug was cordial enough. For the life of her, Maggie couldn't piece together who had initiated it. She took several tentative steps toward the porch, turned to look at him.

"G'night then, Maggie Aron," he said. His face was unreadable.

"Stop by when you get a chance," she told him.

With that he was off down the alley. *Taking his time*, Maggie thought. She watched until he rounded the corner, disappeared from sight. He never looked back.

"Just as well," she muttered as she climbed the porch steps. "We both could use some breathing space."

In spite of herself, Maggie found herself wildly rationalizing the abrupt turn their date night had taken. It was the kind of misunderstanding that happens between friends, that's all it was. *A hiccup. A case of too much too soon.* In a nutshell any or all of it could account for the whole fiasco of an evening. Jake would get over it. So would she.

She opened the porch door, flicked on the light switch, but not before grabbing what she could of the remains of their dinner. Once inside the kitchen, only the steady drip of the faucet broke the silence, that and the clatter of the dishes as she stacked them in the sink.

"Later . . . I'll do them later," she told herself.

Another trip to the porch was enough to erase most of the remaining evidence of the evening she and Jake had spent together. Suddenly exhausted, feeling at loose ends, Maggie ran a hot bath and settled down in the claw foot tub. The steam felt good. It fogged the mirror, glistened on the black and white octagonal tile of the floor.

An island of calm, she kept telling herself as she pulled on her nightgown and climbed into bed—well-earned after Holly's visit and everything going on with Mom Lillian. But tired as she was, sleep eluded her.

A rare headlight moving along the alley cast waves of light over the bedroom ceiling. It was the last thing Maggie remembered before she drifted off into a dream-plagued sleep.

VINCA MINOR or periwinkle is a world traveler. Native to Europe, Northwest Africa and Southwest Asia, the plant has become popular as a ground cover in the United States. Herbaceous, it is known for its long trailing stems and stunning blue flowers. But when introduced in woodlands, it also is considered an invasive species, capable of wiping out native plants.

Growing Pains

The rhythmic droning of the alarm escalated by the minute. "Hell's bells," Maggie muttered, fumbling for the Off switch. Seven a.m. and no time to dawdle.

When she said she needed a break, physical therapy at eight in the morning was not exactly what she had in mind. But there it was penned in on the calendar. *Monthly physical therapy session.*

Tousle-haired and still far from awake, Maggie stared long and hard at the reflection in the bathroom mirror, trying to focus. *A Prufrockian moment*, she thought grimly, measuring out her life to the low whirr of the electric toothbrush.

Floss so you don't wind up with dentures. Shower, but don't forget the moisturizer afterward. When Maggie towel-dried her spiky hair a day removed from the salon, it didn't seem to want to respond as promised. It too had its habits after all those years of growing long.

With some effort a dresser drawer yielded a work-out outfit that appeared only moderately creased from lack of use. Her gym shoes were stashed under the night stand. The results were as good as they were going to get.

Traffic was moving at a crawl, a small town version of the morning rush hour at its peak. The undersized parking lot in the tiny strip mall that housed the therapist's office, a storefront coffee shop and dollar store was already clogged with staff and client vehicles, a mismatched assortment of pickups, rusted-out cottage cars and upscale newer models with out-of-state plates.

Luck of the draw, her therapist—Eric his name badge informed her—had all the resolve and dark skills of a prison interrogator in a grade B spy movie. The sensation was excruciating as he dug in, testing the muscles and trigger points along her hip bone.

Worse, Maggie concluded through gritted teeth and clenched fists, *than having babies*. And at least with childbirth, there was a major payoff for the sweat and agony.

"Try to relax that leg," the therapist suggested as he continued to explore the state of things.

Lying there on her side, hip exposed, on the black faux leather treatment table, Maggie didn't dignify that with a response. Tears threatened. Her whimpering sounds of protest went unacknowledged. Eric just moved on to unconquered territory.

"Tight there." He bore down on the offending trigger point with his elbow.

Maggie gasped, felt the oxygen leave her lungs. "No *fooling*!"

The staccato cracking within her right hip as the bands and muscles let go were audible even to the therapist. "Could be some bone-on-bone going on that hip," he ventured. "Maybe it's time for x-rays."

Maggie's torturer shifted course and zeroed in on the IT or Iliotibal band running the outer length of her thigh.   "Not too bad along the IT band," he grunted as he poked and prodded. The vocabulary driving these monthly physical therapy sessions would have challenged a second-year medical student.

Another sharp intake of breath from Maggie met that pronouncement. "Could have fooled me." It felt so good when he stopped, even momentarily.

The pressure of the fingers moved on to the area where hip and leg connected. "You've been doing your stretches on a regular basis, are regaining some flexibility I see. Piraformus syndrome can be nasty to treat. A lot of people your age just walk in the door on a referral and after a session, maybe two, give up. Easier, they say, just to live with it. I gotta hand it to ya—"

"No. . . yes, and I get people's lack of enthusiasm," Maggie told him. "Have I been faithful about self-flagellation, lying on my back every day with a tennis ball under me, grinding the darn thing into all those knots? You're kidding. No wonder people quit before they even

154

start."

He ignored her. "You're even walking better, I noticed."

"At least I can bend over to weed now without pitching headfirst into the flower beds," she had to admit. Then there were her dance moves at the Bliss Fest—impossible three months ago.

Eric chuckled, shook his head. "Gotta say, you tell it like it is."

"So return the favor. Remind me why I'm going to have to do this the rest of my life . . . presuming I want to walk, that is."

"Mobility," he said. "Flexibility. Happens to the best of us. Why don't you try finishing the rest of the routine on your own?"

Under the watchful eye of the therapist first on the treatment table, then down on the hard gym floor with a foam roller, Maggie attacked the panoply of taut and aching muscles. "One-one thousand, two-one-thousand," she counted under her breath.

Time seemed suspended in a series of slow counts to thirty. Straps and bands aided and abetted the routine of extending and contracting, pushing her reluctant hip to rotate freely. Adductors longus, brevis, and magnus, gluteus maximus and the inferior portion of the adductor magnus. Her body yielded reluctantly to her demands, sometimes more so than others.

A-thousand one, a thousand two, Maggie sighed. At thirty, switch sides and start the process all over again. The hour passed. Beaten and limping, nursing her aching hip, Maggie gathered purse and car keys to head back to the cottage where Ibuprofen was perpetually ready to go on the counter top in the bathroom.

"See you next month," Eric called out to her retreating back as she snagged her purse from the chair alongside her treatment table. He was already on to another victim, a blue-haired woman lying on her slab of a table with a ball the size of a watermelon between her knees.

A humiliating business, those monthly reality checks. When insurance eligibility expired, staff pronounced a client'graduated', ready or not. The expectation was half hours of do-it-yourself misery on the living room floor on a more or less daily basis. What they didn't tell you is the price for maintenance was often as painful as what landed a client in therapy in the first place. And never-ending.

Images shot through her head of running in the spray from the garden hose, sun-dappled flashbacks of skipping down the alleyway behind the cottage for hours on end. Right now she would have settled for a quarter of that spontaneous ability to shift and turn and bend.

"Wasted on the young," Maggie muttered to herself. "Where is all that energy when I need it?"

She parked as close to the cottage as possible. Trying to get out of the car was the worst. Not even a hint of a cooling breeze stirred in the garden. *Wilting fast*, Maggie sighed, like the plants drooping along the path.

The wicker table at which she and Jake had eaten dinner still stood mid-porch where she had left it last night. It took but seconds to slide it back into place against the cottage wall. In the living room, the puzzle she and Jake had been tackling lay sprawled across the card table.

All was as it had been. But then something had changed and Maggie knew it. The calendar now read, *August.*

Sometimes a late season hot spell will fool a visitor into thinking summer goes on forever. But most resort programs end mid-August. And with Labor Day, college and high school kids working in the restaurants and shops head back to classes. Water temperatures in the bay peak then quickly begin to drop again.

The garden too was changing. Leaves of the bachelor buttons were dry and yellowing, ready to be pared back to six-inch stubble for the season. The perennials in full flower were few and far between.

For a lot of snowbirds Maggie's age, gardening became a year-round sport if plant choices were adjusted accordingly. But in Michigan, life in the garden meant only from last frost to first. The growing season along Little Traverse Bay averages a hundred forty-one days, not all that far removed from Alaska's hundred twenty-three. Winter becomes the measure of all things.

And it was coming. The twinges in Maggie's hip were as sure a barometer as the *Farmers Almanac. Time in the sun doesn't last forever*, she grimaced. True of most things we love.

Maggie gave up on her heating pad and set up camp on the cottage porch with her laptop. Friend Sonia strolled past with yet another round of grandkids. Deep down, Maggie half expected to see Jake moseying along the alley as well. But noon came and went with no sign of him.

A leftover slice of lavosh from her dinner with Jake last night made for an adequate lunch. Maggie cleared away the morning and last night's dishes. She stopped to gas up the car, then drove out to the senior citizen complex to see her mother.

It could have been her imagination, but there seemed to be fewer cars in the parking lot. At season-end the population at the multi-care facility would gradually become sparser.

Lillian was ensconced on a wicker loveseat in the solarium that overlooked Little Traverse Bay. She had a book open on her lap. But when Maggie first saw her, her mother's eyes were closed.

"Napping?" Maggie said quietly as she slid onto the loveseat beside her.

Her mother's eyes flickered. "I never nap," Lillian yawned. "Have enough trouble as it is sleeping at night."

Maggie resisted the temptation to laugh out loud. "Just resting then."

"Plenty of time for that after I'm dead."

"Not anytime soon I hope," Maggie sighed.

"Most of my friends are. Don't see what's keeping me going."

"Grit. Pure and simple."

"And you nagging me."

Maggie laughed. "Guilty."

"Well one of these days it isn't going to work," Lillian said. "You better get used to the idea."

Maggie started to protest, but something in her mother's expression stopped her. For all her bravado, Lillian seemed to be struggling to put her recent fall into a realistic context. The power of denial has its limits.

The two of them played a half dozen hands of rummy back in her mother's apartment, fueled by the box wine Maggie kept on hand in Lillian's refrigerator. Mid-afternoon she headed back to the cottage, stopping only long for a pick-up shop at a deli along the route. She met a contractor's truck as she maneuvered her car into the alley.

Jake's cottage. Disgusted at herself for assuming, Maggie wouldn't let herself go there, literally or figuratively.

Sonia wandered over in the evening. "Need a break from that herd over at my place," she said, but not before waxing enthusiastic over

Maggie's new hair-do. "My daughter is on baby-sitting detail. If I hear one more whine or have to complain yet again about 'indoor voices', I'm going to lose it."

Maggie laughed sympathetically as she poured her friend a glass of iced tea. "It's quiet enough over here. Whenever you need it."

Her friend looked at her quizzically. "No Jake?"

"Taking a break," Maggie said, half under her breath.

Sonia's eyebrow raised. "Why do I think you're not telling me the whole story?"

"There's nothing to tell. Summer's almost over. He has a cottage to sell. Life goes on. And I need to concentrate on Mom right now, in any case."

Sonia didn't look convinced. "She's had another set-back, then—problems after the fall?"

"Not really. She's just in a funny mood. Not depressed exactly. Resigned maybe to her fragility. That fall really shook her up—me, too, I guess."

Sonia nodded. "It's hard, thinking about the inevitable. And there's never a good time to deal with the fallout when the end actually comes. I get it. When I lost my mother, it was just days before my daughter got married."

"Awful . . . I remember," Maggie said quietly. A wedding and funeral within a week was enough to knock the stuffing out of her friend for years. "I've been lucky, I know that. But suddenly when I look in the mirror, all I can see is *older generation*."

"Been there. With my in-laws gone, that leaves me."

If and when. Maggie's thoughts kept circling the same reality. When it came to her mother, she was living on borrowed time. Part of her already seemed to be grieving, trying to let go without letting her mother sense it. Part of her was clinging doggedly to denial. Lillian had known her longer than anyone—since before Maggie was born. There would be no replacing that.

She and Sonia sipped at their iced tea in silence.

"But you're right," Maggie said finally, "to wonder about Jake, I mean. I have the feeling I might have given him his walking papers yesterday."

Before she had time to second-guess herself, she launched into an abbreviated account of their ill-fated 'first date', if that's what last night could be called. To her credit, Sonia listened without comment.

"A disaster!" Maggie winced. "I still can't make sense of what triggered it—why Jake's talk about traveling together spooked me so much."

"Exactly what *did* Jake have in mind? Lots of people these days do have traveling buddies. Singles cabins on those trips are usually more expensive . . . "

"Dunno. He didn't really come out and say and I didn't ask." Maggie stared down into the half-empty depths of her iced tea glass. "I guess I panicked, pure and simple. Spending a day together at Bliss is one thing, reserving twin beds in a balcony suite for a cruise down the Loire is in another category altogether."

"You could be over-reacting. Maybe he just—"

"He couldn't get out of here fast enough, Sonia. There's not been a sign of him since."

"And you're okay with that?"

Maggie sighed. "Yes. No. I don't know. Anyway, that proverbial ship seems to have sailed."

For once Sonia didn't try to talk her out of her mood. Their evening trailed off into awkward silence. When Sonia finally called it a night, Maggie felt oddly bereft, worse even than after Jake's abrupt departure. Sonia—the friend who always had an opinion on everything and anything—suddenly wasn't touching Maggie's wisdom or lack of it regarding Jake Faland with a ten-foot pole. Disturbing in itself.

Running on empty, but nowhere near ready to call it a night, Maggie sat down at the half-finished puzzle. She couldn't concentrate. The newspaper lay half-read on the floor alongside the wicker sofa, equally unappealing in Maggie's current state of mind.

Across the living room, her grandmother's battered upright had sat largely untouched for most of the summer. Even from a distance, Maggie recognized a yellowing edition of Mendelssohn's *Songs Without Words* gathering dust on the music rack.

Maggie slid onto the piano bench. When she took the over-sized book in hand, it cracked open on its own to one of the more playable pieces.

"*Agitation.*" Maggie chuckled softly as she took in the composer's title, key and time signatures. *Appropriate enough.*

Tentatively at first, the restless ebb and flow of eighth-notes repeated themselves under her fingertips. Ten years of piano lessons as a child hadn't been entirely wasted.

Mom Lillian never let her forget it. Several summers back, Maggie volunteered to play her way through show tunes at the senior center once a month when her mom was in residence. Lillian seemed tickled. The sound of golden oldies echoing in the center's hallways quickly drew a modest audience.

"Some of these folks can't remember their own birthdays. But those lyrics from their childhood? They can recall every word," the center's program director said by way of thanks.

The promise of youth, Maggie marveled at the time, living on in the words to "Love Me Tender" and "April in Paris." And so it was with the classical repertoire that called her back time and again.

Maggie fudged her way through "The Sighing Wind," felt Mendelssohn's sadness pulsing upward from the keys to far deeper places inside her. She shivered, broke off the final chord.

Irony of ironies, the composer had never been her favorite. As a young woman, the fierce physicality of the Russian and Spanish composers seemed far more exciting. But here in the dark of a Michigan night, Mendelssohn's sparse yet lyrical expressions of love tapped into a quiet longing she felt hard-pressed to articulate.

Songs without Words. Mendelssohn said it all when he named that collection of pieces, she thought. At heart, the human experience can be too elusive to capture on the printed page. And like music itself, the essence of the life journey can prove as ephemeral, as fleeting as the notes on an old upright dying away into silence.

Maggie played on until her eyelids began to feel heavy and her wrists ached. It wasn't the best thing in the world to sit like that in more or less fetal position, arms extended and back stiff and straight on a hard piano bench. Especially after a morning of physical therapy. Exhausted at last, she found herself limping as she began to wander through the cottage clicking off lights, checking doors and windows.

It felt like rain. The air felt still and close. In the far distance over the rooftops of neighboring cottages, she saw the sky lighten for a fraction of second. A rumble or two of thunder later, she heard the wind moving among the branches of the overgrown yew alongside the cottage. The staccato beat of droplets against the shingle roof wasn't far behind.

But for once the sounds of the storm over the bay seemed strangely peaceful. Sleep came, populated with wispy dreams that pieced together faces and decades like the patches of the crazy quilt lying crumpled at the foot of her grandmother's ornate brass bed.

Morning dawned cooler. The front had passed.

Maggie snagged a makeshift breakfast, a handful of blueberries from the fridge, then made her way into the garden, coffee mug in hand. *Grounding herself.* The sky overhead was cloudless. Dew underfoot caught the rising sun and shimmered on the hem of her caftan.

She hadn't expected to see anyone at that hour, much less Jake Faland poised with a hand on the latch to the garden gate. From the look of it, he was as surprised as she.

"You're up early," he said.

Maggie just stared at him.

"I was hoping I would catch you," he added quickly. " Was going to leave a note before you took off for the day. I'm going to be out of town for a few days, didn't want you to think—"

"There's a pot of coffee brewing." The invitation was out there before Maggie could rethink it. It wasn't exactly based in fact either. The contents in her own mug were courtesy of a quick nuking of yesterday's dregs still sitting in a pot on the kitchen counter.

"I'd like that," he said.

Keeping his distance, Jake followed her up the porch and into the cottage. She heard him pull out a chair at the table as she busied herself with the ritual of putting on a fresh pot to brew.

"I almost stopped by last night," Jake told her, "but it was late. I heard the piano. You still play—I remember you doing that. A lot."

Maggie had her back to him at the sink, couldn't help but smile. *He noticed.* "I do play, now and again. It's a little like riding a bicycle."

"Mendelssohn. Not hardly."

Something fluttered inside her, like the first rush of air through the cottage door after the place had been closed up for the winter. Did he truly *know* what he was hearing or had Jake merely caught a glimpse the other night of the cover of the music propped on the rack of the piano? Either way, she wouldn't put it past him.

"Mistakes galore, but fun," she told him as she turned back to the table. "As a girl, I got out of doing dishes if I practiced. Which is probably why you heard sounds of *Für Elise* coming out of the cottage on a regular basis. Amazing how fluently you can learn to read with that kind of incentive—anything and everything that comes to hand. You play?"

"Trumpet," Jake winced. "And sad to say, awful at it. The brass were considered the jocks of our school orchestra but even that didn't inspire me."

They moved on to operas they had seen, plays they enjoyed. Maggie shared a tale of her first and only double-header in Milwaukee during a first and only date with a sports reporter in college.

"The game lasted longer than we did as a couple," she said.

Jake laughed. "Eye-rolling boredom, I gather. But we guys had to play *something* back in the day. Fortunately my teams were usually terrible which allowed for plenty of time standing in the outfield wishing I were somewhere else."

"I wouldn't have guessed." Maggie was remembering the glove slung over the pickets of her grandmother's fence.

"Thornton Wilder," Jake's tone took on a wistful edge. "Do we ever truly know life while we live it, every single minute—"

Our own life or anyone else's for that matter. It was time for the truth. "You scared me witless the other night," Maggie said.

A sheepish smile flickered at the corner of Jake's mouth. "That occurred to me. Unintentional, I assure you. The agenda—if there was one, is that I like your company, want to spend more time with you."

Maggie hesitated. "Relationships get tricker as we get older," she said finally. "Kids like us grow up, build a life, make new friends in new places. In my case that meant a good marriage, family. And then somewhere along the line with the parade of inevitable losses along the way, we start to cling harder to what we know . . . "

"All cloaked in platitudes about pillars of salt and the impossibility of revisiting the same stream twice. No going back."

"Something like that."

They were seated opposite one another at her grandmother's

kitchen table. A deja vu moment, if Maggie ever saw it.

Jake must have been thinking the same thing. He made a show of standing. As he did, he reached out to her across the golden expanse of oak. *Starting over*, she thought to herself.

"Jake Faland," he said. "Pleased to meet you."

Maggie chuckled softly, shook his hand. "We really need to stop doing this. After all, weren't we neighbors—back in the day?"

"That we were."

Jake sat. Maggie poured them both another mug of coffee. The need for apologies had come and gone.

"Anyway," Maggie exhaled sharply, "I've been spending a lot of time with Mom over at the senior center . . . which slowly but surely is starting to get to me."

He chuckled. "I still remember the verbal hiding she gave me when she caught me raiding the raspberry bushes along your cottage fence."

"I can imagine." For a split-second Maggie weighed what came next. "I planned on going over there in a little while . . . "

"How about I keep you company. My plane doesn't leave from Traverse City until late afternoon."

"Nice, but you don't—"

"My pleasure. It must be tough being cast as perpetual visitor-in-chief."

Maggie sighed. "Does it show?"

"No. But since my dad has been in rehab for that broken hip, my sister has drawn the short straw, signed on for check-in duties. Dad was never a good patient. I hear on a regular basis how I got the best of the deal—handling the plumbers and carpenters working on the cottage."

They finished their coffee. With Maggie behind the wheel, they headed out to the senior living center. Jake proposed a quick stop at a market along the way. When he came back to the car, he had a plastic grocery bag in hand, its contents a mystery.

Looking very full of himself, Maggie thought. She decided not to ask.

The corridors at the senior center were busier than usual. Maggie and Jake found themselves dodging wheelchairs and walkers along the

163

way to Lillian's apartment. A morning program must have just ended.

From the look of it, Lillian herself hadn't attended. She was sitting in a wing chair facing the door. Her brow tightened quizzically when she saw her daughter standing in the doorway.

"You're up and at 'em," Maggie said.

Jake had lingered behind while mother and daughter exchanged hugs. But Lillian didn't miss a thing. She took a long hard look at Jake. Her frown deepened.

"I know you," she said.

"Jake Faland."

"You stole my raspberries every summer."

Jake flashed an impish grin. "Best in the neighborhood."

With that he handed her the mysterious package. Lillian peered into the bag, then reached inside and pulled out a thick paper carton brimming with raspberries.

"You wash these?" she wondered.

Jake laughed out loud. "Organic. And clean as a whistle."

"Haven't changed a bit, I see. Sassy as ever."

"Jake is selling the family cottage," Maggie said quickly.

"Anyway, he's here now," Lillian said.

True. Maggie decided it was safer just to let the two of them go at it. Jake dodged everything her mother shot his direction with amazing patience.

He told Lillian about his career as a teacher, stories of life in Wisconsin along the Fox River, his love of travel. In Jake's telling, his motives for selling the cottage came down to simple economics.

"I'm up here, what? Maybe two weeks every summer. Traveling is a higher priority. And taxes being what they are, keeping the cottage doesn't make sense."

"Dangerous nowadays, traveling."

"And dangerous not to. I've always believed it keeps a guy young. New places, food, people. New experiences."

Lillian looked at him sharply. "Restless feet my mother always called it. You never married . . ."

It wasn't a question.

164

"Never found the right girl," Jake told her.

"I seem to remember you and my daughter . . . eyeing each other over the back fence. More than once."

"Mom . . . !" Maggie's face felt hot. "We aren't any of us kids any more."

"Have to wonder what the guy's waiting for," Lillian said.

"It isn't just up to me." Jake was looking at Maggie as he said it.

Amused, Maggie thought. *Enjoying every minute of this.* "All good, Mom. But they're going to be calling you to lunch soon," she said.

Lillian hesitated. "You come back any time," she told Jake.

"I'll do that." Jake nodded.

Maggie had offered her mother an awkward hug and was already half-way to the door. "You coming?" she said.

"Right behind you."

The thud of Jake shutting the door echoed along the hallway. Maggie counted their footsteps to the elevator. All the while Jake was chuckling quietly to himself.

"She's still a pistol I see," he said.

"You gave as good as you got, I noticed."

"Lillian's right, you know. Come a certain stage in life, the clock starts telling us to—"

The elevator bell dinged as the doors opened. *Mercifully*, Maggie thought, *they weren't alone.* An elderly couple were holding on for dear life to opposite handrails bolted to the elevator walls.

By comparison to the dim-lit hallways, the sunlight seemed blinding. Maggie blinked, struggling to remember where she had parked the car.

"Over next to that neon yellow Smart Car," Jake said.

"Hard to miss—I must be losing it." That came out harsher than Maggie intended.

Jake didn't respond.

"Well, that was interesting," she said finally as they settled into the front seat.

Jake was intent on unsnarling his seat belt. "I can't even imagine what Dad would think if we walked in on him like that."

"Probably wouldn't remember me."

"I wouldn't count on it."

"So where next?" Maggie wondered.

"Is that a metaphysical question . . . or just wondering about lunch?"

"I would have thought we had enough of each other for one day."

Jake looked amused. "For a minute there, you sounded just like Lillian."

"You have *got* to be . . . ," Maggie flushed, took a deep breath, released it slowly. "Unfortunately, I guess maybe I did."

Just when had *that* happened? Becoming her mother.

"As role models go, you could do a heck of a lot worse," Jake laughed. "You may worry about how frail she has become. I get that. But from where I stand, the Lillian I knew as a kid is still in there, utterly incapable of going quietly into that dark night."

"Something, I guess," Maggie told him.

Jake's smile faded. "It's everything, Maggie." Everything.

Hybrid Clematis, a member of the buttercup or RANUNCULACEAE family, has been a favorite in gardens since 1862. The plants are mainly of Japanese or Chinese origin, but the name derives from the Greek for 'vine'. For their first several years, the woody plants are fragile, but over time they grow to become sturdy climbers. They do well when allowed to wind and twist around trellises for support.

Old Friends

Jake never explained why he was planning to fly out of Traverse City or where he was headed. Maggie didn't ask.

Typical, Maggie told herself, *for people to come and go as the summer played out.* The easy rhythm of relationships was one of the beauties of cottage life along Little Traverse Bay. From summer to summer over a lifetime, the bonds forged in childhood took on new dimensions as old friends reconnected. No questions asked.

Jake's absence stretched to a week. In the interim, the activity at the Faland cottage continued unabated. Every time Maggie's route took her that direction, a swarm of blue-jean uniformed workmen were hard at it. Maggie concluded the renovations would be finished soon.

The finality of the process left Maggie wistful. Sale of the Faland cottage wasn't just a question of economics or practicalities any longer. Jake wasn't likely to return to the shores of Little Traverse in coming seasons. Another chapter of life would soon be over.

Nice while it lasted—this old friends business, she told herself. Inevitable too that the end was in sight. Time and distance would see to that.

Maggie didn't need Mom Lillian's assessment to realize that she and Jake had cultivated different lifestyles over the years, wanderlust versus the urge to put down roots. "Restless feet," Lillian had told him, never one to miss the chance to call a spade a spade.

Jake had laughed off Lillian's blunt assessment. But the moment remained a powerful reality check to which Maggie found herself returning in odd moments.

The season continued to wind down. A lot of the neighboring cottagers already had headed home over the weekend. Nights were getting cooler. Maggie had been reading in bed for quite a while Tuesday evening, so someone knocking on the kitchen door of the cottage caught her off guard.

It had to be at least eleven o'clock. Immediately wary, Maggie took her time, flicked on the porch light before opening the door. The screen was also hooked. It took a few seconds for her eyes to adjust, for her to recognize the shadowy figure standing there.

"Jake," she said to herself.

But the Jake Faland who had shown up in jeans and rumpled pale blue dress shirt open at the neck was not the man who had left barely a week before.

Older, she thought. In the harsh glare from the porch light, the salt-and-pepper stubble along his jawline transformed his features from strong to grim, even hard. The network of lines and ridges around his mouth and eyes had deepened.

A man in pain. There was no other way to describe it.

Maggie unhooked the screen. Even then, Jake just stood there, looking at her through the fine wire mesh.

He blinked, eying her forties-era chenille robe. A faded salmon with white swirling ridges, it was hard to miss. Maggie had thrown it on over her flannel nightgown as an afterthought on the way to the door.

"I know it's late—"

"I was still up. No problem."

Maggie cracked open the screen in Jake's direction. He hesitated before grasping the door handle.

"Coffee?"

"I don't want to put you out."

"Just give me a sec . . . "

The pot was all set up from the night before. Without comment, Maggie plugged it in. On an audible outrush of breath, she heard Jake ease himself into a chair at the kitchen table.

"Tired?" Maggie wondered as she turned to face him.

"You could say that."

169

"Hard trip?

Jake shifted in his seat. "*I have a son*," he said.

"Say again?"

They made eye contact. It was Jake who finally dropped his gaze.

"A long time ago. I had no idea." He broke off, at a loss for words. "She—his mother Angie and I—we were freshmen in college, dated a few weeks before things got . . . intimate. A month later she was gone, without a word. Dropped out, her roommate said. It never occurred of me to wonder . . . put two and two together."

"And the baby?"

"A boy. Adopted."

Maggie drew in a deep breath. "How did you . . . did he—?"

"My sister Chloe and I've lived a half-hour apart the last twenty years. So after Dad broke his hip, we moved him from Indiana to a care center near us. When she called asking me to fly home . . . I just assumed Chloe was worried about Dad. In fact, I barely set foot in the airport when she hit me with the truth. This guy had shown up on her doorstep, said he had been digging through records for decades, but finally found his mother. Before the woman died she told him my name—all he had but it was enough. I was here of course, in Michigan, when he tracked down my Wisconsin address. A neighbor pointed him in my sister's direction."

"And so you met him."

"Yes."

The coffee maker sputtered and sighed, gave Maggie an excuse to collect her thoughts. She retrieved two mugs from the cupboard. As she poured the dark, steamy liquid her hands were shaking.

What do you say to someone in that situation? No clue, she told herself as she set one of the mugs in front of Jake on the table. On autopilot, she headed for the opposite side of the table. She continued to stand, gingerly clutching her own mug, warming herself.

"He's an accountant. An irony in that, I guess—Dad would certainly approve. He ran track in college, sails. Has a wife and two kids, sons." Jake sipped at his coffee in silence. "Makes me a grandfather, I guess."

"More fun than parenting. Trust me."

Jake looked uncomfortable. "I wouldn't know."

"Does he . . . your son—"

"Mark."

"Does Mark want you to meet his family?"

Jake nodded. "Eventually . . . yes, that's what he said. He was angry, cautious. To be expected, of course. But to his credit, he listened. —ridiculous in a way wanting to know anything I had to say. There certainly was no point in my defending the indefensible. He's . . . I got the impression he's a good kid. Not a kid anymore, but still . . . "

"A lot," Maggie said. "After all these years."

A muscle worked along Jake's jawline. "Which only goes to show . . . *something.*"

The 'why' of it all began to hit home, starting with why Jake had sought her out immediately—a relative stranger—when he needed to get his bearings with the ground shifting underfoot. Oddly enough, it made sense. She and Jake had been children together. He had barely left boyhood behind when unknown to him his life had changed inexorably. Granted, it took a lifetime to realize just how.

Do we ever recognize life while we live it, every every second? The words of *Our Town*, the play that shaped her own young adulthood came back to Maggie with stark clarity.

Fools, maybe. And poets. Some.

To the rhythmic throbbing in her temple, Maggie felt the turning of the minute and second hands pursuing their circled course, relentlessly lurching forward, churning up memories in their wake. Joy, regret, guilt—and no one was immune. The pace seemed dizzying.

Maggie set her coffee mug on the table, pulled out a chair opposite Jake and sat. "So what now?"

He looked at her blankly. His shoulders lifted—not a shrug so much as an expression of absolute helplessness.

"You've missed a lot," Maggie persisted.

"True."

There was a bitter awareness in Jake's voice. *Some things,* Maggie thought, *don't allow for do-overs.* This was clearly one of them.

"Did you love her?"

Jake winced. "I was seventeen. It was the sixties. God help me,

I've spent the last sixty-some years trying to answer that question—admittedly dealing with a changing cast of characters . . . and I'm not proud of that, by the way."

"We all have our moments," Maggie said. She was thinking about her own journey through the family albums earlier in the summer. All the years she missed with Joe. A career grounded on if-onlys.

Jake looked at her, started to say something. Stopped.

"I'm . . . grateful," she said, "grateful you felt comfortable sharing this."

"Guys don't do guilt," he said. "I'd say this is one hell of an exception. He . . . Mark would have grown up here I suspect, as we did. Those unending summers with grandparents."

"Holly did. It's no guarantee of anything. I suspect—know, in fact—if I decided to pack it in anytime soon and draw a line under this place, put the cottage on the market, she might protest but not too hard. To be honest, she suggested as much."

"I never imagined myself as a father. Not once. My own paternal role model as boy wasn't exactly . . . stellar."

Jake had more than hinted that his relationship with his banker father had been anything but positive. "Not all that rare to feel that way about parenthood," Maggie said, "until it's thrust upon us."

The incredulous look on her husband Joe's face when she told him she was pregnant the first time had stuck with her all these years. Half disbelieving, that look said, half scared to death.

Maggie couldn't suppress a hint of smile. Jake caught it immediately.

"Ludicrous, I agree," he said.

"That wasn't it," she told him quickly. Maggie shared her husband Joe's reaction to the news that he was about to become a father. "Unplanned, by the way. It happens."

Jake drew in a harsh breath, let it out slowly. "In any case, I shouldn't have . . . I've probably already overstayed my welcome. This isn't your problem."

"We're friends," she said. "You can trust me."

The flicker of a smile didn't reach his eyes, all steel—the color of the bay on a gray and foggy morning. "Good to know."

With that he was on his feet, coffee mug in hand. He started for the sink to dispose of it, had to pass her in the process. Maggie quickly stood, reached out and snagged his arm.

Her fingers closed on the starched cotton of his sleeve. A lifelong love affair with the piano had unintended consequences. That vise-grip stopped him dead in his tracks. Jake flinched, but held her steady gaze.

"Don't be a stranger," she said quietly. "I mean it. There are times when life threatens to get the best of us. If you need to talk, I'm here. You can count on that."

Maggie's voice was calmer than she felt. Jake's expression was inscrutable. When she withdrew her hand, he continued on his course to the sink but not before checking her mug for contents.

"I'll take yours, too," he said.

The mugs clattered against each other as they disappeared into the depths of the enameled farm sink. For a split-second on the way to the kitchen door, Jake broke stride. He turned and started to say something, visibly struggling to master whatever it was he was feeling.

"I just want to—you're an amazing woman, Maggie Aron," he said.

She didn't react, except to try to follow him. Her robe was a trifle too long, a tripper, kept getting underfoot.

Jake was already outside on the porch. When he turned to look back at her through the screen, the porch light was behind him. His face was lost in shadows.

"Thanks again for listening."

Jake's voice was barely audible. He didn't give her a chance to react. He was down the porch steps, picking his way along the path toward the gate. At the alley, he turned a final time to make sure he had closed the latch behind him. Maggie thought she saw him cast a quick glance her direction.

Framed in the doorway by the halo of light from the kitchen, she waited until he was out of sight. *That's what friends are for.* The song was a favorite and it came to her now. *You can count on me.*

A lot of friendships would have gone aground on a lot less than the devastating secret Jake Faland had unpacked around her kitchen table. But alone under the midnight sky, all Maggie Aron could think was how desperate Jake must have been to have come to her like that.

173

How alone.

She tried to rehearse in her head how Lillian would react. Or Sonia. Those who have escaped from foolish choices unscathed can be brutal, merciless in judging those for whom the day of reckoning actually comes.

But then this was her secret to keep. Jake knew that or he would not have come. Their relationship mattered to him—even knowing his blunt confession likely had changed it forever.

Hard, she thought, when we learn a friend has feet of clay. Hard for all parties involved. But then it's impossible to live as long as the two of them had and not appreciate how rarely people one admired truly had it all together, appearances to the contrary. If she had to put a name to what she felt as she walked through the cottage clicking off the lights, it was simply *sadness*.

Sleep eluded her. When she finally gave up, threw on her caftan and headed out to the garden, the gray of the dawn matched her mood.

A frenzy of weeding left the area in front of the hollyhocks clear of weeds. The wild mustard with its delicate yellow flowers was on the rampage again.

By the time the sun broke through the clouds, Maggie was done for the day. She settled down on the wicker chaise in the living room, tried to read, but drifted off to sleep. By the time she woke, it was past noon.

She showered and changed into a favorite teal tunic and jeans, anticipating a visit with her mother at the senior center. Their time together was short, strained. If Lillian suspected something was wrong, she didn't confront it. She didn't ask about Jake.

Mercifully, Maggie thought. For once after all the years of verbal lunge and parry between them, she really didn't know what she would have said.

The drive home proceeded by rote. Only when she pulled up in front of the Faland cottage, did she realize what she was intending. All the things left undone in her life rose to the surface. This was one regret she was going to remedy and the sooner the better.

Clad in jeans and faded dark blue tee, Jake was climbing down off a ladder propped against the wall near the front door. He didn't seem to hear her coming. By the time Maggie pulled over, cut the engine, he hadn't quite hit solid ground.

The car door slamming shut behind her finally got his attention. He turned to see her picking her way through the random mounds of dirt that still littered the front yard. The look on his face almost stopped Maggie in her tracks.

Just behind him under the ladder, nestled up against the Faland cottage, the hosta she had given him had begun to rally. But then all she really noticed were Jake's eyes searching her face for some clue to what had brought her here.

The workmen apparently were gone for the day. No neighbors in sight, the two of them were alone.

Whatever Jake was intending to say by way of greeting was lost as Maggie reached out and hugged him. His body went rigid at her touch. She felt his breath warm against her hair, each and every painful breath until he finally gave in, allowed himself be held.

"I thought maybe you needed that," she said as she slipped from the awkward embrace. "Everybody needs a hug once in a while."

At that his face worked. The raw emotion Maggie read there was beyond the power of words to describe.

What surprised her most was the incredible calm she felt, from the moment she pulled up in front of that cottage to her spontaneous suggestion of a walk along the bike trail in the direction of Harbor Springs. She simply resolved to offer the only thing it occurred to her to give. *Acceptance.*

Jake grabbed a long-sleeve dress shirt on the way out the door, threw it on over his workaday tee, a smart move considering the stiff wind blowing along the trail. Hand-in-hand they cut down to the shore at Tannery Creek where there wasn't a windbreak in sight.

The popular expanse of sand adjacent to the state park was all but deserted. Here the wicked headwinds were pushing water toward the shore, creating near-surfing conditions. Only a few bigger kids were in the water, struggling with what looked like surf boards in miniature.

"Lots of luck," Maggie laughed. "My grandkids all have one of those things—"

"Boogie boards," Jake shook his head. "Somebody is making a fortune on that one."

"Our cue, I suppose, to complain how very different things were back in the day," she teased. "Before conspicuous consumption turned kids' brains to mush chasing down each and every electronic fad of the day . . ."

"Actually," Jake turned the idea over in his head, "I was thinking how insanely resourceful human beings can be—creating new ways to have fun out of relatively nothing at all."

"You're right, of course," Maggie told him. "Regardless, what *is* different nowadays is our response to all those changes, fast and furious, enough to make a guy's head spin. Back in the day, Mom used to let us know on a regular basis how rough they had it—the Depression and all. To her credit, no more. Watching even from afar how her grandson is raising his two kids, her only comment was she wouldn't try parenting now for all the tea in China."

Kids, parenting, the generational divide, they couldn't seem to stay away from the topic. Maggie hadn't thought how Jake might feel about Lillian's pessimism. Especially given what he had ahead of him.

It was on the tip of her tongue to apologize, steer their course in safer directions. But then Jake's new normal made it all but impossible to soften the shock of relating to a family he never even knew he had.

Shadows were beginning to lengthen. Maggie was glad she had worn that tunic. The days were noticeably shorter and cooler now. If they set a brisk pace, they might make it to the waterfront near the cottage just in time to catch the sunset over the bay.

They sat on a porch swing across from the old Victorian inn where Maggie had worked those many decades ago, mesmerized by the play of light on the water of the bay. A dark cloud bank on the horizon made for a jaw-dropping spectacle. The sun flamed first orange then red. Broad golden ribbons of light stretched out across the water, setting the roiling white crests of the waves alight. For a few seconds as sun and clouds met, a dazzling explosion of light shot upward. And then it was over.

Darkness came quickly. Maggie hadn't left her porch light on. The two of them wound up picking their way single-file through the garden and up the porch steps into the Aron cottage with only the familiar light from his cell phone to guide them.

Together they assembled a makeshift dinner of pasta with the last basil of the season from the garden, wine and a small Caprese salad. For desert, Maggie scrounged up a half-empty bottle of port and hot-pepper flavored dark chocolate squares.

"A chocolate fix my son calls it," she said. "Apparently all the rage in the restaurant business."

"He's a chef?" Jake wondered.

"A surfer—given he settled in Hawaii. That and food critic for of a small newspaper chain."

"I'm impressed."

"You would like him, I think."

"I'm sure of it . . . if he's anything like his mother."

When in doubt, work. Maggie made a show of picking up after their impromptu feast. At her suggestion, Jake got a blaze going in the field stone fireplace that dominated one wall of the living room. Suddenly exhausted, Maggie was content to sit alongside him on the wicker love seat in front of the fire, watching the dance of the flames in the grate—now blue now red, until nothing remained but glowing ash.

For the life of her, she couldn't have pieced together much of what they talked about or even if they talked at all. Finally with the fire all but out, the room began to cool down quickly.

Maggie shivered. *Too beautiful to last.*

As if sensing her mood, Jake checked his watch. "Midnight. The witching hour—I ought to be going," he said. But then he made no move in that direction.

Instead it was Maggie who seized the moment. She struggled to her feet, stretched out her hand in wordless invitation. The confusion on Jake's face begged an explanation.

"I should have done this last night," she said, "and didn't. I regret that. You're tired—I'm tired. Not a long drive back to the hotel maybe, but then we've had our share of vino. It makes sense for you to stay."

"Busted . . . a DUI is all I need right now." Jake sheepishly glanced around at the possibilities. "You've got a couch somewhere—"

"Not just all this undersized wicker, you mean," Maggie's laughter sounded strained, even to her. "Absolutely, and there's a guest bedroom upstairs too for that matter—though those aren't . . . it doesn't have to be what I'm talking about . . . "

His brows tightened in a puzzled line.

"We're all adults here," she finished hurriedly. "It's supposed to get down in the low fifties tonight. Grandma Aron's brass bed is massive and my feet will be freezing by morning. Besides, if it makes any difference, you're not the only one who's feeling . . . *vulnerable* at the moment."

Her voice cracked on that admission. *So much for the illusion of independence she had so carefully crafted for herself.* Tears stung her eyelids, but Maggie wasn't about to let them fall. This was absolutely no time to feel sorry for herself. Raising her chin, she looked him straight in the eye.

"I haven't kept the family bundling board," she told him, "but we're smart people. I think we can figure it out."

It was Jake who blinked first. The emotions washing over his face were those of a man with his guard down, beyond the power to pretend otherwise. After what seemed like an eternity, without a word he exhaled sharply, got slowly to his feet.

"All right then," she said evenly.

To her relief he followed, albeit at a discreet distance, in the direction of the bedroom. Thoughts racing, Maggie made a show of her usual routine, locking the kitchen door and clicking out the kitchen and hall lights behind them, pointing out the door to the bathroom.

Intimacy or passion had nothing to do with what followed. Compassion, forgiveness—the shared pain of life and loss can assume guises that anyone younger might have never understood, much less thought possible.

Once at the bedroom, Maggie went on ahead. Several steps behind her, Jake hesitated in the doorway.

"You're sure about this?" his voice was raw, barely audible.

By way of answer, Maggie pulled back the coverlet and sat down on the edge of the bed. She made quick work of shrugging out of her jeans, let the teal knit tunic which came halfway to her knees serve as a make-do nightshirt. The sheets felt cool and welcoming as she slipped under the covers, like the glassy water of the bay after a storm has passed.

Jake watched all this from the footboard, his face inscrutable. At her welcoming hint of a smile, he shed his work boots and jeans. Then still wearing the long-sleeve dress shirt and weather-worn tee from their hike along the bay, he eased into the bed alongside her.

I lied, Maggie thought. Turns out, Grandma's bed was big, but not *that* big. Jake found it no easy feat trying to keep his distance. When Maggie leaned over to turn off the switch on the converted oil lamp on the night stand, bedsprings creaked and swayed like a ship at anchor.

Darkness wrapped itself around them like a quilt. A branch began to tap out a quiet tattoo against the bedroom window. Through a gap in the curtains, moonlight spread a cold river of light across the bedroom floor.

It needed to be said. "At the end of the day," Maggie said quietly, "you're a good man, Jake Faland."

With a stifled sigh, he reached out for her in the darkness and gently coaxed her against him. Maggie felt a sudden rush of relief as she snuggled into the curve of the body alongside her.

Two spoons in a drawer. Theirs was the spontaneous pact of good friends sharing a sleeping bag on the last camp-out of the season, keeping the cold world around them at bay.

The last thing Maggie remembered before she drifted off to sleep was Jake still holding her, the slow rise and fall of his breathing against her hair. It seemed to her the most natural thing in the world.

LAMIUM or Dead-Nettle is native to Europe, Asia and North Africa. In the United States this hardy, frost-resistant plant has become naturalized as a 'weed' in many different habitats. The genus of plants itself consists of both annuals and perennials, its status dependent on the climate zone. Leaves often have striking patterns and the lobed flowers appear in a wide range of colors, from white and yellow to lavender.

Weather Forecasts

Maggie woke to find the covers alongside her pulled back. Jake was nowhere in sight. But from the direction of the kitchen, she caught the reassuring smells of coffee brewing and bacon frying in a pan.

"When in doubt," her mother Lillian had told her when she was first learning to cook, "get the coffee going, fry up some onions or bacon. It'll do the trick while you figure out the rest."

Maggie yawned, stretched, half thought about going back to sleep. Instead she sprinted barefoot down the hall to the tiny bathroom. She had come to make her peace over the course of the summer with the face that stared back at her from the mirror. Or maybe the deteriorating silver nitrate surface after more than a century—all the crackles, specks and foggy patches behind the vintage glass—simply made the image more forgiving.

Smoke and mirrors, Maggie smiled. Smoke and mirrors.

The water in the shower was lukewarm. Jake must have had the same idea. So Maggie decided to pass, instead threw on her favorite caftan and wandered out to the kitchen.

Breakfast was a work in progress. The table was set for two. A newly arranged collection of flowers from the garden had materialized in the blue and gray salt glaze pitcher that always stood on the top shelf over the refrigerator.

Humming tunelessly under his breath, Dressed in his work clothes from the day before, Jake was using a fork to transfer bacon to a mat of towel paper laid out on the kitchen counter. His back was turned. He obviously hadn't heard Maggie coming.

"The man *cooks*," she said.

Startled, he half-turned with fork in hand. His face lit up when he saw her. "I couldn't guess how you liked your eggs," he told her. "Scrambled seemed safest. As for the bacon—we've got everything here from charcoal to raw. Take your pick."

"Slept well, did we?' Maggie smiled. "I never even heard you get up."

"Tried not to wake you."

"I was probably snoring like a lumberjack."

Amused, he cocked his head to one side. "Faint, high-pitched like a porch swing in just a hint of a breeze."

"Lovely."

"Actually, *cute* pretty much fits," he said.

Maggie laughed out loud. "Have you thought about investing in hearing aids?"

"Not lately. For years I've needed orthotics in my running shoes but aural acuity-wise, the Faland gene pool seems to have come through. Common sense, as it turns out, maybe not so much."

Suddenly dead serious, Jake had laid down the fork and took several tentative steps in her direction. "Whatever that was last night," he said evenly, "I'll never forget it. Just to set the record straight."

A hug was her only reply. Though it lasted a split-second longer than absolutely necessary, it was just what the doctor ordered, warm and reassuring.

"I'm not sure what I've done to warrant any of this," he told her, his relief evident, "given what I dumped on you about my checkered past."

"You're way too hard on yourself—"

"Not hard enough, I suspect." He drew in his breath, let it out slowly. "But I appreciate the thought all the same."

"No thanks necessary," Maggie said brusquely. "I'll settle for the bacon and eggs. Don't know about you, but I'm starving."

"Coming right up!"

Jake made short work of plating the breakfast and arranging the platters on the table between them. Not much time for Maggie to collect her thoughts. But it would have to do.

The coffee was hot and plentiful. By the second cup, Maggie had summoned sufficient Dutch courage. "So then, we always come back to the moment of truth," she said. "What exactly *is* happening here? . . . as you see it."

She left the 'with us' unsaid. But a pained expression signaled Jake had been waiting for this particular shoe to drop. "I'm not in the best of positions to answer that with any kind of credibility," he told her.

"Jake," she sighed, "by any standards, you were so—"

"Stupid."

"I was thinking, *young*. But that too. In a word, human."

"And with not much of a track record ever since."

Maggie wasn't buying, let him know it. "If I'm honest, I suspect my own Vita would qualify as . . . *boring*. Predictable. Downright ordinary as lives go."

"Try . . . creative. Perceptive. Funny as hell now and again."

She shifted in her chair. "Not exactly the stuff of epics."

"Vastly over-rated. Teaching 'em for the better part of my adult life, I know whereof I speak. The Ring cycle, the legends of Roland and Gilgamesh were all thoroughly depressing reads."

Maggie laughed. "So much for aspiring to Wonder Woman. It's the gardener in me speaking now, but I like to think at least I'm capable of growing. That's something."

"Everything. And that's coming from a slow learner."

Jake laid down his fork. Maggie was fiddling with the linen napkin alongside her plate. Like a genie out of the bottle, it wasn't going to go back into the ring.

His hand reached across and closed on hers. "I can do friends. If that's what you want. Your call."

Maggie looked down at their two hands clasped against the dark, battered wood of her grandmother's kitchen table. "Friends are . . . good," she hesitated. "But then so are a lot of other possibilities."

Jake's eyebrow arched. "I would say we have all the time in the world. But then if we tally our combined seniority—"

"In dog years we would both we dead!" she finished for him.

Their laughter felt good. "Life," Mom Lillian once said, "is just one darn thing after another." Clock ticking or not, there were worse ways to live than for the moment.

"For starters," Maggie volunteered, "it occurred to me you must be spending a fortune on hotel bills. An official invitation, if you're wondering."

Jake's smile faded. "Sensible in theory," he told her. "But at least the way things are going, I can't guarantee how your no-sofa policy is going to end up."

"We can cross that bridge if and—"

"Or not," he offered quickly. "That's in your hands . . . technically feet if you decide to kick me out of bed. Let's keep our metaphors straight here."

"Now you *are* playing unfair. At this stage in life, a good foot massage is the most effective foreplay I know."

To his eternal credit, Jake's face actually reddened. "Duly noted," he told her.

Offer made. Offer accepted. Jake was moving in, no strings attached.

"It will take me a while to check out at the Perry," he told her before he headed downtown to retrieve his stuff. "So if I'm not back within the hour, don't be surprised."

"Duly noted. I'm not going anywhere."

After Jake left, Maggie spent a good half hour in the garden, staking up hollyhocks and sunflowers. High winds were forecast for later in the day. It was where Sonia caught her.

"Saw the lights on late over here last night," Sonia said.

"Jake and I had dinner together," Maggie shrugged. "Nothing out of the ordinary."

Sonia knew her friend—knew mendacity when she heard it. She shot a pointed look Maggie's direction. "Okay, kiddo, come clean."

Maggie flushed. Her friend was not one to be put off the scent so easily. It was either share now or explain later.

"I told Jake it was okay to bunk over here until the cottage was done. Just a week or two. He's downtown collecting his stuff."

Open-mouthed, Sonia just looked at Maggie. "You did . . . you said *what* . . .? And to which he said—"

"Thanks. He said thank you very much," Maggie told her. "You're looking for drama where there is none. I have two guest bedrooms . . ."

Not exactly a fair representation of where things stood between them. Sonia didn't look convinced for a minute.

"Maggie . . . I hope, really hope you know what you're doing."

"Helping out an old friend. It's what you've been hinting all summer—that we get together. Well, we are. You know the resort rates around here. And nobody ever finishes contracting jobs on time."

"Girlfriend, girlfriend . . . "

Maggie shrugged. "You asked."

"Have you told Lillian?"

"Nope. She has enough on her plate. And the last time she saw him—"

"Jake went to visit her?"

"With me. Lillian had a field day. The less she knows about Jake Faland, the better."

Sonia sighed. "Sounds like I've missed at least two-and-a-half out of three acts here. What can I say? If you need it, I'll be around to help pick up the—"

"It won't come to that. I'm going into this eyes wide open. Once Jake sells that cottage, he's out of here like a shot, I'm sure. With no excuse to come back whatsoever."

Maggie's words rang hollow even to her. Hopes and fears aren't opposites, she told herself. They're two sides of one coin. When it came to emotional costs, her friend may have every right to worry.

"So anyway, if you see Jake letting himself in the kitchen door," Maggie told her, "don't panic—or call Security. This too shall pass."

Sonia clearly would have welcomed an invite to coffee, but Maggie wasn't in the mood. As confident as she had been going into the conversation with her friend, second thoughts already were beginning to rear their ugly heads.

Instead, Maggie quickly leaned down and used her ever-handy shears to cut her friend a bouquet for her dining table. Bloomed-out astilbe would last forever. There were a lot of coneflowers, some sprigs of silver-leaved perennial artemisia and a lily whose heady perfume would fill Sonia's cottage for days.

"You better get them in water," Maggie said. "The artemisia stems can be a bit finicky . . ."

If Sonia suspected her friend intentionally had created an excuse to cut the conversation short, she wasn't making an issue of it. Flowers in hand she gave Maggie a lingering hug, started back down the alley.

"Take care of yourself, Maggie girl," she said.

"Always."

Maggie watched her go, feeling vaguely guilty at dismissing her friend that way. They hadn't seen each other much all summer. And the accumulation of half-truths about Jake had begun to weigh heavily on her heart. Maybe Sonia was right about trying to protect herself.

Jake was leaving the boundaries up to her. And she was going to have to set them from Day One, starting with a quick change of linens in the larger of the upstairs guest rooms.

The day felt stickier as it went along. Not exactly beach weather, Maggie thought as she wrestled with fitting the bottom sheet to the heavy mattress. Humid as heck, one minute clear, one minute overcast. It seemed like nature was having issues of its own making up its mind.

Feels like a heck of storm, she decided. A check of the Doppler websites wasn't anymore enlightening than the radio.

It was a standing joke that the Chamber of Commerce and local stations had been colluding for decades. Down along the bay, it could be hailing icebergs but the announcers would be predicting eventual clearing late afternoon. By evening—guaranteed—there would be a Million Dollar sunset. Somewhere under the thickest overcast, the weather gods were always smiling.

Just before noon, the sound of Jake's cottage car rattling down the alley foretold his return. He cut the engine, leaned over the back seat for the longest time before emerging with a threadbare vintage two-suiter travel bag in hand. Maggie went to meet him on the porch.

"You're back," she said. "It took a while."

Something in her tone must have gotten Jake's attention. "You know, if you're having second thoughts, we don't have to do this," he said. "I've been putting off a move . . . but apart from the dust level, one of the bedrooms in Dad's cottage might be more or less usable."

Maggie said casually. "Too late. I've already gotten one of the guest bedrooms ready just in case. That way you're guaranteed some privacy, can come and go as you please."

"Fair enough," Jake nodded, his expression unreadable. He pocketed the key she held in his direction. "Though I'll apologize in advance for the ton of stuff I've been stashing at the hotel this summer."

Maggie had taken note of the odd heap of boxes stacked to the ceiling in the back seat of the Toyota. "You're going to need help."

"Thanks, but I'm better off on my own with this," he told her. "A lot of the wardrobe I've been pirating from the cottage all summer is headed straight for either a dumpster or the thrift shop.

Maggie laughed knowingly. "We all do the same thing up here—hang on to our vintage Lily Pulitzers, Birkenstocks and Doc Martens. Even if we know darn well we'll never fit in most of it again."

She gave him a quick tour of where he could store his things. Second floor bedrooms were small but serviceable. The upper floor had never been plumbed.

"So if nature calls," she told him, "you're out of luck. The lone bath is off the kitchen. And if you shower, you better do it quick. The water heater is electric and undersized. When the hot water's gone, it's gone."

"Cold showers," Jake winced. "You aren't taking any chances, I see."

Flustered, Maggie didn't dignify that with a response. She offered once more to help with the move, then gave it up. Payback time came watching him haul what he needed up those steep, narrow stairs.

When he caught up with Maggie in the kitchen, he was out of breath, trying to work the kinks out of his back. "Good thing I didn't shell out for a gym membership," he told her.

"I offered to help, you know." She handed him a sizeable tumbler of ice water into which she had tossed a sprig of mint from the garden. "Then again, if you really want a workout, I can come up with quite a list. Small trees have taken root in the gutters. Some maples have sprung on the east side of the cottage—backhoe material if they aren't pulled soon."

Jake looked pained. "Now I get it. What you really have in mind is a take-it-out-in-trade deal here."

"Suit yourself," Maggie teased. "I just threw it out there, in case climbing around on your Dad's cottage isn't enough for you."

While Jake disappeared upstairs for an hour with his laptop, Maggie grabbed a quick shower. She traded her caftan for a pair of black dress slacks and a bright magenta summer-knit sweater.

Fall colors. She checked out the results in the mirror on the back of the bathroom door. Breezy pastels in her closet were in short supply thanks to one of those at-home fashion parties a couple of decades back. Sonia had hosted the thing—excruciating, but Maggie couldn't very well refuse to go.

"Think winter solstice," the wardrobe consultant gushed. "Your Northern European skin tones are like a snowy landscape. The brighter everything around you, the better."

Break the monotony—her challenge in life, Maggie lamented. Nothing worked quite like nursing a chardonnay on the back porch.

Guys like Jake could brown like chestnuts and get by with it. Her own adolescent experiments in tanning always ended the same, with several days of a painful orange, then peeling like a lace curtain for a good month. A carcinoma and Mohs procedure in her late sixties only clinched the magnitude of her folly.

"When in doubt cover up" became the rule ever since. The sizeable scar on her calf reminded her on a daily basis what was at stake.

Sonia never stopped teasing her friend for her habit of wearing her caftan when she went out to weed in the pre-dawn cool of the morning. "I would garden in a burka," Maggie told her. "If it would let me see enough to tell a weed from a perennial!"

Changes, Maggie thought. We adjust or not. But either way, those moments of truth never got any easier.

She was going on her second chardonnay when Jake finally re-emerged from upstairs. He had traded yesterday's jeans and work shirt for khakis and an olive polo that made him look even tanner than usual. His hair was still damp from the shower.

"Cottage casual," she told him. "I'm impressed."

"Don't be," he laughed. "I'm down to the sartorial dregs after ignoring the laundromat for a month."

He was toting an unfamiliar bottle of merlot and a wine glass he had snagged from the drainboard in the kitchen. The cottage had accumulated a sizeable collection of the mismatched crystal stemware over the years courtesy of garage sales.

"Boho chic—nice," he chuckled as he filled the glass, set the bottle down on the wicker coffee table in front of her. Leaning against a porch post, he stood watching her.

"You brought wine," Maggie said. "The label isn't familiar."

"The least I could do. And the next mega-shop is on me, by the way. I may be homeless at the moment but solvent, I assure you."

"Well tonight's taken care of. I have a quiche ready for the oven," she said. "Homemade."

"Perfect. Though one of these nights I want to take us out for dinner in Harbor Springs, walk the waterfront."

"You don't have to feel obligated to entertain me."

"Plying you with gourmet fare hardly qualifies. Not when the alternative is eating out alone. You know, Maggie, we really have to stop . . . *tap dancing* around each other like this. Otherwise it's going to be one very long couple of weeks."

Maggie broke eye contact, sipped distractedly from the wine glass she was clutching in her two hands. "Was I all that obvious?"

"Notice I said *we* not *you* . . . "

Deliberately, Jake set his own wine down on the railing. Closing the distance between them, he reached out and set Maggie's glass down as well on the coffee table before gently coaxing her to her feet.

Her voice was shaking, barely a whisper. "Jake—"

Whatever else she intended to say became irrelevant as he drew her into his arms. The looks of unspoken longing that passed between them as he held her did the rest. Jake's mouth found hers, tentative at first, then more insistent. Maggie closed her eyes.

Time felt out of synch, stopped entirely. When he finally let her go, Jake seemed genuinely as stunned as she. "Now that we've gotten *that* out of our system . . ."

His voice trailed off. The attempt at levity was fooling no one.

Maggie just stared at him, incapable of speech. She could still feel the ragged rise and fall of his breath against her hair. *God help me,* a voice inside her whispered. Sonia was right. Except her long-time friend didn't suspect the half of it. *She was falling in love with this man.*

"Would it help to know I'm as out there on the edge as much as you are right now?" Jake told her softly.

"Not really. No."

"I get it. Any sane person would peg me as one of those commitment-phobes your mother probably warned you about . . . guys who pride themselves on emerging unscathed from more relationships than you can possibly suspect. But all that said, Maggie Aron, you have got to know by now that what I—what I think *we're*—feeling is something else entirely . . ."

He had dodged the L-word at least. Maggie's throat suddenly felt tight. The air seemed oppressive, closing in on her, making it impossible to breathe. Trying to clear her head, she brushed awkwardly past Jake to the porch rail and leaned out toward the garden. But even there, not a whisper of a breeze stirred among the silent stalks and stems and blossoms.

She wasn't prepared for tears. A solitary rivulet, followed quickly by another already had escaped along her cheekbones and into her hair. That trickle became a torrent. Maggie's face worked. Her shoulders shook with the effort it took to stifle a sob.

Jake's shirtfront materialized out of nowhere, seemed to be the only thing still holding her upright. Never, even early in her marriage, had she felt this kind of soul-shattering vulnerability. The need to be seen for who she was. The need to share the aloneness that afflicts everyone if they manage to live long enough.

The young *assume*. A sense of entitlement protects them. After nearly a decade on her own, Maggie could count on none of those things.

"I would never . . . it's not my intent to hurt you," Jake kept telling her. "Not for the world."

Eyes red-rimmed and stinging, Maggie managed to lever enough distance between them to see his face. Her heart began to beat itself out of her chest at what she read there.

"This wasn't supposed to happen," she said dully. "I've loved and been loved, have had a wonderful life, a beautiful family. I've been on my own for almost a decade—"

"Maggie, Maggie . . . believe me, you're too young to be writing your own obituary."

"I'd like to think old enough to know better. Both of us." Her mouth felt stiff. "Why do I get the feeling we're the only two people on the planet who didn't see this coming."

"So that's what brought this on. Lillian," Jake guessed. "She must have said something."

"Give her time. She hasn't had a chance. Though out of the blue, Sonia gave me quite an earful this morning—asked point blank if I were losing my mind. It never occurred to her to wonder if I might actually be . . . falling *in love* with you."

"When you put it that way, it sounds like a fatal condition."

"Be realistic. At our age, a definite possibility," Maggie snapped, immediately taken aback how harsh she sounded.

Jake's exhaled sharply, started to let her go. "What can I possibly say that would—?"

Help came from a most unexpected quarter. In that precise moment, the solitary cloud overhead chose to drop its contents. A crack of thunder shook the porch, close and deafening.

"What the *hell* . . .?"

The force of the gale made communication impossible. Jake braced a hand against a porch post. With the other, he shielded Maggie as best he could from the wind.

Rain poured down in buckets with a ferocity bordering on hail. Droplets massed into thick gray sheets so dense it was impossible to see the garden less than ten feet from the porch on which the two of them were standing. The rush of water sounded like straight-line winds tearing through the evergreens alongside the cottage.

Even with Jake positioned between her and the apocalypse, Maggie was getting soaked. Like spindrift on the bay, the water swirled and danced around them.

"We need to get out of here," Jake shouted over the roar.

It seemed the words were barely out of his mouth when the downpour stopped—abruptly, as if someone somewhere had thrown a switch. A few gusts, random droplets and a final rumble of thunder in the distance signaled the rampage was over. Thin trails of water cascaded noisily over the rain-clogged gutters. The air smelled of ozone and mint, leaves and the earth soaked through, releasing the scent of things growing.

Dazed, Maggie and Jake stood looking out over the garden at the flattened phlox and coneflower. Only her careful staking had saved the hollyhocks, though their deceptively sturdy leaves appeared more torn and dimpled than usual.

"I take it, that was some kind of *message,*" Maggie said.

Their laughter sounded shaky, uncertain. There had been a seismic shift in their relationship. Maggie knew it as surely as she knew what had to come next—or she would regret it the rest of her life, however long that proved to be.

"I keep thinking," Jake said. "What was that old commercial—?"

"It's not nice to fool Mother Nature."

"That's the one," Jake said. "When I was a kid, we used to call those close strikes, *boomers.* Afterward everything smelled of green."

"Like clothes just out of the laundry. I loved that smell. Nothing beat it, except maybe the feel of mud squishing between my toes in the garden when a storm blew itself out—the only time I really loved to weed without being asked . . . "

Silence settled in between them, momentarily awkward. "Unfortunately, some storms I could name don't get it out of their system that easily." Jake was looking at her intently as he said it. "Does it really matter what Sonia . . . or what anybody else thinks for that matter?"

It wasn't really a question, Maggie realized with a wry twist of a smile. Not any more.

"Just us," she told him. "You. Me. Problematic enough right there. So all things considered, I vote for *practical.* Kids can afford to be spontaneous. By ten o'clock tonight, we'll both be going on fumes."

Jake's eyes narrowed with awareness. "You . . . is what I hear you—?"

Maggie let her fingertips do the walking, let their gentle pressure against his mouth stifle whatever he was about to say. Any labels on the intimacy they were proposing didn't seem relevant any longer.

"What do young people nowadays tell each other . . . time to get a room," she told him. With that, Jake ventured a smile, took the hand she offered him and they retraced the familiar route to the bedroom.

At least she had the foresight earlier to make the bed, Maggie thought as she let herself down on Grandma Aron's pieced coverlet. The quilt was tied at intervals with woolen yarn to hold the batting in place. Over the years the knots had softened and fluffed to the texture of moss that grew in dense patches around the cottages, wherever the sun shone too little and the tree roots grew too thick for grass to take hold.

Jake shed his running shoes alongside the bed. Her head resting on the pillow sham, Maggie waited, far calmer than she felt.

"You realize, this isn't something I've done in a long . . .very long time," she told him quietly.

"In my case maybe *never,* given what's at stake here."

Maggie just smiled.

Over seventy, love in broad daylight assumed a dynamic of its own when it came to the what, when and how. Maggie became grateful for the smallest of favors, anything that obscured or flattered.

Jake's abs were no longer an adolescent's version of a six-pack. Cellulite in Maggie's world was a fact of life. But what she saw as she looked at him, the expression on his face as he held her had nothing to do with any of those things.

With aching tenderness, Jake seemed to know just when to hesitate, when to carry them both along on the tide. Patience, restraint, gentle humor. He employed them all. And after he couldn't hold back any longer, he thought only of her, what it took to let her join him in that last powerful moment of fulfillment.

Maggie's low wordless cry told him what had transpired between them. Surprised at herself, she embraced the new normal, let herself become a woman she had not seen or known in a long, long time. What she read in Jake's eyes left her beyond the power of speech.

Who would have thought it possible, she told herself as spent and glowing, they snuggled alongside one another on the coverlet.

"I love you, Maggie Aron," he breathed against her hair.

He had said it first. The words caught in her throat. "You don't have to say that."

"Yes," he said. "Believe me—yes, I do."

Spiderwort or TRADESCANTIA is a native species found from southern Canada to Northern Argentina. In the 17th century they were introduced as garden plants in Europe and quickly spread to most parts of the globe. Some species have flowers that open in the cool of the morning, but fold in on themselves during the heat of the day.

194

In the Moment

Corn was ripening. Markets were carrying locally grown produce. The annual sidewalk sales had long since come and gone. The upstairs bedrooms at the Aron cottage had been reduced to warehouses. Everything personal Jake Faland owned in the north country was stashed up there—wardrobe, laptop. He and Maggie were sleeping together on a regular basis.

"Stupid, huh?" Jake had trudged up the steep staircase yet again to the second floor to retrieve his running shoes.

Maggie laughed. She couldn't help herself.

"Not funny," he grumbled. "You have no idea how often I climb up there only to forget what brought me there in the first place."

"Senility is no excuse. It'll keep you fit."

His response was to wrap her in his arms. *Loved*, she felt him reminding her.

Preoccupied as Jake was with seeing the work on his dad's cottage through to completion, they found the time to walk the beach together for days after the most recent storm, looking for Petoskey stones. A stash of them now occupied a vintage fish bowl salvaged from the Faland cottage. Maggie kept them covered in water to bring out the unique 'eyes' visible in the fossilized coral.

"*Millions and millions of years*," Jake told her in a credible imitation of Carl Sagen. "Incredible how these primitive organisms have left their mark on this place. While we humans—our arrogant claims as a 'higher species'—let our greed and selfishness wreak havoc with any real chances we have of leaving anything notable behind."

Some time ago, Maggie had brought Jake up to speed on the debate over Pipeline B across the Straits of Mackinac, the disastrous potential for polluting those pristine waters. Signs opposing the project had sprung up all over the area, had caught his attention. Jake seems to have taken her stand on the subject to heart.

"A budding activist," she smiled. "Who knew?"

"You," he said. "Your doing, every bit of it. It seems what I didn't know about this place would fill a good-sized library."

She flushed. The aloof and distant Jake Faland of her childhood was receding into memory—replaced by a Jake of his seventies who was growing more involved in her world, more supportive with every passing day.

Her garden had been a mess after the latest storm. Jake insisted on helping her re-stake the bedraggled army of plants that had suffered from the micro-burst of wind and rain. All of which involved a great deal of bending and stretching, a tough physical workout.

"The last thing you need," she told him as they laughingly raided her stash of Ibuprofen. For days now, he had been wrestling on his own with the landscaping at the Faland cottage as well.

"Worth it," Jake said quickly. "Even the most fragile stuff out there seems to be bouncing back. Good to see."

Only the tomato plants, trapped in their cone-like metal cages, remained broken and stripped of their harvest. Maggie brought the salvageable green tomatoes indoors and left them stem down to ripen on the kitchen window sills. *Would we were all that resilient*, she marveled.

Whenever Sonia saw her friend and Jake together now, she would stop and engage them both. *Downright cordial*, Maggie had to admit, whatever reservations her friend might still be harboring. At times the look on Sonia's face could have passed for wistful.

Privately there was no talk of the future with Jake, only the now. But as Maggie felt their bodies mold themselves to each other in the night, she knew in her heart and gut that *now* was enough. It is all we really ever have.

"We don't come with guarantees," Maggie told Sonia in one of their rare moments alone. "No warranties. Life is what it is, to be lived as fully and honestly as we can. Whatever is going on with Jake Faland,

Lord only knows, I'm trying to remember that."

Sonia sighed. "Still, it must be *tough*, waiting for that For Sale to go up at the Faland cottage. All those traditions and memories—"

"*Tradition*. I looked it up," Maggie said quietly. "Latin roots, from the verb *to hand over. To give over for safekeeping*. I truly believe that is Jake's intent and I respect him for it. He's moved beyond this place—I may not agree, but I get it. Even I have trouble now and again reconciling the need to divest as I've gotten older with the instinct to hang on for dear life. As if somehow the tighter I cling to the past, the more I protect myself from the unknown."

It occurred to Maggie that 'growing older' could be taken in one of several ways. Older and wiser, perhaps—or still growing, as in cultivating flexibility with the march of days and years. Or worst case scenario, to age or grow old before one's time.

Sonia's silence smacked of politeness.

"I've been looking all week at those shredded tomatoes hiding behind their wire cages," Maggie told her. "Even steel all around them didn't help them much when the wind started howling. We all tend to do that I think—assume that if we build enough walls for ourselves, we'll be safe. Or if not safe in some cosmic sense, at least *safer*. A mistake."

"Anyway," Sonia said stiffly, "I hope that we're not going to hear that you're putting this place on the market anytime soon."

Maggie just laughed. "Not hardly. But I am trying to get off dead center, try new things. Jake and I have committed to a wine and castles cruise along the Mosel in spring before the hordes of tourists descend. Plan is to stay on a week afterward in Berlin on our own. He studied there when he was younger—has always wanted to go back."

"Wow," Sonia said. "You really are throwing caution to the winds."

"Risky not to, the way I see it. Now or never."

"I hear you," Sonia sighed.

Maggie wasn't so certain she did. But she let it pass.

Jake's arrival from down the alley saved Maggie and her friend from traveling a road in their relationship that was becoming increasingly uncomfortable. For both herself and Sonia, Maggie suspected.

"Sonia," Jake called out as he joined them in the garden. "Just the person I wanted to see. You would never guess who just stopped by the cottage."

Sonia looked puzzled. "No idea."

"Will. Will Moller."

Sonia looked at him in open-mouthed disbelief. "That . . . guy who . . . we were all in Rec Club together?"

"The same. He shaved his head, just spent a month in a monastery in Tibet or Bhutan, some such place."

"A monk."

Jake grinned, "Who would have guessed, right?"

Maggie found herself watching her friend anxiously. Whatever folly had fueled her own childhood fantasies about Jake, Sonia's teenage pursuit of Will Moller had been disastrous.

Will was the consummate Bad Boy of their childhood, the one who never got caught. He evaded detection through repeated nights of pot and booze behind the sail shed. A rampage of toilet-papering the cottage community had led to police calls but no arrests. Ditto after the incident over the stolen nets from the tennis courts that wound up used for trawling at the State Fish Hatchery down the road. The escapades about which Maggie knew had to have been the tip of the iceberg.

As for Sonia, making out in the woods bordering the community with her Dream Date left her teary-eyed for weeks and with a highly embarrassing case of poison ivy that landed her in the emergency room. For the rest of that awful summer, Maggie had listened to her friend's agonized soul-searching over Will, both appalled and fascinated. This wasn't the way anyone wanted to come of age.

Jake couldn't have known that history, at least not Sonia's role in it. Maggie had to hope that after so many years, memories dim. But in the case of Sonia, she doubted it.

On some level, picturing Will Moller as a devotee of any kind of discipline, spiritual or otherwise—much less Buddhism—was hysterically funny. For Sonia's sake, Maggie restrained herself from showing it. She flashed a pointed look Jake's direction which he either missed or ignored.

"By the way, Sonia, Will asked about you," he said.

At that Maggie saw her friend freeze momentarily like a deer in the headlights. Then before anyone could intervene, she took off through the garden and down the alley toward her own cottage, as if half-afraid Will was about to pop out from behind every random bush and tree.

"Stove," Sonia called out over her shoulder. "Really gotta go! I just remembered . . . one of the burners must still be on— "

Stunned, Maggie and Jake stood watching the exodus.

"What was that all about?" Jake wondered.

When Maggie shared the story, he looked genuinely chagrined. "Of course, you couldn't have known that," she told him.

He ran a hand in frustration over his close-cropped hair. "Next time I insert foot in mouth, you have my permission. Kick me or something."

"Easier said than done. But I'll tuck the idea away for future reference."

When Sonia didn't rematerialize, Maggie decided to give her friend space to put the episode behind her. Confronting her on the subject would have only made the situation worse.

Another day passed. Maggie called Sonia but got the machine. Her car wasn't parked in the alley as usual. From the lack of activity at the cottage, Maggie assumed she had gone downstate, out of the line of fire. But then more and more cottages were sprouting shutters on the windows these days. Parking was no longer a problem at the post office—all sure signs the community's population was on the downswing for the season.

Jake was having his mail forwarded to her box now. Maggie couldn't even guess what speculation that arrangement might be stirring in the old neighborhood if the postal clerk chose to share that little tidbit. Usually Jake made the trek to the post box, took the time to sort out his mail from hers, any bills from among the heaps of glossy flyers.

Mid-day on Monday ensconced at the kitchen table with her computer, Maggie glanced up to see Jake emerging from the den where they had installed his printer. He was holding a single sheet of bond. Something in the way he frowned, reread the contents caught her attention.

"Trouble?" she asked.

Jake handed her the letter but didn't wait for her to read it. "Mark wants to come up over the weekend with his family," he said. "Labor Day is the following weekend so the boys will be back in high school.

They've never driven across the Upper Peninsula. Plan seems to be making both a visit and mini-vacation out of it."

Maggie looked blankly at the page in her hand, gave it back to him. "All good, right?"

A muscle worked along the ridge of Jake's jaw. "In theory. Question is, do they stay at the Faland cottage—or where? Ideally Dad's place would let them get a feel for what it was like growing up here. The crews won't be working on the weekend."

"Can we make the place habitable by— ?"

"Hate to put you through all that work, just for a few days."

"It was going to have to happen sooner or later anyway," Maggie told him. "If done right, we would be helping stage the place for the realtor."

"I'll sleep on it," Jake said. "Moving everything would be brutal."

Maggie had never seen the interior of the Faland cottage. Privately the prospect sounded intriguing, a link to the Jake of her childhood. She woke next morning to discover he had made a few quick phone calls, had called off the workmen for the rest of the week. Together the two of them wandered over to the cottage after breakfast to assess what needed to be done to get the place ready for visitors.

Even on the outside, the Faland cottage was very different from the one in which young Maggie had spent her summers. Gingerbread was conspicuously absent. An enormous porch ran the entire front of the cottage, dominated by massive pillars straight out of *Gone with the Wind*. Maggie couldn't remember what the original paint color had been. Jake had chosen a rich blue-gray paint job for the siding which made a stunning contrast against the brilliant white of the window trim. Stacked on one corner of the porch stood a jumble of vintage wicker furniture, spray painted in matching cool-white all-weather enamel.

"Perfect for sunset watching," Maggie said. "And easy enough to spread all these wicker pieces around the porch."

Jake was fiddling with the ornate brass lock on the beautifully refinished oak double doors. The beveled glass windows set into the wood obviously were still the originals. Centered on the recessed panel below one of the heavy panes, Maggie spotted what had to be an unusual brass manual door bell.

"Never saw one of those before," she said.

"Works like a charm," Jake told her. "Why don't you give it a whirl?"

When she turned the strange mechanism in a clockwise direction, the result was a loud, raspy bell-like sound. Startled, Maggie jumped a foot. "That will get a guy's attention," she laughed.

The vintage door bell was only the beginning. If anything, the interior was even more attention-getting. An open living area ran the entire width of the house, the size of a small dance hall. Beyond it Maggie could see the dining room, separated by an arch trimmed with a pair of elaborate wooden ball and rod screens meant to create a curtain effect on either side of the wide opening.

There were doors everywhere. One opened to the kitchen and another to what turned out to be a master bedroom, connected in turn to a full bath and still others linking the rooms to each other. Behind another, Jake told her, she would find a staircase to the second floor.

Although the kitchen itself was tiny, it was well laid-out with lots of beadboard cupboards and gleaming butcher block counter space. "Oh my gosh," Maggie breathed. "You even saved the old stove." The green and black enameled beauty dominated one entire wall of the kitchen.

Jake winced. "Don't remind me," he told her. "The thing operates on gas—took a small fortune to restore."

"Worth it. It's stunning."

The woodwork in the kitchen, as well as the rest of the cottage, had been painted the same dazzling white as the trim on the exterior. Typical wide floor boards from the late 1800s had been sanded and refinished without sacrificing the patina.

"A shame to lose the open stud walls," Maggie ventured. "Though I have to admit that pale gray coat of paint on the drywall is elegant."

"In a word, *insulation*," Jake said. "This place was like a refrigerator, heat bills a nightmare. I figured comfort and cost trumped quaint if I was ever going to sell the place. Though I'll confess, I felt a bit guilty going that route."

"You kept the original furnishings?"

Jake nodded. "Absolutely. Though right now it's all crammed

into one of the bedrooms upstairs."

From clawfoot tubs upstairs and down to converted gaslight fixtures in the hallways and bedrooms, the cottage decor was a mix of vintage chic and contemporary minimalism. When together the two of them took a look at the furniture, Maggie saw that it too ranged from late Victorian to the thirties era with a penchant for cabbage rose upholstery. They would have their work cut out for them spreading all those furnishings around two floors of empty rooms.

"The cottage is . . . stunning," she said. *Purposeful*, all of it, unlike the outworn fittings and furniture that had accumulated in the Aron cottage over the years.

Jake was in the process of extricating a large Morris chair that had been stashed on a matching loveseat, gave up. "I'm going to hire a couple of kids from down the street to help. This stuff is heavy, awkward or both."

Maggie checked out a large cardboard box among a small mountain of them piled to one side of the bedroom door. From the contents that were visible, the carton appeared to hold a collection of typical cottage treasures—children's painted wooden sailboats minus the sails, a covered wooden box decorated to look like a metal-bound chest, a picture frame with shells glued around it. Jake may have bowed to trendiness with the drywall and color palette in the cottage, but he hadn't tossed tradition entirely out the window.

Maggie couldn't resist a peek in the treasure chest, discovered a horde of metal pirate coins inside, glued to the gold painted bottom. On the undecorated wooden underside stood the boldly executed block-print initials, JBF.

Jake's handiwork. Maggie wondered.

He caught her at it. "Pirate week," he said sheepishly. "I must have been eight, nine tops at the time."

"My grandson made one just like it couple of years back when he spent a week up here. Amazing—that kids today can still identify with Jolly Rogers and pirate booty."

"Thank the Disney series with Johnny Depp. Who could forget a character like Captain Jack Sparrow?"

Maggie laughed. "I did, obviously."

"At least I didn't carry all these quaint local customs and folklore to their ultimate extreme. I don't plan leave food in the fridge the way the owners did before Dad bought the cottage. Maybe a bottle of bubbly, but that's as far as I'll go."

"Sensible," Maggie said. "By the way, I noticed the initials, JBF. You never did tell me your middle name."

"Jacob Bard Faland. Now there's a mouthful."

"A Shakespeare fan in the family."

Jack chuckled. "Nothing that high-toned. My mother's maiden name, Bard."

Maggie hesitated. "You never told me much about her."

Jake looked uncomfortable. "Indiana aristocracy. Her dad was a state representative for twenty years. Mom spent most of her marriage polishing the elegant wedding silver, entertaining with style—and drinking a great deal in her spare time. I had a live-in nanny, Anna Galette, until I hit age six when Mom caught Dad getting it on with the woman in the front seat of the family Mercedes. After that, the nanny was out and I was more or less on my own with two younger siblings. When Dad would go on one of his rants, Mom retreated into the bottle. She died of complications from cirrhosis when I was in graduate school."

"I'm sorry—"

"Don't be. Thank God, I was lucky enough to have anyone genuinely care for me as long as Anna Galette did. She had lived next door for years, had no kids of her own. After a messy divorce she could have wound up on the streets if my folks hadn't taken her in, put her on the payroll. Turns out she and I needed each other . . . "

Hard to trust, after something like that growing up. "I can't even imagine—"

"I survived," Jake said bluntly, met her steady gaze.

"Well . . . if it's any consolation, Mom and I have had our dicey moments too along the way," Maggie told him. "Eventually we wound up friends. I'll always treasure that."

"You haven't seen her today. My doing—sorry about that."

"No problem," Maggie said. "You're right about hauling all this stuff around in the cottage. We would kill ourselves. While you're organizing a moving crew, I could dash over to the senior center. It's likely to take most of the week getting this place ready for your son. I *could* skip a day at Mom's if necessary."

"I don't want that," he told her.

They had a plan.

§§§§§

The last stretch of the road out of town toward the senior center was hilly, lined with meadows and swampy ground that miraculously thus far had escaped development. Field flowers flourished here in abundance, whatever the season. On impulse just beyond the semi-abandoned railroad tracks, Maggie pulled the car over and set to work creating a bouquet out of anything she found at hand.

A labor of love. Maggie hummed tunelessly as she worked. These were Lillian's favorites.

Goldenrod and asters, dried stalks and seed heads found their way into the impromptu arrangement. Rarer now were July's gauzy Queen Anne's Lace, jaunty white daisies and sky blue chicory. As if overnight, the landscape had begun to clothe itself in the rich purples and golds, deep rusts that only mid– to late August in Northern Michigan can provide.

Ironic, Maggie thought, *though oddly fitting that nature should choose to save the finest, most dramatic for last.* She bundled the stems temporarily in an empty plastic grocery bag she found lying on the floor in front of the passenger seat before she headed on her way again. Lillian's apartment was bound to have something that would pass for a vase.

For a gardener especially, fall represents an acquired taste. As a girl, Maggie's favorite season of the year had been the spring, flush with its trillium and May apples popping up after a long, brutal winter. New life was asserting itself, new beginnings. In adulthood, summer held pride of place. The unfolding of her garden played out in a succession so glorious that the gardener in her could almost forget how sadly brief the spectacle was.

Fall took some getting used to. The chill of morning and early evening were daily wake-up calls. Winter was coming, sooner than later. And yet Maggie came to identify with fall's fierce bravery, the urge to flower with such abandon even as the growing season itself was on the cusp of ending.

Her wildflower arrangement in hand, Maggie navigated the familiar stairs and hall to her mother's apartment. *Would she be lucky enough to have Holly make similar pilgrimages some day?* The thought struck like an emotionally charged suckerpunch—disturbing as it was unexpected. Hand on the doorknob to her mother's room, Maggie fought to regain her composure.

Under normal circumstances, she wouldn't have dreamed of opening her mother's door without knocking. This once she did. Lillian was sitting in a chair in the living room facing the open doorway. *If looks could kill*, Maggie thought.

"What are you doing here?" Lillian demanded. "I told you before, I didn't want to go to lunch."

Maggie blinked, double-checked her watch. "*Lunch . . .* that would have been over a while ago, Mom."

"Well then, whatever it is you're selling, I don't want it. My daughter isn't here either so don't bother."

Not here? "I brought some flowers, Mom. Your favorites."

"Goldenrod," Lillian sniffed. "A lot of people are allergic, you know. My daughter would have known that."

At that a vacant look came over Lillian's face. Maggie felt a rising sense of panic.

Dropping the wildflowers unceremoniously on the coffee table, she turned and bolted out of the room. At the nursing station, only a lone caregiver was on duty. Dressed in starched pale green pull-on scrubs and a neon flowered shirt, the woman was scribbling notes in a file on her clipbboard. She was one of the older caregivers on the staff, had gotten to know Lillian over the past two summers.

"Something's wrong," Maggie breathed, half-choking on the words. "I just went to see Mom . . . Lillian Aron. She had absolutely no idea who I was. None at all."

The woman looked up, momentary confusion on her face. "Lillian. Yes, we noticed symptoms this morning. I thought someone had called you. We think your mother must have had another TIA

205

episode last night—"

"A stroke."

"Tansient ischemic attack, yes," the woman nodded.

Her mother had TIAs before, mini-strokes in popular parlance. Lillian was taking aspirin and blood thinners as a deterrent. In Maggie's mind any stroke was cause to sound alarm bells. "Should she be hospitalized?"

"She was refusing to go. I guess they couldn't reach you. The doctor saw her, said to keep her here for now—only move her to nursing care if necessary. The symptoms could reverse themselves . . . aren't usually permanent. Lillian's already taking preventative medication. There really isn't much else to be done."

Maggie drew a deep breath, let it out again. "I should have been called."

"Sorry about the mis-communication—"

"Non-communication," Maggie corrected her sharply.

The woman seemed visibly uncomfortable. "Would you . . . I could have you talk to the director."

Lillian's doctor had warned about this very possibility. Making a federal case of it wouldn't help her mother at this point.

"Not necessary," Maggie said stiffly. "I just want to make very sure . . . is there anything I can do at this point?"

"Your mother still seemed agitated?"

"Yes. And I wasn't sure how to—"

"Try quietly to help her put your presence in context. Otherwise it's best just to go with the flow. Give her a chance to figure it out. Talk about things that interest her and tie her to you or people she knows. If she remains upset, maybe it's best to try again later."

The walk down the hall this time to her mother's apartment seemed like a death march. Fearful of what she would find, Maggie waited for a response after her knock, trying not to give the impression she was intruding.

Lillian was sitting where Maggie had left her, staring off into space. The same magazine lay unread in her lap.

"How are you feeling?" Maggie wondered.

Lillian looked at her blankly. "Fine. Why on earth do people keep asking me that?"

"Because they care about you. They worry."

"A waste of time—worry," Lillian sniffed. "I don't worry about anything."

"A good thing," Maggie said, knowing how ridiculous it sounded. In fact, her mother had no trigger points which could set worry's wheels in motion, no memories or clues to what had happened to her.

"You don't have to keep checking on me," Lillian persisted.

"I want to."

"For no reason at all, as far as I can see. All this company." Lillian frowned. "You should be out with your friends, Holly. Not hanging around here."

Still disoriented but trying to fake it. Maggie felt the tears well up behind her eyes, fought them back. "I'll come again tomorrow."

Lillian had already moved on. "No need."

"I love you, Mom."

Their usual hug might only be perceived as upsetting. Anything else Maggie could say sounded hollow. She turned and walked out into the hall, shutting the door gently behind her.

"Oh, dear God," Maggie gasped.

Outside in the dim corridor, she stood hunched over momentarily like someone who had just taken a hard blow. Her breath came in deep, painful gasps. When she finally managed to keep going, the twists and turns of the halls and staircase left her confused and disoriented. The car was parked right out front, a rare occurrence. Maggie had no memory even of having snagged the spot.

Landmarks on the drive back to the cottage rose up with the unsettling detachment of a 3D pop-up book. The waterfront with its forest of masts stood out against the skyline. The brick steeple of St. Francis Xavier. Facades of the turn-of-the-century buildings in the Gaslight District.

Eventually Maggie turned off the highway, then into the alley behind the Aron cottage. Jake was sitting on the porch. He smiled and gave her the high sign, but at the sight of her emerging from the car he abruptly stood. In a dozen strides, half-sprinting, he reached the garden gate only seconds after Maggie herself did. She was still fumbling with the iron latch.

"Good God, Maggie—what happened? Is Lillian . . . ?"

For the life of her she couldn't answer, even with his hands cradling her shoulders in support. Naked alarm reflected in his eyes. He reached up and brushed at the trail of tears along her cheekbone.

"Mom had a stroke last night," Maggie told him in a rush. "A TIA actually. She hasn't the slightest idea what happened to her . . . thought I was *Holly*."

Jake exhaled sharply. "Maggie, I'm so very sorry. When I saw you get out of that car, I was worried sick."

Her laugh was choked, ended on a sob. "Trust me, *Lillian* isn't worried. She told me so repeatedly. Said I was visiting too much."

Jake drew her into a quiet embrace. "I can't imagine what you must feel. Dad lost mobility when this happened, a major stroke after all. But through it all, for better or worse, his memory has stayed intact."

So much for living in the moment, Maggie grimaced. Lillian suddenly had become the poster child for the mantra—with past all but gone and no meaningful links to what lay ahead. Human existence depends on our sense of time, those connections between past, present, future. Bereft of that compass, the *now* becomes meaningless, one series of disconnected events after the other.

Maggie's sigh conveyed the magnitude of her helplessness. "They suggested I come back later. Tomorrow. I left it at that."

"I'll go with you . . . whenever," Jake told her.

She shook her head. "No. Best not. Not until they assess how she is progressing. She would be mortified for you to see her like that."

Maggie followed Jake single file through the garden to the porch. "Coffee?" he wondered.

"No need to wait on me . . . I can—"

Maggie stopped mid-stream at the sound of her mother's words playing back at her. She let herself down on the closest piece of wicker at hand.

"Yes—coffee," she managed finally. "That would be nice."

Through the screen, she heard Jake rattling around in the kitchen, the closing of cupboard doors, water running in the sink. Around her the garden was humming with life. A small army of bees darted from plant to plant. Butterflies swooped in long restless arcs. A stray breeze cooled her burning cheeks.

Jake was intent on pampering her. Maggie let him, long enough anyway to fortify herself with caffeine and his hastily thrown together Caprese salad for lunch. When he proposed she rest, finally Maggie had enough.

"Put me to work over at the cottage," she demanded. "Jake, please. Cleaning, moving stuff around, anything to take my mind off Mom."

He looked at her long and hard. "You mean that."

"I just can't, won't fall apart like this."

On a sigh, Jake did as she asked. In her absence, he had corralled a couple of beefy college kids in the neighborhood to blitz reshuffling of the furniture from the upstairs bedroom to the rest of the house.

"We only have the crew until six," he said. "But it's a start. Meanwhile there are a good dozen boxes with lamps, pictures—you name it—to unpack."

"Perfect," Maggie told him.

Armed with a hammer and picture hooks, she turned the assignment into a quest to get herself as well as the decor back on an even keel. A tin-punched sailboat wound up on a narrow strip of wall between a couple of doors. She paired it with a small shadow box trimmed in brass that housed an intricate collection of sample sailor knots, all carefully labeled in a child's hand. Jake's doing again, she suspected.

A large painting of a cottage garden that looked suspiciously like Grandma Aron's wound up over the large wicker sectional in the living room. Though more of a scrawl than a signature, Maggie could have sworn the name of the painter looked like 'Faland'.

"An artist in the family?" she wondered out loud as Jake deposited a sizeable box with lamps next to the carton Maggie had been emptying.

"Mom's work," he said.

"Oh my gosh, it's lovely—"

"The only thing that gave her peace, painting. She would disappear for hours on end early morning or late afternoon with easel and paints. To catch the light, she said."

"So all these other paintings of flowers and Little Traverse Bay?"

"Also hers," he nodded. His eyes had a far-away look.

"She had a real gift," Maggie said.

Jake made eye contact. "Heaven help me, I didn't appreciate it at the time."

"Human enough," she told him quietly.

The only clue to Jake's state of mind lay in an abrupt change of subject. "Speaking of unsung and unheralded," he said evenly, "it looks like you're making real progress here."

"I'm going for homey, trying to find a place for all the family treasures you've accumulated over the years. I would like to believe your son . . . Mark and his family should appreciate the chance to experience what it was like for you growing up."

"Or potentially awkward." Jake grimaced.

"You'll figure it out."

By evening, the place had become downright livable. Maggie's favorite hands-down was the master suite downstairs. Made of oak chambered panels, the headboard alone stood seven feet. Along the top edge the craftsmen who made it had installed a raised wooden scroll-work border of leaves and flowers. Just inches shy of the ceiling, the headboard took a great deal of sweat and maneuvering on the part of Jake and his crew to get it down the staircase and into its rightful spot.

Mopping his brow with his forearm, Jake stood looking at the results. "Quite a bed," he muttered.

Maggie laughed. "I thought you and those two guys were going to come to blows moving it."

"A distinct possibility. I think I wrenched something in my back on that turn in the landing."

He gave her a hand outfitting the bed with the linens Maggie had found in one of the dresser drawers. Sheets and pillow cases were a creamy white onto which someone in more recent years had sewn heavy handmade lace borders. For a quilt, Maggie had singled out an elaborate crocheted coverlet. Over time both the lace and the coverlet had aged to a deep ivory.

"A true museum piece," she told Jake as they admired their

handiwork. "With the vintage prints spread over the walls, the filmy lace curtains, the room looks incredibly romantic. Straight out of a British costume epic."

"Is that a hint?" Jake teased.

Maggie's brow crinkled.

"We could set up camp here tonight," he persisted. "Though after moving all that furniture, I'm not sure how successful anything we start might end up."

She flushed. "Just *look* at me. I'm hot, sticky—"

"You look pretty darn good to me," Jake said.

With that he drew her into his arms. Maggie should have taken it as a colossal turn-off. Somehow it was anything but. Jake's kiss was deliberate, lingering. Worn out as she was, Maggie melted against him.

"Oh, God, Maggie," he whispered against her hair. "I can't imagine what any of this would have been like without you."

"One thing for sure. We are not going to muss up this beautiful room," she said as with some difficulty she squirmed out of his grasp.

"So we change a few linens again," he told her. "Just once I would like us to be together in this place. Cook something, crack a bottle of prosecco . . . spend the night—"

"Shower. Clean up around the head, as my grandmother Aron used to say. Sit out on the porch and watch the lights winking at us across the bay at Harbor Springs."

Jake sighed. "*Buzzkill* !"

"A train wreck. Right now, I'm hell bent on putting my feet up."

He laughed. "You win. For now. But it doesn't mean I like it. With Mark and his family here this weekend and the realtor chomping at the bit to get this place on the market, we haven't got a lot of time to pencil in a rain date."

Turns out, the forecast precipitation for once actually materialized, a steady drizzle that had all the makings of hanging on for a day or two. The cooler air provided a welcome relief after all their hard work. Maggie and Jake cleaned up and changed clothes at the Aron cottage. Eventually she gave up and let him put together a hamper with goodies for a picnic out on the Faland front porch overlooking the bay.

"A moveable feast," she told him. "Smart. That would keep the cottage kitchen spotless for company on the weekend."

Jake organized tableware and glasses from the Faland cottage for their impromptu feast. *Nothing mismatched here*, Maggie thought. The vintage etched crystal stemware had been in his family cottage for a century. Plates were a one-of-a-kind design, scalloped edges with a bold art-deco border in gold, rust and black.

"So, how do you see this whole weekend happening with your son and his family?" Maggie wondered as she and Jake sat side by side on the porch watching the rain.

She couldn't pretend to know how Mark was going to react to all this splendor, the wealth and taste of generations of Falands on display. By comparison, the Aron cottage was quaint, bordering on primitive.

Jake hesitated. "I thought I would stay with you, give his family privacy here," he said. "If you have no objections, that is. Your grill works. The one here hit the dumpster very early on—totally rusted out. So maybe you would be willing to play hostess for a cookout Friday night."

"Whatever you think," Maggie said. He was making it plain he expected her to be a part of the weekend from the get-go. "But if they want the time alone with *you*, I totally get it. Do they . . . does your son even know that you're—"

"Seeing someone? It came up, of course. He would think it strange if they didn't meet you. His family and I have all day Saturday and Sunday morning to be on our own if it comes down to that."

Maggie couldn't ignore the tiny caution light that kept blinking on and off in her head. She kept visualizing every war story she ever heard regarding first encounters between adult children and significant others. Jake's situation was more fraught than most.

Maggie drew in a deep breath, let it out slowly.

"You're worried," he said.

"Cautious might be a better word." But then the logistics of the visit were his call.

"It'll be fine." Jake wound an arm around her.

Maggie shivered. The rain had stopped though the night air still felt damp. A gust of wind muscled through the porch rails, threatening to wreak havoc with the remains of their improvised picnic.

"Time to pack it in," Jake said. "I for one am not moving one inch from the spot."

Maggie didn't protest. She felt no more capable than he of hauling the leftovers from dinner back to the Aron cottage. The heat of the day still lingered, close and still, in the Faland kitchen. Together they hand-washed the dishes. And afterward they fell asleep holding each other in the shadow of that ostentatious headboard.

"I love you," Jake told her as he drew her to him in the darkness.

Beyond romantic, Maggie found herself thinking. She was becoming a part of Jake Faland's life, his story, in the deepest sense.

"You're sure about all this," she wondered sleepily before she drifted off. "My meeting your son—"

"Everything's going to be all right," Jake told her. "Trust me. The worst is behind us."

With every fiber of her body, Maggie wanted to believe him.

Datura is a night blooming plant in the SOLANACEAE or 'nightshade' family that includes poisonous and toxic plants such as mandrake. Known as Devil's Trumpets or Witches Weeds, the plant has been used since ancient times as everything from an aphrodisiac to the ingredients for spells and potions causing delirium and death. The stunning plant and large bell-like flowers are closely related to the so-called Angel's Trumpets or BRUGMANSIA which can be equally deadly if ingested. Rarely cultivated except in arboretums, the plant has been known to pop up as a volunteer in home gardens.

Fathers and Sons

Feeling sleep-drugged and aching, Maggie woke to find herself in a strange room and strange bed. As her eyes adjusted, she recognized her surroundings, the master bedroom in the Faland cottage. Her cell phone was lying on the night stand where she had left it, still on.

No messages. That was a relief at least. Lillian must have had an uneventful night.

Alongside her under the heirloom lace-bordered linens and coverlet, Jake hadn't stirred. Barefoot with only one of Jake's dress shirts as a nightshirt, Maggie slipped quietly out of bed and down the hall to the bathoom.

One look in the mirror almost sent her back down the hall again. They had slept a good ten hours. Even so, doing the math couldn't alter reality—she looked spent beyond the power of a hot shower to remedy. She hadn't given a thought to bringing her hair brush or makeup.

The leftovers in the fridge from last night's picnic on the porch yielded an adequate breakfast of French bread and cheese, green grapes and some prosciutto. By the time Jake wandered into the kitchen, Maggie had assembled the fixings on the kitchen table. He pulled out a chair for her, then sat himself.

"Tired?" she wondered.

Jake sighed. "I don't know what possessed us to do most of the arranging and rearranging of furniture in a day. Not a smart move."

"We had help. That wasn't a given the rest of the week. And the job's done, amen to that. Your son will be impressed."

Jake had a pained look on his face. "Compared to the coziness of your family cottage, this place smacks of Taj Mahal. I had forgotten just how . . . over the top it was."

"All relative. Back in the day, I suspect a lot of the pieces here would have been considered factory rejects from your family's downstate home."

"*Still*—"

"You're anything but a snob, Jake Faland. Surely your son already knows that."

"A guy has got to hope."

Although the landscaping out front of the Faland cottage was nowhere near finished, Jake insisted on leaving it that way. "We aren't lifting one more shovelful," he told her.

Instead, the two of them drove to the Petoskey waterfront and hiked along a stretch of the trail to Bay Harbor. The morning was cool, fresh. Late summer wildflowers were at their peak and some of the maples showed significant traces of red and gold. The water of the bay was a vivid periwinkle with horizontal steaks of purple and black.

The trail rose and fell with the terrain, now close to the shoreline, now high above and more distant from the water. Distracted and aching from yesterday's marathon move, Maggie lagged behind, finally coming to a dead stop at a clearing high over the bay. The panorama spread out below was riveting.

Eventually she sensed Jake had come to a stop himself. He had turned to see what was holding her back. Concern stamped the tight set of his brows.

"I'm fine," she told him before he could ask. "Just looking at the water."

"Thinking about Lillian?" he said.

Maggie sighed. "That. And your family. I guess I've been in avoidance mode on all fronts. I really should drive over to see Mom when we get back."

"We can both go—stop somewhere for lunch on the way back to the cottage."

"Your place or mine?"

Jake hesitated. "Yours. We cleaned up well last night at Dad's.

The laundry situation for the master bedroom is under control. Whatever still needs to be done before Mark comes, it'll keep."

She caught the purposeful shift, Jake's choice to identify the cottage solely with his father. "Do I sense someone else is in denial here?"

"Let's just say, I realize it's time to draw a line under the Faland legacy. Whatever the relationship becomes with my son going forward, it needs to be about the now, not the past."

Maggie laid a hand gently on his arm. "Still, he's bound to be curious. And you're doing the right thing, honoring that."

Jake exhaled deeply. "I've got to hope so."

By the time they got back to the parking lot, it was mid-morning. Jake aimed the aging Toyota off the highway, picked his way cross-country to the senior center. As they drove, Maggie felt a tight knot building in the pit of her stomach, uncertain what they would find.

Lillian was sitting where Maggie had left her the day before, minus the book. She looked up to see her daughter and Jake standing in the doorway.

"Maggie . . . ?"

"It's me all right," Maggie told her. "And Jake Faland. You remember him—one of our old neighbors."

"*Old*." Lillian frowned. "Last time I saw him he was learning to drive. Made an awful racket in the alley in that junker his dad let him drive."

Jake laughed. "You noticed."

"Hard to miss."

"Jake drove me over here," Maggie told her.

"Hope he's slowed down some. Drives way too fast that kid!"

At least Lillian hadn't lost her feisty edge, Maggie sighed. "Jake has been doing a lot of work over at the Faland cottage. He's getting it ready to sell."

"Change . . . it never stops," Lillian muttered. "Can't seem to keep up with it."

"You're feeling better today though," Maggie told her.

"Still breathing anyway."

"Jake and you can visit a bit. I'm going to go see what you're having for lunch."

"Looking to talk behind my back, more likely," Lillian said pointedly. "The help around here never lets you alone."

Maggie managed a wry smile. *Her mother sure didn't miss a trick either.* "I'll be right back."

In fact, it took a good five minutes to locate the woman on duty in Lillian's wing. Maggie caught her on the sofa in the break room, feet up on the coffee table. She was one of the younger aides, blond and a pound or two overweight, had been working there only a few months. *Looking pretty much like I feel*, Maggie thought.

"You're here to see Lillian," the woman said. Awkwardly she scrambled to her feet, straightening her uniform in the process.

"Mom seems better today."

"It comes and goes. She's not quite her old perky self, but yes."

"Being difficult, I gather?" Maggie grimaced.

"I wouldn't say that. But she certainly keeps us on our toes."

"Sorry about that."

"No need. It's sad when they start losing that . . . spunk. Just give up."

"Well, I'm grateful," Maggie told her, "for all you do. Mom likes it here and that means a lot."

What should have been minutes had turned into more like fifteen. The aide went back to her rounds. Maggie retraced the route to her mother's apartment. Even with one hand still on the doorknob, the first thing that greeted her was Jake's burst of laughter.

"What's so funny?" Maggie wondered by way of greeting.

"Lillian was just giving me some marital advice," Jake told her.

Maggie's eyebrow arched. She started say something, decided against it.

"The Faland kid—makes sense now," Lillian sniffed. "You always did have your heart set on this guy."

Maggie flushed. "A bit of an exaggeration, Mom."

"Well, he's a keeper."

"I'm sure Jake doesn't need your—"

"Blessing," Jake chimed in.

Maggie heard the laughter in his voice. "Opinion," she corrected him under her breath. Leave it to Lillian to remember one of the few things about Jake that Maggie preferred to leave unsaid. That, and where he did or didn't fit into her life at the moment.

Time to change the subject. Maggie couldn't even imagine what had transpired between Jake and her mother in her absence. On some level, she didn't want to know.

"In any case, Mom, the aide says you're doing a lot better."

Lillian frowned. "Better. That covers a multitude of sins."

"Well, you haven't lost your vinegar, I'll say that." The actual expression was significantly cruder, but Maggie figured her mother would get the point.

Jake was watching the two of them go at, a bemused expression on his face. "Mothers and daughters," he shook his head.

Maggie had it on the tip of her tongue to remind him they would be finding out soon enough how fathers and sons handled the generation gap. But she caught herself in time. She suspected Jake already had thought of that—plenty.

"Mom, we really should go. Jake is having family visit this weekend. He's got a lot to do before then. I'll be over to see you though, as usual."

Lillian, in fact, was looking tired. Over the loud speaker, they heard the lunch chime. "Happy Friday, residents! Lunch will be served in the dining room in ten minutes."

Maggie located her mother's wheeled walker wedged against a chair in the corner of the living area, obviously unused yet again. "We'll walk you that far," she said. "I'll get your bike."

Coming up with a less loaded name for a 'walker' hadn't helped much in getting Lillian to use it. At least this time she didn't protest, though she looked at the thing with visible distaste before she reached for the handlebar-style grips. At the door to the dining area, she came to a dead stop.

"I can manage on my own," she told them.

Jake laughed, made a point of holding the door for her. "Nice seeing you again, Lillian."

She ignored him, didn't give Maggie a chance for a hug. Like a shot, Lillian bolted through the door and on her way toward the nearest open table.

"That was interesting," Jake said, still chuckling as he and Maggie made their way to the exit.

"One way to describe it," Maggie told him.

Once outside, she struck out at a brisk pace toward the farther end of the parking lot. Except for the life of her, for a split-second she couldn't recall which car they had driven to get here, hers or Jake's.

If he noticed her hesitate, Jake was too polite to comment.

"Senility," Maggie grumbled under her breath. "Must be contagious."

"Good to see that Lillian seems to have shaken off whatever happened yesterday."

"Pretty much what the staff said," she told him. "It sure isn't like I imagined it to be, this aging business—all downhill after a certain point. Mom's been on a roller coaster for a while now. There's no predicting the ups or downs."

"Stressful. I get it, trust me. My sister unloads on me every couple of weeks about Dad's status, pretty much the same pattern."

Maggie sighed. Tough as the situation was, it wasn't unique.

"I used to be so smug as a kid," Jake admitted, "watching my grandparents struggle. I informed anyone in earshot that if I ever got that old, somebody should just shoot me."

Maggie laughed. "Worse, as I remember it. Anybody over thirty was pegged as on the road to dementia. The colossal arrogance of our generation seems almost funny now . . . we deserve whatever we get."

"I shudder to think what my son makes of all this. You've had a chance to grow gradually into parenting and grandparenting. To say I feel clueless is a vast understatement."

Maggie shot a quizzical look in Jake's direction. His hands were flexing on the wheel as he drove. From the set of his features, she knew he had moved on from second to fourth or fifth thoughts on the wisdom of his son's visit.

They were almost downtown. "We don't have to eat out," she said.

Jake exhaled sharply. "We need a break. At least I do. How about the City Grill, whatever it's called?"

220

"The old Annex bar where Hemingway used to sit and write."

"That's the one." Jake eased the car into the metered public lot.

The large open dining room with the massive wooden bar along the full length of a sidewall was crowded. Maggie welcomed the chance to people watch, a time-out from the issues of their own family, young and old. A couple of hard ciders and the restaurant's signature cheese-biscuits tided them over until their soups and salads arrived.

"Lillian had a point, you know," Jake said after a while. "About us."

Maggie chewed on a hunk of romaine in silence.

"We haven't talked about down-the-road stuff," he observed quietly.

"Summers can seem like a lifetime up here," she told him. "But if we're honest, we haven't really known each other all that—"

"Also fact—time's in short supply at this point in life."

"I get that."

"*But* . . . ?

There were no 'buts' about it. Maggie's silence spoke volumes.

"I have to believe these past weeks haven't been just a classic case of childhood revisited," he told her. "Or unfinished business, for that matter.

"I care about you, mean it when I use the l-word. Truly do," she said. "And I'll admit I've been surprised, taken aback at times how . . . *well* we get along. It wasn't what I would have suspected after all these years. Not at all."

Jake drew in a long breath, exhaled sharply. "Fair enough. Which leaves us right where this whole conversation started."

"Your son is likely to wonder the same thing."

"Also true."

A fleeting smile teased at the corner of Maggie's mouth. "Somebody might say if we could figure out how to relate after all these years, then so can you and your son."

Jake returned the smile, but Maggie noticed it didn't reach his eyes. "I guess we'll find out soon enough," he said.

§§§§§

Mark had called his dad from the Bridge, roughly thirty miles from Petoskey mainly on two-lane roads. Warned of their arrival, Maggie and Jake were waiting for them on the porch of the Faland cottage when the newer model Chrysler mini-van pulled to a stop out front.

At Maggie's sharp intake of breath, Jake looked over at her. "You okay?" he said evenly.

"Fine."

Like father, like son. With a shock, Maggie took in the resemblance between the two men—lean and chisled, the consummate Marlboro Men. It hit her the moment Mark climbed out of the mini-van and walked around to help his wife and teenage boys do the same.

"Mark," Jake called out. "Good to have you here. Sorry for the mess of a yard."

Mark and his family started picking their way over the muddy stretch of lawn, avoiding the puddles left over from the intermittent showers in recent days. It didn't help that Mark and both boys were wearing khakis and rugby shirts. Heather's slacks were white and she was sporting a blue and white striped boat top.

Maggie felt suddenly self-conscious in her dark slacks and flowing tie-dye tunic. It was a favorite of Jake's, but under the circumstances she wondered, maybe just a bit too sixties for the occasion. Jake had opted for jeans and dress shirt.

"I'd like you to meet the troops," his son said as his family reached the safety of the wide staircase to the porch. "My wife Heather, son Tom and his younger brother Peter. This is Jake Faland, your . . . grandfather."

Jake didn't hesitate. "And this is Maggie—"

"A neighbor," she threw in quickly. This was no time, Maggie decided, for worrying about niceties or definitions.

Jake shot her a puzzled frown. "We grew up together. I think I told you that."

Once on the porch, father and son met in an awkward embrace. Jake thrust out a hand in Heather's direction, then greeted Tom and Peter in similar fashion. Maggie followed suit.

"So this is the family cottage?" Mark said, looking around at the wide verandah with its oversize white wicker furnishings. "Bigger than most houses, I'd say."

"The place goes on the market in around a week, once the landscaping is finished. If it ever stops raining. Your timing was good. I thought it might be fun for the kids to see some of their roots before the old place goes. Why don't you let Maggie give you a guided tour while I deal with the luggage. We thought we would get you settled in, then maybe take a walk through the neighborhood. The cottages around here were all built around 1900, give or take. Fascinating architecture. No two alike."

Heather perked up at the offer. "I took an art history class in college," she said. "Walking around would be great."

"The boys can help with the bags," Mark said.

Tom and Peter were looking around them as if newly landed from some alien planet. Jake started back to the van with them while Heather and Mark followed Maggie into the cottage.

"Wow," Heather gasped as she and Mark looked around at the cavernous living area with its gleaming white wicker furniture, colorful floral chintz cushions and mirror finish hardwood floors.

"Jake and the contractors worked out a great plan for restoring the cottage," Maggie told them, suddenly awkward about her role. "Those wide hardwood floors alone would have been quite a job to refinish. Most of families painted them over the years."

Mark seemed at a loss for words. Heather more than made up for it. "I . . . we've never seen anything like this," she said. "It's not really fair to call them cottages, is it? Though you can only use them in the summer, I've read online. Your family has a place here, too?"

"A whole lot smaller," Maggie told her. "These waterfront cottages were the flagships—perfect for sunset watching. You'll see it's a sport around here. On any given evening, quite a few locals and a couple dozen tourists try to catch those last moments before the sun disappears beyond the Great Lake out there. It's usually quite a sight."

"The antiques, all the furnishings are just . . . *wow* . . . !"

Heather's reaction seemed to be defined in a single word—disbelief. Maggie's mouth felt stiff. "It's a tradition to sell the cottages furnished," she said. "The Faland family has owned this one for quite a while now—"

Heather had wandered over to a small side table decked out with a half-dozen framed photos in various sizes, mostly faded to sepia now. Only one was of more recent vintage with three tow-headed kids standing on the cottage steps. The oldest was holding a puppy.

"Jake?" Heather wondered. "Mark, take a look at this."

He hesitated, then joined her. His back was turned as Heather handed him the frame. Whatever Mark was thinking, Maggie hadn't a clue.

"I think so . . . yes," Maggie said. "And Jake's sister and younger brother."

"You knew each other as kids?" Heather persisted.

Something in Heather's voice caught Maggie's attention. "We participated in day camp activities together," she said, choosing her words carefully. "But then he . . . Jake was a couple of years older, so in a different group. Boys and girls had separate activities. Still do."

Heather ran her hand over a crude wooden bird house with a license plate for a roof. "Must have been a fun place to grow up."

"Some think a bit too sheltered in some ways, but yes," Maggie told her. "Kids pretty much can roam free without a lot of supervision."

Heather looked back at Maggie. "Not your average childhood nowadays, that's for—"

"Or even back then." Mark abruptly set the photograph back on the table.

The silence was uncomfortable. "Anyway," Maggie offered, "I should be helping you get the lay of the land. The kitchen is off to the side through that door behind the archway."

From there they went on to the bathroom and the master bedroom. Heather seemed mesmerized by the seven-foot oak headboard. "*Wow*," she breathed. "That's quite a bed."

"Jake thought you and Mark could sleep down here. Each of the boys can have their own room upstairs." With Heather and Mark trailing behind, Maggie took the rest of the cottage at a brisk pace.

By the time the three of them were downstairs again, Jake and the boys had piled the luggage at the foot of the staircase. "All here, except for yours, Mark and Heather," Jake said. "I left your luggage in the master bedroom."

Heather laughed nervously. "That oak headboard certainly is *intimidating*."

"You didn't have to go all out for us," Mark said. "We could have stayed in a motel."

Jake started to say something, stopped. "It's no problem at all. Since I've been staying over at Maggie's, you guys can have some privacy over here. We'll be just down the alley out back if you need anything."

Maggie caught the quick look that Heather shot in her husband's direction—recognized the silent message sent, message received. Mark's eyebrow arched. Without further comment or objections, he sent the boys upstairs with their suitcases. He and Heather excused themselves and headed along the hallway to their bedroom.

Alone in the living room, Maggie and Jake made eye contact. "I thought that went . . . *well*," Jake said.

Maggie laughed, but it didn't sound convincing. "I'm not sure it was a good idea to foist me off on—"

"You're part of my life. I'm not about to pretend otherwise."

Maggie let it drop. Jake's voice had taken on a don't-mess-with-me edge that she rarely if ever had heard before. In the distance, they could hear a low undertone of voices. Heather and Mark were making their way back along the hallway.

"How about we give the kids a few minutes before we start exploring," Jake suggested. To his visible relief, the sound of footsteps on the upstairs landing signaled the gesture was unnecessary.

With Jake in the lead and Maggie bringing up the rear with the boys, they all set off. The group was strung out enough that Maggie often missed Jake's running commentary. Tom and Peter seemed to be purposefully in adolescent foot-dragging mode. Maggie's repeated attempts at finding things of interest to them met with polite silence or eye-rolling indifference.

Only when the whole bunch of them were down at the waterfront with its small gaggle of young female swimmers did the boys' attention improve dramatically. "Jake . . . your grandfather used to work as a lifeguard out on the pier," Maggie told them.

Tom and Peter grinned. A knowing look passed between them.

"Some guys have all the luck," Tom said. "Must be nice. Dad has us bussing tables and washing dishes. Says it builds character."

Maggie laughed. "I worked my way up from the dish room in ninety degree heat and a hundred percent humidity to waiting tables. Believe me, I get where you're coming from."

Peter scowled, crinkled his forehead. "Can't believe you guys would have to do anything," he said. "I mean . . . looks to me like most of the cottages are humungo. Worth a bundle."

"They didn't tend to be quite so . . . upscale back in the day. I think my grandparents paid a couple of hundred dollars for their cottage. Most of that generation of cottagers were preachers or school teachers, people who either could get time off in the summer or couldn't afford much travel. Friends my age who bought their own cottages thirty years later still found nice places for around three to five thousand."

"You're kidding," Peter told her. "I was counting the Beemers and Audis around here. The ads for cottages at the post office said some of the bigger ones hit close to a million."

Maggie winced. "Changing times. Anyway, my family's cottage certainly isn't in that league."

Tom and Peter didn't look convinced. But as they picked their way back along the alley to the Aron cottage at the end of their junket, Maggie was relieved to see they had relaxed a little.

"How lovely," Heather told her as Jake stopped at the gate and garden that dominated the back of Maggie's cottage. "Did you design this garden yourself?"

"Actually, it was my grandmother's doing. I just tried my best over the years to keep it going."

"Those hollyhocks are gigantic."

Maggie smiled. "Hybrids. I'll admit I'm cheating a bit there. You know flowers I gather?"

Heather laughed. "A brown thumb when it comes to perennials. But I've managed to keep annuals alive for most of the season anyway."

"I would love to show you my family's cottage," Maggie said.

"There's some sun tea and fresh lemonade in the fridge. We can sit on the porch and cool off while we decide what to do about dinner."

"Sounds wonderful."

Following Maggie's lead, Heather began making her way through the garden to the porch. Jake, Mark and the boys followed at a distance.

Once inside the kitchen, Heather looked around her approvingly. "Cute," she said. "I love all the little gee-gaws. It makes the room look so personal."

"The grandkids' doing. Grown up as they are now, they expect to see their treasures on full display every time they visit."

Lost as the group had been in the wide open living room of the Faland cottage, here the congestion level had increased exponentially. "Feel free to poke around," Maggie gestured in the direction of the living room, "while I put together some goodies."

Heather and the boys took her up on the invitation at once. It was only then that she noticed Jake and Mark had lingered behind on the back porch. They were deep in conversation, from the look of it, though in an undertone that made it impossible for Maggie to catch what they were saying.

By the time the two men wandered into the kitchen, she had a tray organized with home-baked cookies and two brim-full pitchers, one in the shape of Noah's Ark and the other an etched coral colored glass. The glassware beside them was one of the few matched sets still intact, pale green Depression glass in a ribbed pattern.

"Help yourselves," Maggie said. "Heather and the boys are still in the living room."

She looked up and even before Jake said anything, Maggie knew that something had gone very wrong. Jake's face was like a thundercloud. Mark's jaw was clamped tight and he wasn't making eye contact.

"We'll set up camp on the porch," Jake said. "Tell everybody else not to hurry. Don't you still have a puzzle going in the living room? Maybe the guys would like to—"

"Good idea," Maggie said. Whatever was going on between father and son, one look at Jake's face told her that distance was the best policy right now.

Excusing herself, she loaded four glasses onto the already crammed-full tray and disappeared in the direction of the living room. Hauling gigantic aluminum trays into public dining rooms all those years had its advantages, she smiled to herself. How odd it had seemed to have the boys assume a level of wealth that once was anything but the truth in much of this place—at least in the Aron household.

Heather and the boys were standing alongside the puzzle table looking down at the latest project, a scene consisting entirely of vintage license plates. It was all the opening Maggie needed.

"This puzzle is driving us nuts," she told them as she set the tray down on a coffee table in front of the nearby sofa. "How about we help ourselves to something to drink and you can try your hand at it?"

Heather gave the boys a pointed look as she joined Maggie at the coffee table. "Sounds like fun. Lemonade, I think you said. Tom and Peter would probably like that best. I'll have the tea."

Maggie forced a smile, reached down and poured two glasses for the boys. Heather did the same for the tea. There were four chairs around the puzzle table, enough for everyone. But Maggie chose to stay on the sofa, subtly watching the boys at work. She kept trying to picture Jake at those ages. The resemblance was tempered by Heather's freckled features, but the shocks of sandy hair had 'Jake' written all over them.

Fortunately, Tom and Peter genuinely appeared up for a challenge. While Maggie and Heather sat watching, the two boys went at sorting pieces with a vengeance. Consulting the puzzle box now and again, they started to get a feel for where some of the plates belonged.

"Are the guys . . . Mark and Jake, okay?" Heather asked after a while.

"Sure. Fine. They're out on the back porch."

But when she wandered out to the kitchen on her own to replenish the cookie supply, Maggie saw to her chagrin that she was mistaken. From where she stood looking out through the screen door, there was no sign of either of them.

"Problems?" Heather had left the boys and followed Maggie to the kitchen.

Startled, Maggie drew a deep breath. "No. I hope not anyway."

"This is all new to Mark. Certainly for Jake as well," Heather said.

"True," Maggie said carefully.

"After all these years of wondering, speculating, trying to find his birth father, I'm really not sure Mark thought through how he would feel when he actually met him."

"He . . . Mark had a hard time growing up?"

Heather looked uncomfortable. "Yes and no. He always knew he was adopted—good people though a lot older than the parents of his friends. They owned a small dairy farm in central Wisconsin. Mark went to public school in town, kind of rough for the farm kids."

Maggie nodded sympathetically. "I can imagine."

"We met there . . . Mark and I, in high school. We both wound up at the same state college. Mark studied accounting and business. I took a teaching degree, but didn't quite finish. I stayed at home until the boys were in school, then I went to work in a pre-school. All of us helped his folks now and again on the farm. He sold it after his parents died—that's ten years ago now."

"I'm lucky still to have my mom," Maggie told her. "She stays nearby in assisted living during the summer."

"My own parents died young," Heather said. "Mark finally found his birth mother after his adoptive parents were both gone. Locating Jake took longer, as I suspect he's told you."

"I'm sure there's no simple way for the two of them to . . . connect after all this time." Maggie couldn't help thinking of the shared memories between herself and Jake, growing up in this place. "Jake was hoping that maybe if Mark saw what his family was like, that would help."

Hushed voices outside in the garden cut short anything else Heather might have told her. Footsteps sounded on the stairs, then the screen door opening. Jake held the door for Mark who strode abruptly into the kitchen without a word.

Heather walked over to him, tentatively laid a hand on his arm. "I wondered where you had gone," she said. Mark just stood there as if rooted in cement.

"We took a walk down to the bay," Jake told her quickly. "Lots of sail boats in the water, races this weekend from the look of it."

With a rising sense of unease, Maggie tried to get the emotional lay of the land. "Anyway, now that we're all here, I have the makings of burgers thawing on the—"

"Thanks, but no," Mark cut her off. "There's no need to put yourself out like that. We talked about picking up a pizza for dinner. The boys must be stir-crazy by now, might want to go for a swim."

Maggie blinked. The water was bound to be freezing cold compared to anything they had experienced. "Actually," she said, "the two of them seem to have gotten into the puzzle we started a few days ago. We haven't heard anything coming from the living room in quite a while."

Jake's back was turned so Maggie couldn't see his face. Glass in hand, he was running water in the sink. When he finally turned and made eye contact, Maggie knew it was pointless to continue to protest.

"But then it sounds like you have a plan," she said.

Mark forced a grim smile. "It's been good to meet you, Ms.—"

"Maggie," she said dully under her breath.

But then Mark wasn't waiting for a response—or wasting any time hustling his family out of there. While Heather awkwardly stammered her thanks for the both of them, her husband made a beeline for the living room. From a distance Maggie caught the gist of the exchange between Mark and the boys. She had been right. Left on their own, Tom and Peter seemed more than willing to stay if given any say in the matter.

Jake watched the whole day unraveling before his very eyes, a look of utter helplessness on his face. Maggie followed him to the sink, stood directly in front of him, her back to the room.

"You have *got* to go with them," she told him softly.

He searched her face. "I don't want to leave you like—"

"You have no choice."

Still protesting, Tom and Peter were following their dad into the kitchen. Awkwardly, they mumbled their goodbyes to Maggie. Their dad was already halfway to the door. That finally galvanized Jake into action.

"I'll be back," he told Maggie. In a few quick strides, he pursued his family out the kitchen door and down the porch steps.

Shell shocked, she followed but the screen door swung shut between them. The family made short work of navigating the path through the garden. Jake hung back at the gate to make sure it was latched, looked back momentarily in her direction. His face was terrible.

The air of disaster was so palpable, Maggie could taste it. On the counter, the burgers were still lying untouched where she had left them. She temporarily moved the package back to the fridge.

Split them up, refreeze them, that looked like the only option. Based on what had just transpired, she wouldn't be needing them any time soon.

Going on adrenalin, Maggie separated the burgers into smaller packages and popped them in the freezer. That accomplished, she cleared up from the impromptu snack, washed the glasses and put them in the cupboard. At loose ends, she wandered the cottage, fluffing a pillow here and adjusting a lampshade there.

Deck chairs on the Titanic, she smiled grimly. She picked up a stray puzzle piece from the floor and put it back on the table.

The boys had made good progress on the project. Several sections of white and gold license plates had been filled in, Oregon and Illinois, a multi-gold-red-white plate for New Mexico. Several piles of pieces were well-organized by color, just waiting to be connected. She poured herself a chardonnay and settled down at the table.

Would life were as easy as a jigsaw, she thought wryly. And if relationships could be made whole again with precious little evidence of all the break points, pain and heartache that had gone before. Getting the weekend right had meant so much to Jake. The results, it seems, had proved anything but what he had hoped.

Picking up where the boys left off, Maggie chose to work on the license plates in vivid blues, colors of the pristine waters that lay so close not just to her doorstep but her heart. New Jersey took shape —the Garden State, then Oregon and Montana. Big Sky Country in white letters swam into focus on a blue ground.

As she blindly fit together piece after piece lying on the table in front of her, Maggie gradually began to feel like she could breathe again. Eventually her neck grew stiff from looking down at the puzzle. She retraced her path to the kitchen, warmed up leftover zucchini pasta only to find she had no appetite.

She saw she must have spent more time with the puzzle than she thought. Through the screen, the sky flamed a burnished gold, died quickly to a pale coral and teal, then velvet gray. Twilight had come earlier than ever.

The glow of lights from neighboring cottages was rare now, even on weekends. Familiar silhouettes of the delphinium and astilbe, the hollyhocks tucked against the picket fence gave the impression of trusty friends surrounding her with their presence. In fact, she had rarely felt more alone.

Sonia had gone downstate again for a couple of days. Jake and his family were nowhere to be seen. Maggie couldn't even imagine what was going on over in the Faland cottage. The devastated look on Jake's face as he latched the garden gate behind him was permanently etched into her memory.

Maggie roamed through the cottage, turning on lights. She went back to the puzzle but couldn't seem to concentrate. The music on the piano rack was open to Mendelssohn's *Sadness of Soul*—definitely not reassuring given her mood.

Nine o'clock. The rough physical work of getting the Faland cottage ready for visitors had begun to take its toll. Maggie poured another glass of chardonnay and settled down on the wicker loveseat with her cell phone, checking the news, Facebook and email. Her son had texted a photo of granddaughter Naomi on a campus visit in California.

Was it always thus? Maggie wondered, shook her head. Despite saccharine platitudes about no place like home, young people seemed obsessed with leaving theirs as quickly as possible. A sign of the times.

The mailbox yesterday had yielded a Saturday edition of the paper with its usual crossword. Maggie found a pen and tackled it with a vengeance. Another hour crawled past.

Around eleven o'clock Maggie gave up, took a shower and got ready for bed. The face that greeted her in the bathroom mirror appeared to have aged in just a matter of hours.

"It's over," a voice inside her head kept repeating. The mantra was only stating the obvious. And still the minutes crept past without any sign of Jake.

The piece quilt seemed far too warm, but Maggie kept it draped over the footboard just in case. Alone in that massive bed, she felt ridiculous in her spaghetti strap black satin nightgown.

Maggie had just started to drift off when she heard the distant closing of the kitchen screen door, then silence. The random creak of floorboards was followed by the sound of water running in the bathroom. Eventually a dark shape silhouetted in the bedroom doorway confirmed the obvious. Jake had returned.

For an awful moment, Maggie thought he wasn't going to stay. But finally he cautiously picked his way toward the bed, dodging furniture and scatter rugs along the way. He pulled back the coverlet and slid into bed alongside her.

"You're back," she said as she turned over in his direction.

Jake drew a ragged breath, let it out again slowly. "I was trying not to wake you."

"No problem. I wasn't asleep. Though it has to be—"

"Late. Nearly midnight."

"You must have had a lot to talk about," she said after a while.

Silence greeted that assumption. "You could say that," he told her finally. "Things didn't . . . none of this turned out remotely the way I hoped."

Maggie lay so still in the darkness, she could hear her every heartbeat, waiting for the shoe to drop. It wasn't long in coming.

"I haven't been fair with you," Jake said. "Maybe at first. But certainly not since my son came into the picture."

"There's no need to—"

"Apologies are the very least I . . . face it, anything I can say is a drop in the bucket," he said harshly. "You've been nothing but straight-up, understanding through all of this. I knew Mark was seriously . . . conflicted. And then I toss you square into the middle of that."

"He doesn't approve." It wasn't a question.

"Of any of this. As he sees it, I didn't care enough to be there when he and his mother needed me. That trumps everything else. From his perspective, I ought to be out there shooting hoops with my grandsons. And instead I'm repeating the same damn patterns all over again when it comes to relationships—"

"He can't know what motivates you. Or me for that matter," Maggie told him.

"Then there's his opinion of the Faland family and what he sees as pretentiousness. I'm not even going to go there. He could be dead-right on that score. But when it comes to you, that's another story entirely. My son has no right to make you a lightning rod, to drag you into what he's feeling. I drew the line there, God help me. That one's on me, my responsibility and mine alone, to have let things go this far."

"Do you have any idea how *arrogant* that sounds?" she said quietly. "There are two people in this bed. And at least speaking for one of them, it's of my own free will."

Jake exhaled sharply."Maggie, you deserve better than this."

The anger that had been building in the darkness flared white hot. Maggie sat up bolt upright in bed. The thick brass posts behind her felt cold, unyielding against her back.

"Better than what?" she said. "Jake you never implied or promised any more than you've given. And from where I find myself—that's a lot. The gift of feeling like a woman again, not just a widow of a certain age or somebody's mother or grandmother. Most of my friends would mortgage the farm to feel that way once more in their lives, to feel truly wanted. For however long it lasts—"

The words died in her throat. It was so still in the room, Maggie could hear the steady click-Click of the manual alarm clock on the night stand alongside the bed, the heightened rise and fall of Jake's breathing alongside her.

"God help me, I love you," he said in a strangled whisper.

"But if it comes to a choice between me and your son . . . ? There is no choice," she told him dully. "Parenting 101. And 'fair' has nothing to do with how your son reacted either, to any of it. He hasn't had an easy time of it. You owe it to him to be there after all these years."

"And you—*us*?"

Maggie heard the anguish in his voice. For what it's worth, she wanted to tell him, I love you too. But the next twenty-four hours were going to be tough enough to handle without that reminder, for both of them.

Get your act together, then we'll see, she wanted to tell him. But time wasn't on their side. To pretend otherwise was worse than foolish.

"How did you leave things?" she said finally.

"With me pretty far out there on the limb, saw in hand. I half thought he might pack the bunch of them up tonight and head back across the Straits."

"And his wife . . . Heather?"

Jake managed a laugh, raw with irony. "She likes you. But then, who wouldn't? The woman tried her darndest to defuse things before she gave up, went out on the porch with the kids to watch the sunset—at least that didn't disappoint. If they're all still at the cottage in the morning, I would say it's her doing."

"Something I guess."

Maggie herself had gone from thinking Heather a snob—resort togs and all—to genuinely liking her. The khakis, boat shoes and all the cruise ship window dressing stemmed not from pride but massive insecurity, the desire to fit into what the family assumed was the standard for resort life in this part of the world.

When Jake didn't respond, Maggie found herself weighing the alternatives, none of which seemed to allow for a win-win by any wild stretch. "Regardless, you are going to have to go back there to the cottage—somehow figure out a way to start rebuilding bridges."

"Easier said than done."

"It always is," Maggie sighed. "As for the rest—"

"Us, you mean?"

She reached out in the darkness and gently laid a hand against the hard planes of his face. Jake flinched at the touch as if half expecting something far harsher. His skin felt warm to her touch. Her fingertips traced the familiar stubble along the ridge of his jaw.

"We've had a good run, Jake Faland," she told him quietly. "In two weeks you'll be gone either way. We always knew that something like this was likely once the repairs on the cottage were finished. And we're both old enough, wise enough I have to believe, that we can admit happy endings are in short supply after a certain point in life. It all becomes too complicated. And try as we might, one way or the other, things . . .*end*. Though I for one will never regret a single minute of—"

On a groan of awareness, Jake drew her to him in the darkness. Everything had been said and not nearly enough. Where words failed, their bodies filled the void—touching and holding with an intensity that left them both spent and silent alongside one another.

They slept. When Maggie woke, the first traces of gray were flooding the room. The covers of the piece-quilt had been carefully eased back into place as if they had never been disturbed. Jake was gone.

Milkweed or ASCLEPIAS is named for the Greek god of healing. But when the stems of most plants in this species are damaged, they produce a milky latex-like substance that is highly toxic. Sometimes called the "American silk", the fibers from the plant's seed pods are used for insulation and for cleaning up oil spills. Milkweeds abound in the wild in much of the U.S. Some varieties also are used as a showy garden plant.

Labor Day

Jake didn't have to leave a note on the kitchen table. Maggie saw immediately that come morning, his things were no longer in the bathroom. He would likely wait until after the weekend was over to reclaim the rest. Her brave call to duty last night would carry her only so far in the merciless light of day. The prospect of being there, watching him systematically walk out of her life was more than she could bear.

But what to do? Maggie checked out the contents of the fridge and packed anything likely to spoil in the next days or weeks in a plastic bag for disposal outside in the heavy-lidded trash container meant to discourage stray wildlife. A few of the less perishables wound up on the lower refrigerator shelf. That accomplished, she got dressed, locked up the cottage and willing herself into autopilot mode, aimed her car in the only direction that made any sense at all, downstate and home.

Maggie avoided any temptation to check out what if any vehicles were still parked in front of the Faland cottage. She stopped just long enough en route at Sonia's cottage to slip a note under the door:

> Something came up. I need to be in Lansing for a bit. Set aside some things for you in the fridge that will spoil if they aren't used, ASAP. You'll find the key under the mat.
>
> Maggie

And with that Maggie Aron began the first day of the rest of her life.

There would be plenty of time for tears later, the grieving that her friend Sonia had predicted was inevitable. Right now, the only thing that mattered was the traffic and getting home to Lansing in one piece.

The route unfolded in a blur of pine-covered hillsides that mid-state gave way to board-flat fields of soybeans and the inevitable congestion that comes with civilization. The potted plants on the front porch and patio of the family homestead were dried out, beyond saving. Maggie jerked them up at the roots and disposed of them in the compost bin out back.

The place desperately needed airing out. She restarted the hot water heater. A bath could wait until later.

Maggie ticked off the rest of the familiar end-of-summer to-do list with grim efficiency. When in doubt, keep busy. Half-way through the routine, she remembered with a shock that her mother wouldn't have the slightest idea what had happened to her. A quick call to the nursing station at the senior center assured her that Lillian was fine. Maggie's absence, however long would not be likely to cause either lingering notice or alarm.

Not so with Holly. Maggie retrieved the latest ongoing message string with her daughter and crafted a text that wasn't likely to send up any warning flags:

Downstate for a couple of days. A friend is having some problems—needs my help. Back up north later next week. Love and hugs.

Not exactly a lie, any of it. Except the friend in question was Jake. And he was back along the shores of Little Traverse dealing with who knows what. The only help she could give was to do exactly what she had done, regardless of the personal cost to either of them.

There wasn't a breath of air stirring, so Maggie hauled a fan out of the closet and positioned it between two open windows. A neighbor spotted her car and brought over a couple of lattes from the nearest Starbucks as a welcome home gift. That killed an hour.

Maggie hadn't eaten since yesterday. Suddenly ravenous, she pulled a pizza out of the freezer, brushed off the freezer burn and heated it up. It tasted awful but edible. She saved the leftovers in plastic wrap—that would take care of breakfast tomorrow.

An early evening run to the nearest big box store yielded a couple of promising fall plants from their discounted plant rescue department. With the glow from the faux Edison bulbs on porch and patio, she had just enough light to plant and water them.

Though exhausted when she climbed into bed, Maggie stared at the ceiling until well past midnight before drifting off to a restless sleep. She woke tousled-haired and cranky to a sticky downstate late summer day. Storms were forecast. Judging by the burned up lawns around the neighborhood, the predicted rain down here was long overdue.

Maggie drove over to the discount hair salon in the neighborhood and talked the girl on duty through a badly needed trim. She painted her toenails a cheery coral, then swam a half dozen laps in the community pool.

The sky was getting darker by the minute. By the time she got home again, thunder was rumbling in the distance. Michigan Doppler radar showed the line of storms sliding north and east, pounding the lower half of the state but just missing Little Traverse Bay. In her Lansing neighborhood a few cracks of lightning already sounded disturbingly close. Rain poured down in buckets.

The downpour matched her mood. She sat on the family room sectional with a view over the patio, mesmerized by the sheets of water cascading from the eaves. The lights flickered once or twice but eventually the storm moved on.

She called a friend and took in a dollar movie. Neither one of them had paid any attention to the playbill, wound up in a depressing feel-good film about couples in their senior years finding love and adventure on motor scooters and hang gliding.

If it seems too good to be true, Maggie told herself, assume it is. The leading male actor had enough plastic surgery to look just that—plastic.

"Wouldn't it be wild to live like that?" Maggie's girlfriend gushed. "Like all the ninety-year-olds we read about who are jumping out of airplanes and climbing Everest?"

Sounds exhausting, Maggie wanted to say, but chose not to rain on her friend's parade. One storm a day was quite enough.

Several days passed in similar fashion. Whenever a text popped up, Maggie held her breath. But true to their middle of the night pact, Jake kept his distance.

Wednesday she heard from Sonia. If her friend read more into Maggie's abrupt trip downstate, she didn't let on. In their flurry of back-and-forth texts, she thanked Maggie for the groceries, promising a cookout when both were back at their respective cottages. Labor Day would soon be upon them. Maggie took the reminder as a hint.

A call to the senior center proved more sobering. "Lillian has had a bad couple of days," the nurse on duty said. "She's been asking for you."

Resigned, Maggie said the only thing she could say under the circumstances. "I'll drive up tomorrow," she said wanly. Her desperate search for emotional asylum had ended as abruptly as it began.

She got an early start. For a Thursday morning, traffic headed north was appalling. Through neighboring vehicle windows, Maggie spotted kids galore. Families were making one last getaway before school started.

The thought of Jake's son and his family in matching khakis standing in front of the Faland cottage popped unbidden into Maggie's head. Her hands tightened momentarily on the wheel. She didn't dare close her eyes. The moment passed.

Ten miles sped past, then fifty. Maggie lost count, attention riveted on the lane markers stretching out ahead of her into the far distance. At Gaylord, her route veered from interstates on to a series of two-lane roads. Signs of fall color were in evidence everywhere. While families might be closing up cottages for the season, soon these same routes would be over-run with tour buses full of tourists intent on photographing hillsides blazing in reds, orange and yellows. In winter came the skiers and snow boarders.

Just like the garden, the human landscape of this stunning part of the world had rhythms all its own. While some locals resented the seasonal ebb and flow of tourists, Maggie saw the periodic transitions as part of the area's charm. From morel to salmon season to cross-country skiing, there was an allotted time for everything.

On the outskirts of Petoskey, Maggie forsook the usual route to the cottage and drove directly to the senior center. After so many months of daily visits to her mother, she couldn't help a twinge of guilt at having abandoned the routine.

The parking lot of the center was unusually full for this time of year, most likely due to families visiting from out of town for the Labor Day weekend. On her mother's wing, the caregiver on duty was occupied with another resident, but waved at Maggie in passing.

Cheery enough, Maggie thought. The stressful ups-and-downs of dealing with an elderly parent manifested themselves two seconds inside Lillian's apartment. Maggie found her mother deep in conversation with a woman she recognized as another resident on that same floor. The two women were laughing. Lillian's hair was newly done in puffy clouds of silver-white. Maggie hadn't seen that particular pants suit in a while. All good.

"What are you doing here?" Lillian asked.

Maggie gave her a pained look. "Missed a couple of days so I thought it was time to check in."

"I'm doing fine. So I'm letting you off the hook—go play some tennis, go swimming. All's well over here."

Her mother hadn't seemed this perky in months. So much for a couple of bad days.

"Okay then—have fun," Maggie forced a smile, waved.

The joviality faded the minute she closed the apartment door behind her. Relieved as she was at her mother's state of mind, the emotional tug of war was beginning slowly but surely to take its toll. Shaking her head in disbelief, Maggie trekked back to the car parked on the grass at the far end of the lot.

With the weekend crowds on their way, it made sense to get other errands out of the way as well. There were several groceries close by and Maggie used the opportunity to power shop. With a stack of on-sale TV dinners and a pint of Tom & Jerry's melting in the trunk, she made a beeline for the bay and home.

The weather had blossomed into a crisp fall day with puffy white clouds resting on darker layers scattered from horizon to horizon in all directions. Little Traverse Bay was a solid cobalt blue. Only faint lines of foam marked the low lines of waves coming ashore.

Maggie got the worst over with when it came to Jake as well. Instead of heading directly into the alley behind the cottage, she made a quick detour that took her past the front of the Faland cottage.

241

Jake's car was MIA. No workmen were in sight either, but a brand new *For Sale* sign had sprouted on a recently leveled and seeded lawn. A variety of deer-resistant bushes had been dug in around the cottage foundation. Mid-yard stood a new grove of young birch trees, supported by a system of thin support posts and wires.

Although she felt a knot of unresolved emotion twist inside her at what the developments meant, Maggie kept going. She pulled up behind the Aron cottage, cut the car's engine and parked.

"Home," she breathed. Safe enough for the moment, she sat there—hands on the wheel—in no hurry to get out.

Beyond the white picket fence, her garden too had begun to take on its fall colors. Badly in need of radical dead-heading, she sighed. Soon enough it would be time to get out the weed whacker and put the entire garden to bed for the season.

Hells bells, she swore softly under her breath. The ice cream would be soup if she didn't do something about it soon. Hurriedly she rummaged through the grocery bags and grabbed the ones containing frozen food. A quick sprint through the garden and she stashed the contents in the freezer. The Tom & Jerry's already felt squishy to the touch in its paper carton.

It took a handful of trips to haul the rest of the groceries into the kitchen. Maggie dug in and unpacked everything else into the cupboards before she called it quits.

The drive had been hard, the anxiety over her mother's condition equally exhausting in its own way. Maggie had just vowed to skip lunch in favor of a nap when her cell phone rang.

Sonia, the caller ID said.

"What's up?" Maggie wondered.

Her friend laughed. "You're back. I just came back from a walk and saw your car sitting out there with the hatch open."

"Groceries," Maggie said. "In another hour the lines will be twenty instead of ten deep everywhere."

Sonia laughed. "You wouldn't have had to stock up on my account. How about coming over for dinner tonight? Just the two of us so we can catch up."

"Great," Maggie told her.

It was and it wasn't. Maggie knew the issue of Jake would come

242

up. Avoidance when it came to Sonia was not the best policy. Her friend would guess or find out what had happened sooner or later. Sonia would be miffed. Maggie would never hear the end of it.

She was going to need her wits about her, that much was certain. Snagging a handful of raw almonds from an open container inside the door of the refrigerator, she called it lunch and headed down the hall to the bedroom.

Maggie didn't bother to take the time to shed her sweaty clothes from the road. She crawled under the top quilt. A quickie mid-afternoon nap always took the edge off. Thoughts a jumble, she managed to fall into a sound and extended sleep.

When she awoke, the room looked considerably darker than she remembered. A glance at her watch confirmed the worst.

Five twenty-seven. She had less than a half-hour to make herself look human before heading to her friend's for the cookout.

Maggie lurched down the hall and turned on the shower. She was in and out before the water had a chance to get completely warm. No time to fool with hair dryers either. She towel dried her hair and brushed it more or less into shape. This occasion called for serious makeup, anything that said 'Confidence, I Know What I'm Doing'.

A dash of nude palette eye shadow and concealer could work miracles. Maggie pulled on a black shell and black crop pants with a row of three matching buttons decorating the outer seam. Pedal pushers, she remembered calling them in the day. But then maybe those were shorter.

She spotted a gauzy black and white top in the closet, but went with a short-sleeve lime green over-blouse instead. A funereal look was not going to send off the right vibes under the circumstances. She rummaged in her jewelry box and topped things off with a trendy floral necklace she had purchased on a whim off ebay last summer. When the tiny package had arrived in Northern Michigan covered with custom stamps and Chinese writing, the postal worker had taken the time to hand-deliver it at the door.

"China," he frowned. "Never saw a package like that before."

Maggie fought a smile. The guy obviously worried the thing was packed with explosives and detonator or something equally sinister.

A pair of matching earrings and black strappy sandals completed the look. *Way over the top for an impromptu evening with Sonia*, Maggie concluded as she caught a glimpse of herself in a dresser mirror. But she was going to need every bit of spunk and sass she could muster to pull this off.

With that she was out the door, through the garden and on her way down the alley to Sonia's cottage. Smells of something grilling wafted to greet her through her friend's backyard. Maggie was about to start up the back stairs when Sonia herself appeared in jeans and a flowered tunic top, platter in hand.

"Wow," Sonia came to a dead stop on the porch. She blinked, taking a second look. "You look . . . amazing."

Maggie smiled. *So far so good.*

"And to what do I owe this elegance."

Maggie hesitated. "It's been a while," she said. "Thought I would go for festive. Between all your company and the general craziness this summer, we haven't really seen much of each other."

"True." Sonia picked her way carefully down the steps with the empty platter. "You don't usually go downstate in August either. Jake, I gather, is—"

"Back in Wisconsin, I assume."

Sonia shot a hard quizzical look in Maggie's direction. "Are you trying to tell me something?" she said.

Maggie forced a smile. "I think I smell something burning. . . "

"Oh m'gosh." Sonia sprinted for the grill in the corner of the yard which was smoking profusely. When she lifted the lid, a cloud of acrid gray smoke poured out around her.

"So much for medium rare," Maggie laughed.

Sonia was leaning into the swirling inferno, gingerly hauling out burgers with a long-handled spatula. "Very funny," she grumbled.

"It *is* actually," Maggie told her. "We try so hard to control our outcomes and . . . woosh! It all goes up in smoke. As Mom always said, if you don't laugh, you die. I'm beginning to agree with her."

Looking sheepish, Sonia closed the grill, turned it off and headed Maggie's way. On the platter she was carrying what looked like the early stages of charcoal briquettes. "Maybe we should order a pizza."

Maggie laughed. "I vote for my grandma's trick—scrape off the worst and break out the horseradish sauce."

Together the two of them did just that. Then still laughing about the grill fiasco, they settled in on the front porch of the Gunderson cottage for dinner. Though less ostentatious than the Faland cottage, it too boasted a spectacular view for purposes of sunset watching.

Sonia had set a wicker card-table with her vintage blue and white Currier and Ives place settings and matching cobalt blue glasses—all, Maggie recognized, courtesy of gas station or grocery store promotions back in the day. Her friend had raided the farm market up on Mitchell Road for fresh tomatoes, basil and sweet corn that more than lived up to its name.

"You've been busy," Maggie told her.

Sonia sighed. "It's been one of those summers. I also noticed Jake and the contractors really went to town the last couple of days, too. The place looks done. Some realtor came over early this morning and pounded in the For Sale sign."

"The crews weren't expecting to finish things off for another week at least," Maggie said dully. "Apparently Jake lit one heck of a fire under the landscaper—trying to catch the holiday weekenders."

Sonia was studying her friend's face intently. "Why do I think you're not telling me something?" she said.

"We decided it wasn't working," Maggie told her straight out. "I suspect Jake thought it made sense to head for the hills as quickly as possible."

Nothing different than she herself had done, she admitted to herself. But the prospect made her sad nevertheless.

"Go back to that first part," Sonia said slowly. "Exactly what wasn't working?"

"Us, of course. The relationship. Nothing that hasn't happened to a lot of couples our age. You get kids in the picture, families, and things can get pretty . . . complicated in a hurry."

"Kids." Sonia looked confused. "You said Jake wasn't married. And I got the impression that your Holly seemed okay with the two of you."

"Turns out he has a long lost son. Mark."

Sonia started to say something. Her jaw clamped tight. "Why am I not surprised?" she said finally.

"You're not being fair," Maggie told her. "We're talking about

245

something that happened when Jake was seventeen. He had no idea that he had a son until Mark tracked down his birth mother which eventually led him to Jake. The minute Jake knew—we're talking less than a month ago, he tried to do the right thing."

"Breaking up with you, you mean? Trying to hook up again with—"

"She died." Maggie's voice hardened. "And for the record? *I* was the one who called things off! Sonia, you and I are parents. Of all people we should understand the instinct to move heaven and earth to maintain that relationship with our kids. I wouldn't have expected anything less of Jake."

Sonia dropped her gaze, processed what Maggie told her in silence. "I get it," she said finally, "may not like it, but I get it. How are you holding up?"

"Keeping busy, the old remedy for anything and everything. It's hard, but then you already warned me on that score. I'm moving on. And Sonia, I'm going to need your help with that."

Sonia's smile was sad. "So what now?"

"Just let it go—both of us. Keep busy. You and I go out to the fish hatchery and hike. I've always wanted to go up to the Dark Sky Park near the Bridge. Sounds like much more fun with somebody than alone."

Sonia stood up. "I'll get my calendar."

Maggie was also on her feet. As they hugged, Maggie felt the tears begin to well up but forced them back.

No tears. No self-pity. Maggie thought.

"Tell me one thing. And I promise to ask this once, never again," Sonia said. "Did you . . . do you think you loved each other."

Maggie stared thoughtfully at her friend before responding. "Yes, on both counts. Did. And . . . do."

Sonia drew in a deep breath to clear her head. What Maggie read in her friend's face wasn't judgment or pity. It was simple human concern.

"We've both lost people we've loved, you and I," Maggie added. "Unlike fairy tales, love isn't always enough."

§§§§§

Labor Day came and went. Work and plenty of it became Maggie's operational mode. The Labor Day holiday over, she bought a gallon of paint and redid the downstairs cottage bathroom. Shark's Fin, the sample swatch said. It was only after the fact that she realized it was the same shade Jake had used for the bathrooms in the Faland cottage.

Sonia was out of town. Maggie called another friend from down the block to drive up to Cross Village for lunch along the Tunnel of Trees. Always one of the most scenic highways in the state, it reached a highpoint of popularity in fall. On any given day, the narrow two-lane road that wound and twisted along the lakeshore north from Harbor Springs was likely to deteriorate into a sixteen-mile-long parking lot.

In fact, traffic could have been worse. Maggie never tired of tiny Cross Village with its burgeoning artist's colony and Legg's Inn, the historic Polish restaurant decorated inside and out with carvings and amazing driftwood art that had washed up from Lake Michigan over the years. It owed its name to the collection of cast iron stove legs mounted like an ancient Greek frieze all around the top of the building.

Most recently she had gone there with Jake and her daughter in July—something else she had forgotten when she planned the outing. It had been raining then. The three of them had eaten indoors. Spending an entire lunch reconstructing the smells, sights and sounds of that precious time together felt way beyond Maggie's comfort zone.

Despite the chill in the air, she suggested she and her friend sit outside for lunch. "The gardens and view of the offshore lighthouses and passing ore boats is so special," she insisted.

"The wind's coming straight off Lake Michigan," Maggie's friend protested, teeth chattering, as they waited for the wait staff to take their order. "Would have made more sense to sit inside."

Maggie sighed. She was remembering that gosh-awful B movie she saw a few days ago about senior citizens going wild. *Ridiculous*, she thought, the extremes at this stage of life—the urge to base jump or find a snug and cozy corner out of the wind.

"I've got an extra sweater in the car," Maggie told her friend. She made no move to change their choice of seats.

The attempt at damage control did Maggie no good. Privately her memories already had leapt from driftwood art to another weekend with Jake just down the road at Bliss. Exotic rhythms played themselves out in her head. If her current luncheon companion sensed something was wrong, she didn't show it.

Was it inevitable, Maggie wondered, to give up as this neighbor of hers obviously had done—follow the path of least resistence, do the sensible thing. "Start acting your age," as Grandma always described it.

Maggie had arrived at a fish-or-cut-bait point in her life and she knew it. Jake was gone. She had done the right thing, had no doubt about it. But was the alternative to retreat into the safety of the familiar—to substitute mindless busy-ness for genuinely caring about something or someone outside herself?

Fortunately Maggie had driven. She could control their departure. The inland route back from Cross Village went much faster without all those twists and turns. All the while her neighbor chattered on about her grandchildren, her book club, the weather and traffic. As the woman saw it, too many tourists, not a typical Little Traverse summer at all.

Maggie silently agreed. Though for entirely different reasons.

She stopped at her neighbor's cottage long enough to leave her off. But instead of returning to her own cottage, Maggie aimed the car up the bluff into Petoskey. Set back in a tree-lined clearing stood a distinctive stone church straight out of a British novel. Maggie and her husband had attended Episcopal services there on and off over the years when they summered together along Little Traverse Bay. After Joe's death, her presence in the place had become conspicuously sporadic.

The parking lot was in back, the church doors open. Maggie parked, then followed the maze of hallways into the sanctuary. The space was dark and cool, its gray block walls interrupted at regular intervals by rows of jewel-tone stained glass windows. Over the organ pipes and the ornate wooden screen behind the altar area, a large rosette made up of smaller glass medallions bloomed in the half-darkness.

Maggie slipped into a pew near the front. Everything about the room said 'sacred'. The other-worldliness permeated her troubled soul. Streams of tears that she so carefully had held in check for weeks now began to course freely down her face.

To do right is not always easy, at any age or stage of life. Maggie felt the bitterness of that truth more so than any time in recent memory, on so many fronts. Jake, her mother, absent children she dearly missed all played a role in her choices and the losses that went with them. Half-blinded by her tears, she stared at the rose window above the altar as somehow the illuminated panes contained the answers she was seeking.

Like a jigsaw, she thought. The challenge of her life had become to piece together the Big Picture, to see the whole emerging from the many disconnected parts—a lonely struggle at times. And yet, it was the overriding presence of something larger than herself moving alongside and within her that quietly prevailed. As she sat in the darkness, she felt the knot of anxiety and grief inside her begin to unravel, thread by painful thread.

Eventually her vision cleared enough to look around her. Sticking haphazardly out of one of the wooden racks mounted on the back of the bench in front of her, she saw a random sheaf of papers left over from a previous Sunday. One of the ushers apparently had missed it when scouring the church on pick-up detail after a service.

Maggie thumbed through the odd-sized assortment of pages. An old bulletin with the order of service and a slim sheet with upcoming weekly events lay on top of the stack. Tucked within them was a printout of Biblical texts for a previous week and a printout of a homily that must have gone with it.

"We crave certainty," the writer of the essay said.

We tell ourselves it is the natural order of things. But in fact, that instinct to cling to tradition and the 'known' to anchor our lives is only an illusion. Hanging on to the past as a measure of the future will not make us any safer or happier. When we sense the hunger for certainty beginning to close in and limit our lives, our truest instinct should be one not of comfort, but of deep suspicion.

On the spiritual journey at its most powerful and fulfilling, it is *uncertainty* that molds us. Uncertainty causes us to rethink. It keeps us forever searching for what it means to be our best selves. The healthy impulse to doubt, to question is what urges us ever deeper into an understanding of what our lives are meant to be.

Maggie stared down at the crumpled page as if it were alive.

The truth of the writer's insights cried out to her with a still, small voice that would not be denied. Wallowing in her sense of loss was leading her nowhere. It was only in embracing the unknown that her future made any sense at all.

There was life to be lived. She had to take the first firm steps along the road to finding it. In the entryway, Maggie had passed a large cardboard box labeled Food Pantry. A poster on a corkboard near the door outside the sanctuary asked for help with women fleeing marital abuse. Still another sought support for the working poor.

Over the years, Maggie had tried to interest cottage friends in joining her to volunteer for area charities, to little avail. "I'm so up to my ears with all that kind of stuff during the rest of the year downstate," a neighbor told her bluntly. "When I come up north to the cottage, frankly I just want to take a break from all that."

Maggie was genuinely shocked. Off-season in Northern Michigan meant lean times for a lot of people working mainly in the hospitality and service industries. So much so, a recent newspaper article claimed, that a high percentage of kids in the local schools qualified for free lunches.

I get it—battle fatigue, Maggie wanted to tell the woman. *Problem is, these are the very families who handle our landscaping and odd jobs, who wait on us in stores and restaurants. We can't exactly close our eyes to that.* What stopped her was the realization that she couldn't pretend to have done enough herself over the years. That, she vowed, needed to change.

But this was now. In the flower beds along the curving paths that lead to the parking lot, Maggie had spotted weeds galore. And that need was something she *could* deal with on the spot.

Dressed as she was in heeled sandals, black linen slacks, tank top and over-blouse she wore on the luncheon in Cross Village with her friend, she began to search out the Lambsquarters and Creeping Charlie. Despite its elegant name, amaranth hung on as a stubborn garden pest better known as pigsweed. Buckhorn plantain and crabgrass were on the march. Dandelions crept out from under the leaves of the hosta.

Come, labor on. Redeem the time; its hours too swiftly fly. The night draws nigh.

She had no tool but her two hands. Maggie tugged until her fingernails were broken and stained with dirt. A pile of uprooted greenery on the sidewalk behind her grew into a small mountain. Sweat poured down her back. The manicured toes sticking out of her sandals became tinged a vitriolic green.

At the corner where the bed turned to follow the outline of the building, Maggie finally stopped. Behind her in the bed where she had sweat and toiled, bare dirt lay exposed where previously a jungle had thrived. Back aching, she stood and stretched. As she was surveying her handiwork, she heard another car pull into the lot behind her.

"Great work," a voice called out to her. The woman was about her own age, dressed in jeans and a yellow tee shirt. Her scuffed gardening shoes and the tools in her hand spoke of a similar purposefulness to get the job done.

Maggie smiled. "See a weed—pull it. Sorry I made such a mess of the walkway in the process."

"No problem. I'll get a broom downstairs from the utility closet. You've already done your share. Most people would have just taken one look at that crop of spindly sow thistles getting ready to shed their seed and walked on as fast as they could in the other direction. Grumbling, of course, at how badly the beds were kept. "

"Weeds don't pull themselves," Maggie told her.

The two of them shared a moment of laughter. Their own little private gardener's joke, starting with the truth of how unsung the job of keeping a bed weed-free could be.

What Maggie really wanted was to admit out loud how painfully narrow her own vision had become of late, how small the plot she had been willing to tend. The walls had been quietly closing in on her for years. And even now, breaking free seemed a daunting task.

On a sigh, Maggie said her goodbyes to the woman and made her way back to the parking lot. Retrieving the keys from her purse, she unlocked the car and drove back to the cottage. The evening news was obsessed with destruction from an early hurricane moving its way through the Carribean. On impulse, Maggie went online and clicked on an agency setting up a disaster-relief fund. She scrolled through the screens and fired off a donation. It was a start.

See a weed and pull it. Her own life may be borderline out of control, but she still had the power to engage with her world in ways that counted. All it took was to spot the need and then act upon it. That much, Maggie resolved, she could do.

The thought fresh in her mind, she redirected her internet search to the cottage owner association blog. For some months now, an ongoing war had been waging over the problem of stagnant cottage sales and asking prices for properties in the community. The dialogue was contentious, driven by increasingly ugly polarization among those who saw the solution as isolationism versus those advocating a more open door policy. With friends on both sides of the controversy, Maggie had chosen to stay strictly out of the fray.

No longer. The words poured out as her fingertips moved over the computer keyboard:

> We are becoming dinosaurs while the world changes all around us, changes for the better I like to think. Our grandchildren represent every skin color and ethnic heritage imaginable, every sexual orientation, faith and creed. It is folly to cling to a monochromatic, white bread vision of the ideal community. No wonder second and third generation cottagers are moving on.
>
> As a gardener, I cast my vote for the power of diversity. All red roses do not a garden make. If we are to survive as a community, we must be willing to open not just our doors but our hearts in welcome. We need to redefine what it means to be a neighbor or we will lose the very soul of this place. The time for holding back the future is over. We can and must do better.

For a long time, Maggie sat staring at what she had written. Then on a sigh, she clicked Send.

For what it was worth, she had taken a stand. At one time she might have felt fearful that friends could consider her public declaration a defection, or even betrayal. Instead, she felt only a deep sense of relief.

The truth needed to be told. It was long overdue.

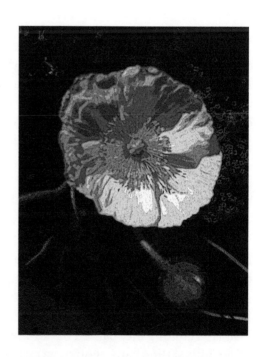

In the language of flowers, poppies (family PAPAVERACEAE) symbolize peace, sleep and mortality. Since ancient times—including the culture of early Egypt—some varieties have been used for alkaloid producing painkillers such as opium or morphine. A red-flowering variety common in the fields in Flanders has come to represent "remembrance" following the brutal battles fought in that region and heavy loss of life during World War I. Poppies can be annuals, biennials or short-lived perennials.

A Cold, Hard Rain

Rains began that evening across Northern Michigan with a cold drizzle, more like a spray of mist swirling over the bay. By midnight, Maggie heard heavier droplets pelting against the uninsulated roof of the cottage. When she made her middle of the night bathroom run, the downpour was steady, a thick wall of water blotting out the street light in the alley, her garden and the cottages beyond.

Morning dawned gray and still. But by eight o'clock it was raining again. The hollyhock resisted at first, then succumbed to the relentless downpour. Wood smoke hung heavy in the chill air. And still it rained.

The mud and showers kept Maggie out of the garden. But outfitted in her gardening boots and a yellow poncho, she walked the paved bike trail toward the waterfall in the city park at the base of the steep hill below the Gaslight District. At one time the area had been a limestone quarry, the source of the cement and building blocks for the historic gem of a city carved out of the wilderness. In recent years, the waterfall's setting had become a scene out of South Sea island brochure.

Fed by the rains, an impressive quantity of water poured under the highway and over the face of the limestone. Ferns and colored algae thrived in the shadows and niches. The spot was a favorite with brides and graduates wanting to immortalize their life experiences surrounded by such wild beauty.

Maggie made the return trip through the puddles to the cottage, chilled to the bone. Leaves were falling everywhere, way too early. But then the drought in June had seen to that. Environmentalists at the Ag Extension office had been warning for years that global warming was having a dangerous impact on the sprawling maple forests of Northern Michigan.

Maggie witnessed proof positive all around her. Not all human endeavor is created equal, she thought sadly. A little like the cliff face above the waterfall pounded daily by tens of thousands of cars on an average summer day, things overused or misused will crumble.

She couldn't imagine the traffic nightmares ahead when the department of transportation was slated to move the highway back away from the edge. Some sections along the upper walkway already had been closed for a good decade due to the danger of collapse.

A hot shower and change of clothes revived Maggie's flagging spirits. Comfortable in jeans and a navy blue sweatshirt she had bought at the sidewalk sales with the five Great Lakes embroidered in white on the front, Maggie drove out to the senior center to see her mother.

Lillian had been on a roll, the staff said. Her memory lapses didn't keep her from enjoying company or endless rounds of rummy. Lillian was amazing at the game. She routinely drew high count cards and trounced her daughter accordingly.

"Not today," Lillian said when Maggie proposed a game or two. "I'm tired."

Instead she talked about the 'old days' growing up on the farm, her teachers at the one-room school and the flour sack dresses Grandma Aron had sewed for her as a girl, the austerity of the Great Depression.

"So many friends are gone," Lillian sighed. "Losing people takes the stuffing out of you after a while. Whatever happened to Jake? He hasn't been around lately."

The question hit like a thunderbolt. Sketchy as her mother's memory had become of current events, Maggie wasn't expecting it.

"He's back in Wisconsin," Maggie said.

"A shame. I like him," her mother told her. "Funny. Someone who wasn't afraid to talk to an old fogey—but then he isn't exactly a spring chicken himself."

Maggie winced. She could only imagine what had gone on between the two of them whenever they were alone. It was on the tip of her tongue to tell her mother what had happened with Jake—and to her as a result, but the moment passed.

"And that blond girl you used to play with? Scandinavian. What was her name?"

"Sonia."

Lillian shook her head. "Wait until you get my age," she said. "You stop counting the missing and concentrate on who is left. For me that's down to the fingers of one hand."

Maggie felt a stab of recognition. Her own husband had been gone nearly a decade. The list of deceased high school friends whose names appeared in the periodic alumni emails had grown exponentially of late. She thought about Jake in a different category entirely, but then his absence still loomed raw and freshest of all.

"I can't even imagine, Mom," Maggie said.

"Gets to a point," Lillian sighed, "when even the ones who are left don't remember you. Suddenly, you're Harvey the Invisible Rabbit."

Our memories become our mirrors, Maggie realized with a shock. Held in the hands of the friends and family who know and love us, we see our identities reflected back at us. And without those anchors and reference points in our life, we lose bits and pieces of ourselves over time. Those living memories are our history.

"Well, at least I'm glad you have friends here. And the staff really likes you."

"Friends—hang on to the ones you can," Lillian told her. "It takes a lot of work to keep making them. Wears a guy out. You figure out after a while the younger the better. You lose fewer that way."

Maggie smiled. "You haven't lost your spunk. That you have to admit."

Her mother sniffed. "Just too darn stubborn to die that's all."

At that Maggie laughed out loud. "I love you, Mom."

When she leaned down to give her a kiss on the way out the door, Lillian reached up and caught Maggie's face between her hands, held it. "You're a good daughter, Margaret Aron."

Tears glittered in Lillian's eyes as she said it. Maggie felt a lump in her throat that momentarily robbed her of speech. "And you're my best friend," she said. "Are and always will be."

Hang on to the friends you have. Lillian's salty take on life lingered as Maggie found herself back at the cottage. On impulse she picked up the phone and invited Sonia over for an evening of Scrabble. She was down to her last bottle of merlot, but it would do. So would the jeans and comfortable Great Lakes sweatshirt she had donned especially for her visit to Lillian earlier in the day.

The curving shape of those five unique bodies of water, carved out by the glaciers of the Ice Age, were emblazoned on her memory. On her soul. *Places can anchor too*, she thought, for all the problems that they too accumulate over time.

Maggie filled her friend in on the visit to the senior center, everything Lillian had said. "It must be exhausting for her," Sonia shook her head. "Telling the same stories over and over again. She constantly needs to start from scratch with a new cast of characters in her life."

Maggie sighed. "And to add insult to injury, they call us senile when we do. No wonder we lose track of who knows what and who doesn't—wind up repeating ourselves. We can't win."

When they got tired of fishing around for words on the Scrabble board, Maggie lit a blaze in the fireplace. She dug out the old metal camping forks and the two of them made S'mores.

The graham crackers had sat in the pantry for a while, forgotten in their box. But layered with gooey marshmallows and rock hard chocolate that melted in the assembly process, the results were a blast from the past, straight out of childhood.

"I'd suggest we sing camp songs, Kumbaya or Someone's in the Kitchen," Sonia said, "but maybe that's just a little too funky." Yawning, she told Maggie it probably was time to call it a night.

"What does it mean anyway?" Sonia wondered. "Kumbaya?"

Maggie laughed. "I looked it up once—means something like *come on over*. And I hope you will now that we're both on our own for the rest of the summer."

"I'll do just that."

Maggie walked her to the kitchen door. Their hug was the warmest they had shared in a long time.

"Gotta be done," Sonia grumbled as she opened her umbrella and made a dash through the garden.

The air was thick with rain and trails of mist. It was impossible to tell where the earth left off and sky began. Sonia disappeared into the inky blackness long before she reached the gate and alley beyond.

Yawning herself, Maggie started to close up the cottage for the night when the phone rang. The woman's voice on the other end of the line was agitated, unfamiliar. She introduced herself as one of the night staff at the senior center.

"Lillian fell a half hour ago," the woman said. "We think you had better come."

Just that fast the ground shifted underfoot. Maggie hadn't changed out of her jeans and sweatshirt. It only took seconds to pull on a pair of garden boots and a rain slicker, grab purse and keys and sprint to the car. On impulse she grabbed the medical power of attorney papers that hospice had given her the last time Lillian had fallen—what seemed like eons but in fact had only been a month ago.

If anything, the rain was coming harder now. The windshield wipers were having trouble keeping up. Late as it was, few cars were on the roads. Headlights from the vehicles Maggie met washed across the windshield like a strobe, momentarily blinding her.

Apocalyptic. Her mouth hardened in a grim line.

For once, the parking spaces in front of the senior center were virtually empty. Maggie swung the car into a spot right out front without a thought for the painted yellow lines separating them.

"The worst park job of my life," she grimaced.

Ducking her head against the downpour, she plowed ahead through the puddles to the front door. Her unwieldy rubber boots squeaked, left a soggy trail along the floors of the empty corridors.

Hydroplaning. Maggie almost slipped, then slowed her pace. There had been one accident—no sense in inviting more.

The hallway outside her mother's apartment was quiet. But once inside, the situation was anything but.

Two women dressed in street clothes greeted Maggie at the door, cell phones in hand. One introduced herself as the hospice nurse. The other had a clipboard, weighed in as the social worker.

"Lillian doesn't want an ambulance," the woman with the clipboard said. "But we think she's broken her hip."

Those last three words kept churning in Maggie's brain. One look at her mother's face told her the rest. Lillian was lying on her bed, face twisted in agony, while two night nurses hovered over her. This was an endgame playing itself out, something no ambulance or hospital or surgeon was going to change one iota.

"You do not do hip surgery on somebody pushing a hundred," a hospice doctor had told her bluntly the last time Lillian fell. Lillian herself already had weighed in on the subject.

"Don't you dare let them do that to me," she told her daughter. "No emergency rooms, none of that hardware, no tubes—none of it."

Maggie blinked.

"Promise," her mother had demanded.

The two made eye contact. "I promise," Maggie said.

The power of attorney documents were orange, encased in a plastic sleeve. They suddenly felt like tablets of stone, uncomfortable and heavy. Maggie's jaw tightened. "Whatever happens next, it happens here," she told the woman with the cell phone. "Mom is not going anywhere."

"We'll have to move her to the nursing center. And she needs x-rays."

By then the hospice social worker had joined them, far too many people in that tiny bedroom. "Hospice has portable equipment. I'll send for it."

"That's as far as it goes." On instinct, Maggie raised the crumpled power of attorney for emphasis.

"Hang on to that," the social worker told her grimly.

What followed was a nightmare of hastily administered painkillers and a trip by gurney under the canopy through the rain to the skilled nursing wing. The staff tried its best to keep Lillian comfortable. Even in pain and disoriented as she was, Lillian would not agree to anything resembling an ambulance run. Maggie held her mother's hand through as much of it as she could.

Lillian clearly had no memory or sense of what had happened. "Mom, you fell—broke your hip," Maggie kept saying. "They can't take care of you in your room, need to move you to the nursing center. You are not going to the hospital. I promise. Your friends . . . you'll be just across the courtyard. Everyone can still come visit—"

Maggie's voice broke. Eyes wide, Lillian tried to take in what her daughter was saying. All the while Maggie saw her mother slipping farther and farther away in a haze of painkillers.

It took a couple of tries to adjust the medication. The occasional breakthroughs of pain that followed were awful to witness.

Through it all, Lillian grimaced but never cried out. She bit back the waves of pain with the same fierce force of will that had carried her through nearly a century of the best and worst life can offer.

The grapevine in the senior living community did its job. By early morning a ragged band of neighbors accompanied by an on-duty aide on Lillian's corridor showed up in the nursing wing. Whatever they had been told about Lillian's fall or condition, it hadn't prepared them for what they encountered in that dim and silent room. The five of them stood along the foot of Lillian's bed like a Greek chorus, suddenly uncertain of its lines.

Lillian blinked several times when she finally saw them. A smile of recognition flickered at the corner of her mouth. She tried to raise a hand in greeting but the morphine held her back.

Hang on to your friends as long as you can, Maggie told herself. Tears glittered in her eyes and she had to look away.

This woman lying on the hospital-style bed had been with her from the beginning. She had witnessed Maggie take her first halting step, utter her first broken syllables, literally books full of such defining moments. As a mother, Lillian had steered Maggie through the shoals of what could otherwise have been a rocky adolescence. She had cried at graduations and pressed a lace handkerchief embroidered in blue into her daughter's hand at her wedding.

"Something borrowed," Lillian had whispered.

And now a lifetime later, in an instant of unsteadiness, her mother's life had been reduced to just that. *Something borrowed*, Maggie breathed to herself as she looked down at her mother's pain etched face.

As suddenly and with precious little warning as we come into the world, life ends. Her mother's final gift to her was in mustering the courage to leave it.

The hospice chaplain picked that moment to show up. Prayers were said. Maggie heard none of them. All the while, clutched in her hand, crumpled and sweaty by now, was the medical power of attorney, the directives that were guiding them all.

Snippets of a Sunday School faith flooded back as Maggie struggled to ground herself in the moment. *So teach us to number our days.* It had to be a Psalm, that poetic admonition to live life to the fullest.

She walked the chaplain to the door after a while and out into the hallway. Rummaging in her purse, she pulled out her cell phone. Holly's number was on speed dial. Maggie launched right into what had brought on the call.

"It's Grandma Lillian," she said evenly. "She fell and broke her hip tonight. It isn't good—"

"I'll get a flight," Holly said.

"Don't do anything foolish. You won't get here on time. She won't last another night . . ."

Maggie bit off the rest of what she was going to say—*if she were lucky.* Truth was, for her mother's sake her prayer was simple. That this would end sooner rather than later.

"No one could want your Grandma to linger like this," Maggie said. "No one."

Holly's sharp intake of breath left no doubt what she was feeling. "Don't worry about me," she said. "I'll fly in to Traverse City as soon as I can get a flight. Or Pellston, whichever is quicker. I'll rent a car. You shouldn't be handling this alone, Mom."

"I'm alright, really."

"And while I'm waiting for a flight or whatever, I'll call my brother. Anyone else you think—"

"Your uncle would want to know."

"Done," Holly said. "Tell Grams . . . tell her I love her. We all do."

With that the connection broke. Maggie stood phone in hand, trying to reorient herself. By comparison to the empty hallway outside her mother's apartment, the corridor of the nursing center seemed cluttered with equipment, staff comings and goings. There was a fierce energy in the air, the aura of life and death at war with one another.

Maggie straightened, drew a deep breath and went back into Lillian's room. It was only then that she noticed her mother was not alone, hadn't been this whole time. Halfway across the width of the room, a white grommeted curtain had been pulled into place. When drawn, it created a second area just big enough for another bed. Behind the veil, Maggie heard hushed voices and an occasional low whimper of

261

distress.

Lillian was oblivious to all that. Maggie sat alongside the bed on the hard metal-framed chair and held her mother's hand.

"I love you, Mom," she told her. Her mother's eyes would flicker in recognition. The expression on her face bordered on luminous.

Lillian's bed was situated on an inner wall right next to the corridor. From there in the distance Maggie heard the occasional buzz of voices, footsteps hurrying along the tiled floor. Without a window and only the dim lights in the room, she lost all sense of day and night.

"You really ought to eat something," one of the aides told Maggie on a regular pass-through to check medications and Lillian's vitals.

The woman later returned with a soggy cheese sandwich, glass of iced tea and chunks of fruit in a small sauce dish. Maggie picked at it, anything but hungry.

Faces of the aides around them suddenly became unfamiliar, a shift change. The same questions were asked and answered. Maggie had been monitoring the morphine breakthroughs. They became fewer and farther between. Much of the time, her mother's eyes were closed.

The hospice social worker was back briefly, going off shift herself, she said. She handed Maggie a booklet which described the stages of the vigil ahead.

Lillian's breath became shallower. There were times it almost appeared to have stopped entirely. Instinctively, Maggie gripped her mother's hand tighter. Lillian's eyelids flickered. She winced.

"Sorry, Mom. I didn't mean to get so carried away."

Lillian looked over at her, recognition in her eyes. She tried to smile, Maggie realized with a shock. But instead she closed her eyes again. The ragged breathing returned.

Her son called from Hawaii. Her brother phoned as well. The hushed long-distance conversations steeled Maggie to return to her mother's side.

Eventually Lillian's breathing would stop long enough that Maggie found herself counting. A second, two, ten, more. There were times when Maggie thought she was gone. And still Lillian clung to life.

The end when it came took Maggie by surprise. Her mother's eyes shot open and Lillian's face transformed itself into what only could be described as a look of awe and wonder. It was as if she saw something coming toward her—too incredible to be believed.

And with that, it was over. Maggie sat there tears streaming down her face. An aide peeked her head in, sensed what had happened.

"It's best if you step out in the hallway for a bit," the woman said.

Going on autopilot, Maggie complied. Staff came and went. When Maggie returned to the room, Lillian was lying as she had left her. The bed clothes were tucked carefully around her now. Evidence of the oxygen feed was gone. She looked as though she could have been sleeping. Maggie sat down along the bedside, took her mother's hand.

"You can consult with family, do what you need to do to make arrangements," a passing nurse told her. "We don't have to hurry here."

Maggie nodded. She and Lillian had never talked about this contingency. Their plans had always assumed the end, when it came, would be downstate. But hospice had left her with a list of possible mortuaries. Lillian's only request had been to be cremated and laid to rest along the shores of Little Traverse Bay.

"No shipping me around in a box media rate," she said. "I don't want to get lost in the mail."

Goodbyes came hard. Eventually armed with the ragged pile of paperwork that had been given her, Maggie started for home. The rain had stopped. The tense vigil had blurred in her memory until she had no idea how long she had been at Lillian's side, what time or day it was.

From one moment to the next, Maggie had become the older generation. The weight of that truth closed in on her like the walls of the car, reducing her world to inches. She could reach out and define the measure of it with her two hands.

When she arrived back at the cottage, Maggie found a message from Sonia waiting for her on the back porch along with a tin of zucchini bread. "Let me know how I can help," the note read.

Holly must have called her friend, Maggie concluded. One less call to make amid far too many. She set the cookie tin and note on the kitchen table, along with the papers from the senior center and hospice. The magnitude of what lay ahead of her left her bewildered, uncertain where even to begin.

She brewed herself a pot of coffee, thick and black. With a mug in hand, she wandered back on the porch, intending to survey the damage the rain had done to the last of the flowering fall plants, anything to get her bearings.

The stems of the phlox and stockier field asters were lying sideways, mud splashed and bedraggled. Maggie could empathize. She had been living in the same clothes for two days. Debating whether to throw them in the laundry hamper or burn them, she headed back inside the cottage and took a shower.

An hour's worth of phone calls later, Maggie had arranged to meet with a mortician who in turn would work with the senior center to start the arrangements. She donned gray dress slacks and a coral long-sleeve shirt the color of the sunset. "No running around in black," her mother had told her. Then just as Maggie about to head over to the mortuary office, the phone rang.

"My plane's about to board," Holly's voice told her from the other end of the line. "I should get in to Traverse City early evening. After that it's a two-hour drive, depending on traffic."

"I was going to start making arrangements," Maggie said, "but it makes sense to wait now until you're here."

"Did Grams ever say what she wanted?"

Maggie chuckled soundlessly over that one. Did Holly truly doubt that? "No viewing. Cremation."

Those blunt directives had come from Lillian a decade ago—reinforced every time she had witnessed the funerals of friend of hers. "Ridiculous to make a public display," Lillian had insisted, "when you're starting to look like an alligator handbag. Ditto when it comes to a fuss. I'd be dead, couldn't care less at that point."

That left only absent family matters to consider. "The rest of the tribe are staying put for now," Holly told her mother. "Waiting to see what the plan is."

"Lillian wouldn't want some grand spectacle. She was absolutely clear on that," Maggie said. "Plus the greatgrands in Hawaii are just starting school—no time to yank them away from all that. I'm thinking, better wait until Thanksgiving when a lot of us stand a reasonable chance of getting together. Unfortunately the cottage has to be closed up by then. So maybe we could even wait until next summer and hold a service here when we have her ashes laid to rest."

"Great idea," Holly agreed. "Grams would want us celebrating her life—not feeling sorry for ourselves. She was always happiest when we were together at the cottage, admiring her garden, walking together along the lakeshore, watching the sunsets."

"Then summer it is. You just worry now about getting over here in one piece," her mother told her. "I'll call the rest of the crew and let them know what we're doing."

"See you tonight. I love you, Mom." Holly broke the connection.

Maggie brought her brother, her son and his family up to speed. That accomplished she called the mortuary back and postponed the meeting to arrange the cremation. Holly was on the way. It made sense to give her a chance to participate in the decision-making.

One less thing to handle right now, Maggie thought. That left just enough time to catch a short nap before Holly showed up. She suddenly felt so exhausted, she couldn't seem to keep her eyes open.

The bed was still made, unslept in, the way she had left it. Maggie crawled under the coverlet. Almost as soon as her head hit the pillow, she fell into a troubled sleep.

When she awoke, midday light filled the room. The rains were definitely behind them. The glare from the windows hurt her eyes. Sleep-drugged and light-headed, she got up and wandered into the kitchen. Although food was the last thing on her mind, she knew she better eat something.

The coffee had been warming for hours. It had become thick and bitter tasting. Maggie grimaced but poured herself a mug. She set a low-everything frozen dinner in the microwave and pressed the power button. That gave her all of four minutes to clear her head. No sense standing around to watch the thing cooking. Throwing open the screen door, she made her way onto the porch, coffee in hand.

Over the top of the garden fence, Maggie noticed there was an unfamiliar SUV parked in the alley where it hadn't been before. She blinked, not once but twice, convinced she was mistaken, seeing things. Maggie's forehead knit in a puzzled frown. Fumbling with the latch to the gate stood the last person in the world she expected to see.

Jake. The word kept turning itself over in her head like someone hearing a foreign language for the first time. *Jake Faland.*

The mug dropped from Maggie's hand and shattered. Coffee and shards of stoneware spread out across the wooden porch floor. At the resulting crash, Jake looked up.

Maggie saw him silently mouth her name as he caught sight of her. "*Maggie . . .?*"

Dressed in jeans and a rumpled dress shirt, he looked as tired as she felt. His eyes appeared red-rimmed from lack of sleep. He must have started driving in the dead of night. The trip across the Upper Peninsula under the best of circumstances took seven hours. With the time change, that meant eight. Inconceivable what that drive had been like—starting out in the rain, dodging deer and an imposing potential list of smaller wildlife. Towns of any size and even human habitation were few and far between, the darkness endless.

As if in slow motion, Maggie watched the gate swing open. Jake began to pick his way through the rain-drenched garden in her direction, dodging the fallen stalks and stems.

His voice was strained, raw. "Holly called me . . ."

With that he was up the porch steps. Maggie choked back whatever questions were churning in her brain, simply let him hold her while she poured out her tears onto his shirtfront.

He didn't need to say a word. His presence was enough. Finally her outpouring of grief slowed, then stilled. With his arm around her propelling her gently forward, they took refuge on a wicker loveseat on the porch. Its cushions still felt wet to the touch from the rain. But then so was Jake's shirtfront. The coffee and wreckage of the mug that had held it lay strewn perilously underfoot.

None of that mattered. He had come. Maggie felt no longer utterly alone in the deep well of sadness that enveloped her.

"She . . . Mom had been doing so well the past week," she told him bleakly. "Then out of the blue, this."

"A broken hip, Holly said?"

Maggie nodded. "We always knew this could happen. And Mom didn't want surgery . . . or trying to prolong the inevitable. I could tell the minute I walked into her bedroom that she wasn't going to last long. Morphine slows the system. And with her heart . . . "

"Lillian was quite a woman. I'm truly sorry."

"I'm sorry that you . . . it wasn't necessary to make that awful drive in the middle of the night. But I'm grateful you're here. And in one piece. When Holly called you, she must have assumed—"

"That we're still together. A reasonable assumption. It's been hard staying away, trust me." Jake hesitated. "And now someone has made an offer on the cottage . . . "

It sold, after just days on the market. Soon he would have no reason to come at all. Maggie's heart sank. "So fast then," she said.

He grimaced. "I wasn't expecting it."

"And Mark . . . your son?"

"They stuck out the weekend. He's called since, twice. I suspect that may be his wife's doing. All in all, things have been more . . . civil between us."

"Does he . . . I assume you didn't tell him you were coming back here."

"I got going right away when Holly called. There wasn't any time. First things first."

"My daughter's on a plane, will get into Traverse City around dinner time. She's bound to sense something—about where things stand with us, I mean," Maggie said after awhile. "I don't know how or what I'm going to tell her. She likes you."

Jake looked pained. "Ditto. I can't help comparing her reaction with that of my son."

"In retrospect it was probably a mistake," Maggie sighed, "introducing me into the equation that weekend."

"I don't think it would have mattered—only brought to a head what already was cooking in his skull. There was all that anger, especially when Mark caught a glimpse of the Faland family's so-called cottage and what he interpreted as a privileged lifestyle. Frankly, I can't blame him."

"You couldn't have known any of that in advance," Maggie told him.

"But didn't want to either, on some level. I can't claim moral superiority here, I'm all too aware of that. Still, I expected more of him."

Maggie sighed. "Well, for what it's worth, on her last good day, Mom . . . Lillian asked about you," she told him.

Jake chuckled softly. "We hit it off, she and I. Though I suspect she also saw right through me."

"Give yourself more credit than that. Mom was never one to suffer fools gladly." Maggie told him about her last conversation with her mother earlier on the day of her accident. "You never made her feel . . . ancient, irrelevant, as if she didn't count."

"You'll miss her. A lot."

Tears started in Maggie's eyes, but she forced them back. "Already do."

"Priority number one, you need to take care of yourself. Holly said as much on the phone. She sounded worried."

"Lovely," Maggie muttered "I'll have two of you riding herd on me."

Jake's jaw hardened in a grim line. "You can count on it—starting with lunch. I'll bet you haven't eaten."

"Good grief," she muttered. "I left it sitting in the microwave."

He aimed her in the direction of the kitchen. Maggie managed to salvage the soggy TV dinner. Jake insisted on cleaning up the mess on the porch while she nuked something that passed for lunch for him as well.

"I'll bet you drove straight through," she told him. "This isn't gourmet fare, but it's edible."

By the time Holly's rental car appeared in the alley, night had fallen. Jake had moved his overnight bag into the cottage. "Downstairs bedroom," Maggie said evenly. "In case you're wondering."

A smile teased at the corner of his mouth. "I wasn't going to presume."

"I appreciate that," Maggie told him.

As late as it was once Holly arrived, there was nothing that could be done about Lillian's funeral arrangements until morning. After a round of hugs, Maggie, Jake and her daughter settled down in front of the fireplace with a bottle of wine and Thai take-out that Jake produced from a restaurant in Petoskey. The blaze felt good. Nights had grown chillier.

Eventually it was Jake who broached the elephant in the room. "You've caught us mid-rough-patch," he told Holly in Maggie's presence. "I love your mother—no news I suspect. But life, it seems, is rarely as simple as we might wish it to be, has a way of throwing curve balls when we least expect it."

And then Jake shared a halting account of his meeting with the son he had never known and the disastrous weekend with Mark's family at the cottage. "I never should have subjected your mother to that nightmare. She was far more understanding, cut me a great deal more slack than I probably deserve."

At that Jake hesitated, weighing every word that followed. "So when your mother proposed we . . . *cool* things between us, I didn't necessarily agree. But I had to respect her sense of priorities. After all, she's been a parent—something I'm only beginning to appreciate."

Holly listened without comment through the blunt narrative. "I appreciate your honesty," she told him.

Jake's jaw tightened. "Probably not as . . . harsh as I ought to be about my own role in the situation, from the get-go."

"Adult kids are tricky," Holly sighed. "And much as I hate to admit it, on some level we're always kids, whether five or fifteen or fifty. There are times in my own life I likely would have resented the two of you—times I would have raised total hell for the mere whiff of anything 'Mom'. Maybe still am capable of the ridiculous, I suppose. But watching Mom try to support Gram Lillian these past years has been very . . . *instructive*. I only hope I can manage to cope as well."

Tears sprang up in Maggie's eyes. She bit them back.

"I'm proud of you," she told her daughter finally. Her voice was raw with emotion. "Whether you give me hell or not."

Holly chuckled softly. "So, you won't get on my case if I call it the way I see it then."

Maggie's eyebrow arched, her uneasiness apparent.

"Mom, I watched you all those years with Dad," Holly told her. "And trust me, I recognize compatibility when I see it. For all Gram's bravado, living on your own is not all it's cracked up to be. And for the record, Jake . . . you're not immune here. Your son is hurting—I get it. But being a part of his life shouldn't depend on giving up one of your own. When he stops making up for lost time in the 'brattiness' department, I think he'll figure that out. Meanwhile . . . none of us are getting any younger, least of all, you two."

Maggie looked over at Jake, made eye contact. "Point taken," he said evenly.

"So, if it's an official endorsement you're waiting for, here it is.

And if my brother gives you grief . . . well, he won't. I've already told him my version of what seems to be going on here in his absence."

Maggie laughed. "You remind me of your grandmother."

"I hope so," Holly told her. "I certainly hope so."

Life moved on. They shared Lillian stories until midnight. By the second bottle of wine they had cracked the family albums and were poring over the grainy photographs with more laughter than tears. Finally drained emotionally and physically, the three of them called it a night.

Holly laid claim to her childhood bedroom upstairs in the cottage overlooking the garden. At the base of the staircase, she turned and looked back at her mother and Jake still standing there in the kitchen side by side with their backs to the battle-worn farm sink. Not touching.

"G'night, you two," she told them, smiled.

Maggie knew she must have looked to her daughter like a kid with a hand caught in the cookie jar. "Are we all that obvious?" she wondered under her breath.

Jake reached out and wrapped an arm around her shoulder. "Apparently."

She sighed. "I don't know what's more debilitating—kids who match-make or ones who type-cast parents as old fogies, way beyond all that."

"Your Holly's a good egg."

"She has her moments."

"So then," Jake made eye contact. "Are we going to take her advice? In any case, we have world travels together in a couple of months. Quality alone time, whether you want it or not."

Maggie chewed thoughtfully on her lip. "I had forgotten that."

"I hadn't," Jake smiled. "Not for a minute."

Friends with benefits, Maggie wondered for a split-second. Is that what he believes we're becoming? But then the reality of Jake's presence—what had brought him here—laid that last vestige of doubt to rest. Loss and death forge far more powerful bonds than tales idly told of ships passing in the night. She and this man standing alongside her were on a first-name basis with both.

Maggie slipped out of his arms, headed for the light switch. "If

270

you go ahead and turn on the hall light, I'll shut things down in the kitchen," she told him.

The bedroom still smelled of rain and damp. The fire in the living room grate had gone out. That left the wall furnace to take the edge off. Maggie adjusted the thermostat on the bedroom wall, heard the familiar woosh of gas igniting. A wave of super-heated air spread into the room.

Jake was waiting for her alongside the bed. "It's supposed to get down in the forties tonight," Maggie told him.

His response was to draw her toward him. On a sigh he rested his chin against her forehead.

Here's to a warm body on a cold night, Maggie told herself. Sometimes love doesn't get any more complicated than that.

The Day Lily in the genus HEMEROCALLIS derives its name from two Greek words, 'beautiful' and 'day', perhaps because one of its flowers lasts only twenty-four hours. Native to Asia, the plant's long blooming season and showy flowers make it a favorite with gardeners all over the world. The orange variety commonly found along North American roadsides is considered invasive. A stand of these 'naturalized' perennials frequently marks the spot where a now-abandoned pioneer farmstead once stood.

Consider the Lilies

From the look of it, the mortuary now occupied what had been the turreted mansion of a lumber baron or an entrepreneur who had made a fortune from one of the mills spread along the steep slopes of Petoskey's Bear River valley. That was the early 1900s. In their death throes, the once flourishing factories left deep scars on the landscape, the rubble of foundations, heavy stone mill wheels and massive dismantled and rust-covered pieces of equipment their purpose no longer comprehensible.

But given time, nature does what it does. It heals.

A jungle of vines and brush covered the barren hillsides. Thick trunks of maples created a dense canopy over the churning waters of the Bear River. Wildflowers carpeted the banks. Scenic trails and footbridges followed the river's rocky course down to Little Traverse Bay. Only the most experienced of kayakers braved the foam-crested rapids.

As a cottager Lillian Aron had witnessed those changes from girlhood onward. Standing in front of the erstwhile mansion now a mortuary, her daughter and granddaughter surveyed the vestiges of wealth from those earlier times with mixed emotions.

The facade was monumental. "Looks like a battleship," Holly muttered under her breath.

Top to toe the building was clad in camouflage-green wood shingles. Between floors and under the gables of the epic Queen Anne structure, the decorative patterns of the shakes were dizzying. They morphed from herringbone to fishscale—hexagons, octagons and rounds, diamonds and arrows. The chambered and raised-panel friezes were bordered with a wild array of Greek key and dentil moldings.

Even in the halls of death, whimsy triumphed. "Gingerbread gone amok," Maggie grimaced. "But somehow it works."

Jake handled the heavy wood and beveled glass door to the place but it took two hands. Inside the cavernous entryway, a massive staircase wound dramatically upward. Its wooden spindles and bannister gleamed a rich mahogany.

The sound of high heels tapping on the parquet floor told them they weren't alone. "You must be Margaret Aron," a woman's voice called out as she rounded the corner from one of the sitting rooms adjacent to the entry.

"Maggie is fine. This is my daughter, Holly. And Jake."

A friend and more than a friend. Lovers. A couple. Sometimes in defining how we connect, less is more, Maggie decided.

"My office is just through this front parlor, if you would like to follow me. We'll be more comfortable there."

Lillian would have marveled at the collection of authentic period chairs and side tables. Vintage loveseats from the period had been meticulously restored, outfitted in reproduction turn-of-the-century upholstery.

Odd, Maggie thought, how achieving a new millennium abruptly made a whole vocabulary assigned to styles of art and furnishings confusing at best—*Fin de Siecle*, end of the century, but which one? The tyranny of time eludes all those who presume to master it. In a high tech world, a guy can arbitrarily celebrate the New Year through a blur of rolling time zones. Weary jet-legged travelers battle with days lost and gained. Through it all, humanity seems no closer than ever to making sense of its todays, tomorrows or yesterdays.

The woman from the mortuary's office was all business. A gigantic corporate board table dominated the consultation room. Floating shelves on the walls housed an impressive display of urns, ranging from simple to gaudy.

A few of the containers for ashes could pass for downright feudal, Maggie thought. Or 'Goth' as her grandchildren would say. Others overflowed with cherubs and hearts, so over the top that they gave credence to Shakespeare's comments about 'protesting too much' when affection was involved.

At the end of one shelf, tight up against the wall, Maggie spotted an oaken box, conspicuous for its simplicity amid all that excess, beautiful. The patina and grain could have passed for the dropleaf on Grandma Aron's kitchen table.

"That's it," Maggie said, pointing in the unusual urn's direction.

The woman from the funeral home pulled a disappointed frown, deprived of the chance to trot out her well-rehearsed litany of options. "It's a floor sample. The woodworker doesn't make them any more."

"All the more reason. It looks just like a board out of the dining room table when Mom Lillian was a girl."

With visible reluctance the woman hauled down the box. Maggie opened the lid. The walls were a good inch thick. It was rare even to find wood like that any more.

The woman wasn't giving up so easily. "We have this lovely hand-thrown salt glaze pottery suitable for cremains. Only four hundred—"

"The oak," Maggie persisted. The surface of the wood felt warm in her hands, almost alive. She waited, eyebrow raised, anticipating a price.

"Two fifty, as is. Though we can deal with the scratches and wear points. It has been sitting on the shelf for quite a—"

"No need. Just dust it off. Or maybe try a little Murphy's Oil Soap on a rag."

The rest of the logistics were equally uncomplicated. Maggie herself would pick up the urn with the ashes, would arrange for the interment on her own.

"I assume you'll want some kind of memorial service."

'No." Maggie shook her head. "Mom was clear about all of that. No viewings. No doom and gloom. We'll figure out something with the family when they show up next summer at the cottage."

Open-mouthed, the woman stared at her as if she had somehow grown a second head. "If it's what you want."

"It's what Lillian would have wanted," Holly told her.

Another generation had weighed in. And with that, paperwork was produced—slowly, as if somehow in the interim Maggie would come to her senses and change her mind.

Their ragged exit through the cavernous front parlor led by the funeral home representative seemed interminable, beyond awkward. Maggie managed a grim smile. She could imagine her mother as a funeral guest here, surreptitiously admiring the antiques, the lush Persian carpets—tickled pink as long as any over-the-top display of mourning going on was not aimed in her own direction.

Outside on the sidewalk, Maggie came to a dead stop, took a deep breath. Leaves were drifting down prematurely from the maple along the boulevard, visible signs of a hardwood in distress. Sadly, predictions about the future of that venerable tree in a changing climate were not off the mark.

Maggie was so intent on the tree, she didn't notice the uneven patch of pavement ahead of her. Holly's hand shot out and cradled her mother's elbow, steadying her.

"Hang in there, Mom," Holly said. "You've done good through all this. Grams would most definitely approve."

Jake had fallen behind. With the wind behind it, that massive entry door was no less tough to handle coming out than going in. Sounds of the city around them seemed a refreshing contrast to the artificial hush of the funeral home.

"Senior moment—what say we walk a couple of blocks and have lunch at that Hemingway place . . . the name escapes me?" Jake said as he caught up with the two of them. "Lillian shared a story the last time I saw her of how he had written some of his early Nick Adams stories sitting on the end of that long wooden bar."

"City Park Grill," Maggie said. "Right now, the ghost of Ernest isn't the only one on the hunt for a good stiff drink, that's for sure."

Holly laughed. "I thought that poor woman back there was going to break down in tears when you eye-balled that oak box."

"Truth was, I was pretty worked up myself at the time. That gorgeous wood all but cried out, *Lillian.*"

"Well, Grams would be pleased."

The three of them hunkered down at a table at the front window. Foot traffic on the sidewalk outside was heavy for a weekday. Moms with strollers, a few men and woman in business attire and older couples—tourists from the look of it—passed by the historic eatery on their way downtown.

Outside their fish bowl of grief, Maggie thought, life went on. A page had been turned. The finality of her loss suddenly seemed overwhelming.

While Holly and Jake chatted around her, she sat largely silent watching the passersby, the autumn sky. Vehicle traffic eased in and out of the city parking lot tucked alongside the old rail route through the heart of Petoskey—now a well-groomed parkland. Several years back, most of the tracks had been ripped up and unless tourists knew it, they most likely would have missed that chapter in the area's history entirely.

Maggie had read somewhere that at the peak of tourism in the early 1900s, a dozen or more trains had plied the routes from Cleveland and Chicago and Detroit to this destination along the shores of Little Traverse Bay. What remained of that history was a beautifully tended stretch of grass where the tracks once ran. On the lawn outside the restaurant where a major resort hotel had stood, a jewel box of a white painted bandstand had been installed, along with markers testifying to Hemingway's Michigan and a bronze casting of the author himself as a young man.

Milestones of lives lived in this place, Maggie thought.

Her mother Lillian's legacy was destined to be far more ephemeral. First and foremost it was measured in flesh and blood, the shared DNA of mother and daughter seated around a table.

Maggie struggled with a sense of her own mortality in the rise and fall of every breath. In the presence of loss, it seemed the only possibilities were denial or to embrace the fragility of life and move on—destination unknown, like the ragged parade of humanity lurching zoetrope-fashion past the restaurant window.

Holly and Jake left her alone as she wrestled with her thoughts. Maggie was grateful.

"I'm going to make a bathroom stop, Mom," Holly said finally after the waitress began clearing the remains of their lunch. "Want to come along?"

Maggie shook her head. "I'll pass. We'll hold down the fort until you get back."

She watched as her daughter turned and headed toward the back of the restaurant. It didn't occur to Maggie that she too was being watched until Jake reached across the table and laid a hand on hers.

"You okay?" he said.

His hand felt warm, strong and reassuring. "Yes. No. As well as can be expected," Maggie told him. "I was thinking about stopping off at the church on the way back to the cottage—just need to think."

"Understandable."

"You and Holly don't have to stay. You could pick me up later."

"I can't speak for her, but it's no problem to wait."

Maggie sighed. "It's overpowering—all of this. Holly suggested we wait until next summer to hold a memorial service, when we can get the whole clan together. That helps. And Lillian would be totally okay with it. Her life is what she would want us to celebrate, not her passing. But still—how does someone decide?"

"Settling estates is no easy business either. You have that ahead of you too, I assume."

"Right now some things won't wait," Maggie told him. "We have Mom's apartment here to empty, then the one downstate. With the meter ticking in assisted living both places, it makes sense to blitz the move as much as possible."

"Storage?"

"Not my garage, that's for sure."

"Bear in mind," Jake said evenly, "I'm with you for the duration. We'll do what we have to do. Rent a truck. Get it done."

They made eye contact. "I can't . . . won't ask you to do that."

"You don't have to," he sighed. "I get why you booted me out that awful weekend my son was here. But your daughter's right. The more I thought about it, the more I'm convinced that letting that scenario stand is just plain . . . *wrong*. I am not going to walk away from our relationship without a fight."

He waited for Maggie to object. When she didn't, Jake went on. "Holly told it like it is. My son is going to have to come to grips with reality, sooner or later. And destroying our relationship is not going to solve or expiate anything. I can't undo what happened to him or his mother, but I can do something about us. And that's exactly what I intend to do."

Silence greeted that pronouncement. In the near distance, Maggie saw her daughter threading her way through the tables in their direction. Something in Maggie or Jake's body language must have caught Holly's attention.

"Am I missing something?" Holly frowned.

Jake looked up at her with a knowing smile. "Your mother and I were just wondering what comes next," he said. "She suggested a stopover at her parish. Then maybe the three of us can tackle Lillian's apartment—scare up some boxes en route."

Holly didn't appear convinced that he had been entirely forthcoming, but let it pass. "I've taken off ten days," she said. "Compassionate leave. And yes, the semester has just started. But Mom, you're going to need help clearing both of Grams' apartments."

"Three sets of hands make quicker work," Jake nodded.

Maggie exhaled sharply, let herself be managed. The air outside the restaurant smelled of fall. Jake was driving. Maggie quickly gave him directions to the stone church on the hill. The doors around back were unlocked though the lights in the hallways and sanctuary were off.

While Maggie slid into a pew near the front of the sanctuary, Holly and Jake stayed behind to check out the office. Through her tears, the brilliant reds and blues and greens of the rose window once again danced and swayed to some unknown breeze.

Something about those disjointed medallions of glass kept calling out to her. She had spent endless hours on Sundays over the decades picking out the stories and symbols in those glowing panes—angels and chalices, orbs and doves, icons of the faithful over the centuries.

Silent and alone, dwarfed by the massive gray walls, Maggie reached inside her for fragments of that certitude. But the Holy to which she found herself clinging in the stillness after a lifetime of living was intensely personal, rooted in the now and not the hereafter. *I am with you, always . . . to the close of the age.*

Words came flooding back about the wisdom of dying to self in order to live more fully. Tough stuff, being prepared to lose everything we hold dear as a price tag for the examined life. The girl in her might still cry out for absolutes. But the woman she had become was learning to find hope and a measure of peace in embracing life's losses in the presence of some great, eternal Mystery.

Dust we are. And to that dust we all return. Gardeners knew that better than anyone.

Reluctantly, Maggie found herself trying on for size the role Lillian had left her. *Mater familias, matriarch, the older generation.* There was no escape. The inevitability of death became the ground from which new life grows, rooted deep in a new and ever changing reality.

If certitude existed, it was that life was meant to be lived. The only prayer that came to mind was to find the courage to do just that, as Lillian had, boldly and unafraid.

Maggie had no sense of time passing. Eventually the side door to the sanctuary swung open. Holly slid into the pew alongside her.

"I had forgotten how beautiful it is in here," Holly breathed.

"In an austere sort of way. I like to come here when life seems spiraling out of control. The silence has a way of getting me back on an even keel. Or at least close enough."

"As a kid those stone walls always reminded me of a medieval castle, full of secret passages and great halls that echoed with the sound of armor clanking." A look bordering on awe crept over Holly's face. "I half expected knights on horseback to turn up any minute."

Maggie smiled. "Their armor shining, I assume?"

"More like Don Quixote, as I remember it, a bit tarnished around the edges. But impressive all the same."

"Growing up," Maggie told her. "It happens to the best of us."

Mother and daughter embraced in the dim silence. Maggie let herself be held. After a while, her breathing steadied again. The tears that were on the verge of falling receded to that deep well of sadness inside her.

On the way out of the church they passed the so-called Hemingway window. Holly immediately caught the irony of the donor plaque attributed to the author's family. She couldn't help it, started to chuckle.

"You're right, of course," Maggie told her. "I doubt sincerely that Ernest himself ever darkened the door of the place."

Jake was waiting for them in the parking lot behind his SUV. The hatch and both back passenger doors of the vehicle were open. He was trying to consolidate a small mountain of paper cartons so that Holly had room in the back seat.

"I thought I would save us some time and make a box run," he told them. "The package store over on Emmet had a decent collection of wine cartons."

Doing what needed to be done, Maggie smiled. She wasn't surprised, but found herself touched nonetheless by his thoughtfulness.

Lillian's apartment seemed stuffy, unnaturally still. While Holly and Jake hauled up boxes from the car, Maggie threw open the windows and got a fan going. Crisp fall air quickly filled the tiny space.

"Clothes, shoes and linens—we can take them right over to the thrift store," she said when her daughter and Jake finished the last of the trips to the car for empty boxes. "Personal things we can box and label for sorting later. I found a black permanent marker in the desk"

Maggie had used the pen earlier in the summer to label masking tape strips on the dresser drawers. Lillian was starting to wear the same thing every day, complaining that she couldn't find anything.

"Makes sense," Holly said. She grabbed an empty box and began to tackle the shoes lined up neatly in pairs on the floor of Lillian's closet.

Jake set to work accumulating and weeding through a small assortment of books that were stashed around the apartment. "There's a library downstairs," he said. "If you can pick out the ones you intend to keep."

Maggie made short work of the task, moved on to drawers and shelves. Holly seemed to have the closet in hand. When in doubt, both Holly and Jake turned to Maggie for decisions that defied easy solutions. By late afternoon, the living room was heaped high with two mounds of boxes, one labeled Keep and the other Donation that would be headed wherever made the most sense.

Sweaty and moving a great deal slower than they had at the beginning, the three of them settled down on the sofa, the only piece of furniture still accessible, to survey their handiwork. Reduced to cardboard cartons, the measure of a life seemed even more finite than it had four hours ago.

At Jake's suggestion, he called several thrift stores and arranged for pickups. Commandeering wheeled carts from the senior center's cafeteria, the three of them began the cumbersome trek down the elevator to his SUV.

"We can make a run to the cottage with some of this stuff," Holly said wearily, "and then pick up Mom's car and my rental. It'll go quicker with three vehicles—mean fewer trips."

By sundown, the apartment was emptied of anything that required further sorting or that Maggie intended to keep. Too tired to unload their respective vehicles, the three of them sat out on the porch of the Aron cottage and watched the shadows deepen over the garden.

"I'm not even hungry," Maggie said after a while, "but we really ought to eat something."

"Pizza," Holly told her. "Delivered." Smartphone in hand, she had dialed the number of one of the places downtown that made deliveries.

Comfort food, Maggie thought. Solid and no-nonsense. And in the end, they found themselves hungrier than they thought. The cleanup afterward went quickly.

"First dibs on the shower," Holly called out as she finished wrapping the leftovers and stowing them in the fridge.

At loose ends, Jake and Maggie found themselves on opposite sides of the puzzle table. "Just what we need," she sighed, "more problems."

Jake laughed. "I see you moved on from license plates to a musical score. Though I'm not sure it's an improvement. There are an awful lot of sixteenth notes running around on those staffs."

"I thought of playing some snippets, using the picture on the box lid but never got around to it. I have absolutely no idea who the composer is—or if it's courtesy of more than one."

"Black and white with no shades of gray whatsoever. Appropriate under the circumstances, I guess," he told her.

"We . . . Holly and I couldn't have managed without you. I want to thank you for that."

He met her steady gaze. "No thanks necessary. I cared about Lillian too, you know. And you would have done the same for me."

Maggie blinked. Jake was giving her more credit than she likely deserved. She couldn't honestly say that she would have had the courage, made the first move—have shown up on Jake's doorstep at the first hint that he needed her.

"Somewhere along the line," she said evenly, "I lost my capacity to risk. And I'm not proud of that. If we want to be morbid about it, every new breath is taking a chance it will be our last."

"You're gutsier than you think." Jake smiled. "I will never forget you showing up in the front yard of the cottage sporting that spiky new haircut of yours—gorgeous by the way. Fearless, prepared to forget about what had always been and look at us—you and me—as people, as we are now. You were ready to see doors opening, not slamming loudly shut behind us."

Maggie laughed. "You make the summer sound far more intentional than it was."

"Whatever the motivation, I want . . . need you in my life, Maggie Aron. The few days apart—little more than a week, if you add them up—seemed like a lifetime. One I don't care to repeat any time soon."

Maggie chewed on her lip, bit back the tears. "I missed you too," she said softly.

With that Jake stood and moved around the table until he was standing directly in front of her. Gently, he coaxed her to her feet and into his arms.

It was as if they had never been apart. His mouth felt warm and insistent. Maggie felt the tension draining from her as she gave into his lingering embrace.

"Okay, you guys," a voice called from the kitchen doorway. "Time to get a room."

Startled, Maggie and Jake turned to see Holly standing there, a look of undisguised amusement on her face. She had snagged a bathrobe from her mother's closet. Her feet were bare and her hair was wrapped in a bath towel.

"Did you go easy on the hot water?" Maggie teased.

"Of course. At least next man up will have enough. I can't guarantee the same for three-on-a-match."

Jake laughed. "When it comes to the prospect of cold showers, I guess it's up to me to volunteer."

Maggie wriggled out of his arms and headed toward the kitchen. When she passed her daughter, she gave her a playful hug. "I can remember a time when you would have used every last drop."

Holly winced. "Ah, adolescence. What can I say?" She wandered over to the puzzle table and promptly fitted a piece into place.

Jake shook his head. "An expert," he told her.

"Beginner's luck," Holly shrugged.

The last thing Maggie saw as she turned the corner and headed toward the shower was the sight of her daughter and Jake with their heads bent over the table. Their laughter followed her down the hallway.

After an uneventful night, the three of them took their time getting started next morning. Maggie got on the phone and contacted the local memorial garden, made tentative arrangements for her mother's ashes. The boxes from Lillian's apartment were still stashed in the three vehicles where they had left them, ready to transport downstate.

"We're going to be strung out along the interstate like ducks headed for the pond," Holly lamented as the three of them stood together on the cottage porch, looking out toward the alley.

Maggie laughed. "Makes more sense anyway for you at this point to fly back to Arizona from Lansing," she said. "Not Traverse City. So regardless, you would need to have the rental with you."

The trip to the East Lansing suburb where Maggie and Lillian lived clocked at a tad over two hundred miles. Post Labor Day during the week, the traffic on the northern stretch was thin. Traveling at the rear of the pack gave Maggie relative leisure to watch the landscape unfolding outside the windows.

She knew the drill, had fled along this same route after the disastrous weekend with Jake's son. *Days, barely a week—a lifetime ago.* Rolling pine and hardwood forests gradually gave way to flat fields of soybeans and corn. Traffic increased along with the population density. By the time they hit the Lansing area it was approaching noon. The three of them stopped for lunch at a fast-food place at a convenient exit.

"Why don't we leave our overnight bags at the homestead?" Maggie suggested. "And then head over to Mom's apartment."

"Sounds good," Holly told her. "Then we can take our time figuring out how to deal with Grams' stuff. It's bound to be more complicated than the Petoskey move. That place up north was furnished."

This last stretch of the drive was Maggie's home turf. She took the lead. Jake punched the address of the homestead into his smartphone but managed to keep up as she navigated the maze of shortcuts no GPS would ever suggest. By the time Jake parked and cut the engine, Maggie and Holly were already heading up the front walk to the homestead with their overnight bags.

Maggie hadn't given any thought to what Jake might make of the place. *Deja vu all over again,* she winced. Except this time isn't wasn't a case of Mark trying to reconstruct his father's childhood based on his first sight of the Faland cottage. It was Jake himself trying to make sense of *her* story confronted with the parade of elegant white porch columns spread out across the front of the homestead, an impression of understated wealth.

Things aren't always what they seem, Maggie could have told him. Grama Aron's decision to add on to the farmhouse and take in boarders, followed by Lillian's later sale of the acreage for development were the only things that saved the family financially over the years. Lillian never grew tired of reminding Maggie of that fact.

"Plain folks, the Arons," Lillian said. "And never forget it."

Widowed young, Lillian had inherited the sprawling two-story farmhouse after her own parents died—which is how in turn Maggie wound up spending her high school years in that imposing relic from another era. When Lillian sold off the farmland piecemeal to suburban developers, the neighborhood quickly sprouted with a whole community of high-end single family homes.

The cycle of generations repeated itself. Newly widowed herself, Maggie sold the small Craftsman bungalow in which she had raised her own family and moved into the homestead. Lillian went into a senior living center nearby. The downsizing that went on as mother and daughter made the transition was chiseled in stone in Maggie's memory. So much history in those walls.

To have explained all that would have smacked of defensiveness, Maggie decided. And to Jake's credit, he didn't say much except to marvel over the powder-blue water silk wallpaper in the foyer. While Holly headed upstairs to the attic to case out the storage situation there, Maggie gave him a quick tour of the downstairs.

"Out of another century, I'll admit," she told him. "And pretty much the way Mom left the place when she moved into an apartment at the senior center. Dated, to put it mildly."

Jake flashed a wry smile. "I'm no one to talk. My own sense of decor stopped somewhere back there around Mid-Century Modern."

"I simply didn't have a major overhaul in me when I moved in here." Maggie said. "My son and Holly have told me from the get-go this place looks like a bottomless money-pit—urged me to buy a condo. Better late than never. The housing market is pretty good right now—I've decided to bite the bullet and put this place on the market."

Jake's eyebrow arched. "And then?"

"I know, I know," Maggie sighed. "A lot on my plate right now. I thought I would bank the cash for the moment—buy some time to figure things out. Maybe down the line invest in a condo near Holly. Michigan winters don't get any easier"

"Figure out what?" Holly said as she joined them in the living room in front of the massive fireplace.

Maggie told her about her decision to sell. "About time," Holly said. "There's sentiment and then there's sentiment. Nobody but nobody lives like this any more."

"First things first then," Maggie said. "If I'm going to sell, there's no point in hauling anything from Mom's apartment over here. There are some storage units about a mile from here. We can just stash her treasures there. And when I downsize this place, I'll just combine the stuff until I know where next . . ."

"Make's sense," Holly told her. "Though downsizing won't be a walk in the park. I saw a whole heap of boxes up there in the attic—"

"Including a bunch labeled *Holly's Toys.* Time to claim 'em. Or out they go."

Holly looked chagrined. "Oops . . . "

"Well said. Trust me, I've moved the darn things for the last time," her mother said.

Jake just laughed.

On that note, the three of them piled into their respective vehicles and made a beeline for Lillian's apartment in the assisted living complex. "Over-furnished, that's for sure," Holly grimaced as they stood inside the front door trying to get a measure of the job ahead.

"Most of the stuff you see is headed straight to the Hospice thrift shop," Maggie told her.

"Some of Gram's pieces are priceless." Holly's voice sounded wistful.

"Okay, good—they're yours. No way would Tony want me to ship any of this to Hawaii. My brother already claimed whatever he wanted back when Mom was downsizing last time."

Jake wisely seemed to have taken a measure of the situation, was looking for the exits. "Time to get out of the line of fire," he chuckled wanly from the safety of the apartment door. "While you two reconnoiter, I can make another box run—"

Maggie laughed. "Smart man. By the time you get back, we'll have a plan."

The bedroom of Lillian's apartment quickly became Ground Zero for everything that fell into the 'keeper' category. Holly tore into organizing and boxing her grandmother's clothes, anything meant for donation, and hauling it into the living room. Maggie sorted out jewelry and collections of old photographs, any keepsakes that merited saving.

Wrapped in tissue in a box from a long-defunct department store, Holly found a fur muff that Lillian's husband Benjamin had given her the first year of their marriage. In a yellowing envelope, Maggie unearthed a braid from her first haircut as a girl. The fine, chestnut strands sun-streaked with blond were tied in a pink bow with a blue thread pattern running through it.

Now and again, tears welled up in Maggie's eyes as she handled the precious relics from her family's past. What to do with it all would come to her later. Right now, the goal was simple. Give away as much as possible. Grieve the loss and move on.

The value of most of the objects lay only in the memories behind them, whether the grainy photo of Lillian on a Sunday morning in suit and gloves headed for church or the intricately embroidered caftan she had picked up on a trip to the Holy Land decades ago. On such things price tags are meaningless, letting go was far easier said than done.

When Holly started to flag, Maggie kept reminding her daughter of the steep by-the-day rental charges in assisted living. "A powerful incentive to keep going, kiddo!"

The day passed, measured in tired backs and arms that ached from lifting and stacking boxes. Two more days and the job was done. Jake rented a truck and together he, Holly and Maggie hauled the boxes to storage that were destined for further sorting or ultimate division among family members. A quick series of phone calls located several thrift stores of local charities that agreed to pick up what remained.

"Life reduced to a pile of furnishings, pots and pans and shoes with the price tags still intact in some cases," Maggie sighed. She and her daughter had just made one last run through the apartment looking for any treasures they had missed.

"Enough to make minimalists of us all," Holly said.

Jake smiled sympathetically. "All in all, we done good," he said. "I would never have thought we could make such short work of this."

"Thanks to you," Maggie told him.

"I would say, my pleasure. But then putting the past to rest is never fun."

True enough. Visibly worn out, Holly wearily shifted her plane reservations to fly out of the Lansing airport next morning. Compassionate leave from her teaching job would be running out soon enough.

Maggie insisted as a kind of last hurrah to treat them all to dinner at a well known restaurant near the family home. It was a strange experience, fraught with laughter, tears and long periods of silence.

Holly drove herself and the rental car to the airport. Jake stayed with Maggie who insisted while she was at it to engage a realtor.

"No time like the present," she told him. "Before I lose my nerve."

The agent's tour of the homestead was a stark reminder that all their hard work, the packing and downsizing of Lillian's apartments, was only the beginning. "You're sure you're okay with this?" Jake wondered afterward.

He and Maggie stood alone together on the lawn looking at the homestead and the *For Sale* sign out front. Those seven words in bold type had a non-negotiable air of finality about them.

"Fine," Maggie told him bluntly. "This is long overdue."

Her bravado didn't ring entirely true. Mortified, Maggie knew Jake must have caught the tremor in her voice on that last disclaimer. He wound an arm around her shoulder, the universal silent gesture of support when words fail.

"Gutsy," he said finally.

"Stupid timing . . . but necessary," Maggie grimaced. "I'll worry about the great throw 'em out and adding my stuff to Mom's in storage later—if and when the place sells. Right now, all I want is a good night's sleep. And to get out of Dodge."

Which is how things unfolded. Crack of dawn, Maggie and Jake were on the road again, retracing their route north toward Little Traverse Bay.

Jake took the lead. The silence was deafening as Maggie fought to maintain a safe distance behind his mercifully spacious SUV that had served them so well over the past few days. They stopped for lunch in Gaylord, on the home stretch.

Rounding the last hill on the outskirts of Petoskey, the panorama of Little Traverse Bay spread out before them under sullen skies. The water was a steely gray. On the horizon, the forested hills around the ski resort resorts north and east of town had begun to shed their leaves in spots.

When Maggie pulled into the alley behind the cottage and parked, Jake had beaten her to it. He was standing outside the gate looking toward the garden beyond. When he turned her direction, his face was like a thundercloud.

Maggie felt a knot tightening around her heart. She climbed out of the front seat, started to shut the door behind her.

"*No! Don't . . . ,*" Jake said sharply, then softened his tone. "Maggie, sweetheart, you are not going to want to see this . . ."

As she joined him at the gate, the sight that greeted her all but sent her to her knees with shock. She clutched at the pickets of the fence to steady herself. "Dear God . . . !"

Where her carefully tended garden had stood, only scattered stubble and rough mounds and clods of bare dirt remained. This wasn't winterizing. The garden was simply *gone*, plants and roots and all.

Random slabs that had marked the path through the perennials lay scattered and upended. And behind that wasteland, on the wall of the porch, someone had scrawled in bold black brush strokes a series of ragged swastikas. The message and intent was clear.

"Who in the hell could have done something like this?" Jake persisted.

Maggie gasped. "I have . . . no idea . . . "

The words were barely out of her mouth when she recognized the likely cause of all this. "The blog," she breathed. It had to be.

In a halting voice, Maggie told Jake how she had posted comments about diversity and inclusiveness on the community's blog. With it had come an impassioned plea for tolerance.

"I never dreamed it would lead to something like . . . *this*."

Dry-eyed and in shock, Maggie felt the ground slipping out from under her. Jake reacted in a heartbeat. Stifling a gasp of alarm, he pulled her into his arms.

Death. Loss. Their ugly presence surfaced where Maggie least expected it. *The loving work of three generations was gone—vanished in an instant.*

Maggie leaned hard against him or she would have lost her footing entirely. She felt herself thrust back into childhood, the gentle pressure of her mother Lillian's hand moving against her back to comfort her. Only now that hand was Jake's. Distraught himself, he grasped at anything that would get Maggie to stop shaking.

"I'm so sorry," he told her over and over in a strangled whisper. Oh God, Maggie—we will get through this. We will make this right." Nonsense, and they both knew it under the circumstances.

Her grief was beyond tears. Eventually on an anguished sigh, Maggie wriggled free, forced herself to stand on her own. Her head ached. Like a sleepwalker awaking from a bad dream, she turned back to survey the desolation. She had not imagined it.

These were not the actions of hate-peddling strangers. Behind this vandalism was the venom of someone she likely knew—a neighbor or even a friend, a child or grandchild who heard too much over the years, damage calculated to inflict the most emotional pain and harm possible. The Aron garden had survived, lovingly tended, for a century. It had personally grounded Maggie throughout her lifetime. That garden had served as her compass in unsettling times. Its loss was immeasurable.

"What or who would . . . I can't even imagine what it would take for someone to do this," Jake said quietly.

Maggie recoiled. "The damage speaks for itself," she said.

"What are you going to do?"

She drew in a breath. For a split-second the landscape—trees and pickets, the gingerbread of the cottage gable—seemed to be spinning wildly out of control. Maggie's answer came as a desperate prayer.

"Replant," she said dully.

"The police ought to know about this," Jake told her. "This is a hate crime . . . by any definition."

"It won't change anything."

Jake's voice was hard. "*Still*—whoever did this shouldn't get by with it."

Maggie had moved beyond him through the gate. She wound up standing ankle-deep in the loamy soil, looking around her in lingering disbelief.

Gone. The word kept repeating itself in her head.

"We really shouldn't be disturbing the scene," Jake said quietly. "Or at least keep our footprints to a minimum."

Maggie just looked at him, kept going. From a mound of dirt just inside the fence, she retrieved a broken stem from what had been the massive stand of hollyhocks. The seed heads looked all the world like dried and weather-creased figs torn from a Christmas fruit basket. It would take years if not a decade to replicate what had been growing here.

"Anyone who would do this . . . I'm not convinced you're safe here," Jake said after a while.

Maggie just looked at him. "For decades we never even locked the doors around here," she said.

"Locks or no locks," Jake's jaw tightened, "I am *not* going to let you stay alone"

Maggie managed a shaky laugh. "Is that an order?"

"A proposal," Jake told her—clearly making it up as he went along. "These cottages will all shut down in a matter of weeks. With the homestead on the market in Lansing, you could be homeless sooner rather than later. I'm rattling around in a house way too big for me in Wisconsin . . . not the most idyllic place to spend the winter. But if you insist on keeping this place, we could come back up here in spring, try to put the garden back together."

Jake's voiced hardened. "Correct that—starting *now*. I'll make a hardware run now for house paint. At least it's still warm enough to get rid of that *obscenity* scrawled on the porch wall."

"You don't have to—"

"Yes. I do," he told her. "Whatever I do or don't feel about this place right now, I love you, Maggie Aron. And I am not about to let you deal with this *brutality* alone."

At that, Jake knelt down, took a handful of soil and let it run slowly through his fingers. Maggie stared in wonderment,. This from someone with a self-professed un-green thumb.

"Can you even find nursery stock this time of year?" he said thoughtfully.

"Some maybe. End of the season stuff. It's a huge risk of course, transplanting this late in the growing season. Some of the independent nurseries would have all but closed up shop by now when it comes to perennials."

Jake stood up and met her bleak gaze. "What have we got to lose?" he said.

What, indeed. Overwhelmed at how vulnerable, violated Maggie felt, she didn't protest.

Jake sprang into action. While Maggie watched helplessly from the safety of the wicker loveseat on the porch, Jake unloaded their luggage from his SUV and set everything inside the kitchen door of the cottage. "We'll need the room," he said. "Those big box stores on the highway should have enough to get started. Paint. Plants."

As an afterthought before they left, he grabbed his smartphone and snapped a series of photos of the porch and the garden, documenting the damage. Maggie sat in silence as he drove them out to the State Police Post. Though the day shift had already clocked out by then, an officer on desk duty took their statement.

"A hate crime," Jake said as he showed the officer the images on his phone.

"Looks like it." The officer uploaded the photos into a computer file, which took a while.

"We'll send out investigators first thing in the morning," the man said. "Meanwhile, don't touch a thing. If you have to go through the scene into the cottage, keep footprints at a minimum."

Jake nodded. "Understood."

Back in the car, Maggie sat stone-faced staring out the windshield. When they passed the turnoff to the cottage, she finally couldn't hold back any longer.

"Jake, you heard the officer," she said bleakly. "We aren't going to be able to replant if they . . . when the police map out a crime scene, it could take weeks, months even to be allowed—"

His hands flexed on the steering wheel. "Trust me," he told her, jaw tight. "We are going to replant."

Her misgivings were dead-on. Pickings were slim when it came to finding nursery stock. The plants on sale weren't the sturdiest, the variety limited. Depressing, but Jake coaxed Maggie into selecting enough to make a start.

The trunk full of black pots, undercoat and white outdoor paint, they returned to the cottage. Clouds of sandy dust rose as they made repeated trips from Jake's SUV to the porch with their purchases. As the officer requested, they were careful to limit themselves to a solitary narrow path through the wasteland.

Once inside the cottage again, Maggie sank down into a chair in the kitchen to catch her breath. The magnitude of the day's events, the surrealness of everything that had happened finally began to register. A profound sense of dis-ease left her silent and shaken.

"Take-out," Jake searched her face thoughtfully. "When in doubt keep it simple, right? You seem exhausted. I can go alone this once, pick up some wings, salad, maybe some vino. Whoever did this is likely to lay low for the moment—you should be safe enough."

Maggie looked at him blankly. He was right, of course. But it took every bit of willpower not to give in to her fear at the prospect of staying behind alone in the silent and empty cottage. What she had unleashed was so monstrous that it had sent her world spinning off its axis. She could count on nothing but Jake's ultimate return.

As she waited in the gathering darkness of the kitchen, Maggie strained to spot his SUV picking its way down the alley. Her thoughts swirled and rustled like the dry leaves drifting down outside the kitchen window.

They could and would replant the garden she had nurtured the better part of her adult life. Paths could be reset. Paint could cover the symbols of hate that desecrated the cottage walls.

But for all that, Maggie knew that some things are not so easily repaired. And simple trust was one of them. The community she had embraced and loved for a lifetime, idyllic and epitomizing the kinder, gentler time of her childhood, had ceased to exist.

Or had it? A nagging voice kept whispering in her head. There was an uglier, sadder possibility. Had the Brigadoon she treasured in her heart all these years ever been truly real or merely a fantasy that for once and for all had vanished into the mists?

The girl with the cornrows. The professor from India—Jake's friend who was made to feel 'her kind' wasn't welcome. And from deep within Maggie's own memory banks, a solitary image from childhood kept cropping up, unbidden. It was of that elderly neighbor woman those many years ago who had so solemnly speculated about the origins of the name Aron.

A Jewish name—Aron, the woman had wondered out loud. As if somehow pronouncing judgement. Once sown, the seeds of prejudice can bear ugly fruit when and how we least expect it.

A member of the ASTERACEAE family, asters bloom deep into fall, long after most perennials have gone dormant for the season. Their name comes from the Greek for 'star-like'. Hungary's Revolution of 1918 was named the Aster Revolution because protestors wore the flower as a symbol of their solidarity. The showy flowerheads are actually tightly packed clusters of multiple tubular blooms.

Putting Down Roots

Maggie slept the night, but fitfully. The sun was barely up when a knocking on the kitchen door of the cottage woke her. Curled in the circle of Jake's arms under the winter-weight crazy quilt her grandmother had sewn so many decades ago, Maggie stirred, immediately alert.

"Jake, there's someone at the door . . ."

He groaned softly in protest, sat up. "Stay put," he growled. "I'll get it."

The floor must have been cold underfoot. He made short work of shrugging on his jeans and a fisherman's knit sweater draped over the footboard of the bed. Still barefoot, he headed for the bedroom door.

The knock was more insistent now. "On my way," he called out.

Maggie sat up in bed. From down the hall in the kitchen, she heard the muffled sound of voices. With the chill in the room, this was no time for indecisiveness. Scrambling on tiptoe, she retrieved a furry robe from behind the bedroom door. As she passed the wall mirror, the face reflected back at her looked wan, sleep-drugged.

The kitchen was empty and the porch door open. Out in the yard, in the wreckage of what had been her grandmother's garden, a uniformed state trooper and Jake were surveying the damage. Armed with a camera, the officer was zeroing in on patches of dirt along the picket fence.

"Footprints," Jack called out when he noticed Maggie standing on the porch.

Their own had blotted out any evidence left along the direct path from the gate to the porch steps. But apparently along the edges, the intruder or intruders had left tracks behind.

"Small shoe sizes," the trooper said. "Two different pair. Kids or most likely teenagers from the look of it."

Eventually he turned his attention to the graffiti on the porch wall. Once again the shutter on the officer's camera clicked repeatedly. The hateful symbols well documented, the officer and Jake started back up the porch steps in Maggie's direction.

"I'll put on the coffee pot," she said.

"No need," the officer told her. "I don't want to put you out—"

"We could sure use it," Maggie told him. "It's no trouble at all to make an extra cup."

Tired as she had been, from force of habit Maggie had set up the coffee machine, raring to go, the night before. To get it brewing took no time at all. Jake and Maggie sat side-by-side, opposite the officer at the kitchen table. Taking notes had gone digital, she noticed, as with just about everything else in their lives.

"Do you have any idea why or when all this happened?" the officer wondered.

"Sometime in the last three days. My mom passed away and we've been down in Lansing. The garden was fine when we left."

The officer nodded. "Sorry to hear about your mother. It couldn't have been pleasant coming back to this."

"I shouldn't have been surprised," Maggie told him. She shared her internet posting on the community blog, weighing in on the side of inclusiveness and diversity. She sensed at once that the officer was well aware of the tensions in the community over the issue.

"Do you have any suspicions who might have done this?"

"No." Maggie's brow tightened as she found herself returning to the conversation with a neighbor a lifetime ago that first had raised the ugly specter of anti-Semitism. To mention it now seemed patently unfair. "Though it makes sense to suspect kids, teens in the neighborhood anyway who might have heard their parents sounding off about the controversy."

"They used one of those small electric tillers from the look of it," the officer told her. "You have that electric outlet on the porch. I find it hard to believe no one noticed strangers in the yard."

"It's off-season," Maggie said. "Most of the closest neighbors have been gone for weeks, since Labor Day certainly. It's altogether possible that someone could have done this undetected."

"Or maybe passersby thought you hired someone to do a job."

"Not likely. Everyone knew that garden was growing there since my grandmother owned the cottage."

The officer nodded. "It must have been spectacular. Do you have photos—that would help."

Tears started in Maggie's eyes. She didn't trust herself to speak. Her fists were clenching and unclenching in her lap.

"Yes, it was. One-of-a-kind," Jake chimed in quickly. He reached out and took Maggie's hand in his, drew it onto his lap as they sat there together. "And yes, we do have photos. I'll see you get them."

"You're right too on another score," he told the officer. "Whoever did this knew exactly what they were doing. I suspect an adult had to have some part in this—at the very least."

"And the swastikas?" the officer speculated.

Maggie hesitated, found her voice at last. "My last name supposedly has Jewish roots," she said. "And I did talk about religious diversity in my online post."

The officer eyes hardened. "So we're dealing with a hate crime then, pure and simple."

"It appears so," Jake chimed in.

Maggie sat clutching her coffee mug in one hand. Jake was still holding the other one in a gentle show of support. "So what now?" she forced herself to ask.

The officer shifted in his seat. "Canvas the neighborhood. Try to figure out who has a rototiller. This was likely a crime of opportunity carried out, I suspect, in broad daylight. I can't imagine someone renting a tiller to pull a stunt like this. And if this had been done by an outsider, it probably would have drawn notice."

"Are they likely, whoever did this . . . do we need to worry that something like this might happen again . . .?" Maggie's voice trembled, broke. She felt Jake's hand tighten around her own.

The officer hesitated. "No guarantees, but I would say it's

unlikely the perpetrators will make a return appearance. Especially if they've spotted my cruiser in the alley. What they did the first time was sufficiently . . . vicious that they would have gotten whatever was bugging them out of their systems."

Jake nodded, looked relieved. "My thought as well."

"That said," the officer told them, "I realize folks around here aren't big on locks. But I would advise you to get in the habit of closing up tight from here on in."

"You're saying it could have been worse?" Jake said.

"Somebody out there is darn angry and feels relatively safe lashing out," the officer said carefully. "I would guess they knew your schedule, knew you were out of town. Better safe than sorry."

Maggie's voice was low. "And the likelihood of finding out who did it?"

"Probably not too good," the officer said slowly. "We've . . . there have been incidents like this before in recent months, going back several years actually. Some folks aren't shy about resorting to violence when it suits them. And afterward, they are used to stonewalling. Sad, but true."

The officer stood, took one last sip from the mug Maggie had given him. "Thanks for the coffee—for being so helpful."

Jake stood and extended his hand. "You'll keep us posted?"

The man nodded.

"You have photos," Maggie said quietly. "Can we deal with the garden, the damage to the porch?"

"Of course," the officer told her. "I have everything I need at this point. Do whatever you have to do."

Jake followed the trooper to the door. Maggie watched them go, her two hands clutching her now-empty coffee mug.

"Thank you," she called out to the officer's retreating back.

He turned and looked back at her. "No problem, Ma'am," he said. "Sorry for your loss."

Awkward, she thought. Genuinely disturbed by what he had seen.

Maggie heard Jake and the officer's voices disappearing in the direction of the gate. After a significant pause, she heard the sound of an engine turning over and the sound of tires navigating the uneven surface of the alley.

When Jake didn't immediately return, she got to her feet and headed out on the porch. On his way back to the cottage, Jake had begun to unearth and level the flagstones that had been randomly strewn around the bare dirt. From the look of it, he had remembered exactly where the path had been.

"You've started," she said.

Startled Jake looked up and met her quizzical gaze. "If you tell me where to place the pots we came up with, I'll dig in the plants as well."

Maggie looked down at the nursery stock at her feet. "Let me think about it. But I'll get dressed first."

While she was gone, Jake kept busy leveling and setting the flagstones in place. Maggie had grabbed a pair of jeans herself and a faded sweatshirt emblazoned with the motto, "Gardeners Find All the Best Dirt".

The motto turned out to have a basis in fact. Desolate as the landscape of the yard appeared, the earth itself was rich and loose, welcoming. Maggie stifled her rising sense of despair. With a black nursery pot in each hand, she headed out into the empty terrain.

"Asters over here," she said as she set the two pots down to the left of the gate. "They're tall. The hollyhock seed heads over on the right side won't do much the first season. But at least from the alley, we can get some height going to conceal how bare the rest of the space might look."

Jake headed her way with a shovel in hand he had retrieved from the cottage utility closet. "Marching orders are helpful," he admitted with a wry hint of a smile. "Otherwise, I haven't a clue."

Maggie laughed though there wasn't really any humor in it. "Late in the season like this, everything is likely to be pot-bound. Despite folk wisdom on the subject, it is not a good idea to rough up the roots too much. Unkink them a bit around the edges, but the less we disturb them, the better the chance of minimizing transplant shock."

By way of demonstration, she maneuvered one of the pots on its side, tapped carefully on the plastic as she turned it in a full circle. When she tried to lift the plant from the container, it easily came loose—dirt and roots and all. As she had predicted, the spidery tangle of roots all but absorbed every bit of dirt in the pot.

"Placement?" Jake said.

Maggie used the empty pot to make an indentation in the ground to guide his spade. In a few quick thrusts he had created a hole roughly the size of the root ball.

"A bit larger on all sides," Maggie advised. "Give the roots room to spread out."

He nodded. "Gotcha."

Armed with Maggie's quickie lesson in Transplanting 101, the two of them systematically worked their way through the plants on the porch. When they were finished, they collected the black pots and stashed them neatly in two stacks against the porch. On a sigh, he wrapped an arm around Maggie as the two of them stood looking out over their handiwork. In that vast space, a dozen-plus perennials barely made a dent.

Tears sprang up but Maggie forced them back. "This is going to be a long-haul proposition. And given the randomness of the plants available, we can't ever hope to replicate Grandmother's garden. Maybe . . .," she hesitated, "it might make sense to seed some of this in grass for the time being. Buy us time to let at least part of the garden fill in."

"No way," Jake said curtly. "We'll make a plant run every day until we close up for the season. If we do what we can now and come back at it hard in spring, we can . . . and *will* do this !"

Maggie managed a weak smile. His choice of words was telling. The promises of 'us' and a coming season.

They dug in the contents of a small forest of black pots over the next few days. With each and every one, Maggie kept willing those shelf-stressed, rootbound plants to struggle—to reach out to one another, to fill the emptiness in which they found themselves.

With a sinking heart, she could identify with the magnitude of the task ahead of each and every one of those fragile perennials. The garden she had inherited and loved for a lifetime had ceased to exist. By default this ground was now hers and hers alone to abandon or nurture, painful and overwhelming no matter what she chose to do.

In a microcosm, Maggie felt herself planted in similar alien territory. The community she loved had become something else entirely, something far darker. But then as Jake reminded her daily, she wasn't

301

facing that bleak and uncertain future alone. However frail, that tendril of hope sustained her as she and Jake scoured the surrounding area for anything green and growing that could help them attempt to replace the irreplaceable.

Rootbound. She had been there. No more.

While she rocked peacefully on her porch, hatefulness had been spreading like wild mustard or bindweed through her supposed Eden. Tackling it even tentatively had brought down a storm of ugliness that had left her world in tatters.

There was no going back. Evil only thrives, she told herself, when those who know otherwise choose to do nothing. The author of that bit of wisdom eluded her. It was up to her to make those brave words her own. The time for denial and tolerance of intolerance had passed.

"Burke. Edmund Burke," Jake told her when she quizzed him on the subject. "An Irish philosopher and politician who protested against religious discrimination during the time of both the American and French revolutions. Appropriate as sources go—considering."

It was mid-morning. For the umpteenth time, they had run out of plant stock. "I couldn't have handled this without you," she told Jake quietly as she surveyed the results of their labors. Her voice quavered, fell silent.

Jake made eye contact. "I love you, Maggie Aron."

She recognized the quiet truth of it, the reality of what came next. "I love you, too," she said.

And that simply, the ground-rules changed. Love can't undo what hatred or violence might accomplish, Maggie told herself grimly. But it is the only thing that enables any sane human being to survive it.

"We still have . . . what? Several weeks until the powers that be shut things down for the season?" Jake said. "Time enough to keep making a dent here. I checked the weather forecast. It should be warm enough by mid-day to apply the first coat of primer on the porch. It will likely take several to cover completely. By week's end, we could finish the job."

"But first, breakfast," she told him. "I don't know about you, but I'm starved."

"No scrounging. We're eating out, my treat. Pick your poison."

Maggie laughed. "Junk food. Zero social merit or nutritional value for that matter. But fast."

He looked down at her with a smile. The look on Jake's face told her everything Maggie needed to know. Her mother's death, putting her family home on the market, the terrible loss of her garden—none of it had the power to derail her life.

She was not alone. They were in this together. To live, like creating a garden, was not a destination. It was a journey.

Maggie's confidence did not always prevail. The mere prospect of filling that terrible void with new life at times proved overwhelming. But whenever she found herself breaking down, sitting on the bare dirt with tears rolling down her face, Jake would coax her gently to her feet.

"We can do this," he said. "But the clock is ticking. We need to keep at it as quickly as we can before the season ends."

The two weeks flew past, measured in blistered palms and aching backs. There was no time to think about the future. There was only the now and making sure each and every perennial they planted had the best chance of survival. When a few passersby saw what had happened, learned what Maggie and Jake were doing, they returned with root stock themselves—day lilies and hosta, phlox and astilbe.

"Almost enough to restore a guy's faith in humanity," Maggie said wanly as she and Jake added these contributions, sometimes from absolute strangers, to the mix of plants.

On the last weekend before they had to vacate the cottage for the season, Maggie finally mustered the courage to wonder out loud, *What next*. They were out among the plants, staking up and mulching, whatever was called for. Jake took his time answering her.

"I know the realtor in Lansing has had showings on the homestead. Most likely it will sell sooner than later. But after the downsizing of Lillian's apartments, I can't even imagine your going back there—not until you have to, if and when the place actually sells. You were wise not to rush into thinking beyond that, where and how to invest the profits from the—"

"In a word, homeless," Maggie chuckled softly.

Jake winced. "I wouldn't blame you either for forgetting or ignoring my solution with all that's happened since," he told her. "And Wisconsin winters can be brutal, to say the least. But I hope despite that you'll consider my offer, move in with me. Think through your options without a gun at your head. The future will be what it will be . . ."

Jake was watching her intently through that calm laying out of possible options. Maggie met his steady gaze. The tight knot building inside her seemed to loosen a little.

"You're sure . . .?"

Jake's jaw tightened. "We're too old for games, Maggie."

She nodded.

"Are you telling me . . . I hope that's a Yes," he said evenly.

"Yes."

An outrush of breath told her Jake had been far more anxious about her response than he was letting on. "So . . .what now . . .?"

"Most of my winter wardrobe is downstate. But I just can't bear another trip down there. I'll scrape together as much warm clothing as I can from the closets in the cottage," she said. "Monday morning we have to be out of here. Though Lord help those poor plants once we're gone. I hope it rains."

It did. All weekend. And at the start of another day of gray and vaguely threatening skies, the two of them crammed their luggage into Jake's SUV. Last thing in the world Maggie wanted was to make the drive across the U.P. alone. They stowed Jake's cottage car and her Scion in a garage they rented together in Petoskey and headed north toward the Straits.

The fall color season had peaked early. Leaves were showering down red and gold with every raw gust out of the north. Jake got the SUV's heater going to take the chill out of the air. As they traversed the dunes area west of the Bridge, only a narrow strip of beach separated the scenic two-lane road from Lake Michigan. Flowing sheets of sand swirled and eddied across the asphalt.

Maggie shivered. "Winter's coming."

Jake shot a quick glance her direction. "Is that a bad thing?"

She hesitated. "Gardens go fallow. And after all that's happened, I guess I for one need down time to pull myself together."

"Being stuck at my place for weeks on end could drive us crazy . . . cabin fever on a grand scale. Or it could be good for us both," he said, eyes fixed on the road ahead. The crosswinds were making it hard to hold the wheel. "No distractions."

Maggie fell silent, her thoughts roiling like the wind-driven grains of beach sand encroaching upon the roadway. Truth was, she hadn't the faintest notion where she was headed or what she expected or hoped or wanted the future to hold. Much less, what living day-in and day-out with Jake Faland would entail.

She loved this man—his dogged focus on the journey. And she knew in her heart of hearts that those feelings were reciprocated. Beyond that she saw only the trees swaying and bending in the wind.

Change, she thought. The word summed up not just the risk, but all the pain and heartache of what she was leaving behind her. She tried not to worry for those tender shoots and stems in her newly planted cottage garden. Their survival was by no means certain.

But even in the face of all that danger and doubt, she and Jake had forged ahead. *A lot going for them*, she admitted.

The subtle swaying of the vehicle became hypnotic. Sleep had been in short supply the past two weeks. Eyelids heavy, Maggie felt herself drifting off despite the occasional buffeting of sideways gusts.

No dark dreams intruded. After all that had happened, the grief and loss on all fronts in her life, Maggie embraced the respite for what it was. She felt at peace.

§§§§§

The trek across the semi-deserted southern shoreline of the Upper Peninsula has a mathematical preciseness about it. Eighty-plus miles from Petoskey to Manistique are followed by a series of fifty mile stretches. Manistique to Escanaba. Escanaba to Marinette-Menominee. Menominee to the turn-off to the Fox River Valley area.

In between comes a change in Time Zones. Now and then the roadway wanders inland whenever a peninsula juts out into the Great Lake Michigami. Road signs become milestones of sorts. There's the exit to Tahquamenon Falls and the Big Spring Kitchitikipi. A row of quaint cottages, no longer in use, mark the exit for Bailey's Crossing.

In Marinette, Maggie felt the SUV slow before turning sharply to the right. She woke to find Jake easing the vehicle into a parking spot

305

in front of a landmark Scandinavian restaurant that had been a fixture downtown for several generations.

"What's up?" she yawned and stretched, trying to rouse herself. "Sorry . . . I haven't been much company."

Jake smiled. "Lunch. I don't know about you but I'm starving."

"Makes sense. Stiff as we are from all that digging and hauling, if we don't un-kink once in a while, we may wind up permanently in fetal position."

At that he laughed out loud. "I'm trying to picture that."

"And I can share the driving too," she said. "For what that's worth."

"I may take you up on it," he told her as they headed for the door of the restaurant. "But first, I'm thinking pannkakor and lingonberries. Maybe salmon if we're lucky."

"Scandinavian?" Maggie wondered.

"You betcha." Jake laughed. "Chalk it up to my Brit ancestors' brush with the Vikings back in the day."

It was past the lunch hour. Any rush that might have transpired had come and gone. Only one booth was still occupied with what appeared to be locals caught up in an intense debate over some kind of business proposal.

The Swedish sampler caught Jake's eye. Meatballs, potato sausage and mini potato dumpling served with rutabagas and cole slaw. Maggie settled on potato sausage with lingonberries.

"Ethnic as you can get," Maggie laughed. "Whose heritage, I'm not so sure."

"These places get harder and harder to find," Jake smiled. "I've always gone off the beaten track to find 'em when I get the chance."

"So do I."

"Put a checkmark in the 'Compatibility' column," he teased.

Maggie flushed. "You took care of that list long ago, trust me," she told him. "I'm not sure where I would be or what shape I would be in if you hadn't showed up after Mom died. It's been an awful, awful month."

"Life doesn't get much more stressful."

"True enough."

Where the rubber hits the road, Maggie found herself thinking as the waitress began to serve coffee—strong and black, no nonsense. It is how we relate when the walls are closing in that defines a relationship. She had trusted her Joe that way. Jake had given her no reason to doubt that they were capable of nurturing the same emotional dynamics.

"Anyway, I'm grateful," she told him.

A smile played at the corner of Jake's mouth. "Likewise. I find myself coming back to the supposed folk wisdom about old dogs and new tricks. I've had a good life. No regrets. But it was far too isolated and self-centered for my taste. For the first time in decades, I can see a way beyond it."

"Us."

"Are you afraid of that—that somehow I'm using you?"

"I was afraid of that wanton show of anger and hate in my own backyard. Am I afraid of heading off into the direction of the sunset with a man I hadn't seen since childhood but who stayed around to help me pick up the pieces? No. Nervous maybe. But not afraid."

"Good."

Conversation ended. They talked about their experiences with Scandinavian culture, food fetishes, anything but the weather. Maggie let Jake pick up the tab. And with lunch behind them, they once again headed west.

Maggie drove. As the route took them more in a southerly direction around Green Bay, the winds became less of an issue. Traffic and sprawling areas of road construction added stresses of their own. By the time Maggie followed Jake's directions and pulled up in front of his house, she was exhausted.

"Rough going for a while there," Jake acknowledged.

Maggie's attention was fixed on the curb appeal of the low-slung Prairie style one-story house. It was all but obscured by a jungle of bushes and ornamental trees. The porch light was on. Its amber glass fixture served as a welcoming beacon in the middle of all that foliage.

"You certainly have a lot of privacy," she said.

Jake laughed. "I think what you're telling me is that collection of flora and fauna could stand some drastic pruning."

"Not my intent. But I'm not going to argue with you either."

It took a good half hour to unload the SUV. By the time they were finished, a small mountain of boxes and luggage stood in the entryway.

"The closet in the guest room is empty," Jake told her. "Not a suggestion for living arrangements in general. Just a statement of fact."

Maggie smiled. "Let's get this heap of trippers off the doorstep and safely stashed. Then we can talk about it."

They did. Surrounded by the Stickley pieces in the living room and crackling fire in the hearth, the traditional Craftsman era built-ins around the fireplace, Maggie let herself feel quietly at home.

She told Jake so. "Wish I could say the same for all those plants we left behind us. An exercise in futility if it freezes too soon."

Jake flashed a wry smile. "Taken care of," he told her. "I took the liberty of calling a landscape service. They'll water, mulch, put down dropcloths if necessary if the freeze comes too soon—"

Maggie started to respond. Her jaw clamped tight.

Jake had thought of everything. He had arranged to rent a piano for her—set for delivery next morning. There was nothing left to say but Thank You. That accomplished, she snuggled against him until the flames in the grate burned themselves down to a glowing ash.

Too tired for anything but a good cuddle, the two of them settled down in Jake's queen bed with its turn-of-the-century tufted steel gray headboard. *Comfortable with one another*, Maggie concluded as she drifted off to a dreamless sleep.

Not bad for a beginning. Not bad at all.

SCHLUMBERGERA is an unlikely name for a beautiful holiday cactus—known as an Easter, Thanksgiving or Christmas cactus depending on the time of year the plant blossoms. In its native Brazil, it is called a May Cactus. The plant's flowers are unusual in that the color of the buds and blossoms can vary based on temperature. Unlike holiday plants like the poinsettia, these holiday cactuses are survivors that with minimal care can live for decades.

Transplant Shock

Moving a plant can be a tricky process, Maggie knew. It can take weeks, months, sometimes years for a relocated plant to get its bearings. Case in point, hellebores are notoriously finicky about being uprooted. Once established they naturalize like mad, spreading out at times at the expense of even long-lived stands of perennials around them.

Damage to the roots is the main culprit when a plant struggles to survive a relocation. The plant depends on those fragile tendrils for sustenance, the nutrients and water needed to grow. *Transplant shock* gardeners call it when a plant finds itself under that kind of stress.

While transplant shock is almost unavoidable, the savvy gardener knows it pays to be proactive. Leave the roots intact when setting the plants in the ground. Water well and keep the roots moist, trim back blossoms and foliage so the plant can expend its energy on reviving the roots. And if a plant seems to be suffering, sometimes a weak sugar-water solution can give the boost it needs to snap out of it. Think of those unopenable packets that florists provide with bunches of cut flowers.

Maggie knew all the signs and symptoms. In transition herself, she found herself both amused and impressed with Jake's intuitive gardener's approach to human relations. He was keeping things simple, taking his cues from her. Above all, he followed the one rule that overrode just about everything else when it came to relocating plants that had languished too long in one spot on the nursery shelves. Be patient.

Baby steps, Maggie told herself as well. She shared the news about living arrangements with both Holly and her son in Hawaii. The L–word never factored in Maggie's disclosures, though it was no easy matter to talk about her live-in arrangement with Jake without bandying about words like 'friend', 'companion', 'lover' or anything of the sort. She simply wrote:

> The house in Lansing is on the market and likely to sell quickly, so I have decided to move in with Jake Faland for the winter. Wisconsin isn't exactly a tropical paradise, but I'm grateful for the roof over my head while I figure out where to go from here. Jake and I have known each other since we were kids and are having fun catching up on old times while enjoying new ones. You can always reach me via cell phone or email.

For good measure, Maggie threw in Jake's email and phone as a postscript.

To her relief, her children's reactions seemed equally matter-of-fact—almost disappointingly so. But then Maggie chalked up daughter Holly's casual response to political street smarts. Her daughter was perceptive enough to know by now that spooking her mother with too much enthusiasm was always a risky business.

The realtor made an honest woman of her. As Jake predicted, the agent brought forward a full-price offer on the family home within a month. Maggie accepted and the deal had begun lurching toward closure.

"Yet another move," Maggie groaned as she told Jake about her decision.

He just laughed, shook his head. "I suggest this time you throw money at it."

"No arguments here."

Mission accomplished. Although the two of them flew to Lansing to make the final arrangements, they left to the professionals the actual packing of furniture and items she chose to keep, as well as the maneuvering of everything to storage.

The feast of All Saints on the first of November finally triggered a major meltdown. Maggie looked up the address of the closest Episcopal church. When she expressed her intent to attend the traditional

311

service, she was surprised to hear Jake volunteer to go with her. They had never really discussed religious matters although Jake knew Maggie was an Episcopalian. She hadn't pressed him, always assumed he was an agnostic at best.

It only took a quick last-minute conversation with the priest to get Lillian's name on the list of those who had died. Seated alongside Jake in a pew of the tiny church, Maggie found the tears streaming down her face as her mother's name was read out loud. Jake fished in his pocket for a tissue, extended it her direction. His arm wrapped supportively around her shoulders.

The priest was young, the congregation small. When an open Eucharist policy was announced, Jake never missed a beat. He went with Maggie to the altar, knelt alongside her at the rail. The closeness was so intense she could taste it. She bowed her head for the final blessing. But then the greatest blessing of all was already hers. Maggie was not alone in her sorrow.

On the drive home, out of the blue the floodgates opened again. Maggie stifled a sob, stared ahead out the windshield. The tears washed over her burning cheeks. At the first opportunity, Jake pulled the SUV to the curb and parked. He cut the engine. Maneuvering as best he could with the sleek bucket seats, he reached over and drew her into his arms.

"I understand," he told her softly. "Trust me, I understand. Death is never easy. Neither is life for that matter."

Gradually with his quiet coaxing, the torrent stilled. Head aching and eyes puffy, Maggie awkwardly freed herself from his embrace.

"I wasn't expecting to react like this."

Her voice was raw. Her hands clenched and unclenched in her lap. It was not her mother but herself for whom she was mourning, a voice in Maggie's head told her. Lillian had seen nearly a hundred seasons come and go when she passed. For all that, there are no guarantees. Life is short. It is meant to be lived. And that includes telling the people who matter to us just how much we care, when and while we can.

"I love you, Jake," she whispered

His sharp intake of breath signaled his surprise. "What brought that on?" he wondered.

"You. This. . . *ridiculous* self-pity of mine. Berlioz."

"Wasn't he the French composer who wrote—"

"Glorious music. Yes, and in the process oddly enough he also had a lot to say about death. I picked up a gem on a website a while back, randomly googling, *Grief*. Time is a powerful teacher, Berlioz said. Too bad it also does in all its pupils."

"Harsh." In the glare from a nearby street lamp, Maggie saw the deep grooves and furrows bracketing Jake's mouth. Suffering with and for her, Maggie realized with a shock.

"You could look at it that way," Maggie said. "But I took it as hopeful. The ultimate call to seize the day."

"*Carpe diem.*"

She sighed. "Which is what I'm trying to do, I guess. Whenever I ask myself what I'm doing on this side of the lake, in totally unfamiliar terrain . . . "

"Is living together truly all that frightening?" he said evenly.

"Yes. No. Outside my comfort zone, maybe. But I think you already know that. There have been way too many changes, some more . . . *final* and yes, scary than others."

"Which is why I wasn't about to let you celebrate All Saints alone. Times like Day of the Dead, our human rites of passing and services of remembrance all seem to revolve around community . . . family. And as I see it, you and I are the closest thing to family we have right now. On site anyway. . ."

Maggie processed his words in silence. "We were children together—you and I," she said. "All those memories are our stories. They tell us who we are. Saddest was seeing Mom lose that in the last year as her short-term memory all but disappeared. She kept the context of the distant past which grounded her. She knew who we were and could recall an amazing amount from our childhoods . . . some of which she had never shared before. But day to day she found herself trapped in the moment. A true prison after a while."

"I would like to think we're making new memories with every breath, Maggie. And when push comes to shove, I also have to believe Lillian would wholeheartedly agree."

"Except we're not kids eyeing one another over the back fence any more—"

"All the more reason. Maybe with age comes some level of

smarts, wisdom even. No talk of 'settling'. Just the courage to make one last grab at love wherever we find it."

In the almost nonexistent light filtering in from the windshield it was hard to see. Jake's eyes, dark and shadowed as they were, seemed to be looking straight through to her soul.

"So, onward and upward?" he said finally. His hand hovered over the ignition.

Maggie drew in a breath, let it out slowly. "Home, James!" she told him. Whatever the future held, cutting and running was no longer an option.

Daylight Savings weekend had arrived with its usual degree of chaos and confusion. *Fall back*, Maggie reminded herself as she reset the clocks. Gaining an hour at this stage in life was a drop in the proverbial bucket. At eight, a year seems to go on forever. Pushing eighty, an eternity in dog years, every week and month seems a heartbeat.

Thanksgiving now was just around the corner, bittersweet. Despite the raw vestiges of grief over her mother's death that surfaced almost daily, there was a lot for which Maggie found herself giving quiet thanks. Even Lillian's passing could have been so much worse. No one wants to see a parent suffer after a life well and truly lived. And no matter how deeply we love, no one goes living out of this world.

The State Police Post checked in just once. The news proved pretty much as the officer had predicted. They had tracked down rototillers but no viable suspects. If any leads seemed promising, the parties involved knew how to cover their tracks. The case file slid on the back burner.

Jake made a point of calling the landscape service in Petoskey once a week for a running account of the fledgling garden's status. The rain had cooperated. The landscaper's precautions before an unseasonable early snowfall sounded sufficient to avoid disaster. Soon enough the ground would be hard and the garden's fate out of everyone's hands until spring.

Winter took hold and unfolded as it is wont to do in freezes and thaws, holidays and down time. Sub-zero temperatures were not conducive to venturing forth. Maggie and Jake weathered the fallow season with a quiet domesticity. Both had been on their own for a long time. The prospect of shared responsibilities proved an unexpected

314

bonus. If Maggie cooked, Jake volunteered for prep work and vice versa. They both dug in for cleanup duties. Jake's robot vacuum took charge when it came to weekly attention to floors and carpet.

They went Dutch on season tickets to a concert series in Green Bay. Maggie insisted on a similar arrangement for the nagging realities of light and heat and cable bills upon which daily life in the modern world depends. Their lovemaking was at times casual, at times intense—kept real with good-hearted laughter at the vagaries of twinges and aches that come with the years.

For Thanksgiving, Jake tackled The Bird while Maggie took over the sides. When he invited his son and family to share the celebration, to their astonishment, Mark agreed. Time had accomplished a minor miracle and the weekend went off without a hitch. Maggie suspected wife Heather had something to do with that as well. Yet another thing for which to give thanks.

Christmas was more fraught. Maggie and Jake made the trek through glare ice on secondary roads to his son's home for the day. Mark's boys deserved to celebrate the holiday in their own setting.

Jake and Maggie kept their gifts to one another low key. She surprised him with a wine club membership. Her favorite gift from him turned out to be a gigantic Christmas cactus in full and spectacular bloom.

"You remembered," Maggie told him as he returned from the garage where he had hidden the showy cactus in order to surprise her.

Months ago she had mentioned how that plant with the unlikely name of *Schlumbergera* had thrived for decades on her grandmother's sun porch. "The first plant I fell in love with—that and hollyhocks of course," she said. "Schlumbergera is actually a cactus. Its internal clocks are set to the solstice, Christmas or Easter. I found that fascinating. In the plant's native Brazil, people call them May flowers."

"*Flor de Maio*. I had no idea."

Maggie laughed. "Sadly, retailers lump them in the same category as poinsettias and amaryllis. Disposable. But with any care at all, they can last for decades. Oddly enough, the varieties in the genus number less than ten—rare in the plant world."

She hung the plant in the kitchen in front of the large window over the sink to capture the humidity released by the dishwasher, the hot water faucet and steam from pots on the stove. The cactus became her daily wakeup call, reminding her of Jake's thoughtfulness. She quickly discovered the necessity of curbing her enthusiasm lest he attempt to surprise her with whatever momentarily caught her eye.

Time sped on like the casual flipping of pages in a brand new calendar. Days and dates flashed by as blank slates upon which life was being written, with only a stand-out photograph to anticipate the milestone for each month. Relentless.

The New Year dawned bitter cold. Maggie read online that ice caves had begun to form on Little Traverse Bay. She felt a fleeting sense of anxiety about the fate of her garden slumbering under the layers of ice-crusted snow. Outside the window of the bedroom she and Jake shared, icicles gleamed and crackled on the bushes.

When the language arts department at the local elementary school put out a desperate call for 'mentors' to help students once a week who were struggling with their reading skills, Jake and Maggie volunteered. He found himself paired with Santiago AKA Sam, a second grader with energy to burn. Maggie drew a painfully shy third grade girl who loved penguins, an animal she had never seen in the flesh.

"A born parent," Maggie smiled wistfully to herself as she watched Jake seated across the library at an undersized table, patiently working with the young boy. Whether Jake himself knew it or not.

Daughter Holly flew out to visit them late January for a long weekend. The wind howled across the airport runway in Green Bay, drove icy clouds of dry snow flakes in its path. Jake swore softly under his breath as an oncoming plow nearly blinded him with a cloud of airborne white, threatening to send the SUV into a skid.

"You look happy," Holly told her mother when they were alone.

Maggie smiled. "I am."

Holly was dating a surgeon on the rebound from a bad marriage. For the first time in years, she too seemed content. Jake spoiled them both with dinner at an upscale restaurant down in the formerly industrial flats along the Fox River in Appleton. The woolen mills were long gone, replaced by a museum and elegant condos built into the cavernous spaces where massive knitting machines once rumbled and clattered.

On Valentine's Day, Jake showed up with a single red rose wrapped in tissue to protect it from the driving snow. "If I thought you wouldn't run out of here screaming and never look back," he said quietly, "I would have gotten down on one knee—"

Maggie's sharp intake of breath told him his assessment of the situation had been dead-on. "Wise choice," she told him. Her voice was shaking as she said it.

"Seriously—would you ever considering marrying again?" he wondered out loud.

Maggie hesitated a long time before answering. "Yes. No. Maybe. At this stage of the game, I'm not sure what it would accomplish."

His brows tightened. "A hassle in some ways. Legally sensible in others. We both have families to think about—but also each other."

Maggie promptly buried the thought deep on her priority list. Out of sight, out of mind. Jake didn't raise the issue head-on again, but from time to time over the next weeks and months, Maggie caught him looking at her thoughtfully, a world of questions unspoken in his eyes.

Their small ship trip in Europe—once a source of controversy that almost threatened their relationship before it even began—proved adventurous and fun despite bouts of rain. The two of them hiked in their oversized ponchos, sampled the cuisine and local wines way too much. They vowed to do it again.

In April, the trees began to bud. The vivid crimson of the maples and neon yellow-green of the willows unfolded dramatically against the cloudless blue sky. During a rare thaw, brave strands of grass began to pop up around the meltwater forming beneath one of the south-exposure drain spouts.

Spring was coming. Jake spotted the first robin of the season shivering on a budding forsythia outside the kitchen window.

"Just weeks now and we can open the cottage," he suggested in passing.

Maggie looked up quizzically from her computer. "We would freeze our tushies off. I rarely try to settle in before mid-June."

Jake frowned. "And the garden?"

She cast a sheepish look his direction. "To tell the truth, I wasn't thinking of that . . ."

"If you like, in May we could take a few days and check it out—stay in a hotel so we don't freeze to death."

"The later the better. Goodness knows what we'll find. And if we plant again too early, there's a good chance the frost would undo everything we did. I'm not up for that, trust me."

Jake nodded. "Duly noted."

Just before Memorial Day they made the pilgrimage north then east along the Michigan lakeshore. The trillium were blooming, a carpet of showy white in the woodlands along the route. Sunlight caught the crests of the gentle waves spreading like a silvery blue carpet from the beach toward the horizon.

Winter had been hard on those fragile stretches of sand. In spots the distance had narrowed dramatically between road and shoreline. Only tenacious patches of beach grass had averted complete washouts where the water came closest to ballast rock hauled in to stabilize the highway.

Traffic on the bridge over the Straits was light. As they approached the outskirts of Petoskey, Maggie felt her throat tighten. Car dealerships and thrift shops sped past, then the highway leading north to Harbor Springs.

The streets of their cottage community teemed with workmen's trucks and landscapers hard at work. As Jake eased the SUV into the alley behind the cottage, Maggie sat with hands clenched tightly in her lap, willing herself to appear calmer than she felt.

When Jake cut the engine and got out, she simply sat there staring straight ahead out the windshield. He came around and opened the door for her. Stiff from the long drive, Maggie took her time climbing out.

"No time like the present," Jake said quietly.

He extended a hand and waited for her to take it. His fingers interlaced reassuringly with hers. Together they walked to the gate, stood looking out toward the cottage beyond.

Maggie felt her breath leave her in an incredulous rush, baffled at first by what she was seeing. She blinked, assumed she had to be imagining it. But there it was—the garden—sparsely populated with plant stock from last fall, but *growing*. Even the area where Maggie had strewn the hollyhock seeds was bristling with green shoots.

"Oh, my God . . . most of it *survive*d," Maggie gasped. "Not everything, but still . . ."

Jake searched her face, trying to make sense of what they were seeing out there. Slowly, a cautious smile flickered at the corner of his mouth. "Who would have thought it—?" he said.

Who indeed. Maggie had no chance to respond.

As they stood there together staring out over the garden, a stray gust of wind, warm and out of the southwest, swirled around them. Blustery currents stirred the tender green shoots, rustled through the scattering of dry leaves left behind by the landscapers. Brittle and tissue thin, pulled first this way then that, one by one the leaves rose skyward. Slowly they began to dance and circle in harmony above the wakening earth.

Spin, spin, whirl. The breeze whispered and sighed.

Behind the garden, the gable of the newly repainted porch of the cottage seemed to be whirling in synch. Its ornate turn-of-the-century gingerbread melted and flowed like the icicles of winter touched by the late afternoon sun.

Maggie closed her eyes. The sun's rays caressed her upturned face. In her imagination, she gave in to the unseen rhythms all around her. Her spirit moved and spun and turned in joyous abandon, soaring high above the garden.

Spin, *spin, whirl.* **Hol-ly-hock, hol-ly-hock**

Lost in the moment, Maggie embraced the sudden rush of memories—images not just of the girl she had been but the woman she had become, was still becoming. That, and flashbacks of the towheaded boy leaning over this selfsame fence, older now but once again an unexpected witness to her journey.

She had felt life calling out to her here before, felt herself borne aloft on currents of hope and promise that age, even evil or death could not dampen or contain. The very air and ground underfoot smelled of green things growing, of life renewing itself.

On and on the breeze sighed and whispered. *Spin, spin, whirl.*

Tears gathered behind Maggie's eyes. She let them fall, watering the bare earth in silent thanks for the girl that still danced and whirled within her—head thrown back and arms flung wide, reaching out to life, to the world in all its beauty.

Determined. Unafraid. Reaching out to gardens yet to be.

ABOUT THE AUTHOR...

A long-time summer resident of Northern Michigan, Mary Agria is an avid gardener and author of a newspaper column on gardening and spirituality. Five of her eight novels are set in that special area of the country. Common to all her fiction is the human quest to find meaning at whatever stage of life. Her *Time in a Garden* was a regional best-seller in 2006. *Community of Scholars* won a 5-Star rating—"a riveting thriller. . . highly recommended"—from Midwest Book Review. She was named one of two featured Michigan women authors of the year by the Charlevoix Zonta Club in 2016. Her *Time in a Garden* column was awarded a first prize for features in the Michigan Garden Clubs competition in 2017.

Early in her career, Ms. Agria published and worked as a researcher in the field of rural community development, including for the Center for Theology in Land in Iowa. Wife of a retired university president, the author is proud mother of four daughters and a beloved crew of grandchildren. Her love of place and family, faith in the power of community and resilience of the human spirit shine through on every page. *For sample chapters of her work, visit* www.maryagria.com

RANGE OF MOTION
Book Club Questions

1. What is the significance of the title of the novel?

2. Discuss how the 'range of motion' of the main characters are limited as the novel begins.

3. How does the flexibility of the characters expand over time and what factors or events contribute to that growth?

4. Talk about ways in which problems with 'range of motion' apply not just to individual lives in the novel but to the cottage community around them.

5. What do you as a reader consider the most difficult kind of impediment to 'range of motion' you have encountered in your own life? (physical, emotional, spiritual, other)

6. Discuss how a strong sense of tradition in a family or community can be a roadblock to maintaining flexibility and growth. Illustrate this from your own experience and/or the experiences of the characters in the novel.

7. Both individuals and communities may have flaws or biases that go unnoticed. Discuss how Maggie comes to recognize this and tries to move beyond those 'blind spots'.

8. Do you think Maggie will ever sell her family cottage, and why? How does her attitude toward 'home' and 'tradition' change in the course of the novel?

9. What role does gardening play in Maggie's life? Discuss how her experiences in the garden contribute to her feelings about love, loss and community.

10. Discuss how Maggie and Jake's relationship helps and/or hinders their struggles with 'range of motion' in the novel.

11. Reflect on how the garden, the Northern Michigan environment and the cottage community function as 'characters' in the novel?

12. Compare/contrast Maggie and Jake's relationships to their adult children. Do children ever stop being your children?

13. How does Maggie's relationship with her mother change in the novel? How does it change her own view of parenting?

14. What part of the novel speaks most to you personally and why? Discuss ways in your own life for maintaining or increasing your 'range of motion'? Do these change with age?